£2.99

The Val Saga

GW00789696

Volume Three

Odin's Curse

Dr. Gregory Pepper

ISBN: 978-1-4466-3906-1

Cover art by Chris Beatrice ©2011
Typography and page composition by J. K. Eckert & Co., Inc.
Published and printed by Lulu.com

To my mother, Elizabeth Pepper,

and to KJ and Stan; two role models I admire and

whom I will always aspire to be.

Contents

Note: Chapter titles shown in italics are based on original Norse sagas.

Acknowledgments

It is hard to believe that we are already here enjoying this, the third and penultimate instalment in the voyage that is *The Valkyrie Sagas.*

If you are about to read this book then I would like to thank you for so kindly continuing with my tale. If you haven't already read *Mimir's Well* and *Hel,* then do please consider doing so before reading *Odin's Curse.* Your enjoyment will be that much the greater.

Along with my heartfelt thanks to my readers, I would also like to offer my gratitude for the many charming and generous comments I have received about the series. Your kind words are what make this journey worthwhile; the knowledge that I have been able to entertain and enthral you. Without such feedback, any pleasure in writing swiftly withers and dies. Forget fame and fortune. Spreading happiness is the true goal for any author and if I have achieved this, then I am truly blessed.

Throughout *The Valkyrie Sagas* I have tried to foster an interest in the wonderful characters and stories created by the great Norse bards of old. Their eloquent prose was not only graced with great beauty, but also laced with the extraordinary kaleidoscope of life. Pleasure, pain, anger, greed, humour, fear, tragedy, passion; it is easy to paint a picture of their rapt audiences. Huddled around crackling fires on long, cold, winter's nights, these people from times long passed would shiver and joke as they revelled in the telling and retelling of their tales.

For the Norsemen, their gods were not like the gods of today— deities to be worshipped and feared in humble and distant adoration. Their gods and sagas were part of their everyday lives, with lessons and morals gleaned being passed down from generation to generation. Odin, Thor, Freyja, Loki, and all their kith and kin were the soap stars of the day. Adored and respected, yes; but appreciated too for possessing the same vagaries and frailties as their mortal followers.

To these great storytellers of old, life wasn't only a question of black and white; it was all the shades of grey and colours in between. No one god was truly good, and none were wholly bad. Adults and children alike could learn much from the strengths—and the weaknesses—of their heroes. I have tried to mirror this insightfulness in the telling of my tale.

Producing a book requires teamwork, and I would like to thank Chris Beatrice for the truly amazing illustrations he is creating for the series. Seeing my dreams come to life is unbelievably exciting. I would also like to thank Jeff Eckert and his team for their excellent proofreading and stylish typesetting. Their invaluable contribution has presented my story in a manner that beautifully reflects those of ancient texts.

Gods, superstars, politicians, and heroes; the one thing these beings all have in common is the ability to inspire others. At the beginning of this book, I have acknowledged two wonderful men whose footsteps have influenced my life. Neither man is a god, a star, or a politician; but to me they are heroes—true heroes in the complex game of life.

Enough of this moralising already!

Odin's Curse begs to be revealed…

1

Live or Let Die

ilence.

It wasn't exactly how Marcus had imagined 'a chat' with Frigg would begin, but it was her call, and there was precious little he could do about it. He could shout and scream and demand as much as he wanted to; but locked as he was in a small, windowless concrete cell in an unknown location, he doubted it would do him any favours. No; his best course of action was to sit pretty and play along with whatever it was that Frigg decided to do. If he could remain calm and patient, then an opportunity might just come around for him to state his case. The drug charges against him were paper thin, and he felt sure that she must know this, too. For now, if all she wanted to do was to sit in silence on a plastic chair and smoke a cigarette; then she could be his guest. He wasn't going anywhere.

Decision made, Marcus sat back on his coarse, straw-filled mattress and twiddled his mental thumbs. Frigg would have to speak sometime; after all, she was a Valkyrie, and silence didn't become these powerful women.

Frigg would have been the first to admit that making a decision about Marcus was going to be a tough call, sitting as she was, methodically rifling her way through his mind. Like some trained detective, she was sifting through cabinets stuffed full of evidence; carefully opening each and every folder labelled 'Valkyrie.' She had begun with that first, fateful evening when Marcus had laid eyes on Dr. Neal's corpse; and was now ending with his current placid and reflective state. No file was left unopened, and every memory had been read with the greatest of interest.

After all, his very life depended on it.

Finishing her first Gauloises cigarette, Frigg paused; and then lit another. She still wasn't ready to talk just yet; and with Marcus in such a tranquil state, it was an ideal opportunity to take things slow and arrive at a calm and rational decision.

At first sight, the solution to her predicament looked obvious.

He knew too much and must die.

Marcus had met and developed relationships with more than one Valkyrie and knew most of their secrets. He knew about their knives, the power of the mead, the apples, and Asgard. Worst of all; he knew about Frigg's connection to it all. As far as she was aware, no other Midgard mortal knew even a fraction as much and she had had Woods executed for knowing considerably less. Killing Marcus should therefore be an easy decision to make—and yet it wasn't.

There were two reasons; possibly three; if she was being really honest with herself.

The first was the least compelling.

Marcus was one of the good guys, motivated by a sense of honour. He knew all about the mead, and yet he wasn't drawn to its seductive lure—the gift of immortality. Sure; he had seen its dark side, the terrible addiction and cravings; but no one in their right mind would turn down a drug that allowed them to live forever; no matter what its side effects. This had been Woods undoing and the reason why he had come to a premature and watery death; his selfish compulsion to possess the mead and live the life of Midas—courtesy of her fabulous wealth. No; Marcus genuinely cared about the warriors and Jess in particular. He was a good man, untainted by a lust for personal gain. However, as Frigg had previously discovered to her cost, simply being 'a good man' wasn't good enough. Even the most noble and pure of heart would, given time, succumb to the mead's eternal promise. To trust Marcus and set him free would break a habit of a lifetime.

Trust no man.

This motto had served Frigg well, and she could see no reason for breaking it now.

The second reason was definitely the weakest—and yet her favourite.

Marcus had such an adorably boyish face. This hit her weak spot dead centre. She loved a handsome man. Ottar, her current beau, had been fun; but she was now yearning for change. Marcus was right up her street; which made this reason for sparing his life all the more fatuous.

To spare him merely for being 'pretty' would be an act of complete insanity.

The third and final reason was perhaps the most persuasive.

Marcus was the only hero to have ever cheated fate. He had survived being killed, and his destiny had been rewritten. By rights, any one of her assassination attempts, the exploding boat, and Fulla's knife should have dispatched his soul to Valhalla—but they hadn't. Even now, a force she didn't understand was screaming at her to let him live, to let him fulfill his new destiny; the one that served a higher purpose. However, this compelling voice also caused her the greatest confusion.

Was his newfound lease of life purely a figment of her imagination?

Could it be that she had contrived a convenient, fairy-tale future only to satisfy her curiosity and spare his handsome face?

This paradox frustrated her and ultimately left her with no choice. She had to act, and she had to do so now. Reluctantly, she drew a final pull on her cigarette and after dropping it to the floor; she stubbed it out with a single, elegant twist of her immaculate Jimmy Choo's.

"We seem to have a bit of a problem, Detective Finch," Frigg spoke at last, opening her eyes such that they pierced Marcus with their icy beauty.

"Why?" Marcus retorted too hastily, snatching frantically at his bid for freedom. "You know the drugs weren't mine. They were planted in my room by one of your servants."

"Oh, tush; I'm not talking about the cocaine you silly boy," Frigg laughed, waving her hand dismissively. He'd completely missed the point of what she was saying. "I'm talking about your knowledge of us, the Valkyries. You know too much, I'm so sorry."

"Sorry for what?" Marcus enquired innocently, taken aback by Frigg's casual dismissal of his plea. The drugs were the reason for his arrest and incarceration—surely?

"Sorry for this," Frigg replied, before standing up and withdrawing a small revolver from her handbag.

"Oh, come on," Marcus guffawed loudly. "You don't really expect me to believe that you're going to shoot me right here in the middle of a police station? Don't be so daft! That's murder, and you won't get away with it." The sight of a gun in the Contessa's hand was so preposterous that Marcus genuinely didn't consider himself to be in any danger. He wasn't remotely afraid—at least not just yet.

"Hmmm," Frigg paused, and then placed the gun on the chair behind her. "You know, Marcus, you could be right. I really can't make up my mind as to what to do with you. Do I set you free and trust you to keep our secrets or do I shoot you and watch the sharks nibble at your corpse?" Their eyes met. "What do you think I should do?"

"I'm not going to answer that stupid question," Marcus replied, holding her stare. "It's ridiculous. Now go and call the guards and get lost. If you do that this very instant, I promise I won't tell the police officers that you've just threatened to kill me."

"Um, excuse me Marcus," Frigg scoffed, "but what police officers?" Looking around her, she feigned an air of mock surprise. Surely he couldn't be so naïve as to think that they were really in a police cell in Nassau? She had credited him with a lot more intelligence than that.

Marcus wasn't that naive; and his arrogant, blustered display of confidence collapsed faster than a burst balloon. With a sudden, terrible sinking feeling inside, he knew that his bluff had been called. He had half suspected that the police officers were bogus and he might still be on the Contessa's island—and now that fact was confirmed.

An icy fear gripped his heart.

Nervously, he glanced once more at the gun on the plastic chair. Suddenly Frigg's death threat was horribly, terrifyingly, all too real.

"Perhaps now, Marcus, you understand my predicament a little better," Frigg continued cheerily, following his gaze and noting his nervous gulp. "So, I ask again. What would you do, given my situation?"

"Trust me, definitely trust me." Marcus's mouth suddenly felt dry, and his knees had turned to jelly. With a shock, he realised he was pleading for his life.

"Sorry," Frigg mocked apologetically. "No can do."

Picking up the gun, she released its safety catch with an ominous click. Playfully, she toyed with the weapon for a few moments, giving Marcus one last, desperate chance to sing for his salvation.

"Oh, come on, please," he begged. "Give me a break, let me prove myself. I swear I won't tell a soul about anything." His life was beginning to flash through his mind, and Frigg was reading this loud and clear.

"I know you won't be telling a soul," she retorted, winking as she smiled and raised the gun in his direction. "Dead men seldom do."

Marcus swallowed hard. This was it; his end had come. *Christ!* When he came to think about it; the fucking Valkyries had tried so many times to top him, he was beginning to lose count. He knew he should be wracked with fear, but this sudden recollection of deathly brushes made him feel more angry than afraid.

Maybe he really did lead a charmed life and his number still wasn't up?

Marcus rose from the bed. If he was going to die then it would be standing up and with his eyes wide open.

He stared hard at his captor.

"You should trust your instincts, Contessa," he began slowly, "not me. Trust your instincts; because they're the ones that really matter." Marcus didn't have a clue as to where these words had come from, but they slipped from his lips with a calmness that belied his inner trembling.

Frigg returned his stare—and then to his relief, put the gun down.

"You know, you've got a point Marcus. My head is telling me to kill you, but my heart is saying no. I really can't decide. Perhaps we should just leave it up to fate to make this important decision, hey?"

Smiling broadly, Frigg reached into her handbag and withdrew a small, golden coin. It shone brightly in the artificial light, and Marcus knew instinctively that it was the same coin that the Valkyries carried in their purses. He could almost picture the beautiful swan on the front and the strange, geometric symbol on its back.

"A single toss of the coin," Frigg purred serenely. "Heads you live, tails you die." Briefly she pointed out that swans would be heads and before Marcus could utter a word; the coin was on its way. Tossed and spinning upward crazily through the air.

His life; his death; his very existence was all going to be determined by this insignificant hunk of metal.

Returning floorward, Frigg deftly caught the coin and slapped it down hard on the back of her hand. Raising this up, she tipped it and glanced briefly at the golden disk. Without saying a word, she removed this from her hand and placed it down on the chair.

"Well, what was it?" Marcus enquired indignantly. "Heads or tails?" She hadn't even shown him the coin. *How unfair was that?*

Picking up the revolver, Frigg turned and levelled it at Marcus's heart.

"Hey, this isn't fair!" he yelled angrily. "How do I know the coin was tails? It's a stitch up."

Frigg cocked the hammer and chambered a round. She still hadn't spoken, not one single word.

Marcus stared hard at the gun's muzzle, and then screwed his eyes shut. This really was it—and the heartless bitch wasn't even going to let him say a few final words. *Fuck!* His death was happening way too quickly.

BANG!

The gun roared in a deafening explosion and Marcus recoiled back onto the bed clutching at his chest. *Shit!* He hadn't even felt the shell as it ripped through his heart. Inhaling his final breath, Marcus listened to the reverberating echoes of the gunshot as these faded slowly from the claustrophobic cell. The acrid smell of cordite filled his nostrils.

So this was how it felt to die.

The shadow of death masking the pain from the gaping hole in his chest while fevered senses soaked up every last drop of reality before plunging headlong down the road to oblivion. The sensation felt peculiar; his seething mind bursting with fresh and fading memories as the ultimate, fateful question hurtled starkly into view.

Would the white light at the end of his nothingness lead to heaven or hell?

Neither came.

Snatching one last priceless gulp of air, Marcus half opened an eye and looked nervously down at his left breast.

There was no gaping hole—and no spurting blood.

He took another deep breath, and another, and another; his heart pounded in his head. *He was alive, for fuck's sake, HE WAS ALIVE!*

After looking up at Frigg, he glanced cautiously over his shoulder. There it was; a splintered hole in the concrete wall. In the moment he had closed his eyes, Frigg had spared his life.

The coin had been heads.

He was alive, and freedom screamed for him to go.

"It seems, Marcus," Frigg began, pausing as she casually returned the revolver and coin to her handbag. "You do lead a charmed life." Walking over to the iron door that led to the corridor outside, she banged loudly on it. After a few moments, a guard entered and undid the lock to Marcus's cell. He was a free man.

Frigg held out her hand.

"No hard feelings?" she enquired as Marcus shook it lamely. *Fuck!* He should be wringing her scrawny neck rather than shaking her murderous paw.

Smiling broadly, Frigg instructed the guard to handcuff Marcus and then place a thick, black, linen bag over his head. This would be removed when they were safely above ground once more. There were secrets buried beneath the surface of Crescent Cay that she didn't want him to see; secrets that were best kept hidden from any mortal man.

Placing his arm on hers, she led him slowly along the corridors and up to freedom. She grinned as she did so, reflecting on the fickle irony that was fate. Marcus did indeed have a charmed life and one that would now lead to greater things.

The coin had landed tails, and yet she had decided to neither spare nor take his life. In the instant of its viewing, Frigg had made a unique and momentous decision.

Marcus would neither live nor die.

He would suffer the third option.

2

Poison?

*I*t was only when the last rays of a winter's sun had finally crept behind the mountains of Jotunheim that the exhausted Valkyries could leave the battlefield and wind their weary way back toward the castle. As darkness began to fall, the temperature plummeted quickly; with thick clouds billowing in from the Great Sea, bringing with them a spattering of heavy, freezing sleet, and melting snow.

It was the end of an inglorious day in early November and with hearts that felt like leaden weights; the warriors turned and bade their last respects to the battlefield.

It had been a hellhole; and one that had witnessed many hours of bloody carnage.

"HAIL VALOUR! HAIL VICTORY! HAIL ODIN!"

The girls cried weakly as they raised their swords to the sky. Their battle cries should have been filled with wild jubilation; but they weren't. The heroes had saved the day by slaughtering Hel's Berserkers, and they had done this with a display of unprecedented ferocity. However, the manner of their macabre and one-sided victory had given the Valkyries little cause for cheer. The Berserkers had fought bravely and with honour; and they deserved a far nobler death than odious one that they'd been dealt: being blown to smithereens.

The terrible mushroom cloud which had spewed from Odin's cataclysmic weapon still hovered menacingly as testament to their gruesome massacre; while smoke from countless funeral pyres that littering the blood soaked battlefield rose pungently all around them.

One of these hung particularly heavy on their souls.

This was the pyre on which Yuko had been laid.

She had died the Valkyrie way; fighting to the last with a furious passion raging inside her heart. Unlike the warriors, she was still a maid and hadn't yet earned her place in Valhalla. Cremation was the only way to ensure her eternal peace. To have done anything less would have condemned her to an afterlife of torture and slavery in Hel's fiery realm.

The warriors never abandoned their fallen sisters; and between them they carried the bodies of Prima and Mist toward the castle. Their sisters would lie in the Chamber of the Valkyries until the time came to journey to Valhalla. Theirs would be the reward of heroes, to serve in Odin's great army—if only they could believe such a heroic force still existed. The callous display of the metal monsters on the battlefield had cast a long shadow over the Einherjar's grandeur; and their lack of chivalry now troubled the warriors. Their one ray of hope lay in the shattered body of Ben. He too was on a stretcher and had Jameela by his side. He coughed and spluttered as she tried to get him to swallow the life-saving mead.

Only he could restore their faith in Odin's heroes.

On the final stretcher the girls carried from the battlefield lay Ruby. She had been gravely injured by a spear whose intended target had been Elijah. Enraged by her sacrifice, the warriors had immediately surrounded and then captured the leader of Hel's demented army of madness.

They had only one thought on their minds.

Execution.

The beast was a Berserker, and that would be a just reward.

In a moment of sublime inspiration before she drifted into blackness; Ruby had saved his life by declaring him the hero of the day; the slayer of Ragnarok itself. Pointing shakily toward Cole's headless corpse, few could doubt Ruby's words; and their derision turned swiftly to exultation as they hailed the hero as their own. In a bizarre and fortuitous twist of fate, Elijah had switched from being the evil, conquering, commander of Hel's Army—to the saviour of Asgard. Better still, he would be Odin's most honoured guest at the celebrations tonight.

Not that Elijah cared.

His eyes were only for Ruby, and he stuck to her like glue as her stretcher was taken inside the castle and carried upstairs to her chambers.

Bathing that evening became a subdued affair, with the warriors flitting restlessly between Ruby's and Jameela's chambers. Each Valkyrie was a bubbling cauldron of emotion; emotions that changed from moment to moment; suddenly and without warning.

Joy and excitement were fickle, fleeting friends that spread rapidly amongst the girls like a summer chill.

At last a hero had returned from Valhalla, and this gave cause for cheer. Everyone was desperate to hear Ben's words, and yet all were shocked by his refusal to drink the mead. "Poison!" he repeated over and over again as his hand pointed urgently toward his backpack. This lay close by on a chair.

Believing him to be delirious with pain, Silk obliged his insistent urgings by opening his backpack. Here, she discovered the true object of his desire.

A golden apple lay close to its top.

Passing this to Jameela, she sliced it delicately before feeding him slivers of the fruit as he drifted in and out of consciousness. Its life-giving strength seemed to ease his distress; and he quickly settled into a sonorous slumber.

The presence of an apple was a major shock.

Nobody could understand what Ben was doing with it and much less why he was insisting on eating it. The apples were for the gods, not Odin's Einherjar. Heroes and Valkyries drew their strength from the mead of Valhalla; everyone knew that. This bizarre revelation was a conundrum; and one that puzzled them greatly. The matter was so disturbing that Jameela vowed to ask Odin about it during the feast that evening; although she didn't say how or when.

Warming to Elijah, the warriors' earlier hostility turned quickly to curiosity and then admiration. They could see his devotion to Ruby and the love that sparkled from her eyes when she awoke briefly and held him close. His gentle manners and shyness endeared him to their hearts.

He had killed Cole and, as such, he was a hero and friend to them all.

Beside these brief moments of joy, grief hung heavily in the air; smothering the warriors like some grey, autumnal drizzle.

Sudden outbursts of weeping swept spasmodically through the girls. The loss of their fallen sisters burned like daggers in their hearts, and the warriors shed tears openly and with pride. Their comrades had fought courageously and with honour and deserved a mighty funeral.

Relief, too, passed through the warriors' chambers.

As the girls started to dress for their victory celebrations; this emotion skipped gaily amongst them, bringing great bliss that so many had survived the terrible battle.

Everyone knew that they owed their lives to Kat; and that she hadn't returned with them to the castle. Speculation was rife and arguments broke out as warriors and maids deliberated as to why she had the left the battlefield with Hel. After much discussion, it was agreed that Kat must have done so under duress. This would have been the price that Hel demanded for sparing the lives of the sisterhood. Some of the warriors begrudged this deal, especially Silk. She resented being deprived of a glorious death on the battlefield. She missed Balder with all her heart and yearned to ride to the gates of Niflheim.

Along with these shifting and effusive feelings, one emotion stood head and shoulders above them all. It remained a constant, aching dullness in the air; an emotion that brought dread to the warriors—but was never discussed.

Fear.

This stalked their chambers like an invisible serpent, striking at random when they least expected it.

The Valkyries had hoped that this terrible battle had been Ragnarok; and that Asgard was now spared from its destruction. Unfortunately, with Fenrir absent from the fray and Thor still very much alive; the battle couldn't have been the ultimate, decisive conflict; the one where all their fates would be decided.

This bitter truth was tough to swallow.

The battle had merely been the beginning of Ragnarok and not its end. Worse was yet to come, and Hel's departing words clamoured like peals of bells inside their heads. The Queen of the Damned had vowed to return and bring far greater horrors to the battlefield at the end of time.

This thought above all the others struck an icy terror in their hearts.

"I salute you all my dearest warriors. I salute your courage, I salute your determination, and I salute the love you have for our beloved Asgard."

"HAIL ASGARD!"

Odin raised his horn of mead, and the warriors responded to his toast with a rousing reply. After drinking deeply, the warriors sat down and settled back into a hubbub of noisy excitement.

Odin sat down again, too; grateful that at last the tension in the hall was beginning to ease. He had pulled out all the stops tonight, dragging as many gods and goddesses as he could from Valhalla to join their celebratory feast. He wanted the evening to go with an extra zing and to that end; he had asked Bragi, although no match for Kvasir's silken voice, to compose an ode in honour of the day's extraordinary events.

His recital had been much appreciated by all those gathered.

Taking note of Odin's strict instructions, Bragi had waxed lyrical about the valour of the Valkyries and glossed over the role of Odin's heroes. The hostility of his warriors toward the metal killing machines hadn't gone unnoticed; and Odin was anxious not to stoke their anger further.

Not now, not when their destiny was so close to realization. He needed their loyalty just a little longer, and so far—touch wood—he had secured that successfully.

Looking around him, he could see Ull and Tyr chatting merrily with Alex and Priya; and his brothers Vili and Ve cheerily ensconced between Lara and Skogul. Both were beautiful, blond warriors, much to his brothers' liking. The boys were flirting outrageously, but Odin didn't mind. His brothers had urged him to sing their praises for repairing Mimir's well, and he had done so gladly. Now they were busy basking in their glorious role, bragging loudly about their brilliant minds.

Freyr, too, was present at the festivities; although he drifted in and out of the hall with all the subtle charm of a becalmed summer tide. Many of the warriors needed the solace of his embrace; the pleasure of a meaningless, passionate tryst to quench the bloodlust from their veins. Freyr was much in demand—and he didn't disappoint a single woman; not one.

All in all, things seemed to be settling nicely and, after congratulating himself on his cleverness; Odin rose once more, raising his horn as he waved for silence.

He had one last toast to make that was bound to please his guests.

"My beloved friends, let us all salute our brave but foolhardy hero, Ben. His passion for you, my dearest Herja, nearly cost him his life, and yet his courage in the pursuit of love is a shining example to us all. Hail valour!"

"HAIL VALOUR!"

The warriors stood up as one and raised their horns, tankards, and flagons in a loud and stirring tribute. Ben was the most recent hero to pass through Asgard, and he was also one of the most popular.

Seizing the moment as the girls around her slowly returned to their seats, Jameela stepped forward and walked nervously toward Odin's table. She trembled as she did so, praying for strength to see her plan through.

"My lord," she bowed low. "Dear Ben lies gravely injured, and I would like a flagon of mead for his use. It will ease his pain and speed his recovery." Shaking as she did so, she stretched out her hand toward the bowl of mead that lay upon his table.

"My dearest Herja," Odin beamed, stopping her hand dead in its tracks. "I believe one of Idun's apples might be of more help to your beloved Ben." Reaching into his pocket, he withdrew an apple and placed this in the palm of her hand.

After a brief but angry murmur of discontent, the hall fell silent. Turning their heads as one, the warriors' glared suspiciously at Odin. They had all heard Ben's struggle to avoid drinking the mead; and Odin's offer of an apple now seemed to confirm Ben's dreadful words.

The mead was poison.

"What?" Odin exclaimed in bewilderment, looking around him in surprise. He could sense his warriors' hostility but was at a loss to understand where it had come from. "What have I said or done to offend you?" he continued pleadingly.

"My lord," Herja whispered coarsely; barely able to speak through fear of his wrath. "Ben, Ben said…Ben sort of said that, that—" She faltered and then hung her head; unable to finish her sentence.

"—Ben said that your mead is poison."

Interrupting the conversation, Silk finished the words for her. She too was now on her feet and staring icily at Odin. Without Balder by her side, she no longer feared their lord. Her death couldn't come soon enough. Her heart ached terribly, and she felt as cold as the grave. Any fight that might dispatch her to the afterlife would be a welcomed release from this torment.

Odin inhaled loudly and deeply before casting his eye slowly around the room.

So this was it, this was at the heart of his warriors' discontent. He exhaled slowly.

"My dear Valkyries, whom I am honoured to call my loyal friends," Odin began before pausing, heightening the tension in the hall. "Ben is correct. The mead is poison."

A horrified gasp rippled noisily amongst the warriors. They wanted to scream their rage at this revelation, but none did. Silence descended swiftly. More words were poised to follow, and none of the Valkyries wanted to miss a single one.

"It is a poison," Odin continued confidently, warming to his task. "But only if you're a man."

THUD!

Odin had thumped his fist dramatically upon the table, sending mugs and dishes scattering in all directions. The sound echoed like a thunder clap around the silent room such that many jumped in shock.

"For you my dear warriors," he continued resolutely. "It gives you your great strength and your great passion; but for my heroes, it does the opposite; sapping their souls and destroying their will to fight. In small quantities, it can save a life, but Ben is correct. I do not allow them drink my potent mead. I brew it only for you, my noble Valkyries, the greatest of all my loyal soldiers."

Odin raised his horn in salutation, but nobody followed his lead.

The hall remained silent.

What he had said could be true, but nobody was buying it just yet. Their loyalty was frayed, and it would take more than mere words to regain their trust.

"Very well, I see you want more." Acknowledging their distrust and after casting his eye slowly around the room once more, Odin raised both hands in the air and waved one ostentatiously over his diamond-encrusted ring. In an instant he was back and in his arms was a basket full of golden apples, which he placed on the table before him.

He had been to his garden.

"Come, eat if you want," he demanded, beckoning urgently to the warriors to come up and take the apples. "None of you need drink my mead anymore if that is your wish. I will bring fresh apples every day, and you may eat as many as you like."

Plucking one from the basket, he tossed it deliberately at Silk.

"But do this at your peril," he cautioned, wagging his finger threat-eningly. "You will loose your strength in battle and passion in bed. The bloodlust, the source of all your power, will be gone. However, if you crave my golden apples and cannot trust me, then so be it. They're yours. Come, eat, all of you." Odin sat down defiantly and folded his arms tightly across his chest. He was daring their defiance.

Nobody moved.

For now at least, his bluff had worked.

Not one Valkyrie stepped forward to take an apple. Even Silk put hers down without taking a single bite.

Breathing a deep sigh of relief, Odin toyed nervously with the disk in his pocket. It was changing colour far faster these days; from green to yellow and now to a deep orange that was becoming heavily flecked with red. Ragnarok had to end soon, and he needed a trouble-making hero like Ben in Asgard like he needed a hole in the head.

Silently, he cursed himself for not processing Ben the moment he had stepped ashore in Valhalla. All this unpleasantness could so easily have been avoided. He was going soft these days, and this softness extended to his warriors as well. Vali really should have killed the traitorous Kat when he'd had the chance.

Odin cursed her name out loud—and then regretted it.

"My lord," Carmel began, rising nervously to her feet. She was one of the many warriors who had heard his expletive and found it hard to stomach. "Forgive my boldness, my lord; but I do not believe we should curse our sister Sangrid."

Pausing briefly to gauge the level of her support, a ripple of mur-mured approval bolstered her confidence. Carmel decided to con-tinue. "Our sister showed no cowardice when she fought the Berserkers. It was they who gave way and refused to fight. I believe—we believe," she corrected herself to an even louder chorus of approval. "That Sangrid travelled back to Niflheim against her wish. My Lord, were it not for Sangrid's valour, many more of us would have met the same fate as Prima, Mist, and Yuko. We should be praising her, not cursing her."

Carmel raised her horn of mead. "Hail Sangrid!" she shouted jubi-lantly.

"HAIL SANGRID!" The warriors replied, raising their voices in the loudest and noisiest toast of the evening so far. Everybody missed Kat. She couldn't be a traitor, they were certain of that.

Odin shook his head in disbelief.

What was wrong with his Valkyries tonight?

Things were going from bad to worse with Carmel, his latest warrior, now getting all uppity. He had to pull things round before the whole evening went pear shaped.

Luckily, he had been saving his best card to last.

Rising again, Odin gestured for silence.

"My dear Astrid; I hope for all our sakes that what you have said is true. If you are correct, then I would be the first to welcome Sangrid back to my loyal band of Valkyries. I have never concealed my love for the noble Kat, she was like—" Odin paused theatrically, "—like a daughter to me." He continued, wiping the merest hint of a tear from his eye. He was laying his love on thick because he had to.

He had to get his warriors back on side, and playing to their emotions had always been a winning hand.

"Now, I beg of you, we must turn to happier matters," he continued, raising his hands in a triumphant flourish. "I have learned of the deepest magic in the realm, and I now know how to free Balder from his doom."

A hubbub erupted around him.

This was good news, and all thoughts of poisonous mead and treachery were immediately forgotten. Everybody craned their necks to catch Odin's words.

"I will reveal the magic shortly, but first I need you, Gunnr, to go with Hermod to the gates of Niflheim. I want you to confirm that Balder is being well treated. I also need you to offer Hel an ultimatum. Unless she releases Balder at once, I will use my magic. Will you agree to ride with Hermod at first light tomorrow?"

Odin raised his horn in Silk's direction, and she rose instantly, grinning broadly.

"Nothing, my lord, would give me greater pleasure," she retorted, raising her horn of mead. "Hail Balder!" she cried.

"HAIL BALDER!"

The hall erupted once more to rapturous applause, and Odin sank back into his chair for the last time; dabbing at his forehead with a linen napkin. Silently, he thanked Yggdrasill for his narrow escape. It had been a tight squeeze, but with Silk now back in the fold, the rest of the warriors would quickly fall into line. He smiled weakly in Vili and Ve's direction, and they gestured two thumbs up back in return.

All he needed—all any of the gods needed—was just a little more time and, with any luck, Silk's final toast might have just bought them that.

It was in the dead of night that Carmel awoke.

After fumbling around stealthily in the dark, she put on a heavy cloak and slipped quietly out of her room. Loki was lying asleep in her bed, snoring soundly as usual. Pulling the door closed, she tiptoed along the corridor, down the stairs, and then hurried out into the night. It was pitch black, and a fine, chilly drizzle hung miserably in the air. The only light to illuminate her way across the uneven and cobbled courtyard was coming from a faint glow in Thor's workshop. The dying embers of his furnace were still alight, and she headed quickly toward them; tiptoeing like a ballerina to avoid the puddles which spread before her.

The end of the evening's entertainments had finished on a high, despite the warriors initial suspicions about the mead and Odin's damning curse of Kat. Copious amounts of alcohol, and a game or two of charades and 'Valhalla,' had all helped to lighten the mood. A final, high-spirited food fight that pitted the warriors against the gods had eventually cleared the atmosphere. Friends once more, the gods and warriors had all drifted drunkenly off toward their beds.

She and Loki had made up, as she always knew they would. They had sat with Thor, Silk, Tyr, and Skogul throughout the evening's festivities, with Loki being in fine form; drinking heavily, spouting witty jokes, and taking silly jibes at Odin and the other gods. Carmel hadn't minded his brash antics because in truth, she wasn't really paying attention. Her mind was elsewhere, as evidenced by the frequent and awkward glances she exchanged with Thor.

No words were spoken, and none were needed. Loki's handsome grin now competed with the twinkle in Thor's eyes for the love she felt in her heart.

She was torn, and she knew that Thor was, too. Loki had been his drinking buddy for countless years, and now their friendship was going head to head with her sensual, feminine charms.

What a mess they were all in.

Carmel shook her head ruefully at this thought as she pirouetted abruptly; narrowly missing a puddle, which had loomed before her. Recovering her balance, she sidestepped the murky waters and continued on her journey.

She was nearly at the foundry door, and her anxiety was rising fast.

Thor was married, and his wife, Sif, was an arrogant and haughty goddess with powers that matched her status. Even though she hadn't been at the feast, Carmel didn't dare to show her feelings before the other gods. Favouring discretion over valour, she bade everyone goodnight and assisted Loki upstairs to her room. They had made love, and they had made love beautifully; but that was all. There had been no spark, no lustful craving, and no explosive surge of passion as there once had been. Maybe it was just her, the alcohol, the troubled battlefield—or maybe it was something deeper.

She still loved Loki, but his allegiance to his giant ancestors and his evil daughter cast a lengthening shadow over their relationship. Loki was a flirtatious dilettante—a god who could be here today and gone tomorrow. His love was fickle, an undying oath sworn passionately today—but what about tomorrow, and the next day and the next; what then?

Part of her yearned now for something more; a man on whom she could depend and rely. That was why she was where she was now; opening the heavy, creaking door to Thor's heart.

Stepping across the threshold, somebody stirred in the pile of straw that glistened in the warm and welcoming light of the furnace. She knew that that person was Thor; and that he was awake, too.

"Can't you sleep my lady?" came his gruff and dazed voice. Thor had been dozing; not really asleep yet not really awake, either.

Carmel shook her head. "And you?" she enquired, skipping across the room to the straw and settling down beside him. His pauper's bed felt so cosy and inviting.

"Too many things on my mind," he mumbled apologetically as he made a desperate and futile attempt to tidy himself up.

"Am I one of those things?" Carmel continued teasingly, helping him as he plucked pieces of straw from his tangled, ginger beard.

Thor didn't reply. He looked such a mess, and yet his coarse, rugged, features melted her heart. This was where she wanted to be; this was where she needed to be.

"You really shouldn't be here," he finally muttered, catching her hand in his and holding it gently against his chest. "This is wrong; we both know that."

"I'm so sorry, my lord," Carmel apologised, averting her eyes. Awkwardly, she made to get up. Perhaps she'd been wrong; perhaps she'd misread the look in his eyes earlier this evening. Her chest suddenly felt crushed and heavy with pain.

Thor didn't release her hand.

"I said it was wrong; but I didn't say I wanted you to leave."

Pulling her swiftly back toward him, he brushed wisps of hair from her face before tenderly cupping one of her flawless cheeks in the palm of his hand.

Carmel looked up. The look in Thor's beautiful eyes was unmistakable, even in the dimness of the furnace light. His look was one of passion: his look was one of love.

Sighing deeply, she nestled her head upon his chest. She pressed her body against his and shivered violently before snuggling closer still. He felt warm—he felt good. Pulling her cloak tightly around them, Thor wrapped a huge arm across her shoulders and held her firmly in his grasp. Carmel buried her face in his chest and then closed her eyes.

The sweetest of smiles floated across her lips.

She was at peace at last.

3

A Puppy

$\mathcal{T}$ he two Sangrids arrived at the shattered rim of the volcano shortly before dusk; climbing the last few hundred metres to the summit after leaving their horses with a small contingent of Berserkers who were standing on duty. With tremendous foresight, Hel had suggested that they bind Hod to avoid antagonising her dejected army.

Her ploy worked.

With Hod bound as a hostage, an ugly confrontation was avoided. Her devastated troops were in no mood to accept a son of Odin walking freely into their realm.

Scrambling up the slopes toward the wormhole's entrance, the terrible consequences of the massive nuclear explosion quickly became apparent.

Lava hissed loudly as it bubbled and oozed from deep, jagged rents in the ground; and scattered piles of ash and rock lay strewn in every direction. These heaps had been cracked and smelted into a blackened, glassy slag, which was still too hot to handle. The scenery all around them was more reminiscent of the surface of Niflheim than the gentle, rolling hills of Asgard. The sight was shocking; as were the glowing embers of funeral pyres, which now lay far behind and below them. It had been a wretched day, and it was with some relief that Kat finally stepped into the gateway that whisked them down to the sanctuary of Niflheim.

If the landscape around the volcano had seemed shocking, then the scene that greeted the trio when they arrived in Eljudnir (Hel's palace) was truly catastrophic.

Cartloads of body parts had already arrived, and these lay strewn across the blood-soaked floor in countless, jumbled heaps. Hel didn't have the energy to sift through the bits for pieces she could salvage; so she ordered her Berserkers to throw the whole lot out onto the planet's surface instead.

"It'll make good compost," she explained dismissively; much to Kat's disgust.

Damage to the vast, vaulted hall of the Berserkers was extensive and almost beyond repair. Piles of rubble lay in huge ragged mounds, and it was a miracle that the whole ceiling hadn't collapsed; such had been the force of the blast from Asgard. The worst sight for Hel was the presence of her servants, the Guardians of Niflheim. They were now united with their brethren, and the four of them were hovering malevolently close to the wormhole. Their intentions were clear.

They wanted to leave.

Kat had never seen the two servants who had been locked up before; but in truth, she could see precious little of them now. All four were wearing identical long, charcoal grey capotes; with their large hoods pulled down tightly over their heads, hiding their faces from view. She could make out the smouldering, red eyes of one of the pair, but the other didn't seem to have any eyes at all. The sleeves of their cloaks were baggy and long; and each servant had their arms folded loosely across their chests with their hands tucked into their sleeves.

This came as a relief for Kat.

She knew of the terrible power in Ganglot and Ganglati's hands; and she shuddered to think what the other two might do. Hel tried to talk to Ganglot, but after shaking her head violently, her servant had shuffled angrily away. She would not be persuaded to help tidy up the muddle. For now, the four were on strike and not obeying orders. The presence of a gateway had galvanised the Guardians.

Freedom's scent was irresistible and, as long as an exit beckoned, the Guardians would crave for liberty and ignore their duties.

"Won't they try to escape?" Kat asked with some urgency to her voice.

"Oh yes, of course; that's what they want to do," Hel replied with a merry laugh. "But they won't be able to," she added nonchalantly.

"Why's that?" Kat enquired. There were no guards standing between them and the portal; and even if there were, one touch from her servants' hands and the guards would be jelly.

"They have to get my permission before they can leave; and I won't give it to them—well, at least not just yet," Hel replied.

Kat looked bemused, so Hel decided to elaborate further.

"The Guardians of Niflheim can leave the realm only with the permission of its ruler. Even then, there's a final safeguard to prevent them from going."

"Oh; and what's that?"

"Their feet cannot cross the threshold," Hel continued. "If they do, all four will turn to dust. I have to provide transport to carry them out through the wormhole. It's an important failsafe; just in case they trick me into giving permission."

"Are they really as terrible as rumours say?" Kat continued hesitantly. After all, there were only four of them.

Hel turned and gave Kat one of her stares. It was that priceless look of incredulity; the one where she opened her eyes wide while her lips remained frozen in a mischievous, half smile. The expression was comical; but also a little scary. "Trust me, my dear Kat," she warned. "You don't want to know the full horror of an answer. Between them, they make Odin's explosion look like a party popper."

Kat gulped hard. That wasn't good news.

"But come, let's get back to our quarters and get down to some serious relaxation."

Hel smiled once more and, after putting her arm around Kat, she shepherded her and Hod toward the flickering candles of the corridor that led to their chambers.

"Hey Kat," Hel stopped after a while, taking her hand from Kat's back. She had paused outside the door leading to her harem. "Fancy a quick sauna and massage from one of my girls?" she winked with a lascivious grin.

Kat paused, looked at the corridor, and then darted a glance in Hod's direction. Ooooh, it was so tempting; but she knew she would have to pass on the invitation. What a shame. "Perhaps another time, I'm a little tired," she replied disappointedly.

"Hey gorgeous! How's my beautiful, victorious angel?"

A voice hailed them from the direction of Hel's reception room. It was Henry, and he was hurrying toward them with an open bottle of champagne in one hand and a glass bubbling over in his other. True to form, he was scantily clad in a loose T-shirt, bright boxer shorts, a scruffy dressing gown—and slippers. The colours of his ensemble varied from canary yellow to vomit green; not that that seemed to bother Hel. She skipped gaily over to him, flinging her arms around his neck, and kissed him hard on the lips.

"Did my darling little boy do a good job guarding my bedroom while I was away?" she gooed in baby talk; tugging at his cheek while relieving him of the champagne—and the glass. Handing the latter to Kat, she raised the bottle to her lips and upended it; taking huge gulps as the foaming liquid cascaded around her mouth.

"Hey Kat!" Henry exclaimed, hurrying over to her and giving her a friendly squeeze. "Guess what?" he continued excitedly. "We've got a new guest."

"Oh, and who's that?" Kat enquired.

"We've got a puppy!" Henry's eyes glistened with excitement. "You must come and see him; come on," he continued, beckoning enthusiastically with his hand in the direction of the doorway.

Kat shook her head. "Why don't you show Hod first? I need to talk to Sangrid about something." Kat breathed a quick sigh of relief. She had nearly called her sister 'Hel,' and she wasn't sure if Henry yet knew the truth yet about the woman he was besotted with.

"Come on then, let's go." Giving Hod no chance to reply, Henry dragged him up the corridor behind him. Hel slapped Henry playfully on his behind as the pair stumbled away.

When they were safely out of earshot; Kat turned to Hel. "Please would you promise me one thing?"

Hel nodded politely.

"Please don't hurt Henry when you grow bored of him. He really is a very sweet guy and totally innocent. He shouldn't be here in the first place." Kat gestured to their surroundings as she spoke. She and Henry were old school chums, and she really didn't want him hacked to pieces when Hel had had enough of his eccentric charm.

"Oh, you don't have to worry about that, sis," Hel laughed as she put her arm around Kat and squeezed her tightly.

"Why not?"

"Because I love him; stupid. But don't you dare tell him that I said so, because I'll deny it if you do." Hel kissed Kat sweetly on the forehead. She really was in an exceptionally good humour.

"Hang on a minute, Hel. Are we talking about the same person here? You, the most gorgeous and powerful woman in this realm or any other for that matter; are in love with my geeky friend Henry?" Kat could hardly believe her ears. Hel could have any one of the gorgeously handsome, hunky men in her harem.

This had to be a joke.

"Mmmm, absolutely," Hel nodded enthusiastically as she stared at Kat with a dreamy, far away look in her eyes.

"You're having me on," Kat giggled, poking her playfully in the ribs. She couldn't be serious—surely?

"No, absolutely not," Hel retorted, shaking her head as she smiled again. "Foxy has a brilliant mind, is fantastic fun, and worships the ground I walk on. What more could a girl want? Bit like you and your Hod; he adores you. You should value that you know; sincerity is hard to find in a man. Most just want your body for sex." She mused thoughtfully.

Kat gawped in amazement. *How could such sage words fall from her lips?*

Suddenly Kat had glimpsed a deeper side to her sister than she could have imagined possible. It was a refreshing insight; and one Kat decided to reflect on. Perhaps she really should stop hankering for a tasty hunk of man-meat.

"Come on, let's go and see the puppy," Hel exclaimed excitedly, taking Kat's hand in hers as she danced merrily through the doorway to her reception room.

Kat stood dumbstruck, feet firmly rooted to the floor.

There, lying stretched out in front of the fire and filling half the room was Fenrir. His green eyes were sparkling brightly, and his tongue lolled languidly from his mouth as he panted hard in the heat.

The beast looked expectantly to Hel, then Henry, and back again.

"Uh, Henry, I think you'll find that's a fully grown wolf, not a puppy," Kat breathed quietly; hardly daring to speak out loud.

"Oh no, he's not!" Henry exclaimed loudly with an impish wink. "He's our puppy."

To Kat's horror, Henry bounded across the room and flung his arms around Fenrir's neck and started to wrestle with him. Worse still, Fenrir flicked his head round and began to mouth Henry's arm with his razor sharp fangs.

Kat's hand went to draw Talwaar—and then stopped.

To her amazement, Fenrir had rolled over onto his back and was wagging his tail; wriggling from side to side in a frenzy of excitement. Henry had straddled the beast and was playfully rubbing his tummy. Incredibly, the soppy wolf was lapping the attention up. With a tremendous whoop of joy, Hel threw herself into the mêlée and the three of them rolled around in an excited ball of fur and limbs. Wild giggles of laughter erupted from Henry and Hel as Fenrir whined and drooled like a puppy.

It was an extraordinary sight, and Kat took a moment to let it soak in. In one way, it was a terrifying spectacle to see the huge, black beast gnashing at her friends; and in another, it was the most beautiful sight in the world.

Two monsters—Hel and Fenrir—locked in an intimate tussle of love.

Kat exchanged a glance with Hod; he was thinking the same thing.

"I wish we got along so well," he sighed wistfully, turning his eyes to the floor.

Kat sauntered over and after ruffling his hair; she wrapped an arm around his waist and ran her fingernails down his chest. Straining forward, she pecked him lightly on the cheek. "What am I going to do with you, my poor, besotted, lover?" she enquired whimsically, slapping him playfully before giving him a heartfelt hug. "You love me so much, and yet I give you so little."

"I know," Hod muttered as Kat kissed him once more on the cheek. It was good to feel her close; but he wished her kiss had held more passion and been pressed against his lips. It hurt, being so hopelessly, helplessly in love with her.

Before he could complain, however; there was a frantic pounding at the door.

"What now?" Hel yelled with more than a little annoyance in her voice. She was having fun and definitely didn't want to be disturbed.

The door creaked slowly open, and a slave tumbled through it; pushed in by another, even more frightened, colleague. Looking like some startled rabbit, the man threw himself prostrate on the floor and buried his face in the thick, burgundy carpet.

He was terrified—and Fenrir didn't help matters.

Leaping to his feet, he hurled himself across the room and pinned the poor man beneath his paws. Snarling viciously, he drew his muzzle back to expose each and every one of his gleaming, dagger like fangs. These hovered millimetres above the man's head as rivulets of saliva dripped into his hair.

One false move and the man would be in pieces.

"Fenrir!" Hel snapped angrily as she grabbed hold of his head and gave him a short, sharp slap on his snout. "Stop it!" she scolded; pointing for him to return to the fireside.

Although he was at least three times the size and strength of his mistress, Fenrir looked up sheepishly before slinking off whimpering with his tail between his legs. If the situation hadn't been so grave, Kat would have laughed out loud. Hel had scolded him like a naughty puppy, and he was behaving like one, too.

"Come on, out with it you maggot." Hel kicked the slave roughly. Just because she had pulled Fenrir off him didn't mean that he was going to get an easy ride. "This had better be good, or you'll be his supper," she warned, waving her hand in the wolf's direction.

"Your, your, your majesty." The man stuttered, not daring to look up.

Hel kicked him again harder. "Come on, spit it out," she hissed.

"Your, your majesty, there are t…t…two dragons waiting to see you and, and, and they don't look very happy."

Hel leant forward and sniffed at his head. It looked singed and was still slightly smoking. The slave was right, there were dragons in the palace, and they obviously weren't happy.

"Go on, get lost," Hel snarled, standing up abruptly before kicking him roughly once more.

Grateful to be leaving alive, the man exited backwards on his knees and then legged it. Next time, it would be somebody else's turn to deliver news, and they probably wouldn't be so fortunate.

"Oh dear, I had a feeling this might happen." Hel began solemnly, looking slowly at Kat, Hod, and then Henry. Suddenly, and to their surprise, she broke into a broad grin.

"Would any of you like to meet a dragon?" she enquired coyly; as if she really needed to ask.

4

The New Youth Movement

$\mathcal{F}$ rigg's idea of freedom was unfortunately very different from that of Marcus. As far as she was concerned, he was free to roam her island and enjoy its luxurious facilities, but nothing else. He couldn't leave. To do that, he would have to agree to three conditions—and they were non-negotiable.

Feeling somewhat cheated, Marcus listened patiently to her proposals as they walked back through the island's orchards toward the sprawling, single-storey mansion.

The first condition was obvious, the second was a pleasure, and the third, well; that was quite frankly bizarre. "It was to demonstrate his loyalty," as Frigg had put it; and because it seemed more ridiculous than unpleasant; with some reluctance, Marcus acquiesced.

Once her terms had been agreed, they both relaxed, and the rest of the day passed smoothly with the sort of efficiency and congeniality he had come to expect from his glamorous hostess.

Her assistant, Gna or Fulla, (he wasn't sure which one it was, because he only caught sight of the back of her) put in a call to Anna, informing her that a chamber maid had confessed to hiding the drugs in their room. Anna was reassured that Marcus would be released and, in an attempt to compensate the two of them for the unpleasantness; Frigg offered to fly Marcus back to New York on her private jet. She would also ensure that all the dresses and shoes the Contessa and Anna had bought went with him; and the two of them would always be welcomed to holiday on the island whenever they wished.

Highly unlikely, Marcus thought when Frig told him about this part of the conversation. He would have dearly loved to see Anna's face when the Contessa made that offer.

As an extra precaution, a launch was dispatched to police head-quarters in Nassau. On it was a black briefcase containing a sizeable quantity of US dollars. This would ensure the local constabulary backed up the Contessa's story, should his overly suspicious wife try to contact them.

With the cover-up successfully completed, Marcus settled down to enjoy what should have been a very pleasant evening. The food and wine were excellent, the company pleasing, and Frigg had promised him a hostess of his choice for the night; if that was his wish. The gorgeous Lia, who had previously been the senator's exclusive companion, was now available; and Marcus felt sorely tempted. After all, the Contessa owed him and owed him big time.

However, to his great surprise, Marcus decided to decline the offer of exotic company and spent a quiet night alone in his room. He had had so many problems with the Valkyries and their associates; he really didn't want to risk another debacle. He didn't sleep well; his mind being too focused on leaving the island.

After an early breakfast and with a surprisingly friendly hug and kiss from the Contessa; he was up, up, and away and heading north to JFK airport. As he settled back into his seat and sipped at a steaming cup of coffee; Marcus reflected on Frigg's terms.

The first condition had hardly needed stating.

He wouldn't breathe a word about the Valkyries, Frigg's true identity, or anything about the Dragza Corporation's involvement with the warriors. Marcus had asked if it would be all right for him to continue liaising with Agent Woods; and the Contessa had reassured him that it would. However; she doubted he would find him easy to get in touch with. Apparently, he was taking an extended vacation on the island and would probably be staying permanently. Marcus would have liked to have said goodbye to his former colleague, but he remained absent from the mansion for the duration of the evening. "Must have gone to Nassau," Frigg suggested helpfully, although Marcus felt sure this was unlikely. His hostess Christina was still around, and she would certainly have accompanied him had he gone there. Marcus didn't pry further; it wasn't his place. Besides, he and Woods were professional acquaintances, not best buddies.

Confidentiality, as demanded by Frigg, was actually an easy condition to agree to. Marcus had already decided to sever all connections with the crazy cult, and he intended to stick to this resolve. It had almost cost him his life and his marriage. Suddenly the humdrum routine of his daily existence didn't seem so bad after all. At least he didn't get shot at, coshed over the head, and thrown into miserable, stinking cells.

The Contessa's second condition was a pleasure.

After dropping him in New York, her jet would fly across the Atlantic and pick Jess up from Ireland. Marcus had been entrusted with the golden coin and a flask of mead, which he promised to give to Jess as soon as she arrived in America. Jess would know what to do with these items, and Marcus had been told to guard them with his life. He was looking forward to seeing her again, particularly after her distressing plea for help. He felt more than a little concerned for her safety. After seeing how badly the mead had affected Woods, he just hoped Jess wasn't suffering similar levels of withdrawal. The sooner she received a 'fix' from the precious flask he was carrying, the better.

Frigg's bizarre, final condition had left his arm smarting terribly, and it was still sore now.

As a gesture of his sincerity, she had asked Christina to tattoo a peculiar black flower on his shoulder. This was identical to the one that Christina and the Contessa bore on their behinds. Marcus didn't mind agreeing to this, as he could see no obvious reason for not doing so. Although he had never had a tattoo before, the flower was not unattractive and, quite frankly, the whole issue seemed of little importance.

Now, however, he wasn't so sure.

His left shoulder hurt like stink.

Loosening his buttons and carefully opening the neck of his shirt, he tried to peer down and take a peek at the flower. It really was very red and angry, with streaks of inflammation spreading up and down his arm. He hoped it wasn't infected. Frigg had assured him that the needles Christina used were brand new, but she could have been mistaken. Deciding that it was better to be safe than sorry, Marcus determined that, as soon as got home, he would get some strong pain killers and start a decent course of antibiotics.

Despite knowing that he should hate the Contessa, Marcus found he couldn't. Her great beauty and extravagant charm could pardon almost any crime. He still liked her, but he hoped for his sake that they would never meet again. Frigg, Jess, Kat, and all the rest of her crazy gang spelt trouble. When he eventually said goodbye to Jess tomorrow, that would mark an end to his uncomfortable involvement with the sisterhood.

He wished the Valkyries well—but call him never.

"Hi darling, I'm home!" Marcus called out excitedly as Anna bounded out from the sitting room and threw her arms around him.

She'd missed him, madly.

After a flurry of heartfelt kisses and cuddles, Marcus grabbed a beer from the fridge (which was actually chilled—what a novelty) and sat down next to her on the sofa. It was mid afternoon, and it was most unusual for both of them to be at home on a weekday at such an hour. Fortunately, Anna had phoned work on his behalf and advised them that he wouldn't be in today due to a dodgy stomach. This was courtesy of their recent holiday. She had used the same excuse yesterday, rather than admit that he was being held in a police cell on drug charges.

That probably wouldn't have gone down too well.

Pouring herself a glass of wine, she snuggled up next to Marcus to watch a bit of daytime TV. This was an equally rare event; but there was an interesting documentary on—one they were both eager to watch.

With a majestic fanfare of music and the waving of a crimson flag; the half-hour show began.

The 'New Youth Movement' had started from humble origins in Paris, France, in the1960s. Its original name—*Organization Des Enfant Nouveau*—was still used there to this day. This year marked its fiftieth anniversary, and both Marcus and Anna were fans of the movement. Indeed, if they had a child, along with a particular school they had in mind; this was one of the few certainties they had already agreed upon. Boy or girl, they would like their child to join the organisation and benefit from its exciting lifestyle and excellent moral code; hence their interest in the program.

The movement had taken some time to become established, and it hadn't really sparked into life until the early 1970s. This was when its rather bland and lack- lustre founder had ceded presidency to its current enigmatic and energetic leader; one Thirle Flöda (pronounced *flu–dah*).

Thirle was a wealthy philanthropist who had changed little in the forty years or so that he had led the organisation. His date of birth, ethnicity, and source of inherited wealth were somewhat confused and clouded in speculation. He had mixed European blood, which had come from his grandparents; and although his parents were naturalized Germans, he had been brought up in Austria.

The source of his wealth was even more ambiguous and completely shrouded in mystery. No one had any idea where his vast fortune had come from.

Thirle was a brilliant and impassioned speaker, and he had transformed the New Youth Movement. He had done this by riding a backlash against the sloppy, long haired, free-sex-loving, 'tune in-drop out' culture of the hippies. His powerful motto, 'Blood and Honour,' said it all; and the stark simplicity of its message had struck a chord with affluent middle classes the world over.

Much like the *Boy Scouts* and *Girl Guides* movements, the founding principles of the organisation were to respect and honour your family and colleagues; and to behave with dignity and courage. Immoral behaviour was frowned upon, as was swearing. Boys were expected to be well groomed, clean shaven, and to have closely cropped hair. Uniforms were provided free of charge, and the movement had its own flag—the silhouette of a falcon's head set against a simple, crimson background. Its motto was emblazoned in black along a yellow scroll, which ran beneath the motif.

The organisation had started as a charitable venture, with Thirle funding the many camps and brigade headquarters out of his own pocket. However, with so many influential and affluent backers, it had grown into a hugely profitable, multi-million-pound industry. Not that any money was squandered; almost all the revenues and donations were reinvested in the organisation, helping to expand its membership and improve facilities.

Both boys and girls were welcome to join so long as they were over the age of ten. Membership could continue into adulthood, with many former juniors going on to become leaders of individual brigades—or 'Banns'—as they were known. Almost every town and city in America had at least one Bann, and both Anna and Marcus had visited their local headquarters. They had been thoroughly impressed with the spotless premises and the vibrant, healthy children who had so politely greeted them and guided them around.

The aims of the organisation were simple and positive: to encourage young adults to get plenty of fresh air, to become strong and confident, and to live cleaner, greener, and healthier lives. This was done by actively encouraging competitiveness. There were weekly meetings with frequent outings and trips to the movement's many country camps. Here, individual Banns would compete against each other; and the children would learn woodcraft and survival techniques; as well as basic self-defence.

All members were encouraged to attend a least one camp a year and to attend every weekly session. Black marks would be awarded if you were absent without good reason, and few dared miss even one. Bullying was frowned upon, but children (being children) were very good at making their disapproval known. Attendance at all meetings and fixtures was free; and the youths whom Marcus had spoken to were ecstatic about their activities. These included camping, hiking, rock climbing, kayaking, horse riding, archery, and even learning how to shoot a gun. It was like a childhood dream come true; and both Marcus and Anna wished that they had been fortunate enough to join a Bann when they had been children.

To their delight, they could both still enrol as adults and they determined to do so once they had a child of eligible age.

The exact membership of the worldwide organisation was a heavily guarded secret, but it was believed to be in excess of ten million. There were at least as many parents and former members who could probably double that number. The current world crises seemed to have accelerated membership, and the whole organisation was truly global with just two exceptions. There were no Banns' in the Middle East and none on the continent of Africa—South Africa excepted.

This seemed an inexplicable oddity.

The movement made extensive use of the internet, and there was a free monthly magazine called *Comradeship*, which was delivered to all members. The name of this magazine seemed to nicely sum up the closeness of their thriving community. The whole movement was like "Scouts on steroids," as Marcus had once quipped.

As the documentary drew to a close, a final promise made Marcus sit up and take note. In October, Herr Flöda would be making a live, worldwide, televised address to mark the movement's fiftieth anniversary.

He was transfixed.

Marcus had never heard Thirle speak before, and this was becoming an increasing rarity as their aging president became ever more reclusive and reluctant to share his wisdom with the world. Thirle's address would be a unique occasion; an unprecedented opportunity to hear the world's greatest living orator deliver a keynote address.

Marcus drooled at the prospect.

Once heard, he knew he would be better able to understand the extraordinary popularity of the man and the significance of his lively and effervescent movement.

5

Dragons' Poo

Carmel ducked low, instinctively covering her head with her hands. She had heard a loud flapping noise drawing close above and behind her, and had stooped a moment before feeling the powerful downdraft of something very big as it flew close overhead. In an instant, whatever it was—it had gone.

Standing up cautiously, she looked around her.

In the darkness, she could see nothing.

Rubbing her eyes, she continued hastily across the courtyard. It was almost dawn, and she needed to get back beside Loki before he awoke and became aware of her philandering. He could be a jealously possessive god and short tempered to boot. He wouldn't take kindly to her making out with his best friend.

Carmel and Thor had, of course, made love. They hadn't intended to—but they couldn't help themselves. It was exactly the sort of spine-tinglingly powerful, and explosive outpouring of passion that Carmel so desperately craved and needed.

At last, she felt satisfied.

Hurrying up the stairs, she chastised herself soundly for her stupidity and vowed that this would mark the end of their affair. She smiled at the very thought of this and knew immediately that she was kidding herself.

Of course she would be back—as would he.

Love, lust, or whatever it was that was holding them in its embrace wasn't going to let them go without a fight.

Turning the handle carefully to her door, she slipped between the sheets and snuggled up next to Loki. He didn't move, so she gratefully ran her hand around his chest and pulled him close. He grunted but didn't stir. Carmel smiled once more. What she was doing was wrong, terribly wrong, but in a deliciously naughty and twisted sort of way; she was loving every minute of it.

The dangerous, craziness of seeing them both just added to its seduction.

Disaster would strike sometime—of that she was sure, but until it did; she was going to enjoy every minute of her two magnificent, godly lovers.

It wasn't long after Carmel had headed back to the castle—and bed—that the first Valkyrie awoke and hurried across the courtyard in the opposite direction. It was Silk who had arisen early, and she was heading toward the stable block. Glancing up fertively at the sky, she shivered. It was a little before dawn, and the first, cold, grey shadows of daylight were creeping slowly across a bleak and moonless sky.

"Are you ready?" she called out angrily, catching sight of the whisper-thin, leggy figure of Hermod. He was lounging idly at the entrance to the stables and didn't seem at all in a hurry to be off.

"Yes, my lady," he replied politely; turning sideways so that Silk could see a packed knapsack on his back.

"Then where's your horse?" she continued crossly. She was anxious to get away and didn't want to be kept waiting while this bandy, 'B list,' nobody of a god got saddled up.

"I'm just fine as I am; thank you, my lady." Hermod replied courteously, trying not to smirk as he did so.

"Well, I'm not going to be hanging around if you lag behind," Silk cautioned him curtly. "Now being as you've got nothing better to do, why don't you make yourself useful and give me a leg up."

Silk didn't really need a hand to mount Sleipnir, but she wanted to slight Hermod; to treat him like a servant. His nonchalant attitude was annoying her and added to the frustration that he was travelling with her in the first place.

Given the choice, she would much rather have gone to Niflheim on her own. In fact, the presence of one of Odin's half-caste sons as a chaperone made her as mad as a hive of freshly smoked bees. He might be a tracker, but with or without a horse, he would only hold her back. There was no way anyone would be keeping up with Sleipnir; Odin's favourite steed and the fastest stallion in the realm.

Stepping toward Silk, Hermod grinned boyishly before crouching down low and making a stirrup with his hands. Squelching a mucky boot roughly into this, Silk signalled impatiently for him to lift her.

"Careful my lady," Hermod chortled as he raised her onto her steed. Odin had warned him. The Valkyries in Asgard were very different from those that had been processed in Valhalla.

Digging her heels sharply into Sleipnir's flanks, Silk trotted out of the stable block and then broke into a canter; clattering noisily across the courtyard and down the road toward Gladsheim. She didn't look back; he could eat her dust for all she cared.

For some reason, even in the grey half-light of dawn, the square looked strangely different; but she didn't stop to find out why. Her mind was too pre-occupied with thoughts about the day ahead.

With a final, loud flourish of iron shoes as they skittered on flint; Sleipnir cantered across the bridge and then turned eastward to head out across the muddy fields toward Muspellheim. Spurring her stallion once more, Silk broke into a gentle gallop and bade good riddance to the nuisance, that was Hermod, under her breath.

"Tum, tee tum, tee tum, tee tum."

She turned her head in astonishment.

There, jogging casually and humming quietly was the figure of Hermod. He was barely three metres behind her and not even breathing hard.

"Giddy-up, Sleipnir!" Silk yelled as she urged Odin's mount into his fastest gallop. Unlike Vali, who was a shape shifter, Silk had just discovered that Hermod's unique tracker ability was running. However, that would be no matter. No god or mortal could keep up with Odin's stallion when he was in full flow.

Standing up in the stirrups, Silk cut lose and shrieked with laughter as the wind coursed through her hair; ebony locks twisting and twirling excitedly behind her as they joined in the exhilaration of their flight.

Hermod must have been left standing.

"Begging your pardon my lady, but when might be a good time to fill you in with the details of Odin's plan?"

Spinning her head sideways, Silk's jaw dropped. Not only had Hermod moved alongside her, the cheeky god was running backward!

Scowling furiously at Hermod's impish grin, Silk realised that the game was up. Reining Sleipnir in, she sat back down in the saddle as she returned him to a much more leisurely and sustainable trot.

"Would you like a bite to eat?" Hermod enquired politely as he pointed to his backpack. "I have some excellent oat cakes and pickled herrings."

Silk frowned angrily once more; and then burst into laughter. Even she could see the funny side of her pompous behaviour. She apologised for her haughtiness, much to Hermod's delight. "Exactly how fast can you run?" she enquired curiously. Sleipnir was snorting loudly and sweating hard from his exertions; but as far as she could make out, Hermod wasn't even perspiring.

"I don't really know, my lady," he replied with a shrug. "Quite a bit faster than we were going, I guess."

"How long would it take you to get to the volcano, say, if you sprinted as fast as you could?" Silk wasn't going to let him off without giving her something more substantial. She was intrigued.

Hermod looked at the distant cone that loomed as black as coal against the grey sky, and then at Silk. The distance must have been about twenty kilometres from where they were now.

"Truthfully?" he enquired.

"Truthfully," she replied.

"Well, my lady; from the moment we set out, I reckon I'd be just about there by now." And to emphasis that point, he raced round and round the Valkyrie and Sleipnir in such a blur of motion that they all became quite dizzy.

"Well, where is it?" exclaimed Jameela to an extremely puzzled Zara, an extremely tired Carmel, and an extremely bewildered Elijah.

It was mid morning, and the four of them were standing in front of Gladsheim, staring hard at the smoking remnant of the flagpole. They had come to the hall in response to the sound of horns being blown. This was a sure sign that trouble was afoot. The three warriors had fully expected to see a red flag fluttering high above Gladsheim, but they had seen none. Now the reason for its absence was apparent.

There was no flagpole—and hence there could be no flag.

Mystified, the four of them pressed forward and joined the throng of townsfolk who were gingerly squeezing into the hall. Each person was taking the greatest of care to avoid a monstrous, steaming, pat of smelly poo. This had been splattered against the oak doors and was now dribbling its way across the wooden threshold.

The mess stunk to high heaven.

Pressing deeper into the hall, they soon joined a swelling rabble of angry peasants and farmers. These were shouting angrily at Thor, who was looking in exasperation at Odin. He, in turn, lay slouched across his throne, looking more than a little bit glum. This definitely wasn't the best of starts to his day.

Loki was there too, twiddling his thumbs and grinning mischievously; clearly enjoying Odin's discomfort.

Finally growing weary of the crowds ceaseless barracking, Odin stood up and slammed Gungnir down hard upon the floor.

THUMP!

Silence fell immediately.

"Good people," he began with a hint of embarrassment to his voice. "I fully understand why you are all feeling so disgruntled, and I also accept that I am to blame. Please be reassured that you will all be compensated for your losses."

Odin finished his brief speech with an apologetic gesture that he hoped would settle the crowd's hostility. It didn't. More angry shouting erupted, and eventually Odin was forced to use Gungnir once more.

The rabble weren't satisfied.

"Yes, yes, I have heard what you've been saying, and I will do so as you insist. I can promise you all that I'll make such reparations in gold." Pulling a sullen face, he patted despairingly at his pockets. "Unfortunately, I don't seem to have any on me at the moment."

Guffaws erupted from the mob, and somebody blew a loud raspberry.

Odin's hunger for gold was legendary, and each and every coin he offered in compensation would have to be pried from his sticky fingers. Still, they had all heard his promise, and the gods always kept their word—eventually. Somewhat satisfied, the crowd quietened down and eased back a little; giving Carmel an opportunity to press forward and stand behind Thor. Feeling playful, she squeezed his bottom hard.

That should brighten his morning.

Glancing cautiously around him, Thor slid his hand backward and took her hand in his. He winked as they exchanged a brief smile. The whole matter lasted an instant, and in the bustle of the crowded hall it should have passed unnoticed.

Unfortunately, it didn't.

The one person whom they really didn't want to see their actions had caught them red handed. Loki wasn't amused, and a thundercloud flickered across his face. Something fishy was going on, and his hackles were raised.

"Loki!" Odin's voice interrupted him with a start. "When we're all finished with our business today, I want you to get back to your miserable daughter with my chest. Tell her that if she knows what's good for her, she'll fill it with Hellinium. I don't want any more feeble dwarf gold. From now on it's Hellinium, Hellinium, Hellinium; only Hellinium."

Loki nodded.

Usually he would have argued, but he wasn't going to pick a fight with Odin today. The god had Gungnir in his hand and, with the state Asgard was in, he didn't want to risk winding him up. He could do it, but he'd much rather leave that pleasurable treat to his daughter. Besides, he now had other things to fret about.

"Now, my good people," Odin raised his hands once more. "I'm afraid that we are having a small problem with our old friends the dragons. Unfortunately, as you can see, it's affecting us all." He nodded sagely toward the door, and the crowd murmured their agreement.

The smoking remnants of the flagpole bore testament to his loss; and the stinking pile of excrement was the dragon equivalent of farting in his face.

Odin wasn't impressed with these attacks, and neither were the Aesir. They too had suffered similar assaults. During the night, numerous cattle had been taken, hayricks set alight, and several cottages in the town had had their thatched roofs torched. These were all angry and defiant gestures, and Odin hoped that it would end there. Ragnarok had begun, and the last thing he needed was Surt and his dragons ganging up with his enemy.

"What I want you all to do," he suggested tactfully, "and I know it will be hard; is to take a deep breath in and try to ignore their mischief-making. I know I disturbed their slumbers with my explosion, and I'm sure that when they understand it was an accident they will all go peacefully back to sleep. In the meantime, we must all sit tight and tolerate these petty attacks."

Odin paused to catch his breath. He really wanted to crack on with other more important matters, like how he was going to get his son back. "Now then, I promised last night that I would explain the enchantment that will bring Balder back to us."

The gathering hushed once more.

This sounded exciting.

Dragons making mayhem in the night was a nuisance, but nobody had been hurt. Now that Odin had agreed compensation, their antics were yesterday's news. A magical charm, on the other hand, was today's billboard-busting, headline gossip. Intrigue, excitement, and the potential for chicanery all gave wizardry that added, sexy 'wow!' factor; and a spell to raise Balder from the dead looked set to be a corker.

"There is a deep magic," Odin began solemnly, pleased at last to have their respectful attention. "A magic which demands every woman in the realm shed tears of sorrow for my son. If they do, then the spell that binds him to the grave will be broken. He will be able to pass freely through the gates of Niflheim and walk once more amongst the living. That is why I have sent Hermod with Gunnr to visit Hel. Their quest is to check that Balder is being well treated and hasn't been hacked to pieces by its evil and cursed Queen."

Loki opened his mouth to protest Hel's innocence, but Odin silenced him with his hand. "I don't want to hear a peep out of you," he snarled. "When it comes to your bastard child, I can't trust a word you say. That's why I have sent those two to see her. If they say that Balder is whole; then, and only then, will I believe it to be true."

Loki scowled. Odin's arrogance was really beginning to bug him, especially as Hel held all the cards.

How dare he be so damned condescending?

"My lord," Jameela spoke up. "The magic sounds interesting but surely it will be impossible to make? Everybody loves Balder," she paused, allowing a ripple of agreement to drift lazily around the hall. "But to get every woman to weep for him would be impossible."

Odin smiled knowingly and pointed toward an object sitting beside him. It was a plain glazed bodn (large storage jar); one of the two which the dwarves had filled with Kvasir's blood.

"You are absolutely right my dearest Herja," he acknowledged with a grin. "And I would agree if it wasn't for the contents of this vessel."

The nosy crowd pressed forward again, eager to take a look. They formed such a crush that Thor had to get the warriors to help him push them back. There was a very real danger that in their eagerness to see the bodn, its contents would be spilt—and that would be a disaster.

"We will start tomorrow," Odin commanded when the crowd had become more orderly. "I want every musician and minstrel to come to Gladsheim at first light and drink a draught of mead mixed with the potion in this vessel. Once that has been done, I want every woman to wait in their homes for my musicians to come and sing their lullabies."

"What happens if somebody doesn't cry?" a heckler cried from the back of the hall.

"That won't happen, I promise," Odin replied confidently.

"But what if it does?" the irritating heckler continued.

"Then we will just have to tie a string of onions around her neck, won't we," Odin retorted crossly. Slumping back upon his throne, he indicated with an angry flourish that he had finished speaking. It was time for Thor to clear the annoying riffraff from his hall.

Waving his hammer above his head and accompanied by none too gentle pushes from the Valkyries; the crowd was slowly dispersed. Once Gladsheim had been emptied, the Valkyries set off back toward the castle. They, like everyone else, were deeply lost in conversation about the merits of Odin's magical plan. Kvasir's blood—the mead of poetry—probably held incredible power, but even so; the whole spell seemed desperately weak and far too fallible. It would only take one woman not to cry, and that would be that. Balder would be trapped in Niflheim forever.

"Aargh, aargh, AAAARGH!"

The sound of a woman screaming cut through the air like a flight of arrows, interrupting the Valkryies' thoughts. The howls were coming from the castle and, fearing the worst, the girls broke into a run.

Whatever was going on; the screams had to be bad news.

6

Surt and Nidhogg

"**W**ow!" Kat breathed quietly as she tried to take in every detail of the two magnificent dragons that were waddling toward her across the Berserker Hall. Up close and personal, the creatures were so much bigger and far more impressive than she had ever imagined.

With fevered anticipation, the two Sangrids and Henry had hurried down the corridors of the palace to greet their new guests. Hod didn't come; he was tired or crotchety or something, and Henry too had now dropped behind. He had insisted on getting a camera from the royal chambers, although quite why he wanted to take pictures was anybody's guess.

Being dead, who exactly was he planning to show them to?

Unfortunately, the boy couldn't be persuaded otherwise, so growing impatient with his delay; Kat and Hel had trotted off, leaving him to catch up. In some ways, this was preferable. Hel could sort out the serious business as to what the two were doing there, while Kat could spend some time admiring the fabulous beasts.

First impressions confirmed what Kat had already suspected. Pictures and drawings of these mythical creatures were reasonably accurate; but they didn't portray the sheer immensity of their size.

They were easily as big as elephants.

When walking slowly—as the pair were doing now—they liked to waddle upright, moving with gaits reminiscent of extremely bloated

45

penguins. Catching the eye of one of the dragons, Kat immediately knew that their names were Surt and Nidhogg. Surt was the Dragon King, and Nidhogg was his deputy, with Nidhogg being the slightly smaller of the two.

Kat didn't know yet quite how she knew their names; she just knew that she did.

"Surt wants to have a private chat with me," Hel whispered quietly to Kat behind the back of her hand. "He's pretty angry, but I'm sure I can sweet-talk him into calming down."

"How do you know he wants to talk to you?" Kat puzzled. Unless she was mistaken, no words had been spoken.

"Ah, yes, of course. You aren't familiar with dragons, are you," Hel nodded as she stopped Kat dead in her tracks. "Dragons can't talk, so they communicate to you by thought. If you look into their eyes as you say or think your question; you'll receive their answer. Do try to be polite, however, as they do hate rudeness. Oh, and one last thing," Hel chuckled as she spoke.

"What's that?"

"We have sex in our favour." Hel smiled cheekily. "Dragons adore beautiful women; it makes them go all soft and gooey inside."

Moving forward once more, Kat noticed that Hel's four servants had already made their way toward the new arrivals. With mounting horror, she realised one of the group had taken his hand out of his sleeve and was offering this to Surt. Kat tried to yell a warning, but before the words left her mouth, Surt had extended a giant claw—or finger—or whatever he might call it; and had shaken the servant's hand.

Nothing happened.

Surt then shook hands with the three other Guardians without ill affect.

Kat clutched at Hel's arm. "Why isn't he dead, or become sick, or fallen over or something?" she gasped, eyes agog with amazement. Surt didn't seem to be affected by the powers of the Guardians.

"Oh, yes, I forgot," Hel smiled apologetically. "Dragons are not of this world, in fact, I don't think they're even from this universe. Odin brought them to Asgard to help him in the first Elf Wars."

"Elf Wars?"

"Yes, shush Kat. Sorry, I'll tell you all about these later. Look, I've got to concentrate for a bit. Have a good chat with Nidhogg and get some great photos of you and Henry with him, okay? Tell Henry I want to see him kissing a dragon!" With a merry laugh, Hel hugged Kat and then strode over toward Surt.

It was time to get down to business.

"Um, hi. I'm Sangrid's friend, Sangrid, I mean, I'm Hel's friend, Sangrid." Kat stumbled over her words as she held out her hand to shake Nidhogg's claw. Her words were muddled but quite forgivable; after all, it wasn't everyday you got to converse with a dragon, and there were so many questions she wanted to ask.

Looking up into Nidhogg's eyes, Kat got an answer. It wasn't exactly in words; it was more an emotional feeling. She knew that Nidhogg was pleased to see her, and he was laughing at her bungled introduction. He also knew exactly who she was, and he was asking her to relax. He wasn't going to hurt her.

Kat chuckled and immediately felt more comfortable. He seemed quite pleasant.

What are you?

Kat's question brought an immediate response; a fully formed answer popping straight into her head. The sensation was hard to describe—it was as though the entire contents of an encyclopedia entitled *Dragon's for Idiots* had been planted there instantly. What was even more peculiar was that she already knew the book from cover to cover.

Suddenly finding herself an expert on dragons; she decided to take a moment and study the information that Nidhogg had given her. It was really rather interesting.

Dragons were reptiles with thick, scaly skins and cold-blooded bodies. Their shape was not unlike a dinosaur's; with a long, pointed tail and large hind legs that they could waddle on, run on, and even hop on like a kangaroo when they wanted to. Their stomachs were much more swollen than Kat had expected; but Nidhogg had explained this in his answer. They stored hydrogen from the food they digested and they used this for flame throwing and buoyancy when flying.

At this point, as if he was reading her mind; Nidhogg tapped the tips of his claws together and then stretched and yawned, proudly unfurling his magnificent wings.

These were so thin as to be almost translucent in colour.

After a gentle flap, which sent a small ripple of sand and dust scurrying across the cavern's floor; Nidhogg furled them once more such that they lay flush beside his body. They protruded a little, forming a pair of pointed fins on either side of his back.

Nidhogg tapped his claws together once more, and Kat knew instinctively that he wanted her to shake one. She did so; she had been dying for an opportunity to see what he felt like.

Would he be cold and slimy or be warm and prickly?

As it turned out, the dragon was neither.

The texture of his claw felt dry and horny, a bit like a fingernail. Growing bolder, Kat stepped forward and pressed down gently on one of the scales on his body. This felt rubbery. The scales shimmered in the flickering light of the cavern and, on closer inspection, Kat understood why. Their texture was like mother-of-pearl, reflecting and bending light such that Nidhogg changed colour as you looked at him from different angles. This was really quite clever and helped him to stay camouflaged when flying in the sky.

Returning her attention to his hands, Kat ran hers along his. She could tell immediately that he was warming to her touch. Dragon hands were particularly sensitive, and the softness of her flesh was enthralling. She was giving Nidhogg the dragon equivalent of a passionate snog on the lips. He was swooning with delight.

Without wishing to offend his feelings or risk exciting him further; Kat slowly withdrew her hand. Stepping back a few metres, she looked up; following the course of Nidhogg's long, tapering neck until her gaze reached his head.

This was the most extraordinary part of his body.

It was easiest to describe its shape as being a bit like that of a crocodile's, but one that had run into a brick wall. His snout was truncated. Nidhogg flicked his tongue out proudly, and this forked and flickered like a snake's.

He was scenting her odour.

Nidhogg yawned once more, and the gaping chasm of his mouth seemed to be crammed full of sharply curved teeth. Yawning wider still; his lower jaw unhinged with a click, allowing his already huge mouth to nearly double in size.

Kat jumped. Now that really did look scary.

Ha, ha, ha!

Looking into his eyes, Kat could tell that he was laughing at her fright. After waggling his large, pointed ears, Nidhogg tilted his head and lowered this toward Kat.

Up close and personal, his eyes were amazing.

Pitch black in colour and positioned like a crocodile's, they bulged from his head like those of a fly—but were much more exquisite; being sculpted like a pair of shiny, black, teardrop diamonds. Having eyes so large and so well positioned, Nidhogg could see all the way around him, and he could see in infrared, too. This allowed him to hunt by night. Indeed, dragons preferred to do this; finding the brilliance of sunlight far too uncomfortable for their liking.

"Hey, say 'cheese' Kat!"

Spinning round, Kat could see Henry crouching down with his camera.

FLASH!

Henry snapped a picture.

WHOOSH!

Alarmed by the sudden, blinding flash of light; Nidhogg snorted out a huge sheet of flames—toasting Henry's hair. He was lucky not to have been burnt to a cinder.

"Wow! Did you see that Kat? How cool was that," Henry cooed; oblivious to the fact that he had narrowly missed being roasted alive. Shuffling forward, he crouched down and prepared to take another shot.

"No, Henry, don't!" Kat yelled, running in front of him. "Don't use the flash! Dragons can't stand bright lights."

"I'm so sorry," Henry muttered apologetically as Kat hastily pulled his head toward her. His hair had been singed, and she quickly patted out tufts that were continuing to smoulder.

"You muppet," she giggled, slapping Henry playfully on the back of his head.

How did you do that? She entreated Nidhogg with her eyes.

Nidhogg bent forward and presented the tip of his snout toward them. He snorted, encouraging the pair to look more closely at his nostrils.

Studying these intently, Nidhogg rolled back a pair of tiny membranes at the tip of each one. A shiny nugget of white phosphorus popped briefly into view before bursting alight. Turning away, Nidhogg snorted once more.

Hydrogen ignited as a fountain of flames erupted from each nostril.

This was how dragons breathed fire.

Delighted at their newfound friendship; Kat, Henry, and Nidhogg took turns in playing with Henry's camera. Hel did get her photo of Henry kissing a dragon; and after setting the camera up on a pile of rocks; she also got a lovely shot of the three of them posing together, with Kat and Henry perched precariously on Nidhogg's back.

Once he understood how the camera worked, Nidhogg proved surprisingly clever and dextrous. He took all manner of photos, and he was reluctant to part with the camera even when Hel returned from the far side of the cavern.

Listening to Henry's plea, Hel promised to get him one of his own, and he demonstrated his delight at this gift by blowing a magnificent ring of fire. Quite how he did that Kat didn't know.

"All done?" Kat enquired hopefully, and Hel nodded her head.

"Yeh, at least for now," she nodded confidently. "They were all for blaming me for the explosion, but I think I've cleared that misunderstanding up. Surt now agrees that it was Odin's fault. Anyway, they seem to like it here, and we've sort of come to a deal."

"Oh, and what's that?" Kat enquired, but Hel didn't reply.

Turning and raising her voice, she bellowed to the remnants of her Berserker Army to gather round. She informed them that Nidhogg and Surt were going to be their honoured guests and that they had the freedom of the realm. They could roam both inside the palace and outside on the planet's blistering surface.

This in fact was exactly what the dragons had been hoping for.

With their cold-blooded bodies, they found the warmth of Niflheim far more cosy and pleasing than the wintry temperatures of Asgard. To have an opportunity to bask and feed on the planets boiling, rotting surface was like going on holiday. Surprised and grateful for Hel's generosity, they fluttered their eyelids as they thanked her for her hospitality.

Show over, Hel lashed out a vicious kick at a soldier who had dared to cough while she'd been talking, and after bidding farewell to the dragons, she set off with Kat and Henry toward the royal quarters.

Kat yawned; she was exhausted.

"Would you like to have a nap?" Hel offered. "Or would you rather stay up just a little longer and let Hod and I tell you about the Elf wars?"

"Oh, go on, Kat, you can't go to sleep," Henry exclaimed, squeezing her tightly before turning his affections toward Hel. "You've got to tell us about them now, please? I won't be able to sleep if you don't."

Giggling happily and skipping rather than walking, Hel led them back to her reception room.

This was going to be a good story.

7

The First Elf Wars

"ome on!"

Taking hold of Hod's hand, Kat yanked him forcibly out of his chair and onto the rug where she, Hel, Henry, and Fenrir had stretched out in front of the fire. Hod was still sulking, and Kat was almost too tired to move. However, she wasn't going to miss hearing about the mysterious elves that lived on the far side of Middle Sea, even if it meant propping her eyelids open with matchsticks.

Grinning in an annoyingly 'stop-it-I-like-it' sort of way, Hod glanced over to Hel as Kat poured a glass of wine and then pulled him tightly against her. His attack of the grumps was definitely lifting. "Are you going to start, or shall I?" he enquired, revelling in Kat's closeness.

"Why don't you start," Hel suggested. "But do remember, guys, that Hod and I were only children when the wars took place. We may be a bit hazy in places." Settling back into Fenrir's thick coat and clutching both her glass and Henry; she beckoned for Hod to begin.

Riveted with attention, Kat listened as their story unfolded. Closing her eyes, she tried to visualise an Asgard that was very different from the one they knew now.

The First Elf Wars had begun almost immediately after the Aesir-Vanir civil war. This was the time when the original castle walls had been torn down, and gods and men were fighting amongst each other. The whole realm was in a state of chaos as many enemies sought to gain from the terrible conflict and Odin's weakened power. The dwarves were busy making handsome profits from forging and selling weapons to anyone who could afford them; and the giants were wallowing in their success at seizing the parts of Vanaheim, which lay at the foothills of their kingdom.

In these times, the elves lived peacefully in Asgard, and the lands far to the south of Middle Sea were unknown and unexplored. Strange creatures roamed there then as they still did today; creatures with absolutely no fear of gods or man. There were flightless birds which nested on the ground, and deer and badgers that would come right up to you and nibble food straight out of your hand.

Unfortunately, this peaceful situation couldn't last. The Aesir were restless and bold seafarers, eager to seek out and explore new lands.

As soon as the first longboats discovered these strange lands, the sailors and gods had a field day. The place was a cornucopia of food and thick pelts; and they set about the poor creatures with gusto, hunting and killing so many beasts that their boats became so heavily laden they could barely stay afloat.

"What about the elves, do tell us about the elves," Kat interrupted. She wanted to get to the good part before she fell asleep. She was feeling so desperately tired.

"I was just getting to them, if you'd only let me continue." Hod squeezed her in annoyance and then carried on.

Elves were vegetarians, and they abhorred the way men hunted and killed animals. In Asgard, they tolerated it because this was the way it had always been; but hearing of the slaughter of the helpless beasts in the southern realms was a step too far. Their leaders called for a meeting with Odin and issued him an ultimatum.

Stop killing the creatures or face their wrath.

Odin, being the diplomatic god that he was, smiled politely, offered his sympathies, and promised that he would do his best to stop the slaughter. Of course, he did absolutely no such thing. He loved to hunt and didn't give two hoots to their idle threats.

Hod paused and then asked Kat and Henry if this part of his story had a familiar ring to it. They both nodded and agreed. Meaningless promises from political leaders were clearly not restricted to those in Midgard.

Taking a deep gulp of wine, Hod asked Hel to continue with the next part of the story. She did so with a wicked, twinkle of green flashing in her eyes.

Growing impatient with Odin's arrogance and 'couldn't-care-less' attitude (Hel spat in the fire when she mentioned his name); the elves began their campaign.

Now for Henry and Kat to fully understand how difficult a problem this would be for the great god; they needed to know a little of what elves were like. Between them, Hod and Hel took some time in describing the strange beings that had once been their playmates.

Elves were like children, both in stature and mind. They were eternal and had come into creation at the beginning of time. They didn't age, they didn't die, and they didn't have babies. They existed then, now, and forever without change.

There were both male and female elves, although it was almost impossible to tell them apart, even if you knew their elegant but lengthy names. They all had long, curly, golden hair and beautiful faces; with large, clear blue eyes and cherubic lips and noses. Their teeth were distinctive, each tooth being clearly separated from one another (like the milk teeth of infants) and being sharply pointed. All the elves looked as though they were about nine or ten years old, if they would only stand still long enough for you to study them.

"What do you mean by that exactly?" Kat enquired, sitting up a little as she rubbed her eyes. This sounded intriguing.

Just as time in Niflheim passed very differently from time in Asgard; so the elves experienced time in a very different manner from men. For them, everything was speeded up by a factor of ten.

If you could imagine standing still and watching a clock for one minute, then for an elf, the same amount of time would feel as though they'd been standing still for ten minutes. From a human point of view, watching an elf talking and walking appeared as though they were chattering in a high-pitched babble and moving in fast forward.

From an elves point of view, the speech and movements of the gods and Aesir were the opposite; appearing to take place in slow motion. It was almost as boring for them to communicate with man as it would be for a man to converse with a tree. For elves, slowing themselves down to walk beside the mortal Aesir was an excruciating experience.

"I thought you said they were your playmates?" Kat interrupted once more, and Hel nodded.

Hod continued the story this time.

Before the war, the elves were friendly and helpful, particularly to children whom they adored. Unable to conceive themselves, they could always find time for the infants of Asgard. The elves lived in small woodland groups, picking and eating berries, nuts, and mushrooms; and generally minding their own business. They lived peaceful lives and spent a lot of their time nursing sick or injured animals and birds back to health. It delighted them to let children stroke and play with these. Both Hod and Hel had spent many hours playing hide-and-seek with the elves (elf clothing made excellent camouflage), making necklaces from forest flowers, and learning what fruits were edible and which ones weren't. They were blissful days, and it was all very sad when they came to an end.

"This all sounds nice and cosy," Henry interrupted, butting in for the first time. He was slurring a little and had clearly drunk a lot more alcohol than the rest of them. "But I don't understand why they would pose such a problem to the gods. After all, they're only small, harmless kids aren't they?"

"Children, yes, but harmless—" Hod looked at Hel and they both burst out laughing. "No."

Both Kat and Henry looked surprised, so Hel picked up the reins once more.

Being small, well camouflaged, and able to move about ten times as fast as a man; made for a deadly enemy. Using short, stubby swords and bows and arrows to great affect, the elves began their guerrilla warfare. The gods and Aesir were free to wander in the woods, but if they dared to harm animals, then they would be attacked.

In a manner similar to how the Valkyries found the giants slow and cumbersome when fighting; the elves found dodging and stabbing humans a piece of cake. For the gods and the Aesir, the opposite was true. Doing battle with the elves was a bit like fighting shadows; an exercise in futility. Feeling frustrated and growing increasingly annoyed at their helplessness, Odin set off 'well hopping' in search of something—or someone—who could help him defeat them.

"Well hopping?" Kat enquired; this was an expression she didn't understand.

"Yes, well hopping," Hel confirmed. "Travelling from well to well and exploring new realms and universes; Odin loves doing that. That was how he found Midgard and how you and my darling Foxy-Loxy happen to be here with me now!" Laughing wildly, Hel turned and started a tickling match with Henry, who fought back with shrieks of laughter. He was particularly sensitive and in an extremely silly and playful mood.

"Henry!" Kat scolded in an effort to stop the silliness. "Calm down, this is important. Are you saying that there are lots of wells?"

"Oh yes," Hel nodded nonchalantly. "Hundreds, thousands, maybe even millions; who knows. Basically every universe that is habitable has at least one well in it."

Hel spoke in such a matter-of-fact kind of way that Kat was taken aback. This was a stunning revelation. "But I thought your rings only allowed you to visit one or two realms?" she enquired.

"Mmm," Hel nodded, elbowing Henry hard in the ribs because he wasn't paying attention and was trying to start tickling her again. "That's true, but not if you're a senior god like Odin, Frigg, or Freyja. If you look at their rings, they each have a central, larger, slightly blue coloured diamond that acts like a master switch. With that, they can pretty much go anywhere they please."

"So," Kat asked, taking a deep breath in. "What you're saying is that there are hundreds, maybe millions of universes out there?" She was struggling with this concept, and Henry didn't help matters. He was making an action as though he was squashing and then rubbing two slices of bread together. 'M-theory' he mouthed and hoped that she would remember their little conversation back on Midgard.

Kat did; although it looked as though her vision of the 'multiverse' had just got a whole lot bigger.

"Yes, absolutely," Hel replied and then requested a bit of silence so she could finish off their tale. Rolling around with Henry was distracting her and making her think of things other than story telling.

Returning to the tale, it transpired that during Odin's travels, he stumbled upon the realm where the dragons lived. They were a race in danger of extinction. Their planet was very hot and getting hotter still, as their sun made preparations to explode.

"A supernova?" Kat blurted and, after nodding that she was correct; Hel asked her to 'zip it.' She didn't want any more interruptions.

Odin struck a deal right there and then and brought as many of the dragons as he could back to Asgard. They would help him defeat the elves, and in return he would build a place hot enough for them to live.

Now at first sight, getting dragons to fight elves might seem a little strange. Dragons being bigger than men should mean that they were slower.

The truth, however, was exactly the opposite.

Dragons' large, sensitive eyes made them able to detect even the smallest of movements, and they could react to these instantly. Using their tails like whips, they could flick them around in the blink of an eye; stabbing anyone or anything. Even when they occasionally missed; they could always toast the whole area with a spurt of flames from their nostrils.

Just as the elves found attacking and killing the Aesir easy; so the dragons found hunting down elves a doddle. The elves' camouflage didn't help them, either. With dragons able to see in infrared, the elves stood out vividly, even when hiding in the densest of thickets.

In a matter of weeks, the elves were defeated and a truce was agreed. All the elves would leave Asgard and, in return, the gods promised men would not set foot on the lands beyond Middle Sea. To ensure that this bargain was kept, Odin appointed Aegir to watch over the sea. He, in turn, created the giant sea monsters, Jormungard and his colleagues; to sink any boats that tried to make the crossing.

"And they all lived happily ever after?" Kat volunteered cautiously in the silence that followed.

"Yes, we all lived happily ever after," Hod smiled, snuggling up closer to her. He was feeling tired now, too.

"What about the dragons, I want to hear more about the dragons!" Henry chortled; he had loved the tale and didn't want it to end just yet.

"Haven't you been listening, Foxy?" Hel threatened, throwing herself on top of him and pinning his arms and body beneath her. Henry hooted with laughter.

"Odin used Gungnir to raise the volcano and create the realm of Muspellheim," she explained. "This is where they have all lived peacefully until now; curled up in their cosy caves filled with straw— and treasure."

Finishing the tale, Hel instantly regretted using the word treasure. She could see Henry's eyes lighting up. With a tired sigh, she knew that she would have to provide him with an explanation. Looking over to Hod, she pleaded for him to bail her out. Luckily, he did.

It turned out that Dragons were only interested in three things: eating, sleeping, and beautiful possessions. These latter included both treasure and fair maidens.

For a dragon, treasure was very different from that desired by gods and men. It wasn't just restricted to precious gems and metals. Anything that sparkled and looked colourful would do; and they filled their caves with bits and pieces that caught their fancy. Gazing at their beautiful collections was restful and also helped dragons in courtship.

Their caves were more than just places to sleep; lady dragons chose their mates according to the beauty of their caves.

This was why they were so angry now.

Not only had Odin's explosion disturbed their slumber, he had also shattered their sex appeal.

"Are you telling me that a dragon's cave is his shag pad?" Henry guffawed loudly as Hel slapped him sharply for lowering the tone.

"I prefer to use the word love nest; but if that is what you mean by 'shag pad,' then the answer is yes; yes you are correct." Bending over, she kissed him once more. He was forgiven. "Now, talking of love nests, is anybody else ready for bed?"

Henry nodded eagerly; he needed no further invitation.

Staggering drunkenly to his feet, he allowed Hel to take hold of his hand and lead him away behind her. Tripping over Kat's outstretched legs; he winked and giggled cheekily at her.

He was living the dream.

8

The Devil's Spawn

i Jess!"

Marcus hurried over and hugged Jess warmly the moment he spotted her. He was delighted to see her again and hoped that the warmth of his embrace would hide the awful shock he felt inside.

She looked terrible.

When Marcus had first met the Valkyrie, she'd been a gorgeous, powerful twenty-six year old; lithe, energetic, and sexy as hell. He had fallen for her instantly—she being his fabulous, fantasy, dream woman. They had spent a single incredible night of passion making wild and exhilarating love.

Now, however, she couldn't have looked more different; being haggard and old for her sixty-something years of age. Unrecognisable from the goddess he had once known. Her shoulders were hunched, she was walking stiffly with a stick, and her mottled, grey hair bore the lankness of ill health. She had lost a lot of weight, too, perhaps ten kilos; and bearing in mind that she'd never been fat, Jess now resembled a twig. She looked positively anorexic.

"Hi Marcus," Jess hugged him enthusiastically.

"Ouch!" he exclaimed, wincing as an involuntary spasm of pain burnt a hole in his left shoulder. The Contessa's tattoo was still very painful. With as much tact as he could muster, he wriggled loose from Jess's embrace.

"Thank you so much for coming to meet me," she continued, as Marcus helped Jess with her bag and then lent her an arm for assistance. She looked so very frail.

"When you next see Frigg, you must thank her from the bottom of my heart for all her kindness. Without you two, I would surely be dead." Jess paused, hesitantly, before flashing Marcus a pleading look. "Do you have it? Do you, do you have the mead?" she enquired nervously, hoping that her voice and the tremor in her hand wouldn't telegraph her desperation. In truth, the flight from Dublin had been an agonising torture. Every second filled with a longing for the draught.

She could have ripped her own heart out for just one sip.

Marcus stopped and reached into a pocket on the inside of his thin summer jacket. "Are you absolutely sure you want this?" he enquired, looking Jess earnestly in the eyes.

In some ways he hated himself for what he was doing. He felt little better than a pimp, a drug dealer peddling death to a sobbing, teen-aged whore. He could see the strain on Jess's face and the involuntary ticks and spasms, which wracked her body in agonising shocks. Death suddenly seemed preferable than going on living as she was now, craving the evil brew with every fibre of her being.

God! He hated seeing her like this.

Jess stretched out an arm and opened a very shaky hand. She wasn't going to beg for the flask, but her look said more than words ever could. Her once beautiful, ice blue eyes were now two sunken, bloodshot wells burning with only one desire.

Mead.

She had to have it—now, now, now.

Pausing briefly for just a moment longer, Marcus shrugged and then placed the flask in her hand. "I'm so sorry," he apologised and hoped that if there really was a god in heaven he would be forgiven for what he'd just done.

Laughing with uncontrollable relief, Jess ripped the stopper from the flask and upended the bottle to her lips. It seemed as though she would down half the contents in a single gulp. People around them stopped and stared, but she didn't care. Gasping for air, she finally removed the flask from her mouth and wiped her dripping lips crudely with the back of her hand.

The tingling warmth of redemption spread quickly through her body, and within seconds Marcus could already notice a difference. The ghastly, Tourette's style twitching was gone, and her sallow, grey cheeks were beginning to glow again with a delicate shade of pink.

Jess leant back against the wall and raised the flask to her mouth once more. "Don't apologise for giving this to me, Marcus," she began, smiling in a manner that suggested the warrior Brynhildr was rising swiftly again. "I have no choice. You can see the train wreck that I've become. Without the mead, I'll die. Odin owns me body and soul, just as he has done since the day I first set foot in Asgard. That is the price I pay for being a Valkyrie, and I accept my fate gladly."

Thanking Marcus profusely, she took hold of his arm once more and with an altogether firmer grasp and lighter spring to her step; they headed toward the airport café.

They needed a coffee and a chat.

Jess had been away a long time, and she was anxious to see if Marcus had any news about her sisters and Kat; especially Kat.

"By the way, this is also for you." Marcus reached into his pocket and carefully slid the shiny gold coin across the table. "Frigg said you would know what to do with it."

Taking it in her hand, Jess looked down briefly and then squealed with delight. It was her passport home, and she pulled Marcus across the table and kissed him firmly on the lips. "Thank you, thank you, thank you," she murmured over and over again.

"I understand the mead, but I still don't get why the coin is so important," Marcus commented. He couldn't help being curious and, to his astonishment, Jess provided him with an unexpectedly frank answer.

"This is how we get home; this opens the well to Asgard."

Marcus looked surprised, and Jess was suddenly aware that he knew nothing about Mimir's well and the way the warriors travelled between worlds. She decided not to say more. He already knew too much, and any further knowledge wouldn't do him any favours. "How's Kat?" she enquired excitedly, grabbing his hand and hoping that her question would distract him.

It did; and for the next half hour or so they chatted about what each of them had been doing for the last few weeks. It transpired that Jess's mother, Doreen, had an advanced form of dementia and couldn't have told her daughter from a teapot. Her mind was gone, much to Jess's horror. Jess had then tried to introduce herself to her brother's children, but that, too, had turned into a nightmare. As far as they were concerned, their sister-in-law—Lieutenant Jessica Sullivan—had died back in 1972, and that was how she should remain.

Dead, buried, and long forgotten.

There was nothing Jess could do to open their minds. In their eyes, she was a charlatan and a fraud; a blatant and contemptuous gold digger who had come to Ireland to swindle their addled mother out of their inheritance. If they could, they would have run her out of town on a rail, so great was their hostility. It went without saying that Jess had been left alone, heartbroken, and torn to shreds by the constant, unremitting craving for mead.

Her stay had been one long, unmitigated hell from start to finish.

Marcus told Jess all about what he had been up to as well. She was intrigued by the island and laughed at the clandestine name of Odin's company. The Dragza Corporation was typical of his wry and warped sense of humour. Everything seemed to be going wonderfully until Marcus jokingly told her about the tattoo and how it was still so painful. It seemed of such little consequence, but Jess's face darkened immediately.

She looked as though he had run her through with a sword.

"Can I see it," she asked in a whisper. "Not here, in the toilets. We need to be somewhere private." She added breathlessly.

"Sure, no problem."

Marcus stood up, and they made their way outside toward the quietest toilet they could find. Looking conspiratorially around him, Marcus ushered Jess into the disabled loo and then locked the door firmly behind them.

"Are you absolutely sure the tattoo is a flower?" Jess asked nervously as Marcus peeled away his jacket and began to take off his shirt.

"Yeh, a funny looking black one with a red centre," Marcus continued casually. "It looks quite nice." He still couldn't see why Jess was making such a big deal of it.

Jess held her breath and shut her eyes the moment before Marcus stripped the shirt from his left shoulder. She placed a hand upon the wall to steady herself, before bracing herself to take a look. *It just wasn't possible, was it?*

"Oh, sweet Odin!"

Jess gasped and then collapsed back against the toilet wall; head spinning and feeling like she was going to heave at any moment.

There it was; Asgard's worst nightmare.

In an instant, everything she knew about the gods had been turned upside down. The tattoo was a black poppy. Marcus bore the mark of Hel, and it could mean only one thing: Frigg was in cahoots with the Valkyries most deadly enemy—Frigg was one of Hel's Angels.

Odin needed to be informed immediately.

"What?" Marcus enquired nervously, unsettled by the look of horror on Jess's face. A sense of alarm was rising rapidly inside him. It was only a tattoo of a crap flower for fuck's sake!

"I can't say, Marcus, and it would be best for you if I don't say, ever. I have to go; I have to go back to Asgard now." Jess reached into her pocket and withdrew the coin.

"You can't leave me like this," Marcus hissed angrily, grabbing her arm firmly. "You can't go acting all mysteriously and then just vanish in a flash of light. I've saved your life and you at least owe me an explanation as to the meaning of this thing."

Jess felt the strength of his grip and looked up. She wasn't strong enough yet to break free. Her Valkyrie blood was still too weak. "I can't, I really, really can't," she pleaded.

"I'm not letting you go, not until you tell me what's going on," Marcus muttered furiously. If this was going to be his last encounter with the Valkyries, he would be damned if they were going to leave him half cocked with a nasty secret to fret over.

"Please Marcus, you don't understand," Jess insisted, but she could see that he wasn't going to give in. Hero or no hero, he was an obstinate and passionate man—which was why she loved him so much.

She had no choice; she had to tell him. She would have to ruin every minute of the rest of his life—and the next.

"All right, you win. Just let go of my arm first, please."

Marcus shook his head as he refused to budge. He wasn't going to be double-crossed. If she was going to vanish, then she would be taking him with her.

"That flower, Marcus," Jess began hesitantly and then stopped. She had had a better idea. "Do you know the significance of the number six, six, six?" she enquired.

"Yes, of course I do, everybody does. It's the mark of the devil," he replied without batting an eyelid. He still couldn't comprehend the terrible truth that was about to shatter his world.

"Well Marcus; that mark is a lie; it's an urban myth. Your tattoo, on the other hand," Jess pointed to his arm. "That's the real deal. You bear the mark of the devil. You have been branded by Hel, and she owns you body and soul. I'm so sorry, but there is nothing more anyone can do for you now."

What?" Marcus exclaimed, releasing Jess's arm before laughing out loud. *That was rubbish!* She had to be talking nonsense.

Jess didn't smile, and she didn't join him in his laughter. Suddenly his merriment sounded empty and churlish in their tiny room.

She hadn't been joking.

"You can't be serious, surely." Marcus enquired incredulously, pinching himself as he spoke. He felt fine, absolutely fine; and nothing at all like how he imagined one of Satan's servants would feel.

"I'm afraid I am being serious, deathly serious. I'm so sorry," Jess added apologetically before leaning forward and kissing him tenderly on the cheek. "I still love you," she whispered softly, "with all my heart." She began to chant the ancient verse. "Goodbye my love and may the gods have mercy on your soul."

Without giving him a chance to say goodbye, Jess was gone; leaving Marcus standing alone in a chilling and disconsolate silence.

Taking a deep breath in, he tried to recover his senses and get his head around what had just been said.

According to Jess, he was possessed by the devil.

Wow!

Now that was going to take some getting used to.

9

Never Going Back Again

"**A**argh, aaargh, AAARGH!"

Carmel, Jameela, and Zara stopped dead in their tracks.

They couldn't believe their eyes.

There, standing in the entrance hall and screaming with joy, was the unmistakable flame-red hair of Jess. She was dancing up and down, pinching herself, and hugging each and every person she could see. Tears streamed down her cheeks, and the girls flew over and held her tightly in their arms. It was a joyous moment for all of them.

"Thank you, thank you so much," Jess cried when Freyja eventually arrived in the castle. Throwing her arms around their Queen, Jess wept more tears upon her shoulder. "Thank you for making me young again," she whispered.

After kissing Jess affectionately upon both cheeks and returning the warmth of her embrace, Freyja stood back and took her hands in hers. "My darling Brynhildr, it is so very good to have you back in our hour of need. We've missed you greatly; with Asgard lying so close to death, your strength and bravery are sorely needed."

"Look at me!" Jess cried once more as she did a little twirl on the spot. "I'm young again."

Freyja took her hands once more and urged her to calm down. No one could remember seeing Jess quite this excited before.

"It's the well that has returned your youth, not I," Freyja continued quietly, bashfully trying to avoid the lavish praise the warrior was

65

heaping on her. Jess looked quizzical, so Freyja continued with an explanation that she hoped Jess might understand. "When you returned from Midgard, the data from your body must have been so corrupted and damaged by age that it was unrecognisable. The well reinstated the original pattern it held for you in its memory. It is Odin, not I, who you should thank for your salvation."

"Where is he?" Jess enquired, suddenly remembering the terrible news she had to tell him. "And where is my dearest Sangrid?"

The atmosphere fell silent as it slowly dawned upon the warriors that Jess knew nothing about the death of Balder, the battles against the giants, the Berserkers—and Kat's flight to Niflheim.

"I'm not sure where Odin has gone," Zara began slowly. "But I think we ought to talk to you before you go and see him."

"Why, why?" Jess cried; eyes wide open with excitement. She needed to see Kat and beg her forgiveness for the terrible wrong she had done.

Nobody spoke.

"What's up? Where's Kat? Where is she—is she, is she hurt?" Jess demanded falteringly—and then gulped. Fresh tears began to well in her eyes. She would take her own life if Kat had come to any harmed.

"No, no, she's fine," Zara retorted reassuringly, waving for the other girls to disperse, which they did so very reluctantly. Prior to Kat's arrival, Zara had been Jess's best friend, so it was only right and proper that she should tell Jess the news. Secretly, however, all the warriors wanted to join in and watch Jess's reaction.

Gossip was as much a way of life as wielding a sword.

Taking her sister gently by the hand, Zara led her through the doors to the feasting hall and then closed them tightly behind her. So much needed to be said that she wasn't really sure where or how to start.

"My lord." Jameela arose quickly from where she'd been sitting, curtsied, and then bowed her head low. In spite of her previous suspicions, Jameela was still one of Odin's most loyal warriors. To have her lord and master come upstairs to her chamber was a great honour—and most unusual.

His presence in her room was actually quite unsettling.

"Greetings my dear Herja," Odin began, crossing the room in an effortless glide and after raising her hand to his lips and kissing it, he continued on his journey to sit down upon the bed. "And how is our foolhardy patient today?" he enquired.

"I'm feeling much better now, Sire," Ben answered politely, shuffling himself awkwardly up between the sheets as he did so. Odin's unexpected visit had caught both of them by surprise. He, too, was feeling uncomfortable.

"That was a very stupid thing to do, wasn't it Benjamin?" Odin began sternly and after raising his eyebrow and staring solemnly at Ben, he relaxed abruptly and smiled as he ruffled the hero's hair. "But we all do crazy things for love, don't we, hey?" Odin turned and smiled expectantly at Jameela.

"Yes, my lord, we do," she volunteered as she began to ease just a little. Hopefully the worst of Ben's reprimand was now over.

"I blame myself, actually," Odin continued, plucking an apple from a bowl of fruit and slicing it masterfully with a knife. "I didn't let you go to Valhalla when you wanted to, did I, Herja?"

"No, my lord," she agreed cautiously. "But you were right to deny my request. My services were, and still are, needed here with you my lord." She was still unsure as to where the conversation was leading.

"Excellent news about Brynhildr," Odin added as he offered Ben a slice of the apple. "She's a mighty warrior and with her safe return, I can now grant you your request." he paused, giving them both a moments reflection to understand what he was getting at. "In fact, I can whisk you both off to Valhalla straight away," he continued cheerily, munching a slice of the apple.

Jameela looked at Ben and Ben looked at her. After an exchange of hurried glances, they both turned and stared awkwardly at Odin. Jameela decided she should be the first to take the plunge.

"My lord, your offer is most kind and generous," she bowed and curtsied once more. "It's just, it's just—" she paused and cursed silently. She had lost her confidence again.

"—It's just, Sire," Ben volunteered, coming to her rescue. "It's just we would prefer to wait and have a more traditional send off; one that befits Jameela's status. She has been a great Valkyrie and deserves a mighty celebration."

Odin looked up and raised his eyebrows. This wasn't what he'd been expecting. He hadn't prepared a good reason for rejecting this excuse.

Damn! He really should have seen it coming.

"Ah, yes, quite; well, I understand," he blustered awkwardly. Standing up stiffly, Odin took Jameela's hand in his once more. This really was an unexpected turn of events—and one that had him flum-moxed. "I…I…I'm sure that that can be arranged; but it may take a few days. We're going to be quite busy what with Ragnarok upon us and getting all the women to weep and so on and so forth," he contin-ued, visibly ruffled by Ben's suggestion.

"Oh, my lord, that's wonderful news!" Jameela exclaimed. "I'm sure Ben won't mind a small delay, even though he really is most anx-ious to rejoin your mighty army." Thanking Odin and grinning broadly, she skipped cheerily beside him as he made his way reluc-tantly to the door.

"Good, well, I guess then that's settled, isn't it," Odin replied as he kissed her lightly on the cheek once more before glancing suspi-ciously at the hero. "Get well soon, Benjamin. My army needs you," he concluded soberly, before disappearing through the doorway.

Jameela closed the door quickly behind her and then raced over to the bed to fling her arms around Ben's neck. "That was close," she whispered softly between kisses.

"I know," Ben sighed, returning her caresses as he pulled her down on top of him. Her body felt good, pressed so snugly next to his. "I'm never going back," he whispered. "And neither are you. We have to tell the others soon."

"None of you must ever go to Valhalla."

Damn!

Odin muttered and cursed irritably as he walked slowly away from Jameela's room. He wasn't sure if her excuse for not returning to Val-halla with Ben was genuine or not; but he should have anticipated it, he really should have.

Feeling annoyed with himself, he placed his hand in his pocket and withdrew the disk, glancing nervously at it as he did about a dozen times a day. It was an obsessive and futile habit; trying to convince himself that he had more time. Of course it wouldn't have changed colour since his last check, but he could never resist just taking one more reassuring peek. Satisfied that its face was still mostly orange, he returned the disk to his trousers and then paused outside Ruby's room.

He would dearly love to take her to Valhalla too; but now that she was cosying up to Elijah, he wasn't so sure. Elijah had spent an awfully long time with Niflheim's bastard queen, and he couldn't be certain as to what poison Hel had filled his mind with. He couldn't trust Elijah just yet, and for that reason, he couldn't now trust Prudr; which was a shame. Like Kat, she was one of his favourite warriors.

Tutting grumpily under his breath, Odin continued his walk along the corridor. He would dearly love to get Ben back to Valhalla, but in the end, it probably didn't really matter. Ben could be a potent source of mischief, knowing so much about what went on in that realm; but any trouble he could make would soon be academic.

As long as his Valkyries stood their ground and fought hard in the final battle of Ragnarok, that was all that mattered; and despite these recent setbacks, he could at least content himself with the knowledge that they were still his loyal subjects. He was certain they wouldn't let him down.

Sighing with frustration and deeply lost in thought, Odin quickened his pace.

THUD!

"Oh, my lord, please forgive me!"

It was Jess, who had almost knocked him over as she bounded around the corner at the top of the stairs.

Bowing low, she curtsied and apologised profusely. "I must speak to you my lord, it's urgent, I'm sorry." Grabbing him by the hand, Jess dragged her lord to her bedroom.

Odin smiled. Being manhandled by Brynhildr wasn't an experience he'd had the pleasure of before.

"My lord, I have some terrible news for you," Jess blurted as soon as she'd closed the door behind her.

Pressing his finger to her lips, Odin stopped her from speaking further. "I'm sure you have, my dearest Brynhildr," he began, taking her hand in his and lightly kissing it. "But first let me greet you properly and welcome you home." Odin hugged her warmly for a while before slowly releasing her.

It was good to have her back.

"Thank you, my lord, for making me young again," Jess curtsied once more, finally remembering her manners. She hadn't fully understood Freyja's explanation for her new found health and strength, but she didn't really care.

She was young, beautiful, and pain free; and that was all that mattered.

"You're very welcome. The wells can perform so many miracles," Odin beamed enthusiastically. "Now, come, tell me; what news could possibly be so terrible as to have you drag me halfway round the castle?" he chuckled amiably, taking one of her hands in his. Jess had cheered him up considerably.

"My lord...it's your wife," Jess began cautiously before looking dejectedly at the floor. This wasn't going to be easy.

"And?" Odin enquired, coaxing her gently to continue.

"She's a traitor, my lord," Jess spat vehemently as she looked up.

"Oh, and what makes you think that?" he enquired; his voice tinged as much with mirth as it was with curiosity.

What was the warrior on about?

"It's the truth my lord," Jess retorted boldly. "She has allied herself with the devil and bears the mark of the black poppy; Frigg has become one of Hel's Angels. Sangrid has branded your wife as her own."

Odin drew his breath in sharply; the smile vanishing abruptly from his face. "Do you have proof?" he demanded.

"Yes, my lord, she bears the mark on her bottom where it's concealed," Jess continued, curtsying once more as she gave thanks quietly that Odin didn't have Gungnir in his hands. He would probably have levelled the castle by now.

"Thank you, Brynhildr, thank you very, very much. Your loyalty will not go unrewarded." Turning on his heel, Odin walked slowly away toward the window, stroking thoughtfully at his stubby beard as he did so. For a long while he stood in silence, his back turned toward Jess and the expression on his face hidden from view.

"My lord, are you all right?" Jess enquired hesitantly, sidling up cautiously behind him and placing her hand tentatively on his shoulder. Odin laid a hand on hers and squeezed it reassuringly.

Turning around, he faced her.

"Thank you, Brynhildr," he began grimly. "If what you say is true, then Frigg has made a very grave error. To side with our cursed enemy would be—" he paused, "—most unfortunate."

Kissing Jess lightly on the forehead, Odin tilted her chin up with a finger such that he could gaze deeply into her eyes. His face remained expressionless; leaving Jess unable to gauge his reaction to her devastating news.

Her revelation must have hurt him so deeply.

"Now, my dear Brynhildr," Odin began, with a tired sigh of resignation. "Why don't you take leave and go and rescue your sister from the clutches of her despicable, new, best friend? If anyone can save dear Kat from certain damnation, then it's you."

Whooping loudly, Jess flung her arms tightly around his neck. His suggestion would have been her very next request.

"Thank you, thank you so much," she exclaimed excitedly when at last she released him from her embrace. "I will bring her back safely my lord. I swear that on my life."

10

Sucky

THUMP! THUMP! THUMP!

"Wake up Kat-Kin, it's time to get up, we've got visitors."

Hel's unmistakable and surprisingly cheerful voice stirred Kat from a deep and much needed slumber.

What time was it?

She wished there was a clock somewhere in the realm. Some hours must have passed, but it felt as though she had been asleep for only minutes. *Damn it!* Who could possibly be visiting Niflheim now?

Falling clumsily out of bed and after apologising to Hod for disturbing him, Kat lit a candle and then fumbled around to find the skirt and bodice to her Valkyrie tunic.

"Won't be a mo," she whispered, before cursing loudly as she stumbled over a pile of Hod's clothes. *Damn!* She almost now regretted letting him share her bed. He could be so untidy. Exhausted and irritable, she definitely wasn't in a mood for anything other than going straight back to sleep.

THUMP! THUMP! THUMP!

"Come on, Kitty Kat, I'm getting bored now."

Kat found her belt and hastily buckled it tightly around her waist. She could hear Hel giggling, so she knew she wasn't really annoyed. Whoever their guests must be, Hel was clearly eager to meet them.

Finding Talwaar, she admired her sword briefly before returning it to its scabbard. A quick finger comb through her hair and she was done.

"Do you know who they are?" Kat enquired a little sleepily when a few moments later she closed the door to her room behind her. Hel had already turned and was beginning to walk away down the corridor.

She was definitely in a hurry.

"Don't know exactly," Hel mused before stopping abruptly. "The message some idiot slave hollered through my key hole was that a Valkyrie 'gunman' and her mother wanted to see me." Hel turned and shook her head. "I'm guessing the Valkyrie gunman could be Gunnr; but I haven't a clue as to who her mother might be; do you?"

Kat didn't; and after linking arms with Hel; the two Sangrids set off down the corridor once more.

"Hey Kat."

It was Henry this time who hailed her, reaching out a hand from Hel's chambers as he grabbed her by the arm. Apart from a towel wrapped around his waist, he was naked. "Can I have a quick word? It's urgent," he enquired sleepily, hair looking like a haystack and eyes practically gummed shut. Kat guessed he must still be half drunk.

Hel stopped and huffed grumpily. "Go on if you must, I'll wait for you in the Berserker Hall; but do make it quick, Foxy, and remember; I'm watching you," she teased, making a playful gesture with two fingers to her eyes and then stabbing them pointedly in his direction. Laughing merrily, she trotted off. Hel was jealously possessive; but on this occasion she was only jesting, thank goodness.

"What is it?" Kat hissed angrily as she bustled Henry back inside Hel's room. "You know you really shouldn't upset your little angel." Luckily, her mind wasn't so addled that she had forgotten Hel's secret.

"Oh yeh, I forgot about that," Henry chuckled. "Look Kat, just be careful when you go anywhere near Hel's servants. Don't let them touch you, please. Whatever you do, don't let them touch you with their hands."

Kat looked at Henry in astonishment. *How did he know they were dangerous?*

Henry read the expression on Kat's face and chuckled. "Look Kat, I'm not stupid. When you've got a brain as big as a planet, it doesn't take all eternity to figure things out."

Kat stared at Henry blankly. *So what exactly did he know?* It wasn't her place to say anything, so she remained silent. She certainly wasn't going to spill the beans on her sister.

"Oh, very well," Henry huffed in annoyance. "I know for a start that my angel Sangrid is Hel and that the woman I am absolutely crazy about is the Queen of the damned. For god's sake Kat, look at me; I'm dating Beelzebub! The devil incarnate."

"Shush," Kat placed her finger to his lips. "You know how she feels about being called such names. Look, I'm sorry, I should have said something about her sooner, but it's just, well; I promised Hel I wouldn't." Kat hung her head. All of a sudden she felt ashamed. Hel was her sister, but Henry was also her childhood friend. She really should have said something.

"Oh, don't worry Kat; I'm not angry; far from it." Henry grinned. "I couldn't care less who or what she is. I love her Kat; she's the best thing that has ever happened in my life—er, I mean death." He chortled loudly at his silly mistake.

"What else do you know?" Kat enquired cautiously.

"Oh, let me see; well, pretty much everything, I guess." Henry replied without a hint of modesty in his voice. "I know all about the Nastrond for example, the VIP suite, and Hel's little trips for massages from her girls. Oh yes, Kat, I know all about her bloody harem, too," he ended caustically.

"How do you cope with that?" Kat asked; noting the bitterness in his voice.

"Because I love her and because she's changing, thanks to you," Henry added as he took hold of her hand. "She needs you, Kat. You're the one thing in her life she holds most dear. You're more than just a friend; you're her older sister, the mother she never had."

Kat nodded slowly and then pulled him close to her. "You're helping, too, Henry. She loves you, but you're not supposed to know that, okay?"

"Really?" Henry shrieked with delight. For a moment, he forgot about acting manly and pranced wildly around the room shouting like an overexcited school boy. "Oh, you've made my life, or death, or whatever!"

Henry hugged her tightly.

"Hey, steady on, steady on," Kat laughed as she pushed him away. "I said Hel loved you, not me," she quipped jokingly. "Frankly, I don't understand what she sees in you—you, you geek!" She mocked, poking him playfully in the ribs.

"It's my hunky body, that's what it is," Henry laughed as he returned her gesture. "Actually, it's quite the opposite." He continued; suddenly sobering up. "We just get on so well. We like the same films, the same games, we laugh at the same jokes; we even like the same music."

"What?" Kat gasped. "Thrash and heavy metal? Well, I guess that figures," she chortled.

"No, not a bit of it," Henry interrupted indignantly. "That sort of music is all right, I suppose; but we both like something much, much better."

"Well go on, do tell?" Kat asked inquisitively. "Don't you go getting all mysterious on me," she threatened with a smile upon her face.

"I can't say," Henry shuffled coyly. "It's a bit embarrassing."

"Well, now you've simply got to tell me," Kat threatened, making a move toward him with her arms out. She was going to tickle the truth out of him, if that was what it took.

"Okay, okay," Henry capitulated, backing away. Kat knew his weakness only too well. "It's just we both like country and western music—" he paused, and then added with a sheepish grin. "—And Dolly Parton."

Kat threw her head back and roared with laughter. She might have guessed Henry would be so girly; but the Queen of the Damned? The very thought of Hel humming along to *Jolene* or *Coat of Many Colours* as she tortured the dead was just too ridiculous for words.

"It's not funny," Henry snorted as a smile twitched eagerly on his lips. "Dolly has a lovely voice, she's the best ever."

"I know, I know," Kat giggled as she tried to pull herself together. "I'm not laughing at her, it's just, you know; taken me a bit by surprise, that's all. Who would have guessed, hey?" she chortled, reaching for the door.

"You won't leave her, will you?" Henry entreated as he hugged her goodbye.

"No, of course not," Kat replied. "I happen to like her too, very much. She needs both of us. Now go on you, be good!" she commanded, patting Henry firmly on the bottom before breaking into a jog as she headed off down the corridor once more.

She just hoped Hel wouldn't be too mad at being kept waiting for so long.

"Tusk, tusk," Hel tutted angrily as Kat hastened across the dusty floor towards her. Strangely enough, Hel wasn't tutting in annoyance at Kat but rather at the extraordinary sight that lay before her.

She had her back toward Kat with her hands planted squarely on her hips.

"Would you look at these two naughty boys," Hel offered with a gesture as Kat drew alongside. "Give them the run of the place and what do they do, they only go and make pigs of themselves, gorging themselves half to death. Look at them, Kat," she continued. "They're out cold."

Hel lashed out a hefty kick to emphasis her point. True enough, there was no response. She was absolutely right.

Surt and Nidhogg were dead to the world.

Kat took a moment to study the bizarre situation before them. The two dragons were lying slouched, back to back, in the middle of the Beserkers' hall. Their heads were lolling on their chests, and occasional spurts of flame flickered from their nostrils as they snorted loudly and smacked their lips. They looked so comical, she couldn't help but snigger.

"It's not funny," Hel smiled as she too tried to stiffle a giggle. She was hoping to sound cross, but she wasn't being at all convincing. "They're just like cattle," she continued. "Faced with all this good meat lying around; they just didn't know when to stop. Now, with bellies fit to bursting and all this warmth, they're comatose. They could sleep like this for decades, and it's going to be murder waking them up. See for yourself." Hel kicked Surt once more to no effect. It must have felt like a flea tickling his heavily armoured scales.

"How exactly are you going to wake them up?" Kat enquired. Both dragons were out for the count.

"Well I've got a plan, but they're definitely not going to like it," Hel smirked naughtily. "Still, they only have themselves to blame."

"By the way, what exactly was the deal you made with them?" Kat enquired; the mention of a plan had reminded her about Hel's agreement with Surt.

"Oh, don't you worry about that," Hel offered nonchalantly, taking her by the arm as she began to march away toward the gaping wormhole. "Let's go and meet our visitors. I wonder who Gunnr's mother will turn out to be?" she remarked chirpily as the pair stepped into the swirling, black void.

"AAARGH!"

Silk hurled herself at Hel the instant the two Sangrids emerged from the top of the volcano. She couldn't help herself; the bloodlust was too strong.

Caught by surprise, Hel collapsed backward, reeling under the ferocity of the warrior's attack. It was only by sheer good fortune that she happened to have her sword in her hand; otherwise she'd have been a goner.

"You evil bitch," Silk spat venomously; slashing wildly with her sword. "I want Balder back now!"

Hermod stepped forward, and Kat drew her sword. "Stay out of this," she growled. "This is between the two of them."

"Watch out for Hermod," Hel yelled, glancing sideways. "He can run faster than an arrow," she added hurriedly, hastily dodging a lunge, which would have skewered her like a stuck pig. Silk was fighting like a woman possessed while Hel was still struggling to get her bearings.

"Thanks," Kat retorted. "Guards, grab him," she gestured with her sword to the space behind the god.

Her ruse worked.

As Hermod turned to focus on a pair of imaginary guards, Kat lashed out with her foot. This found its target with deadly intent.

"Ooh!" Hermod moaned as he collapsed to the ground, clutching at his groin. His testicles felt as though they'd just been blown apart. He was in agony.

"Sorry," Kat muttered, putting her sword down. Making a fist, she unleashed a crunching right hook to his jaw. Hermod's head flew sideways, and he landed heavily on the ground. He was down and definitely out.

Walking scornfully around his prostrate body, Kat crouched down low and grabbed hold of his trousers. With a single mighty tug, she had pulled these down to his ankles. Leaning forward, she tightened the belt around his shins.

"Let's see if you can hop your way out of this," she chortled.

Standing up, Kat placed a foot firmly on his neck. Pressing down hard, she forced his face deep into the gravel. Hermod coughed and spluttered; trapped beneath her boot. He wasn't going to be running anywhere.

"Nice one Kat-Kin," Hel yelled once more, sounding altogether much more cheerful now. She had regained her footing and was beginning to demonstrate why she was the greatest Valkyrie that had ever lived.

Silk was a master of the sword, but The Black Valkyrie was better.

What should have been a clash of titans soon became a master class, a showcase for Hel's extraordinary talent. Darting from side to side with the agility of a panther and lunging forward with the strength of a tiger, Hel's eyes blazed red and orange as her expression slowly turned from one of surprise to one of scorn.

Gaining the upper hand, she couldn't resist the opportunity of taunting Silk as she battered her into the dust. "So, are you missing your hunky lover, Silky-wilky?" she purred maliciously, slashing her sword as a cat might its claws. "Balder's not missing you, he hates you."

"Liar!" Silk screamed as she lunged forward—and missed.

"What was it he called you, Sulky Silk or was it Sissy Silk?" Hel continued, parrying another lunge and smacking Silk's behind with the flat of her sword as she stumbled past.

"Hel, stop it please. You know that Balder's—" Kat began, but Hel overruled her.

"That Balder's a fabulous lover?" she hollered gleefully. "Of course I know that Kitty Kat; but guess what he thinks about you as a lover, hey, Gunnr? Guess what he thinks about your pathetic attempts at love making." Hel yelled, drowning Kat out. She was determined to wring every last drop out of Silk's humiliation.

"Shut up, bitch!" Silk cursed furiously; she was so frustrated. Not only was she losing, she was being dishonoured as well.

"You suck; Silky-Wilky sucks. Poor, yucky, sucky Silk," Hel taunted as she rained down blow after blow upon her weakening foe. "That's what Balder calls you—yucky, sucky, Silk; yucky, sucky, Silk," she chanted in an infuriating, sing-songy, schoolgirl sort of way.

"AAARGH!"

Blinded with rage, Silk hurled one last desperate assault at Hel. She unleashed a devastating series of blows; a flurry of destruction so powerful that any other warrior would have been hacked to pieces.

Hel, cackling wickedly, blocking each and every blow before retaliating.

Kat had never seen such strength.

Silk was quite literally blown off her feet as one huge stroke after another hurled her body from one side of the outcrop to the other. She was being thrown around like a rag doll. Losing her footing, Silk eventually stumbled, and Hel forced her sword from her hand. The fight was over.

Anticipating what was about to happen; Kat released her foot from Hermod's neck and flung herself on top of Silk. "No, Hel, I beg of you," she screamed as she shielded Silk with her body. "Don't kill her!"

Hel's eyes burned like a pair of exploding stars. With sword raised daggerlike above her head, it took every ounce of control to stop her from plunging it down and staking both Kat and Silk to the ground.

Snarling wildly with the exhilaration of victory, Hel slowly lowered her arms. "That was a bloody stupid thing to do, Kat-Kin," she snorted, holding out her hand. "But bloody brave, too," she conceded with a grin.

Grabbing hold of Hel's hand, Kat jumped to her feet and dusted herself down. Turning round, she helped Silk to her feet, too. "Don't you at least want to know what these two are here for?" she asked.

"Well yes, yes, I suppose I do," Hel nodded and then scratched her head. She had forgotten about that. "But I didn't start the fight. It was all your fault, Sucky," she added picking her sword up and waving it angrily at Silk.

"Get lost, bitch!" Silk spat vehemently, narrowly missing Hel's face. Hel moved forward as Kat stepped in between them; pushing the girls apart with her hands. She wasn't going to take any more nonsense from either of them.

"Come on please," she begged. "Make up for Odin's sake. We're meant to be Valkyries; not vicious, berserker hellcats," she blurted and then immediately apologised for taking Hel's name in vain.

"Shake hands," she continued authoritatively, grabbing hold of Hel's arm and dragging her back toward Silk.

Like a pair of sullen teenagers, Hel and Silk meekly obeyed her orders; shaking hands as limply as though each were catching hold of a dead fish. Deliberately avoiding one another's gaze, Kat wished she could crack their silly, schoolgirl heads together.

"Come on Silk, everything Hel said was a lie; she was just winding you up. Balder has been unconscious ever since he arrived, and he hasn't said a word about you, or anybody else for that matter."

Hel threw Kat a dagger-stare.

"Hel's not the enemy, Odin is. She's a good girl, and a really, really fantastic friend," Kat added hastily; desperately not wanting to appear to be taking sides.

"Thanks, Kat."

Both Silk and Hel thanked Kat at exactly the same time and after realising that they had done so, they laughed heartily. Tensions were at last beginning to ease.

"May I see Balder, please?" Silk enquired once their laughter had subsided.

"Yes, yes of course," Hel nodded as she looked toward Kat. "Why don't you take our sister down to Niflheim with you while I attend to my old friend Hermod."

Kat glanced at the god and noted that he was only now rising awkwardly to his feet. Wincing with pain, he yelped loudly as he tried to stand upright.

"I think you've done Hermod some permanent damage, Kitty Kat," Hel quipped laughingly as she took him by the arm and helped him gingerly over to a rock. "Where did you learn to kick like that?" she continued with a snide chortle.

"You make a great teacher, sis," Kat giggled as a smile spread across her face. Hermod's discomfort felt good. All the fighting between Hel and Silk had caused a surge in her bloodlust, and this hadn't yet been properly satiated.

"Come on, Silk, why don't you tell me why you're here while we go down to see Balder?" Taking her sister by the hand, Kat led her slowly toward the wormhole.

"Ooh," Hermod moaned painfully as Hel let out another raucous, mocking cackle. It was going to be hard for her to feel sympathetic about his broken manhood.

Poor Hermod.

Some days, it just didn't pay to be a god.

11

Father Forgive Me

arcus had been standing on the pavement outside the imposing, arched wooden doors for several minutes. A constant conveyor belt of passersby jostled and huffed as they sidestepped his motionless figure; cursing his torpor as they weaved irritably around him.

Marcus didn't care; his mind and his gaze were elsewhere: firmly fixed on the ornate, stained glass window that lay high above the doors. Its imagery was of a single, white male impaled forlornly upon a cross; a constant and tragic reminder of an atrocity committed two thousand years ago.

Marcus sighed and then looked around him. It was the last day of spring, and tomorrow would be the start of what promised to be a glorious summer. A warm—almost hot—afternoon sun beat down upon his neck.

Having returned from the airport in a crowded subway; he had removed his cotton jacket; but he was still feeling sticky—and he was also feeling stupid. Standing as he was now, with the normality of everyday life passing all around him; Jess's satanic suggestion seemed farcical.

How could he be cursed by the devil?

What he had been contemplating doing was silly; and the fact that he was now hesitating before entering the doors in front of him was sillier still. He had to get a grip on himself. He was only going into a church, for fuck's sake; just a church—Anna's church. That was all. He had been inside countless times before, *so why the big deal now?*

"Marked by the devil."

Jess's crazy words had gnawed at his conscience all the way home from the airport. Over and over they repeated themselves, like some stupid, idiotic, mantra.

This was so typical of him.

Give a dog a bone and what does he do with it? Worry. That had Marcus down to a 'T'; and that was why he was standing where he was now; trying to exorcise those burning words from his mind.

All he had to do was to go in, walk up to the altar, bow, and then get the heck out of there. Nothing would happen, and that would be that; proof of Jess's lunacy. The spectre of evil hanging over the silly, black flower on his arm would be vanquished, and he would be free to get back to his boring, humdrum, everyday existence. No more fantasy thoughts about Valkyries, gods, and the devil. He would be back to plain, boring old conversations with people who were exactly the same as him; plain, boring, and old. This was what he wanted. This was what he needed. And this was why he should give himself a jolly good kick up the arse and get through those doors already.

Mind made up, well almost, Marcus stepped forward; hesitated, and then stepped cautiously forward again.

Shit, come on Finch—you neurotic twat!

Fuming at his cowardice, Marcus paused for the last time before pushing the heavy wooden door open. He was inside, and wouldn't you just know it?

Nothing.

Absolutely nothing had happened. His arm didn't hurt any worse than it had done outside. Jess's words were nonsense.

Still, as he was there, he really ought to prove the point conclusively; just to be one thousand percent, absolutely, concretely sure.

Walking quickly across the foyer, Marcus reached the central aisle and bowed stiffly. Anna was a devout Christian and a Catholic; and Marcus had learnt to respect her religion. He was an agnostic himself, but it would be stupid to be impolite—just in case he'd got it wrong. A quick nod in the direction of the elaborate, gilt crucifix would cost nothing; and it might just spare his eternal soul—assuming, of course, he had one.

Looking around him, Marcus was relieved to see that the dimly lit nave was almost empty. He could just make out the shape of a single, elderly lady kneeling and praying in the pew closest to the transept. Other than that, the place was deserted; which was good.

Gazing up at the ceiling, he marvelled at the thousands of hours of craftsmanship that had gone into creating this beautiful building; the extraordinary dedication and fervour of the hundreds of men who had toiled over the imposing edifice. What made this feat all the more remarkable was the fact that Anna's church was, by any account, really rather ordinary. It was just one of countless thousands of such buildings strewn across the towns and cities of America. For a brief moment, Marcus pondered on how many churches there might be in New York alone; before forcing his mind back to the job at hand.

Right; his task was simple. All he had to do was walk up the main aisle to the transept, bow again; and then head on through the chancel, past the choir stalls, and kneel at the rail in front of the altar. Once there he would say a quick prayer, light a candle, make a small donation, and then leave.

Nothing, on such a gloriously sunny day could be simpler. It was easy-peasy, lemon-squeezy; a walk in the proverbial park.

With the hint of a smile beginning to form on his lips, Marcus started up the aisle; his footsteps echoing on the worn, stone slabs. The air around him felt still and refreshingly cold just as he knew it would be. Even in the middle of a heat wave, the church remained blissfully cool.

Marcus chuckled. He was almost beginning to enjoy himself. He really was an idiot, being spooked by Jess's ramblings.

Shit! It couldn't be!

That had to be his over active imagination?

Half way up the aisle, Marcus could have sworn the tattoo on his arm was beginning to smart. He paused and gave his shoulder a reassuring pat. His mind was playing tricks on him—he carried on walking.

Oh dear lord!

Nearing the transept, the sensation in his arm had begun to intensify, to the point where it couldn't be ignored. Tingling jolts of pain now ricocheted from his shoulder to his elbow and back again. If this was his mind playing games, then it really wasn't funny.

"Detective Finch, how lovely to see you."

Bugger!

It was Father what's-his-name, Anna's priest; and he was making his way down the chancel toward him. Marcus had been about to turn and go; but now he was trapped. It would be a terrible snub to ignore the Father and leave; but he really didn't want to linger any longer. His arm was killing him.

"And how is your charming wife?" the priest enquired politely, drawing nearer and holding out his hand out to shake Marcus's.

Marcus was in agony; his pain intensifying with every step the priest had taken closer to him. Now, with their hands so near to touching; his arm felt like it would explode. This wasn't his imagination, this was terrifyingly real.

The tattoo was alive and writhing in the presence of divinity.

"AARGH!"

Marcus screamed loudly and fell to the floor; convulsing with the excruciating pain. For the briefest of moments, his hand had touched the priest's and in that instant; the gates of hell had blown open. Bursting through these, a white-hot dagger had buried itself deep in his shoulder. The pain it scorched was fiercer and more horrific than any he had ever known.

It was agony in its purest form.

He had to get out of there—now.

"I'm so sorry, Father," Marcus choked, gasping as he staggered slowly to his feet. His head was spinning and he clutched at his shoulder with his hand. "Please, forgive me—I've got a cramp."

Feeling faint and with waves of blackness threatening to overwhelm him; Marcus stumbled drunkenly back down the aisle before literally throwing himself through the wooden doors and out into the warm embrace of the noisy, bustling street.

He collapsed onto the sidewalk; sobbing for air.

Almost as quickly as the pain had increased, the sensation now subsided. His arm still burned, however; and after a few more anxious gulps of air to steady his nerves, Marcus loosened the neck of his shirt and peered at the tattoo.

Even if by some bizarre, weird, schizoid, delusion the pain that he had experienced inside the church had been imaginary; what Marcus saw now was undeniable and all too real. There, where the poppy had been, smoldered a charred, burning blister. He could feel its heat pulsating with the back of his hand.

Replacing his shirt, Marcus straightened his collar and slowly stood up. Around him, the busy, boring, everyday people were still going about their busy, boring, everyday lives; each still cursing him for obstructing their path.

Everything was normal; everything was as it should be—*except it wasn't.*

Marcus was different; permanently marked and changed beyond all shadow of a doubt. He was a black sheep, a man set apart from humanity. He was the prodigal son, a leper—

—Judas.

Looking around him; the terrible nightmare exploded inside his head.

Jess had been right. Marcus was branded by the devil, and the terrifying reality of his situation could only now truly torment his soul.

If the hand of one of God's servants could cause him so much pain; a single, blindingly obvious question screamed starkly into view.

What could the hand of evil do?

12

Murderer

hat?"

Hel's face had that wonderfully, uniquely Hel-licious expression of surprise about it. Standing there, motionless with her eyes wide open and a half smile frozen to her lips; she looked the very picture of bewilderment.

Returning from Niflheim to the volcano's crater, Silk had just finished explaining the details of Odin's enchantment and his demand for Balder's immediate release. The thought of all those women crying for Balder seemed impossible, but with Odin, you could never take anything for granted. If he was confident of success, then you could bet your bottom dollar that his plan was sound.

Kat was sceptical.

Hel was fuming.

"You can tell your scabby lord," she blustered angrily, shaking her head in disbelief. "That if he thinks Balder is going to just rise up and walk out of here, he's got another thing coming. Does he really think I won't stop him?"

"You won't be able to," Silk retorted slyly, relishing the opportunity of pissing Hel off again. She was still smarting badly from her earlier defeat. Valkyries seldom lost, and nobody had ever wiped the floor with her before. She was itching for a rematch, and winding Hel up seemed just the ticket. "Odin's enchantment will be too strong; you won't be able to move a muscle," she goaded.

"You're talking rubbish, Sucky." Hel was like a tinderbox waiting to ignite, and her flashpoint was getting closer. Things weren't looking good.

"Look, ladies, please." Kat decided to step in before things turned ugly once more. "Silk; it's fair to say that Hel isn't going to let Balder go without a fight, and Hel; Odin isn't going to give up on his son either. I don't think there's much more to be discussed. It's a bit of a standoff, that's all that can be said."

Bristling with hostility, Silk and Hel glared angrily at each other. Kat was right; it was a stalemate. Hel wasn't going to let Balder go unless she had her freedom, and there was no way Odin was going to grant her that. It looked as though Odin would just have to bring on his magic, so there seemed little point in bickering—or fighting—further.

"Oooh," Hermod winced loudly.

He was still sitting where Kat and Silk had left him and was in too much pain to contribute anything useful to the negotiations. Hel had kindly agreed to let him stay in Niflheim until he recovered, although quite why she was being so cordial was something of a mystery. Hel's nursing skills weren't exactly playing to her strengths; and the wicked glint in her eyes suggested that any care she might administer was unlikely to be found in a handbook by Florence Nightingale.

There was mischief afoot; you could bet your sword on it.

"Are you coming with me, Kitty Kat?" Silk offered with a shrug of resignation. Kat was right. Further negotiations were pointless, and another squalid fight with Hel wouldn't do any good; much as she craved the opportunity to get even.

"I don't know, I thought you all hated me?" Kat replied cautiously.

"No, don't be so silly, of course we don't. We owe you are lives, everybody says so," Silk smiled, putting a hand on her shoulder. "We need you," she added with a warmth that came as a shock to Kat. She had never felt close to the warrior.

"Would you mind if I went back to Asgard?" Kat asked hopefully, staring hard at Hel in an attempt to read her expression. This wasn't difficult; disappointment was already deeply etched upon her furrowed brow.

"I suppose I can't stop you," she snorted grumpily, before grabbing hold of Kat's hand. "I love you and you're my best friend. Remember that; I love you." A single tear welled and then glistened in the corner of one eye.

"Come here, you," Kat pulled Hel toward her and held her close; hugging her hard. "I love you too, and I will be back, I swear that on my life."

"Promise?" Hel whispered in Kat's ear.

"Promise," Kat replied resolutely, before kissing her cheek tenderly. "I have to go back to Midgard to see Jess one last time, but I promise I won't rest until Odin grants you a pardon. He must let you walk in Asgard again. If he wants Balder back, then he must give you your freedom. If he denies this, then I swear I will leave Asgard forever. You are my sister, and you have my word on that. I won't let you down."

Feeling better and inspired by the sincerity in her voice, Hel released Kat from her embrace. "Take Gold Mane and ride like the wind. I want you back, remember, I want you back—okay?"

With a final kiss goodbye, Kat turned to follow Silk who had already started to walk away down the craggy, broken slope. "I'm sorry for kicking you," she murmured apologetically in Hermod's direction. The god waved to her stoically before letting out another feeble moan. He really was suffering; Kat's foot had been devastating; it must have done some damage.

"You will look after him, won't you?" Kat enquired earnestly of Hel. She had seen a yellow flash in her eyes and that made her feel uneasy. Her sister couldn't be trusted, particularly when it came to Odin's sons.

"Of course I will. I fully intend to relieve him of his agony," Hel sniggered as she tried to put on a straight face. "If that's alright with you; do I have your permission?" she added with a titter.

"Yes, of course," Kat replied. Hel was up to something, she was sure of it. "Remember he's a god, so you must look after him and you have to let him go when he's better."

"Yes, yes I will, of course I will," Hel muttered impatiently as a broad grin spread across her face. "I'll take him down to Niflheim as soon as you're gone. A good rest, the scent of my poppies, and some tender loving care from my hands will soon get him back on his feet."

Tender loving care from her hands—*What was she on about?*

Kat smiled thoughtfully and, after giving Hel a final, affectionate hug goodbye, she hurried away after Silk. Her sister had given her word about Hermod, and that would have to do. Besides, Kat really didn't have the time to fret about his fate. Asgard beckoned and she had only one thought on her mind.

Jess.

"Come on, daddy long legs."

As soon as Kat had disappeared from view, Hel turned and eased Hermod to his feet. With one arm around his shoulders and the other tucked helpfully under his armpit, she gently supported him as he hobbled awkwardly toward the spinning portal.

"I'll soon get rid of that pain for you, just like I promised Kat I would."

Cackling loudly and with a brilliant flash of crimson sparkling from her eyes, Hel helped Hermod into the void.

"I can't believe it, Hildr, Olrun, and Kara. Are you seriously telling me that you haven't seen any of them, not even Hrist? You can't possibly have missed her."

Ruby was sitting propped up on the bed next to Ben and couldn't believe her ears. Jameela's room was crowded with every maid and warrior in Asgard. They had all crammed inside to hear Ben's tales about Valhalla. This was it; the very first time any of the Valkyries had had the opportunity to listen to one of Odin's heroes.

None of them wanted to miss a single word.

To everybody's great relief, both Ben and Ruby were making swift recoveries. Ruby's chest was still extremely sore, but for the first time she had struggled out of bed and, with Elijah's support, she had managed to walk down the corridor to Jameela's room. Of all the Valkyries, she was the most eager to hear about Valhalla. Having saved so many heroes and said goodbye to so many noble Valkyries, this would finally be her reward. An opportunity to hear first hand about the wonders of the realm they craved.

Much of what Ben had already recounted to his enthralled audience was, in reality, old news.

The Valkyries spent most evenings feasting and listening to tales from the gods about the wondrous beauty of Valhalla. Each warrior could probably have described every pebble in the realm, so detailed was their knowledge. However, hearing its description afresh was always a thrill. No one could ever tire of hearing about the paradise that would someday be their home.

The arrival of heroes in Valhalla was well known, yet the warriors still thrilled to hear about the mighty river Thund that the longboat Skidbladnir had to cross. This was a swift and treacherous river that ran deep and teamed with fat, leaping salmon. Ben's description of Valgrind, the gateway to Valhalla, lived up to their expectations; although the Valkyries were disappointed that he didn't know the combination to its ingenious lock. They had hoped to surprise Bragi, Tyr, and Odin with an announcement that they could open the gates for themselves.

Unpicking the lock didn't really matter, of course; but it would have made delicious icing on their cake.

The great hall of Valhalla sounded exactly as Odin had described it; magnificent and vast beyond their dreams. They made Ben laugh when they pressed him as to the exact number of doors leading into the hall. Five hundred and twenty was the magic number they were looking for; and Ben didn't argue. He knew there were a hell of a lot of doorways; and if that was the number that Odin had quoted—who was he to disagree?

Besides, when could he have ever had the time or interest to count them all?

The roof to Odin's mighty hall was perhaps its most striking feature; made entirely from the shields of his heroes. This shone in the midday sun with a brilliance that was blinding in its intensity. The rafters to this roof were festooned with countless spears; and chests of gold and gleaming armour lay strewn amongst the tables and benches lying beneath its magnificent, spreading gables.

As the barrage of questions from his excited audience continued, Ben quickly discovered that he was learning nearly as much about the realm as he was telling the girls. He found his ignorance almost embarrassing at times.

For example, the strange goat that lay tethered outside the hall beneath a large, spreading tree was called Heidrun; and the tree whose leaves the goat nibbled was called Lerad. If the warriors could be believed, Heidrun's milk was the source of the ale the heroes drank each night—although Ben took this with a pinch of salt.

The gods so loved to embellish their tales.

Ben also learned the name of Odin's cook. The excellent food the heroes ate was made by Andhrimnir. Ben had often seen him next to the huge cauldrons all covered in sweat and grime. He hadn't known his name, and he thanked the girls for their enlightenment. He also promised he would stop moaning about the lack of variety in the diet. The meat that was served each evening came from wild boar and not plain, boring old pigs. He apologised for this mistake while the girls had fun in teasing him about his culinary ignorance.

Everything about Valhalla fitted, and the warriors were thrilled by his confirmation of their cherished stories. It seemed the very picture of perfection were it not for one small—but worrying—detail.

Its inhabitants.

During his stay, Ben would have been hard pushed to say that he had seen any more than a couple of hundred heroes; which seemed extremely odd. If Odin was to be believed; his mighty army should number many tens of thousands. Odin would often boast that eight hundred soldiers would thunder from each of the five hundred and twenty doors when the last battle of Ragnarok beckoned. He was quite adamant on this detail, particularly after he had downed a few large horns of mead.

Nobody had done the maths yet, but even an idiot could tell that there should be a lot more than a few hundred heroes training along-side Ben.

Ruby's astonished outburst was where the conversation was now; and it had left her even more perplexed. The heroes should be waited on each night by the Valkyries, and all the names she had mentioned were of warriors whom she had known. These Valkyries had already departed to Valhalla, and Hrist should have stuck out like a sore thumb. Her flame-red hair was even more exuberant than Jess's, and she was twice as boisterous. Hrist was unmistakable, and this trou-bled Ruby greatly.

Where were all her friends?

Fortunately, Ben had given them a clue as to what might have hap-pened to them. Curiously enough, this clue was directly related to his concerns about Valhalla.

Since his arrival, Ben had been the heroic equivalent of a Valkyrie maid. He was serving his apprenticeship until he was ready to receive Odin's blessing and become a true warrior in the Einherjar; Odin's army of the brave. This rite of passage was a formality, and Ben's blessing was now overdue.

The ceremony took place in private in a small chamber beneath the hall. Only Odin, the hero, and one or two of the gods would bear wit-ness to it. The details of the ceremony were shrouded in secrecy and the room was kept securely locked at all times. To attempt to enter the chamber without permission was strictly forbidden, and disobedience would result in instant punishment—banishment to Hel.

Ben's reluctance to receive his rite of passage was the reason why he had jumped from the helicopter; and why he had come to Asgard with a warning. There was something deeply wrong with the blessing; something that made Ben afraid.

Ben wasn't a coward, and if he was being completely honest, he had absolutely no evidence to support his fears. They were just a gut instinct, that was all; but a gut instinct he would cheerfully stake his life on.

The heroes who emerged from the chamber were different from those that went down.

Odin's blessing seemed to change them, but in a way that was hard to define. They looked the same, spoke the same, and behaved the same; but something had happened. They were different.

The nearest analogy Ben could think of was *The Stepford Wives;* but as none of the Valkyries had seen this film, the comparison was wasted. No hero who had received Odin's blessing ever spoke about the ceremony, and shortly after they had received it, they would disappear from Valhalla. Sometimes they would return, and sometimes they wouldn't. Wherever they went or whatever they got up to was never discussed. The subject was taboo. Should Ben try to bring the matter up, the conversation would always be tactfully but firmly steered away. The whole business of joining Odin's Einherjar was a mystery; and until it could be explained, Ben urged the warriors to be cautious.

Something was wrong. He could feel it in his blood.

"Stuff and nonsense!"

It was Ruby who finally broke the air of despondency that had settled upon the gathering. She had made her mind up and was having nothing to do with his silly superstitious warnings of gloom and doom. If it weren't for the fact that she was injured and he was a hero, she would have branded his words blasphemy and whipped him severely. He may well be a mighty warrior, but his suspicions were wrong; they had to be.

Ruby decided to blast Ben with a piece of her mind.

"There is such an obvious explanation for the absence of our sisters and your fellow heroes that I am surprised you haven't tripped over it," she began scornfully, rising stiffly from the bed. "All the remaining heroes are off fighting wars, that's why they're absent from the feasting tables. Had you bothered to stay longer you would have discovered this for yourself. All this rubbish about a blessing changing the heroes is complete hogwash, and you ought to be ashamed of yourself."

Ben blushed. The ferocity of Ruby's rebuttal had taken him by surprise, and he was grateful for Jameela squeezing his hand and blowing him a silent but reassuring kiss. Ruby mightn't believe him, but she certainly did.

"I...I...I'm sorry my lady," he stuttered apologetically. Ben was aware of Ruby's fearsome reputation, and he certainly didn't want to upset her further. "It's just a feeling I have, and I wish I could explain it better. Why don't you ask Odin about the ceremony, perhaps he will tell you what goes on beneath his hall? That would reassure us all."

"I will do no such thing," Ruby retorted angrily. "And I don't want to hear another word on the matter, either. If I find out that you have been spreading this or any other malicious rumour about our lord," she added threateningly. "Then I will whip you soundly, do you hear me? I will whip so bad you will rue the day you ever uttered such evil, blasphemous words."

A gasp of astonishment reverberated around the room.

Most of the warriors had felt the sting of Ruby's tongue at some time or another, but to hear her talk to one of Odin's hero like this was truly shocking. A chorus of heads turned to face Ben and their expressions were all the same; he had their sympathy.

"Come on," Ruby gestured angrily as she ordered Elijah to take her hand. She was leaving and her lover was going with her.

Shrugging empathetically in Ben's direction, Elijah took her hand and helped Ruby from the room. His loyalties were divided. He loved Ruby with all his heart, but he had been around Hel long enough to know the gods of Asgard spoke with forked tongues. There was only one truth in this matter, and it should be heeded well.

No god could be trusted—not even Odin.

It would be a foolish warrior to dismiss Ben's concerns without digging just a little bit deeper.

Jess was the only Valkyrie who was absent from Jameela's room. Even though she was dying to hear about Valhalla, she was driven by a desire that burned still deeper.

A desire to be reunited with Kat.

Having learned that her sister was in Niflheim, Jess had put on her cloak of swans' feathers and sped off toward the smouldering volcanic cone. She flew as fast as she could, not wanting to wait a minute longer than she had to. Every second without Kat's forgiveness stung as sharply as a wasp. She could hardly wait; and it was she who spied Kat first, galloping beside Silk as they streaked across the plain of Ida.

Whooping loudly with joy, Jess banked and then glided swiftly down to the ground. This was going to be her moment of truth.

Quivering nervously; she folded her wings.

How would Kat be after their last terrible parting?

"Look, look up there!" Silk yelled excitedly as the two galloped hard together. Kat could barely hear her voice above the thunderous pounding of their horses' hooves, but that didn't matter. She had already spied the beautiful swan and knew that the bird had to be Jess.

Grabbing hold of the reins, she pulled Gold Mane to a shuddering halt. "Go on ahead!" she yelled after Silk, who had barely slowed down. "I'll catch up later."

Kat wanted her reunion with Jess to be a private affair, and guessing as such, Silk had tactfully decided to carry on. Dismounting in a single leap, Kat held her breath as the blinding flash of light swiftly faded into the shapely figure of her long lost friend.

Any thoughts of awkwardness were instantly banished.

Shrieking with joy, the two girls flew into each others arms; hugging and kissing so passionately that time seemed to stand still. They became lost in their embrace as they wept on each others shoulder. So much longing and pain had elapsed that exhortations of sorrow and forgiveness were unnecessary.

Their love and friendship transcended words.

Whatever had happened had happened, and nothing, absolutely nothing, could change the way they felt for each other.

They were friends, sisters, and lovers—now and for all eternity.

"Murderer," Kat whispered roguishly into Jess's ear as she held her close.

"I know," Jess breathed as she held her tighter still. She knew that she was forgiven and could at last rest in peace.

Some considerable time later, and with Jess now sitting snugly between Kat's arms, Gold Mane trotted into the castle's courtyard. The evening's feasting and festivities were well underway, but neither Kat nor Jess felt any urge to join the party.

Tip-toeing quietly across the castle's hall and up the stairs; the pair hurried to Jess's room and dismissed the serfs who would usually attend to their needs.

Tonight was going to be their special night—a night of tenderness and love. Jess's crime had been forgiven, and their love could spring anew. Absence had indeed made their friendship stronger.

The ecstasy of their reunion was far deeper than either had dared to hope for.

13

Unlucky for Some

uck!"

Marcus cursed angrily before collapsing into a groaning heap on the floor.

"Oh, darling! I did try to warn you; are you hurt?" Anna cried as she hurried into the kitchen and knelt down beside him. She had shouted out a warning about the broken glass; but it had come a moment too late.

True to form, after arriving home, Marcus had kicked off his shoes and gone into the kitchen to get a nice cold beer from the fridge. Now this beer was forgotten as attention focused on an expanding pool of blood. This was slowly haemorrhaging through a soggy, black sock from which a large jagged, shard of glass protruded. Offering tender platitudes, Anna fetched some tweezers from her makeup bag and removed the offending item.

"Ouch!"

Marcus yelped in anguish as the dagger was removed.

What a day.

Hopping precariously from the kitchen to the sitting room, Marcus hurled himself onto the wooden sofa, which cracked loudly as he landed on it. Luckily, it didn't break, but the whole structure now sagged even more alarmingly than it had done previously. Marcus sighed deeply before putting his foot up on the coffee table. Some days, life seemed to go from bad to worse to, well; in this case— ridiculous.

Laughing bitterly, he cursed his rotten luck. His shoulder was still as sore as hell, and now he had a pincushion for a foot to contend with. What a complete 'Fubar' (Fucked Up Beyond All Recognition) of a day.

As Anna carefully packed gauze into his heel and then wound a seemingly endless bandage tightly around his throbbing foot; Marcus sat back and reflected gloomily on events.

The day really had been a pile of manure from beginning to end.

Marcus had already decided not to tell Anna about his experience in the church. He knew this would freak her out, and coping with her hysteria was not going to make his situation any easier.

Limping home, he had also come up with a simple solution to his predicament. Tomorrow morning he would make some calls and check out a private, cosmetic surgeon. He would see what it would cost to have the tattoo vaporised with a laser. That would get rid of the cursed flower, and his problems should then be over. He didn't care how much it cost, how much it hurt, or even if it left a scar. All he wanted to do was rid his body of something he didn't understand, something he didn't want, and something that might very well damn his soul. The sooner he got the job done, the better. If his bad luck continued at the rate it was going, he'd be in a wheelchair before the week was out.

Gratefully accepting an ice pack and two paracetamol from Anna, Marcus settled back for a cosy evening of channel hopping. He'd have to miss his usual sortie to the gym, and that thought cheered him up. It was hard work keeping fit, and on a day like today, a workout was bound to end in disaster.

A night off from pumping iron would certainly ease his pains.

Marcus awoke from his night of slumber knowing only one thing. He had slept like a proverbial log.

Wow! What a difference a good night's sleep had made; he felt so much better. In fact, when he came to think of it, he felt absolutely fantastic. The pain in his arm had gone and, testing his foot gingerly on the floor, the pain in this had disappeared, too. Hurrying into the bathroom, Marcus pulled down the toilet lid and sat on it. Working with all the precision of a blindfolded surgeon wearing boxing gloves, Marcus began to unwind the coils of bandage around his foot. A sense of unease was growing rapidly inside him.

Something wasn't right.

What if...?

"Jesus Christ!"

Marcus swore loudly and then apologised quickly under his breath. He was already in enough trouble with God and didn't need to provoke him further.

"Shit," he continued, murmuring in amazement as he stared intently at the sole of his injured foot. His foot wasn't just better—it had healed completely.

There was absolutely no sign of a cut, scab, or even a scar. The injury was gone; as if it had never happened.

Smiling broadly, Marcus glanced at his shoulder. Sure enough, the blister too had vanished, and the poppy with its shiny black petals and scarlet centre positively glowed back at him.

His miraculous recovery and the tattoo were linked; he was certain of that.

Breakfast was a delightful affair as Marcus enjoyed quite possibly the most fragrant cup of coffee and tasty scrambled eggs he had ever eaten. Somehow he felt more alive and aware of his senses than he could ever remember, even from way back when he was a small boy. His eyesight, hearing, smell, taste, and touch all seemed to be working overtime; making every sensation a treat. He could place sounds, scents, and flavours with an accuracy that beggared description. He felt fabulous, and he patted his tattoo cheerfully as he threw his jacket on and left for work.

Go poppy power!

Enthusing happily, he jumped down the steps outside their apartment block. Today might just make up for the misery that had been yesterday.

The morning and afternoon passed like a dream, although he was tormented for a few hours at first by the delicious aroma of a bacon sandwich. Everybody denied bringing one into work, and it was only after a serious bit of sleuthing that he traced the source of his distraction. The divine scent was coming from a discarded sandwich wrapper left in bin from the day before. *Wow!* Now he knew what a dog must feel like. The smell had been overwhelming.

Throwing screwed up pieces of paper into the bin was a popular pastime in the office; the perfect way to cope with boredom while waiting on a report to be typed or an urgent phone call to be received. Today was no exception, but to Marcus's delight, he couldn't miss; no matter how far he placed the bin from his desk. Bouncing the misshapen lumps from the walls and from chairs, they made their way inexorably into the trash can, each and every time. Marcus revelled in the joy of discarding paperwork with the pizzazz of a basketball player.

Life after poppy tattoo—one; life before—nil.

Leaving work with as much energy and enthusiasm as he arrived, Marcus hurried to the gym for one last test of his now found, godly powers.

He wasn't disappointed.

Cranking the speed dial to max, he hammered out twice the distance of his usual warmup on the jogging machine without so much as a bead of sweat forming. It was bliss. Free weights came next, and to his delight Marcus's super powers continued. He could press twice as much as he had done previously and most probably could have gone higher still.

Bubbling over with delight and after deciding to save energy for a night of serious passion with Anna, Marcus showered quickly before jogging the kilometre or so home from the gym to their apartment.

He was a man on fire, a teenager once more. Life simply couldn't get any better.

RING-RING, RING-RING.

Life most certainly couldn't.

"Hello, Marcus, how are you feeling?" The beautiful and distinctive voice of the Contessa floated down the line.

"Um, rather well, thank you for asking," Marcus replied hesitantly as he entered his flat. Her unexpected call had caught him completely by surprise.

"And the tattoo, is that still hurting?" the Contessa enquired.

"No, it's fine now, thank you," Marcus replied crossly; he wasn't going to easily forgive her for the agony this had caused him.

"Do you think your tattoo could do with a little—" the Contessa paused briefly, "—refreshing?"

"No, my lady, it's fine," Marcus replied in a much more servile tone.

"Ah, Marcus, that sounds so much better." Frigg relaxed; he was in 'the zone' and under her control. "Now Marcus, as I'm sure you will have realised, your body has undergone, shall we say, something of a transformation," she teased cheerfully.

"Yes, my lady," he replied meekly. Marcus could hear what he was saying, but he couldn't control his words.

"Do you like what's happening to it?" she enquired diffidently.

"Yes, my lady," he murmured once more. He felt hypnotized.

"What you must understand," Frigg continued. "Is that for all the wonders you are about to experience, there is a price to pay and that price is the bondage of your soul. You will do as you are bid, and you will serve the same mistress as I do, the Queen of the Damned. Do you understand?"

Marcus nodded without saying a word. Frigg didn't need to hear his voice, her question had been rhetorical. She knew he couldn't say no.

Marcus's soul—the third option—belonged to her now.

"From now on you will address me as My Lady or Contessa; and you will only refer to our mistress as Your Majesty or My Queen," Frigg commanded authoritatively. "You are a very lucky man; a very, very lucky man indeed. You are the first to ever be blessed with the mark of Hel."

Marcus nodded once more. He was helpless and powerless. If the Contessa had asked him to bow down and worship a bar of soap he would have got on his knees and started praying. Her voice was god, and there was nothing he could do about it.

She ruled his body and soul.

"Now then," the Contessa continued with an audible smile upon her lips.

"Are you ready to start working for your queen?"

14

Asgard Weeps

Dawn broke late on the first day of winter, and it was as though the realm knew that its bitter vengeance had arrived. Overnight, the heavy November rain and gales that had been battering Asgard disappeared; to be replaced with a clear and star-studded December sky. Temperatures plummeted such that by the time the first, grey rays of sunshine slithered down the hills; a thick carpet of frost lay twinkling on the ground.

It was a lovely sunrise, but its beauty was wasted on the group of cloaked warriors who stood huddled and shivering in the feasting hall. A great fire had already been lit, but the room still felt cold and uninviting. A cosy bed to snuggle up in seemed a far nicer option than where they were now.

Grumbling and stamping their feet to keep warm, the girls waited patiently for Odin to arrive.

Their lord had requested that they all be up and ready by nine o'clock, and he had entrusted Silk to make this so. Like some pent-up rottweiler, she had stomped up and down the corridors, banging on doors and hurling plaintiffs or abuse at the sleepy girls. When words failed, more desperate measures were called for. At least one warrior had had their bedding stripped, and their legs smacked soundly. Today was the day that Balder would be coming home; and Silk meant business.

No one was going to mess things up by missing the meeting—absolutely no one.

To a fanfare of horn blowing, Odin arrived punctually at five to nine and, beaming broadly, he crossed the hall with Bragi and two slaves. These latter were carrying a large bodn and a flagon of mead. Placing the bodn carefully on the floor, he gave its contents a good stir with a ladle. Odin then poured a horn of mead for Bragi. Holding this up so that everyone could see what he was doing, he carefully dripped three drops of the bodn's thick, burgundy liquid into it.

Kat wriggled her nose in disgust and then snuggled closer to Jess, who wrapped a protective arm around her. Kat knew exactly what the bodn contained—Kvasir's blood—and it made her feel sick. It was a ghastly thought, swallowing the stuff; even if it did have magical properties.

Apart from Carmel; Kat and Jess looked the most exhausted of all the warriors and maids. They had had little sleep, but they didn't mind. Their friendship had been reaffirmed, and it was wonderful to be back together; friends forever.

"Hail Odin!"

After a brief and somewhat half-hearted cheer from the warriors, Bragi downed two large gulps of mead and then made his way over to his harp. He sat down.

This was it; the alleged moment of magic.

Plucking one hand slowly across the harp's taut strings, he opened his mouth and began to sing; quietly and sweetly; a sad lament to the dear and recently departed Balder.

Kat was one of the many warriors who had been sceptical about Odin's plan. However, before the end of the second chorus, she had to admit that she'd been wrong. There wasn't a dry eye in the room.

The sadness of Bragi's words, the sweetness of the refrain, and the power of Kvasir's blood was simply overwhelming. Before the end of the third chorus, the girls were begging the god to stop. Their tears were flowing like rivers, and their hearts felt fit to burst.

The enchanted mead worked beautifully, and Odin was elated; the performance of Kvasir's blood having exceeded even his lofty expectations. Closing his eyes, he prayed silently to Yggdrasill.

He prayed that Balder could feel their love and grief of the women of Asgard.

He prayed that he would return before the day was done.

In Niflheim, Balder did indeed sense the women's tears.

As the warriors wept; a single, cold, grey finger twitched and the faintest hint of pink returned to his sunken, ashen cheeks. These earliest signs of awakening were missed; but by midmorning as his life began to strengthen; all hell would break loose in that ghastly, rotting realm.

"HAIL BALDER!"

After a further, more rousing cheer that felt altogether fresher and enthusiastic; the girls hurried out into the courtyard and prepared to get underway. About a dozen musicians and minstrels were waiting to greet them, and a chaotic scramble ensued as the warriors haggled over who would go with whom and to where.

Several gods were also waiting, and it should have come as no surprise that Carmel had somehow wrangled arrangements such that she would be travelling with Thor. The two of them would accompany Bragi on his mission.

Grinning broadly and with far more jostling, giggling, and bodily contact than was strictly necessary; Carmel climbed into Thor's chariot and stood as close to him as she dared. Their secret relationship was going from strength to strength, and Carmel knew that he was in love with her, although he would never say as such. Each night when the other warriors were sleeping, she would tiptoe down to the foundry, and they would lie there together; chatting, caressing, and making love until they fell asleep in each others arms. They hadn't been caught yet, but there had been several close calls.

Still, with so much touching, flirting, and cheeky shenanigans going on inside the chariot; someone was bound to catch on sooner or later.

Carmel didn't care, even though she knew that it would set the gossip drums on fire. Her heart was burning with a passion, and she ached to scream her happiness from the tallest castle spire. Sif would be furious, but Carmel would deal with her rage when, or if, it erupted. For now, spending a whole day with her bull-like lover was going to be heaven; and the two of them stood sheepishly side by side; grinning like a couple of love-struck teenagers.

Odin's enchantment had a tough schedule.

Each and every woman in Asgard had to shed their tears between nine in the morning and nine in the evening for the charm to succeed. Just one woman left forgotten or with tears unshed and the magic would be destroyed. Odin wasn't taking any chances.

With military precision, the warriors, minstrels, and musicians headed out to their appointed villages and hamlets. Each girl carried a long scroll of names and venues; and it was their role to fly back and forth from the musicians; keeping Odin informed as to how they were doing. Odin himself remained seated comfortably in the great hall, with page after page of inked parchment spread out before him. On these he would mark their progress. With any luck, by nine o'clock that evening, not a single name on his mighty list would be left unchecked.

A magnificent, celebratory feast had been arranged; and Odin was confident that his favourite son would stride merrily through the castle gates and into his outstretched arms.

"What was that? Did you see that, Henry, did you see it? Tell me I'm dreaming, please, I beg you."

Hel was practically spinning cartwheels, she was so overcome with fear.

"He's waking up, no question about it," Henry replied blandly, stating what was blindingly obvious. "Odin must have started his spell."

What Henry had said was true. Almost every time Hel looked at Balder, his body seemed to have become a little more animated. First a finger and then an arm or a leg had twitched and jerked. Now he was smacking his lips, coughing, snorting, and even fluttering his eyelids. There was absolutely no question about it, Balder was coming round.

"We'll soon see who has the stronger magic," Hel fumed as she looked around the room. Casting her gaze upon a large, heavy candelabrum, she picked it up and held it high above her head. "He's not going to be doing any waking up if I can help it," she announced menacingly.

"Hel, what are you doing?" Henry gasped with astonishment, completely forgetting that he wasn't supposed to know her name.

"I'm going to smash his head in, that's what," Hel snarled, raising the candelabrum still higher. "By the way, how do you know my name?" she added as a puzzled afterthought.

"It's a long story," Henry retorted as he made his way across the room to dissuade her. He knew she would regret her actions later. Pausing momentarily and furrowing his eyebrows as he did so, he stopped walking. He had had an idea.

"Go on then, smash your beloved Rhett's brains in. I dare you," he scoffed sarcastically.

"What? Do you think I won't do it?" Hel raged angrily. She wasn't in a mood to be taken for a fool.

"No, not at all. I know you will try to do it, but I also know that you won't be able to. Odin's magic is too strong, it will stop you." Henry replied resolutely, folding his arms across his chest. "Go on then, darling; give him a whack. I double dare you."

Hel's eyes flashed angrily, and without further ado, she swung the candelabrum back behind her head. Nobody ever double dared her—ever. Bringing the ornament forward, she started to unleash her deadly blow.

Suddenly, and with the force of a blow struck by Thor's hammer, Hel felt her arms become lead weights. She could barely move them. The candelabrum, too, seemed to weigh a zillion tons. Loosening her grip, the heavy ornament fell clattering to the floor; narrowly missing her head.

Henry was right, she couldn't strike her blow.

"Rats!" she cursed angrily. "Get me some rope, at once!" she commanded, screaming at a slave who vanished as swiftly from the room as though a swarm of bees had given chase. "We'll see who's in charge around here!" she yelled.

"Binding Rhett isn't going to do you any good either, my angel," Henry began in the most gentle and soothing voice he could muster. "He'll just break free, you watch. He'll break free."

"Oh, do shut up," Hel hissed and, as a frustrated afterthought, she threw a candle in his direction. "You'd better have a really good explanation as to how you know my name my dearest, most darling, Foxy," she teased, chucking another candle at him.

"And if I don't?" Henry offered cheekily as he ducked. A third candle whistled past his head. "You know I don't care who you are," he continued, diving for refuge behind the far side of the bed. "I love you, no matter what."

"Damn you!" Hel cursed as angrily as she could. Henry had never used the 'L' word before, and she couldn't help but smile.

How dare he make her heart sing when she needed to feel mad?

Picking up more candles, she continued to hurl these at him.

"Well come on," Henry chuckled taking a peak over the top of the mattress. "Aren't you going to say it too, my angel?"

"Say what?" Hel giggled mischievously.

"Say that you love me—ouch!"

A candle had struck him squarely on the forehead.

"No. I'm not," Hel replied petulantly with a grin.

"Why not?" Henry teased.

"Because you know the answer already," she chortled. He wasn't going to get her to admit her love; at least not just yet.

With a frantic knock at the door and after a hollered "come in!" the slave returned and threw some thick, plaited twine on the floor.

"Right," Hel continued, still chuckling. "Now that we've got that settled, you can jolly well shut up and help me start tying."

Grabbing a handful of rope, she threw the other end in Henry's direction. Laughing loudly, the two of them began to tie Balder to the bed.

After getting the warriors to weep, Bragi next sang Balder's lament to a packed hall in Gladsheim. This had an identical response; everybody fell about weeping.

Buoyed by their spectacular success, the warriors and minstrels fanned out across the land and quickly set to work. Even the most optimistic of the Valkyries had believed that the task would be onerous, but the reality soon proved very different. So powerful was the song and so potent was Kvasir's blood, that the whole process ticked like a well oiled clock. Women and girls of all ages were falling like flies, shedding tears by the bucket load.

It was almost impossible to finish the lament. Its effects were so devastating that even the hardiest men in the land crumbled, too; weeping like babies. The whole scheme was flying high, and by late afternoon, Odin had crossed practically every single name off his list. He was down to a single sheet. The remaining women on his list came from the furthest reaches of Vannaheim and, with the exception of one individual, he was certain that they would all succumb to his magic.

Thokk.

Now that was a name that bothered him.

Odin chewed anxiously at his fingernails when his eyes alighted on the old crow's name. Thinking about it, he should have really laughed out loud.

Thokk—who's name literally meant 'gratitude'—couldn't have been a more miserable, moaning, and miserly old hag. Her reputation as a skinflint was legendary, and she lived in an inaccessible cave at the top of a steep and treacherous path. Bragi, Thor, and Carmel were on their way to sing to her now; and Odin had made sure that they had plenty of time to reach her; just in case. She would be a tough nut to crack, and the fact that she was as deaf as an old coot certainly wasn't going to help matters, either.

Still, he had three hours to go, and he knew that the group was already on their way. Crossing his fingers and fumbling nervously with the disk in his pocket, Odin held his breath. He wanted his son back; that was the plan.

Balder back by his side and Hel consumed with rage; that was just what he needed.

Unfortunately for Hel, Henry's predictions about the rope proved correct.

No matter how tightly the bonds were tied, somehow the knots managed to work loose, and the ropes became slack and useless. Almost without effort, Balder was soon sitting upright with his eyes wide open. He didn't speak, and he didn't seem to be aware of his surroundings. He was in a trance, an enchantment that enveloped him and kept him safe from harm.

Having watched with horror as her shackles failed one by one, Hel's next line of defence was to lock Balder in his room.

The key wouldn't turn.

Try as she might, Hel couldn't get the door to lock. Weeping with anger and frustration, Hel watched as Balder got up from his bed and began to slowly march through the Palace of Eljudnir toward the Berserker Hall.

"Ha, ha, ha! Serves you right."

"Oh, do get lost, Hod," Hel yelled as he mocked her from across the hall. "If you don't shut up, you'll end up like your stepbrother

Hermod," she sneered malevolently before regretting her stupid outburst.

"What do you mean?" Hod enquired suspiciously.

"Oh, nothing! Just crawl back under your rock or wherever it is you've come from. Can't you see I've got my hands full?" Hel huffed as she waved frantically in the direction of Balder. He was now more than halfway across the hall and the gateway to Asgard was looming large ahead of him.

"Yeh, but not for long," Hod quipped, pointing deliberately at the swirling void. "He's going to be out of here, and then you're for it."

Hel stuck her tongue out and blew Hod a raspberry. Unfortunately, he was probably right.

It was going to take a miracle to stop her dream god from leaving their love nest.

"Oh, gracious me, dearie, you gave me a proper fright and no mistake."

The wizened old woman leapt up from where she had been dozing with a startled jump that almost rivalled Carmel's. After shouting so loudly at the hag that the roof of the cave had shuddered and cracked, Thor had given up trying to arouse Thokk. It was Carmel's gentle poke that had finally done the trick; shocking the old woman back to life.

Looking around and recognising Thor, the woman bobbed a quick curtsey. "My lord, what brings your noble self to my humble cave?" she rasped apologetically in a voice that sounded like coarse gravel.

"We're here to ask you to weep tears of sorrow for the death of Balder," Thor began politely.

"You're what?" The old woman raised her hand to her ear.

"We want you to cry for Balder," Thor retorted more loudly, moving a little closer. He was already losing patience with the hag.

"Can't you speak any louder, my lord? I can't hear a word you're saying," Thokk cupped her hand around her ear as she craned her neck forward.

"WE WANT YOU—"

Thor began once more, bellowing loudly through clenched teeth. His hand was itching on the handle of Mjollnir. One blow and the deaf old bag would be dead, and at least then they wouldn't have to go through with all this singing malarkey. Bent over double and with a hunched back, shapeless, black cloak, and wild, matted hair; she could barely pass for a woman anyway. Thor couldn't understand why they were bothering.

One swift blow of Mjollnir and they would all be put out of this misery.

"Shush," Carmel hushed; placing her hand on Thor's, and gestured for him to calm down. Getting mad with Thokk wasn't going to do them any favours. Turning to the old woman, Carmel waved a hand in front of her face to get her attention.

"And who might you be then, dearie?" Thokk croaked with a wicked glint in her eyes. Hobbling forward, she pinched one of Carmel's cheeks between her fingers. "You're a pretty one, and no mistake. A Valkyrie, I'd wager, and a fine one at that."

Chortling loudly, Thokk circled Carmel and slapped her bottom hard. Carmel jumped. Now that was unexpected.

"Nice, firm buttocks too," Thokk continued with a loud cackle as she returned to stand in front of Thor. It was all Loki could do not to burst out loud into fits of laughter; how he loved this silly charade of playing the miserable old spinster.

So far, none of the party had seen through his disguise, and no one had ventured deeper into the cave to bring about his undoing. Had they done so, they would have discovered Thokk's strangled corpse lying buried under a hastily gathered pile of rubble. Loki had shape shifted and, after taking her form, was now in his element; playing the fool and thwarting Odin's plans.

"Can you hear me?" Carmel asked sweetly as Loki—Thokk—shook his head.

"We want you," Carmel pointed her finger deliberately at the woman.

"You?" Loki croaked quizzically as Carmel shook her head.

She stubbed her finger at him again.

"Me?" he croaked once more, and Carmel nodded her head enthusiastically. He was beginning to catch on to her little game of charades.

Carmel rubbed her eyes theatrically.

"Sleep, sleepy?" Loki rasped and Carmel shook her head. Wetting her fingers, she drew two lines down her face.

"Weep? Me weep?" Loki enquired as Carmel nodded once more and then held up four fingers.

"Sweet Odin!" Thor spluttered loudly. It would have been easier to get blood out of a stone. Carmel pinched him hard as she gestured for him to keep quiet. In this case, patience was definitely a virtue.

"Fingers?" Loki asked hopefully and Carmel shook her head. He knew exactly what she was trying to say, but he was determined to eek out Thor's discomfort.

"Four?" Loki added. "Me weep for—?" He enquired tentatively as Carmel nodded that he was correct.

The next part, however, was going to be the tricky bit. Looking around her, Carmel eventually picked up a pebble and held it out to the old woman.

"You want me to weep for a rock, dearie? Now why in Asgard would I want to do that?" Loki chortled with a sly grin. It was such fun to see his beloved squirm. One day he would tell her of his deception; her face would be a picture.

Looking around again, Carmel first picked up a larger stone and then walked over to a huge rock near the entrance to the cave. She waved at it in an exaggerated fashion.

"A big stone, a really, really, big stone?" Loki mused deliberately. "A huge rock, a boulder! Ah now I've got you my lovely; you want me to weep for Balder!" he exclaimed. "Why, what's he done?" he added soberly as an after thought.

"He's dead, you stupid old goat!" Thor hollered as Carmel drew an imaginary rope around her neck and tugged at it; letting her head slump sideways and her tongue loll out. She couldn't have made a better or more obvious, deathly gesture.

"Oh, is Balder dead?" the hag croaked. "Oh, deary me. Now that's a shame, he was a right handsome devil to be sure," Loki muttered apologetically, and after shaking his head he returned to the pot that was sitting over the fire. Whatever Thokk had been cooking, he wasn't in a hurry to taste it. It looked disgusting; like a broth boiled from an old, chopped up boot.

"Will you weep for Balder?" Carmel asked with a sad pout upon her face. She took one of the woman's hands in hers and beckoned for Bragi to step forward and begin to play.

Thokk was as deaf as a post, but they had to try.

Sitting down beside her, Bragi began to sing. He sang as loudly and as close to the woman's ear as he possibly could. Tapping her fingers and nodding her head, Loki pretended to hum along to the sad lament, smiling all the while as he did so.

Carmel and Thor were both quickly in tears, which made him desperate to laugh out loud. They both looked so silly, unlike him. His eyes remained as dry as a bone.

To pretend to be deaf was easy, but to avoid crying to an enchanted refrain, now that was a different matter; one that would have been impossible. Thankfully, Loki had stolen an idea from Kat. To ensure he didn't succumb to the dulcet tones, he had filled both ears with wax. This had set as hard as stone.

He really couldn't hear a thing.

Bragi reached the end of the lament, paused; and then sang it all over again—and then once more for luck. Carmel and Thor bawled their hearts out, but the old woman didn't bat an eyelid. She wasn't going to cry, not now, not ever. Her tears were dry.

"I'll smash your stupid brains out!" Thor bellowed as he picked the woman up by her shoulders and shook her hard.

"No, Thor, you mustn't hurt her," Carmel yelled, flinging her arms around his waist.

Thor dropped Thokk abruptly.

"I've got one last idea, and it had better work," he fumed as he headed back toward his chariot.

While Thor was gone, a rather surprised and ruffled Loki returned to his seat. He looked suspiciously at Carmel and then out toward the chariot. He had suddenly remembered the incident back in Gladsheim.

Was it his imagination or was something going on between his lover and his best friend?

Loki struggled hard to keep up his façade; he could feel his eyes beginning to burn with jealousy.

"Here you are, you miserable old bag!" Thor yelled angrily on his return, sticking a freshly sliced onion beneath the woman's nose. "This will get those tears flowing," he chortled.

Loki stared at the onion, and after leaning forward and sniffing deeply; he looked up at Thor. "Is this for my pot, my lord?" he enquired cheekily. "Only I've got a terrible cold and can't smell a thing."

Overcome with rage, Thor hurled the onion across the room and then kicked the pot over. Its contents hissed, fizzled, and let off a most hideous smell as they turned to steam in the crackling fire. Mjollnir was in Thor's hand, and he fully intended to kill Thokk. There was no way he was going to let Odin's enchantment fail; his brother's life was at stake and was now hanging by a thread.

"Please, darling don't; I beg of you," Carmel leapt in front of Loki and stood her ground. As Thor pressed forward she wrapped her arms around his waist and twirled him sideways. "You mustn't kill the old woman; that will ensure the enchantment fails. It's not our fault she won't cry, it's fate; trust me, it's fate."

Carmel cooed and held on tightly as she let her lips caress his neck and face. Slowly, imperceptibly; Thor began to calm. To Loki's horrified bewilderment, there before his eyes a dark and terrible secret unfolded. He could do nothing; just watch as the love of his life hugged and kissed his best friend.

Loki's eyes flared like red hot pokers, but neither Thor nor Carmel noticed. They were too wrapt in each others arms and commiserating over their failure.

"You'll hear more of this, I swear," Thor threatened the woman as Carmel pulled him gently from the cave. "This isn't over, not by any means," he continued as the two of them climbed into his chariot and set off down the mountainside.

Loki nodded his head as he waved a limp goodbye.

As soon as the party was out of sight, he kicked furiously at the embers of his fire. He hadn't heard Thor's parting words, but he didn't need to. He had won the battle for Balder's soul—but had lost the war.

He should have been dancing around the cave, whooping for joy—but he wasn't.

Inside, his heart broke as his soul drowned in an ocean of sorrow. The price of victory had been too great. His triumph had cost him his love and the friendship of his best friend. Words couldn't express his anger or his grief; but they could say one thing loud and clear.

Odin, the gods, and all the Valkyrie harlots would pay dearly for this humiliation.

That was an oath—and he swore it with all his heart.

15

Reflections

Odin sat alone in his citadel and reflected on the day that might have been.

It was long after midnight and the time when his dejected warriors had thrown in the towel and gone to bed. The celebration that never was had faded faster than a winter's heat wave. Hardly a word had been spoken since Thor, Carmel, and Bragi returned with their sorrowful news.

What was there to say?

In a heartbeat, Odin's victory had turned to dust.

Fate had spat in Odin's eye, and he had a funny feeling about who was behind that cursed spittle. It had to be Loki; but without proof, he could do nothing. Indeed, even if he did find the damning truth behind Thokk's feat; he still could do nothing.

He couldn't kill his nemesis.

Loki's fate, like everyone else's, lay entangled in Ragnarok; the last, great battle—the one that was yet to come. Oh how he wished he could turn back time and start the day all over again. Maybe then he could have forced a happier ending.

Sighing deeply, Odin went back to the task in hand.

He was sitting on his throne wrapped warmly in his faded, blue cloak, leaning forward such that his elbows were resting on his thighs. His crumpled hat lay upturned a metre or so from where he was sitting, and in his hands he toyed with a pack of aged, yellowing, playing cards.

Taking each card in turn, he turned them over before casually flicking them toward his hat. Some landed inside it, and some landed outside. Some landed picture side up while others picture side down.

It was a lottery—just like fate. Try as he might, he couldn't predict nor influence what happened to each card. Card throwing, like destiny, lay beyond his control.

Odin turned his mind to Frigg.

Fortunately, she was the least of his problems. Although Jess's news had wounded him, it hadn't been entirely unexpected. In a strange way, it completed a circle that had bothered him. He knew all about Hel's Angels and their activities; but he had struggled to understand how they were being tipped off about his heroes and often beat him to the kill.

Now he understood. Now he knew it was his beautiful, duplicitous wife pulling their strings.

Frigg had probably passed messages to and from Hel using Loki as a courier, or maybe she'd used the 'White Room' when his back was turned. It could be either or both, but it didn't really matter. Dealing with Frigg would be easy—other matters wouldn't be.

Looking up, Odin cast a weary eye around his room.

This was dimly lit by a single, feeble candle, and the chamber was freezing cold. Strange and terrifying shadows weaved and writhed on the walls as a myriad, flickering candles reflected back from its nine, vaulted windows. The room was now practically empty. He'd been clearing it little by little, week by week; not wanting to attract any untoward questions or attention as he went about this task.

Lifting one hand, he placed this on the table where Mimir's cask had once lain. His dear friend, too, had now gone. He had taken him first, just as he had always sworn he would.

Poor, dear, sad, Mimir.

He had suffered the most, and Odin was glad that he could finally make good his promise to his dearest friend. Of all the gods, he was surely the most deserving of a place in paradise.

Odin glanced at the knave of spades, which he was now turning over in his hands. It was a fitting card to determine what to do next.

Hel had outwitted him over Balder's resurrection, and this had come as a surprise. He still wanted Balder and needed her to unleash Ragnarok even more so. That need was now pressing. Time was getting short, and his mind strayed once more to the disk in his pocket. It had started to change colour again. The change was almost imperceptibly, but there definitely had been a change.

Ragnarok had to come, and it had to come soon.

Knowing this, he had to play the one, last, desperate gamble he had kept up his sleeve.

Odin tossed the knave of spades and watched impassively as it twisted and spiralled before landing picture side up. It landed inside his hat.

Odin chuckled wryly.

Balder's destiny was sealed, and he would make his announcement tomorrow. Odin was practically certain that his gamble would pay off, but if it didn't; his son would be lost forever. The odds looked good and stacked in his favour, but fate could be such a fickle beast.

He sighed deeply again. He didn't know what he would do if he failed to regain his son.

Shaking his head and shivering bitterly as he did so, he stood up, stretched, and made his way slowly over to a window. Huginn cawed quietly before hopping from the ledge onto his shoulder. Both he, Muninn, and his two wolves Geri and Freki; they would be going with him, too. He would make sure of that.

Digging into a pocket, he pulled out a small treat. After watching Huginn nibble contentedly, he focused his gaze through the leaded glass. Asgard glistened in a heavy frost as it lay still and silent beneath a cloudless, moonlit sky.

It all looked so peaceful, so beautiful, and so eternal.

Odin wept.

He loved this place; the hunting, the fishing, the people, and the countless, wonderful adventures he had had. It was so very nearly perfect but therein lay the catch. It was only very nearly perfect; not perfect-perfect. Not like Midgard, a world that lay but a wave of his hand away.

Damn him! Damn the creator of that magnificent realm.

How had he done it?

How had he rolled the dice and thrown perfection?

Odin cast his mind back briefly to the halcyon days of friendship and youth; the times when he, Mimir, Vili, and Ve had come so close to repeating this miracle.

In Asgard, they had been so certain that they had achieved the impossible; found the unique solution and built a home that was perfect in every detail. But in that infinitesimal instant of creation, fate had intervened and dealt them a crippling blow.

Lambda had been undone.

They had been close, so horribly, tantalisingly close; but in the end, just not quite close enough. They hadn't built perfection, and now everybody would pay the price for their failure. He was going to miss Asgard, and that thought made him feel old; desperately old and oh so very sad.

Odin wept more tears as he continued to stare out of the window.

Asgard was sleeping peacefully.

But it wouldn't be for long.

16

Herr Flöda

"**H**ow would you like your tea?" Thirle asked, leaning forward as he lifted an elegant china teapot.

"Oh, I don't mind. As it comes, but with one sugar, please," Marcus replied politely. He was still coming to terms with the fact that he was sitting opposite a living legend, a man whom he had admired since childhood.

"I prefer mine quite weak, black, and with a twist of lemon," Thirle remarked casually, before looking up and smiling. His words weren't intended to sound snobbish; it had merely been his intention to make polite conversation, nothing more. Unfortunately, his kindly attempt to put Marcus at ease had done exactly the opposite.

It had made him feel so ordinary, so common, and so very plebeian.

On this particular occasion, however, Marcus didn't take offence. Herr Flöda, as he liked to be addressed, was a charming man who defined refinement and sophistication. His silken words had merely reinforced this fact; reminding Marcus of the reason why this man was the charismatic head of a global movement while he remained a humble and lowly police officer.

Thirle's voice was magical.

Calm, quietly spoken, authoritative, and yet glowing with the warmth of an inner passion. Every syllable was beautifully enunciated and every word chosen with the greatest care. Crafting each sentence in turn, he delivered his words in perfect meter and with a laser-guided precision. The accent was subtle, central European, and reminiscent of a Victorian, Prussian aristocrat. The voice was captivating to listen to, so it was little wonder that Herr Flöda had risen to such extraordinary heights as an orator.

Just hearing how he took his tea sounded like a work of art.

If anyone had told Marcus earlier today that he would be enjoying refreshments with one of his childhood heroes, he wouldn't have believed them. It was only through a sublime and fortuitous twist of fate that he was there now; sitting before a man he practically worshipped. They were taking afternoon tea together in Thirle's monstrously large, penthouse suite in one of the finest hotels in New York. It was a bizarre and uncomfortable occasion, but Marcus was loving every minute of it.

It was something he could tell his future children about. I once sipped tea with Herr Flöda.

"Are you satisfied with my security arrangements, or do you have any recommendations you would like me to pass on to my staff?" Herr Flöda enquired, looking up over the top of his small, circular, gold-rimmed spectacles before offering Marcus a handmade, wafer-thin biscuit.

Thirle's manners, like everything else, were impeccable.

Marcus paused for a moment, trying to remember the two-hour discussion and virtual tour of the proposed venue he had endured with his security guards. It was highly unusual for Marcus to be asked to act as a consultant on such matters, but as he was the only senior officer in his precinct available today; the job had been passed his way. It was an honour, and he took a moment to dig deep and come up with a reply that sounded vaguely sensible and intelligent.

"I would probably add a few more plainclothes officers in the audience and double-check the venue foyer for CCTV blind spots," he began measuredly. "Other than that, their proposals look very professional. I suspect they must have done a lot of this type of work before," Marcus quipped, finishing his little speech and noting to his relief that his spiel had evoked a small chuckle from Herr Flöda. His barb about "doing a lot of this before" had hit the mark. Thirle was an obsessive man and notorious within the trade for demanding the highest levels of security; aping those normally afforded to the Pope, the Queen of England, or the American President.

The reason behind this was well known.

Thirle had survived a serious assassination attempt some years back, and that horrific incident was why he was now such a recluse. He didn't just value his privacy; he valued his life, too.

"Good. Well thank goodness that's sorted," Thirle mused contentedly, taking another sip of tea as he stared thoughtfully and silently ahead of him.

Marcus would have liked to strike up a conversation, but it was difficult knowing what to say to a man who lived in the highest social echelons and who criss-crossed the world on a never-ending tour of his New Youth Movement. He was adored by the teenagers and young adults whom he inspired, and he never let them down. That was why he was in New York today; he was in the middle of one such tour. He would be giving a rousing speech to the New York Bann tomorrow, and this would be followed by a sumptuous reception party. After that, he would be back on his plane and off for the next stop on his whirlwind express. He was a marvel, and Marcus surreptitiously eyed the gentleman up and down.

Thirle must be well into his sixties and quite probably pushing seventy, but he had the face and figure of a man at least twenty years his junior. His short, cropped, blond hair was definitely receding, and it had a distinguished, grey-flecked pepper pot appearance to it. True, there was the hint of a growing belly beneath his tweed jacket and mustard coloured waistcoat; but it was no more prominent than Marcus's; a fact about which he felt positively ashamed. Thirle's boundless energy was legendary and a serious wake-up call to other more sedentary mortals. He must have climbed Mount Kilimanjaro with his various Banns on more occasions than Marcus had had hot dinners. His energy seemed inexhaustible, and perhaps that was why he had aged so slowly in the thirty years he had been president of the movement.

He simply didn't have the time to grow old.

"Would you like another cup of tea?" Thirle offered politely, and Marcus was sorely tempted to say yes. He would have loved to spend more time in Thirle's company, but he knew that that would be an imposition. The offer of a second cup of tea was a gentle reminder that their meeting should come to an end. Herr Flöda had far better things to do than make small talk with a New York cop.

After reluctantly declining the offer, the two men stood up and shook hands, and Thirle then accompanied Marcus toward the door.

"That's a beautiful picture," Marcus volunteered as his eyes came to rest on a small, framed, watercolour sitting on an easel. "Did you paint it yourself?" he added, pausing as he did so to take in its detail.

Herr Flöda was a keen amateur artist and once upon a time had exhibited and sold his paintings widely. In more recent years, at his request, his works had been removed from sale, and their value had consequently rocketed. The man had the Midas touch. He wasn't a particularly gifted artist, but his status as a player on the world stage and his reluctance to sell his portfolio had ensured an insatiable collectors' market. It was an unintentional stroke of financial genius, but genius none the less.

The rich, it seemed, just couldn't stop getting richer.

"Yes, I'm so glad you like it." Thirle thanked Marcus politely before apologising and removing the painting from the easel. He was obviously self-conscious about the work, which seemed rather odd. It was a pleasing but rather plain watercolour of the interior of a Bavarian lodge. The perspective was slightly distorted, but other than that, it was a charming sketch and certainly nothing to be ashamed of. Marcus decided not to comment further; quite clearly the painting had been intended for his private viewing only.

Pausing by the door to shake hands once more, Marcus posed a question that had always intrigued him. "Will your wife be joining you for the speech?" he enquired nosily.

"No, well not at least on this occasion. My partner, Miss Brown, is currently soaking up the sun on some paradise of a Caribbean Island." Thirle smiled and then continued. "Given the choice, I suspect I would be doing the same."

After thanking him for his kind hospitality, Marcus shook hands and retraced his footsteps as he left the building. He had never been sure if Herr Flöda was married, and now he knew the answer—he wasn't. For such a public and powerful figure, Thirle kept his private life low key and extremely well hidden. Marcus couldn't remember having ever seen a photograph of his partner, hence his lack of knowledge.

Outside the public façade, Thirle Flöda was a man of mystery and that, it seemed, was how he intended to stay.

Stepping outside into the bright summer sunshine, Marcus pulled his mobile from his pocket and pressed a speed dial button. He wasn't quite sure why he was dialling this particular number, but he knew he had to, and he knew that it was important.

"Good afternoon Dragza Corporation, how may I help you?" It was the delightful Caribbean lilt of one of the company's helpful receptionists that greeted him.

"May I speak to the Contessa, please?" Marcus enquired before adding, "It's Detective Finch calling."

Marcus continued walking while there was a short delay.

"Good afternoon, Marcus, how lovely to hear from you." At last the Contessa answered the phone. "I do hope you are feeling refreshed?" she enquired pointedly.

"I most certainly am, my lady."

"Do you have any news for me?" Frigg continued casually. Marcus was in the zone; his meek and humble monotone betraying the abrupt transition from New York cop to servant of Hel.

"Yes, my lady. Your target is acquired and I await your instructions."

17

A Powder Keg

Jess took hold of the reins to Kat's horse and led her mare slowly over the crest of the hill until the view was to her liking. "You can uncover your eyes now," she sang merrily as Kat did so.

The vista that unfolded before Kat was exactly how she remembered it.

The beautiful bay formed a perfect, sweeping curve that followed the contours of the rugged mountains enveloping it. These majestic peaks sloped steeply downward in jagged, buttressed spurs until they flattened off abruptly and then kissed the shore in a shy and tender embrace. Clinging to the broken hillsides and nestled amongst the endless, swirling, waves of shingle; lay the ramshackle, higgledy-piggledy, huts of Noatun. The gateway to Middle Sea.

This cove was going to be the Valkyries' home for the next few days and the venue for the greatest ceremony in living history. The picturesque, fishing hamlet was a spectacular backdrop to bid farewell to Asgard's cherished son.

Noatun was the perfect location for Balder's funeral.

It had come as no surprise following the failure of his enchantment when Odin announced his decision to cremate Balder's body. The only shock was the speed with which he intended to do so. The very next morning the decree for the funeral was announced and plans set in motion for the ceremony to take place in just two days. Asgard hurtled into life immediately as an endless convoy of carts laden with

127

tents, food, drink, beds, tables, and stools began the slow trundle south toward the sea.

This wasn't going to be any ordinary funeral, this was going to be an incredible showcase, and everyone had been invited. Heralds were sent to every village and hamlet in Asgard and Vannaheim; and messengers journeyed to the realms of Jotunheim, Nidavellir, and Muspellheim. Representatives from the giants, dwarves, and the dragons had been invited as well; and an emissary had been dispatched across the sea to Alfheim.

Even the mysterious Elf Lords would receive an invitation.

The event was going to be huge, and even with the spectre of Ragnarok hanging pregnant in the air; Odin was determined to send his son to the afterlife in style. Absolutely no expense would be spared and, for once, his countless coffers of gold were open wide.

The event promised to be beyond huge; a spectacle beyond imagination.

Bunching closer together as the Valkyries eased their horses gently down the pockmarked trail, the excitement amongst the girls began to boil over. Days of petty squabbles and antagonisms disappeared as the scale of the occasion dawned upon them. The peaceful village of Noatun hadn't changed, but around it a vast and glorious city of tents and marquees had been erected. The greys and browns of the shingled beach had been transformed into a multi-coloured kaleidoscope of reds, oranges, yellows, and gold.

Standing proud and silent in the midst of all the bustle was Ringhorn; Balder's longboat.

This was a mighty vessel and had been hauled out of the sea and set upon huge log rollers. Ringhorn's sail was furled, and dried wood and kindling faggots had been stacked around its single, golden mast. Kat gulped and glanced at the ornate chariot, which had been entrusted to the warriors care. Lying in there on a deep bed of fresh straw and draped in crimson sheets made from the finest silk were the bodies of Mist and Prima. These were the two Valkyries who had perished in the battle with Hel's Berserkers. Theirs would be the honour of journeying to the afterlife with Balder.

Tears welled in Kat's eyes as she gazed down upon the bodies; and she murmured a brief prayer to Odin for their safe passage. Their beautiful, silver crowns fashioned in the form of wreaths of oak leaves were identical to hers. One day, if she was lucky, her body might travel as theirs did now. This thought didn't frighten her—far from it. Her tears were not of sorrow but of a longing to join them in

Valhalla. Even now, a warrior for less than a year, Kat could feel the hunger of the afterlife.

It gnawed at her soul like toothache.

Odin had warned her of its intensity, and now she understood why. Looking around her, she could tell that the other warriors were feeling this desire, too. Valhalla remained their hearts' desire in spite of Ben's dramatic warning.

These extraordinary words had been the cause of much antagonism around the castle over the last few days, dividing the warriors deeply. Some, like Jameela, Kat, and Jess, believed Ben's tale and felt a great hostility and suspicion toward Odin. Others, such as Ruby, Silk, and Skogul, remained staunchly loyal to their lord; rejecting Ben's claims as rubbish and shunning him, much to Elijah's distress.

He and Ben had struck up a friendship, and he was now deeply torn between this and his love for Ruby. Apart from Kat, Elijah had the most detailed knowledge of Odin's duplicity; but out of a sense of loyalty to Ruby, he refused to discuss the goings on in Niflheim. Hel had been a cruel and vengeful queen, but she had also been slighted by the god of gods and unjustly punished. Elijah could see both sides; the good and bad in both protagonists. However, for Ruby's sake, he wasn't going to take sides. For now, he would bide his time; watching and waiting as he thoughtfully digested all the stories about Odin and his troubled realm.

"Look, the Elf Lords. I can see their vessel, look, LOOK!"

Jameela rose up in her saddle and pointed excitedly to the distant horizon. It was a beautiful, winter's day with a cold sun smiling down from a cloudless, powder blue sky. With barely a breath of wind in the air, the waves of Middle Sea had a long, slow, lazy swell to them with nary a white horse cresting amongst them. The girls could see for miles.

Coming slowly over the horizon and shimmering vividly as though it were a mirage was a magnificent, silvered, longboat with a sail of purest white. Jameela had to be right; such a perfect vessel could belong to none other.

Spurring their horses on, the girls began to hurry down the twisting trail once more. None of them had ever seen an elf, not even Ruby. She too was most excited.

Arriving in the village at last, the warriors quickly fanned out and began to stake their claims to the various tents and marquees, which had been allocated to them. Competition was fierce to bag the most prestigious location, and some of the haggling and arguing was most unladylike. Eventually, all disputes were settled, and those that couldn't be resolved with a bit of give and take were decided in the time honoured tradition of bouts of arm-wrestling.

Initially, Kat hadn't been too fussed about where she slept, but she was determined that her tent would be for her and Jess alone. With a shortage of this type of tent, to her surprise, she wrestled and defeated Goll for the right to bed down in the last remaining one.

Kat's strength was still growing, and the other warriors were taking note.

There was an established pecking order amongst the Valkyries with Ruby and Silk at the top. Kat's increasing confidence and power was becoming a worry to many. She was still a much-loved sister, but her allegiance and friendship with Hel cast suspicion over their trust. When the final battle of Ragnarok arrived, many wondered whose side Kat would be on.

Odin's or Hel's?

This thought was troubling.

Amongst the dignitaries already present in Noatun was a contingent of nervous dwarves.

Tensions were high, and the warriors' hands twitched lovingly at the hilts of their swords as they greeted their former enemy. Any excuse to slay a dwarf would be gratefully appreciated; their brutal and greed-driven slaughter of Kvasir and Hlokk were still neither forgotten nor forgiven.

Mindful of this fact, the dwarves were particularly wary and humble; bowing low as they offered the girls beautiful gifts of gold and silver jewellery. The aim of the dwarves was obvious; to make reparations for their treachery. Without Odin's patronage, their kingdom and wealth had been frozen. They had come to Balder's funeral with a clear and unambiguous message; to seek a pardon for their misdemeanours and the opportunity to commence trading once more.

Knowing this, the Valkyries' attitude softened. Beautiful jewellery was, after all, beautiful jewellery; and they couldn't resist such splendid and magnificent gifts.

As the warriors cooed and gushed over their fabulous presents, a strange, high-pitched chatter gradually grew in loudness. With a final, resounding crunch of wood impacting upon shingle; the magnificent vessel from Alfheim beached upon the shore of Asgard. With frenzied excitement, the warriors raced through the camp to greet their new arrivals. Tales about the great Elf Lords were steeped with wonder and mystery.

Kat joined the eager rush, and her first impressions of these exotic visitors matched the story she had been told by Hel and Hod.

Dressed in capotes of forest green and sporting bows with quivers full of dart-like arrows, the elves leapt ashore in an excited cluster. A silence swiftly fell upon the warriors as they struggled to come to terms with their extraordinary visitors.

The elves were indeed about the size and shape of ten-year-old children, with the tops of their heads coming close to chest height on Kat. Their hair was long and curly, and the sunlight danced upon their locks in a beauteous display. However, looking at the elves for any length of time made for a tiring and queasy spectacle.

They moved so quickly that their small gathering was a constant blur of motion; a seething mass of tiny arms, legs, and moon shaped faces, constantly changing position. It was almost impossible to keep track of any one individual; the images captured in the warriors' minds being a pastiche of different smiles and bodies in a multitude of ever changing positions.

Kat tried to shake hands and say "hello" to their guests; but she wasn't sure if she had shaken hands with only one or maybe half a dozen elves. Their grasp was so delicate it felt as though a wisp of wool had been drawn through her fingers. Growing tired and head-achy with the symphony of their squeaky voices, Kat and Jess retired from the throng and set about sorting out their tent.

Keeping an eye on the Elf Lords was going to be taxing work.

"What was that?" Kat looked up and paused with what she was doing. It felt as though a deep vibration, a ripple of thunder or minor earthquake, had shaken the bustling village.

Jess shrugged and shook her head. She had heard the strange sound too and didn't know what it was either, although it did seem to be getting louder. Anxiously picking up their swords, the two girls rushed outside.

The source of the noise was soon apparent.

There, streaming down the hillside behind them was a large gathering of giants led by an imposing, warrior giantess. Her name was Hyrokkin, and it had been widely rumoured that she would be leading their delegation.

Up until now, Kat had considered all giants hideously ugly and the attraction of the gods toward the women of Jotunheim somewhat bizarre. Now, seeing Hyrokkin more clearly as she drew near, she had the first inkling as to why some giantesses garnered adoration. Without being obviously beautiful, their queen was magnificent; an extraordinarily handsome and striking woman.

Standing well over two metres thirty tall, Hyrokkin was full fig-ured with an imperious, heaving bosom and slender, muscular waist. Her hair was coloured jet black and streamed behind her like a trail of fluttering ribbons. Her coal-black eyes smouldered beneath a large, single eyebrow, and her long, slender nose gave way to large, full-bodied, cherry-red lips that accentuated the fairness of her skin and the fierceness of her toothy grimace.

She looked ferocious—and her chariot was no less so.

Carved from wood so black that it could only be ebony; her chariot was drawn by two huge and powerful wolves. Panting hard with tongues lolling from mouths bristling with dagger-like fangs, they looked as menacing as Fenrir. Keeping these monstrous animals in check was no mean feat, and to aid her in this task, Hyrokkin drove the beasts with a huge whip and reins made from snakes. Not merely the skins of snakes but the full, dried carcasses, which had been oiled to make them supple before braiding them into a long, thick, leathery rope. The desiccated heads of the serpents hadn't been removed; and these jangled from the reins with their mouths wide open and fangs flashing in the harsh winter sunlight.

Hyrokkin held her giant whip in one hand, and she wielded this lib-erally, swishing and cracking it with great force as the chariot sped into the settlement. With a single, mighty roar, the giant host shud-dered to a bone crunching halt.

The Valkyries drew their swords, and the Elf Lords stood alongside them with arrows drawn. With the giant host sweating hard and shrouded in a cloud of evaporating perspiration, the Valkyries pre-pared for the worst.

"Lower your arms," Hyrokkin commanded in a slow and faltering tongue. Joining words into sentences was as hard for her as it was for most giants. "We come in peace and at Odin's bidding. We are here to pay our respects to Balder and nothing else." Extending her arm, the giantess stepped forward with what was intended to be a warm smile.

Kat giggled nervously; her lips were crooked, and the smile did her no favours.

In the absence of any gods, Ruby stepped forward and took her hand. "Greetings mighty Hyrokkin, please allow us to escort you to your quarters. Slaves!" she yelled authoritatively. "Fetch food and water for our guests' horses and wolves. Treat them kindly and respect them as if they were your own."

With a huge sigh of relief, the Valkyries sheathed their weapons and gingerly escorted the giants to the tents that they'd been allocated. There were many more of their number than had been expected, so the girls reluctantly vacated some of theirs and began to look for lodgings elsewhere. In this respect, Jess was quick off the mark, dragging Kat away by the arm.

"Come on," she urged Kat gleefully. "Let's go and wait outside Njord's hut. It would be such fun to stay with him, he tells such wonderful tales."

Mystified, Kat gathered up her belongings and followed Jess toward an inauspicious, two-storey dwelling closest to the shore. Its door looked weathered and worn, and the windowpanes were tightly shuttered. The place looked deserted and Kat said as such.

"Oh, don't worry, he'll be along soon," Jess reassured her. "He has to be here for the ceremony anyway. Odin wouldn't start without him; that simply wouldn't do," she added with a mysterious grin. Not willing to say more, she begged Kat to be patient.

Njord's identity would be revealed shortly.

As the afternoon drew swiftly to a close and a fading, ochre sun slipped silently behind the hills that sheltered the bay; a large, oak longboat rounded the tip of the cove and sailed slowly into view.

The slightest of winds had picked up, and its striped, red and white sail billowed and slapped noisily in the lazy breeze. The vessel's crew had already shipped oars, and as the boat beached itself with a gentle crunch against the shingled shore, a white-haired gentleman leapt overboard and hauled its painter ashore.

"Here, come on ladies, give us a hand," the man called out, spotting the two warriors sitting close by. With a sly nudge, Jess ushered Kat to join her as she slithered down the shingle bank toward him.

"Ah, the very beautiful Brynhildr; I am honoured to have your gracious assistance," the man beamed ecstatically before lovingly kissing her outstretched hand. "And who might be your equally majestic companion?" he enquired, grinning broadly as he turned his twinkling eyes and weathered face toward Kat.

"This is the Valkyrie Sangrid, my lord," Jess volunteered. "We would be delighted to help you land your catch, but in return we beg a small favour. May we please stay with you in your hut tonight?"

"But of course, of course! It would be an honour to have two such mighty Valkyries grace my humble dwelling." Stepping forward, the man bowed low and kissed Kat's hand. He smelt of salt, seaweed, and fresh fish; and although his face was old and leathery, it was one of the most handsome faces Kat had ever seen.

"Do please allow me to introduce myself," the man continued as he drew his lips reluctantly from her fingers. "My name is Njord, and I have heard a great deal about you from my son Freyr. He speaks very highly of you, my lady Sangrid; very highly indeed." Njord winked teasingly as Kat curtsied without thinking and without hesitation.

Standing before her was none other than the father of the Queen of the Valkyries and Freyja's lustworthy, fabulously endowed brother Freyr.

Kat glanced swiftly at his hand. Njord's ring had nearly as many diamonds as Odin's. He was undoubtedly a powerful god; the master of Noatun and all the shores of Asgard. Just as Thor was the champion of serfs and farmers, Njord was champion of seafarers and fishermen.

Tonight was definitely going to be special, and as Kat busied herself with hauling the heavy catch from the boat, she drooled at the prospect of the stories he might tell.

18

The Marriage of Njord and Skadi

"**B**rrrrh!" Carmel chattered, shivering noisily as she stumbled quickly across the last few metres of shingle before settling herself down behind Kat. Placing her legs either side of Kat's body, she shuffled forward and slid her arms around her waist.

"Hi, Kitty Kat," she murmured softly, gently nuzzling her neck. Turning around, Kat kissed her affectionately and then rubbed her arm gently. They hadn't sat together for some time, and it was good to feel the warmth of her body again.

Carmel had arrived at Noatun quite a bit later than the rest of the Valkyries. Apparently the strap on her saddle had frayed and surprise, surprise, she had had to wait until Thor could fix it before making her way toward the village. Oddly enough, the two of them had then journeyed together for company. These sorts of mishaps did occur, but the number of convenient coincidences pushing the two of them together was beginning to mount up. Add to that Carmel's sheepish grin, and it wasn't going to be too long before her sisters twigged that she and Thor were having an affair.

"Have I missed much?" Carmel whispered, and to her relief Kat shook her head. She would have been quite miffed if she'd missed one of Njord's wonderful tales.

Following Njord's arrival, Kat and Jess had worked hard helping him and the other sailors bring the wicker baskets of fish ashore. They were amazed at the size of his catch and the shear variety of fish that had been caught. There seemed to be more than enough herring, cod, skate, and other more exotic species to feed all the guests for a week.

As Njord had patiently explained, this hadn't actually been the purpose of their trip. Most of the fish was destined to be salted or smoke dried and then stored for eating over the harsh months to come.

Just as the horrors of Ragnarok would soon be upon them, winter was setting in fast, and fishing expeditions would soon be coming to an end.

After cleaning themselves up using buckets of steaming, soapy water; the two girls had rejoined the other Valkyries as they set about hosting the evening's festivities in the main marquee. Other gods including Thor, Tyr, and Vali had arrived in dribs and drabs throughout the afternoon, and many more would be accompanying Odin tomorrow when he arrived with Balder's funeral cortege. Satisfied that all the elves, dwarves, and even the giants had been suitably fed and entertained; the warriors had taken their leave and then slowly drifted away from the tent village to join Kat and Jess outside Njord's hut.

The god's storytelling was legendary, and the sight of his crackling fire on the beach was an invitation impossible to resist. Settling down one by one, the warriors and maids had pulled their cloaks tightly around them, lifted their hoods high over their heads, and then shuffled as close to the fire as they dared. This was where they were all now, alternately chatting, shivering, and toasting their hands and feet against the winter's chill.

"Does anyone mind if I smoke?" Njord enquired casually as he pulled a beautifully carved, Meerschaum pipe out of his pocket. He began the subconscious ritual of cleaning it by tapping out the bowl in the palm of his hand, and then filling this with tobacco.

Few gods smoked in Asgard, and those who did, usually did so in private. Njord was one of the few who could persuade Odin to bring home wads of tobacco from Midgard; and the sight and smell of his fresh pouch of crisp, golden, shredded leaves proved irresistible. Both Ruby and Ben expressed a desire to join Njord in 'a smoke,' and to their glee he kindly passed the pouch to them. Excitedly they rolled a few, crude cigarettes.

Elijah (who was cuddled up next to his lover) expressed surprise.

He had thought Ruby had given up the habit, and this provoked Jameela to start a debate on the evils of smoking. Self-consciously, Ben returned his 'rollies' unlit to Njord. He didn't want to antagonise Jameela tonight and, besides, he knew that she was right. He really should give them up, too. Gradually, as the debate lessened, Njord asked the cosy throng clustered tightly around him as to what story they would like to hear.

Tales about Jormungard and the other giant sea monsters were always popular, but it came as no surprise when the warriors unanimously settled on their favourite story. This was the one that involved Njord's brief and tempestuous marriage to the giantess Skadi.

All the girls had heard second- and third-hand retellings of this amusing tale, but the opportunity to hear the witty saga from the god himself was going to be a treat.

Before he began, Njord stood up and excused himself from the circle. He disappeared briefly inside his hut before returning with several jugs of piping hot, mulled wine. The warriors cheered and clapped him enthusiastically for his generosity.

Passing horns and tankards around the group, the girls wrapped their frozen hands around the warm vessels and sipped gratefully at the soothing liquid. No one could have asked for a nicer ending to a bitterly cold day; cuddled up amongst friends around a deliciously warm bonfire, listening to tales from a master sage, and of course; getting merrily sozzled.

The stage was set for a magical evening.

The warriors could remember Skadi from the recent Battle of the Bridge. Here, she'd been a gnarled and ferocious leader of the giants, fighting like a wild beast in the fray that had ended in the giants' defeat. True, she was now old and shapeless, but Njord reminded them that she hadn't always been that way. In her youth, she had been a handsome giantess, the equal or better of Hyrokkin herself; and nobody would disagree that Hyrokkin was the sort of buxom beauty who could tempt the hearts of the lustful gods.

Back in the days when Skadi was still young and fetching, Odin had killed her father Thiazi. He was a mighty frost giant and King of Thrymheim; the highest and most inhospitable realm in the whole of Jotunheim. Saddened and whipped into a fury by this brutal slaying, Skadi had set out across the Bifrost Bridge with one thought on her mind—revenge. Riding alone in her chariot, Heimdall had let her pass. After all, what was one enraged giantess going to do at a castle packed with mighty gods? Her fury would be a mere pinprick and quite possibly the source of sport for Odin and his companions.

In those days, Asgard was filled with peace, tranquillity—and boredom.

Njord recounted vividly the moment when he had first set his eyes on the giantess. This was when her glorious, battle chariot had thundered noisily into the castle courtyard.

Skadi had looked magnificent; clad in a chain mail coat and wielding her father's favourite sword. This was engraved with a mystical serpent. Beside her stood a long spear with a shaft of ash, and the shield, which hung upon the side of her chariot, was both beautiful and ornate. It was large and round, and made from layers of wood covered with stretched hide. This had then been richly patterned with effigies of birds of prey, and these were inlaid with gleaming, golden eyes and curled, twisted beaks of vermillion red.

"Where's Odin?" Skadi had screamed leaping from her mount and storming toward the castle's entrance. It had taken Thor, Tyr, Njord, and several other gods and servants some time to wrestle her to the ground and disarm her. She had been a mighty warrior and, make no mistake; as wild and untamed as a tigress.

Njord chuckled long and hard as memories of their ferocious and undignified tussle stirred inside him.

Pacified and securely bound, Odin had eventually joined the crowd of spectators who had gathered to see the screaming hellcat.

Fortunately for Skadi, her bravery and several horns of mead had softened Odin's heart. He was in a humorous and relaxed mood and had no desire for further bloodshed. Releasing her, he apologised for killing her father and begged her to forgive him. He even offered several heaped chests of gold in compensation.

"Pah!" Skadi spat angrily at the unlocked chests, kicking one over for good measure. "What do I need with these trinkets?" she continued miserably, pouring scorn on the vast sum of money Odin had offered.

Skadi was the daughter of a mighty and ancient frost giant and had more wealth in her hall than she could spend in many lifetimes. No, what she wanted were two things that she was certain Odin couldn't provide.

A husband and a damn good laugh.

Just like the gods and the Valkyries, giants could be extremely passionate. Once their hearts had been ignited, their hunger for love yearned to be satisfied. During the struggle on the courtyard floor, Skadi had set her eyes on Balder and along with every other maiden in Asgard; she had fallen for his chiselled, tanned features and golden, sun-kissed locks.

Skadi was smitten, and she begged to take him as her husband at once.

Skadi's bold and brazen request caused considerable mirth amongst the gods. It was so audacious that Odin felt compelled not to let the magnificent and garrulous woman leave empty-handed. Being in a mood for entertainment, he haggled with her and eventually settled on a silly competition for her to win her prize.

If she wanted a god for a husband, she would have to take part in a lucky dip.

The warriors giggled at this point and shuffled closer to the fire and Njord. They all knew the next part of the tale, and it never failed to raise a laugh, particularly when they had had a few drinks.

Taking the hint, Njord got up once more and returned almost immediately with several more pitchers of scorching, mulled wine. These were quickly passed around his eager audience. The potent, fortified liquid tasted delicious and was brewed to his own unique and top-secret recipe. Settling down once more, Njord refilled his pipe, and after lighting the tobacco and taking a few deep puffs, he returned to his tale.

A blindfold was tied tightly around Skadi's eyes such that she couldn't see a thing. Then, the bottom of it was loosened such that she could only see the ground beneath her and a few feet further in front. Laughing wildly, Njord, Balder, Loki, Thor, Bragi, Tyr, and several other gods formed up in a line and then took their shoes off. Odin's mischievous competition soon became clear.

Skadi would choose her husband from the fairness of his feet, not his face.

Smiling slyly to herself, Skadi passed back and forth along the line of gods and studied each pair of feet intently. Some had bunions, some had corns, some were dirty and hairy, and some smelt dreadful. Eventually, happy that she had chosen the most perfect pair, Skadi pointed triumphantly down at them.

The most gracious feet had to belong to the most gracious god—Balder.

"This will be my groom," she announced confidently as the blindfold was carefully removed. Gazing up at her chosen husband, Skadi's mouth fell open. The god she had chosen with such confidence wasn't the dashing Balder but was none other than Njord.

"I've been tricked!" she fumed as Njord cautioned her that the words she spoke would set the tempo for their marriage. Skadi wasn't happy; and she huffed and puffed until a gleam lit up her eyes. She had come up with a way to wriggle out of their agreement.

"Here, Odin, wait a minute," she yelled marching angrily over to him. "What about a jolly good laugh? Remember I did request that you gods make me laugh and have you done so? No, I don't think so. The deal's off and I'm going home."

Skadi scowled down grumpily at the worn cobblestones before stomping away. Hurrying back toward her chariot, her gaze came to rest upon a most unusual and ridiculous sight.

Shuffling his way slowly across the courtyard toward her was what appeared to be a particularly stupid peasant boy. In each arm he had balanced two huge baskets of vegetables, meat, and eggs; and tethered to his body was a troublesome and frisky goat.

Now, unable to hold the goats lead in his hands, or to tie it to his wrist, or to some other sensible part of his body; the idiot youth had come up with the craziest plan imaginable. After tying one end of the leather thong tightly to the goat's beard, he had undone his trousers and tied the other around his scrotum.

Gradually, as he had struggled up the hill toward the castle, his trousers had slipped further and further down his legs. To make matters worse, his goat had tugged and strained excitedly at the leash such that it was now wrapped like a tourniquet around his testicles.

The poor simpleton was in agony!

His pants were around his ankles and his scrotum had turned purple. One more tug from the bleating beast and it looked as though his plums might pop.

At this point the girls rolled about laughing.

The image Njord had painted of this tug of war between the idiot's family jewels and a goat was so vivid it was impossible not to howl out loud. Relaxed by the potent wine, the girls couldn't control themselves and it was some time before Njord could return to his story.

Finally, when the girls had wiped the tears from their eyes, Njord got back to his tale.

Watching in disbelief and with a smile threatening at the corners of her lips, Skadi viewed the struggle between man and beast with increasing amusement. Finally, when it seemed impossible that the gangling youth could walk any further, the boy yanked as hard as he could on the leash. He had to get his goat back in order. With one, last mighty thrust from his hips he heaved the goat toward him.

Letting out a single, loud, plaintive bleat, the creature leapt into the air and as the boy toppled over backward, the goat landing bang, slap, wallop—right in the middle of his crotch.

How the youth howled with pain!

The gods, townsfolk, and Skadi collapsed in fits of laughter, and to everybody's amazement the grinning, blushing, half-witted boy shape shifted immediately into the mischievous figure of Loki. The gods had made Skadi laugh, and she was so grateful to finally be able to enjoy a joke again that she agreed to honour her deal with Odin.

Right there and then, Skadi and Njord were wed.

"So what happened next?" Kat asked curiously when further bouts of giggles had subsided. Everybody knew this part of the story, but Skadi still lived in the frozen wastes of Jotunheim and Njord quite obviously didn't. This part of the tale had always perplexed her.

Were they still married?

"Excellent point, my dear Sangrid," Njord answered with a merry grin. He too had been sipping at the mulled wine and was beginning to feel nearly as tipsy as the girls. Puffing at his pipe once more, he brought them up to date.

Far from being upset at being won as a prize in a competition, Njord was delighted with his buxom new bride. She was a statuesque giantess, and just like the passionate bloodlust of the Valkyries; the prowess in the bedroom of the women from Jotunheim was highly prized. They were highly skilled in the art of lovemaking, and the two of them had enjoyed many a blissful night consumed by the heat of their embraces.

Unfortunately, however, their happiness wasn't meant to be.

Skadi hated living by the sea. The endless mewing of seagulls, the motion of the waves, and the constant smell of raw fish had been hard for her to stomach. Similarly, Njord hated living in her freezing mountain kingdom. The constant howling of the wolves, the barren, craggy mountain slopes, and the freezing sheets of hail that swept down from the glaciers chilled him to the bone.

Eventually, after enduring several months of shuttling between their two homes, the pair had come to an amicable separation. Technically, they were still married; but they hadn't set eyes on each other for many years.

Story finished, Njord stood up, stretched, yawned, and with a merry twinkle in his eyes tactfully suggested that they should all go and get some sleep. Tomorrow was going to be a long and stressful day, and the Valkyries needed to look their most magnificent best for Balder's funeral. Getting up reluctantly, the girls hugged and kissed Njord warmly before thanking him for his excellent hospitality.

Gathering their cloaks around them, the warriors had just begun to head toward their tents when a loud creaking and clattering interrupted them. A large, heavy cart was wending its way slowly through the maze of tents toward them.

Hurrying over to take a closer look, the girls all agreed that they had never seen such a peculiar carriage before.

Drawn by four hefty shire horses, the cart was painted jet black and shaped in the form of a squat, rectangular box. What made this object particularly unusual was that there were no windows, and the door was sealed so tightly shut that its outline was all but invisible.

"What is it?" Jameela breathed quietly as she ran her fingernails along its flawless, glossy paintwork.

"I've absolutely no idea," Ruby admitted with a shrug.

Completely overcome with curiosity, Carmel hurried back to Njord's hut and dragged him, Kat, and Jess over to the vehicle, which had now come to a halt.

Pressing their ears tightly against the box, the warriors listened and tapped at its walls to see if they could work out what was inside. The box was clearly hollow, and they suspected that someone or something was inside it. Despite their tapping, whatever lay hidden inside kept its ghostly silence.

"Do you know what might be in here?" Carmel enquired breathlessly when Njord eventually arrived amongst the warriors.

Scratching his head, Njord wandered slowly all the way around the cart and then for good measure tapped on its wooden walls with the bowl of his pipe. The box certainly echoed with a hollow emptiness; but no sound came from within.

"I'm not rightly sure," Njord mused, rubbing his chin. "I have my suspicions, but I wouldn't like to say, not at this moment. Come on ladies, there's been enough excitement for one night. Whatever lies inside this carriage will surely wait for the morning. I'm sure it will all become obvious by daylight." Turning and urging Kat and Jess to return with him to his hut, the god waved a tired goodnight to the puzzled girls.

Njord was ninety-nine percent certain about the contents of the squat and intimidating box, but he wasn't going to let on. If his suspicions were correct, the visitors inside hadn't been seen in Asgard for millennia.

Shuddering at the prospect of these mysterious and sinister guests, Njord began to appreciate just how powerful and how far reached Odin's influence stretched.

19

Ice Cream

"Mmmm, delicious," Vili murmured after he had given the wheelchair a little push, paused; and then taken another spoonful of ice cream from his bowl.

"Mmmm, mine too," mumbled Ve; licking at a spoonful before pushing the wheelchair a little further along the bumpy, pot holed path. "What flavour's yours?" he enquired eagerly.

"Chocolate chip and something else, but I'm not sure what. Mmmm, whatever it is, it's delicious," Vili smacked his lips greedily.

"Mine's all fruity. Peach Melba, I think," Ve added before stopping yet again to scoop another large helping from his bowl.

Their ice creams were melting fast.

It was mid afternoon, and the sun was beating down ferociously between the dappled pools of shade provided by the clusters of palm trees surrounding the sprawling mansion. Odin's brothers had just helped themselves to two obscenely generous portions of ice cream, and they were greedily trying to scoff these while pushing their patient along a loose, graveled path toward the beach.

They were almost at their journey's end, but it had taken them an age; and the frail, greying gentleman who they were pushing would have complained bitterly if only he'd been able to talk. Dressed in a pair of ill-fitting, striped pyjamas that were at least a couple of sizes too small; his face was all but hidden beneath a floppy, old, battered, straw hat. Paralysed from the neck down, the man probably wasn't in the best of humours.

"Ahhhh, that's better," Vili sighed appreciatively when the trio eventually arrived at the beach. "Do you think he's in the shade?" he enquired, pointing a spoon coated in gooey chocolate at their charge.

"I think so," said Ve. "Should we put some more suntan cream on him?" he suggested helpfully. "He's looking a bit red."

"Good idea," Vili retorted, getting up from the sand. Pulling a bottle of suntan lotion from beside their patient, Vili removed the man's hat and ham fistedly slopped a layer of cream all over his face. Satisfied with his handiwork, he replaced the hat and sat back down again.

"Why don't we give him a bit of ice cream?" Ve proposed generously. "I'm sure it'll be all right."

"We shouldn't," Vili cautioned, looking thoughtfully at the sallow, haggard face of their patient. His eyes were tightly shut, and his mouth was furred and lolling open; he really didn't look at all well. "But it might cheer him up," he agreed optimistically as he prepared a heaped spoon of melted chocolate chips and marshmallow chunks to give to their friend. "Open wide," Vili chuckled as his laden spoon glided slowly towards the man's mouth—chocolate blobs dripping and dribbling onto the front of his pyjamas as he did so.

"Boys, boys, BOYS!" Frigg yelled, suddenly breaking into a panic stricken jog. "What in Midgard do you think you're doing?" she enquired angrily when at last she reached the three of them. "Are you trying to kill him?"

Grabbing Vili's hand, she hastily removed the spoon. "How many times have I told you that he must only be fed stewed apples until he can swallow properly?" she ended in exasperation.

Vili looked blankly at Ve—and Ve looked blankly at Vili. Frigg's message clearly hadn't gotten through to either of them. It needed reinforcing.

"Come on, give me your hand." Frigg demanded authoritatively, and after taking Vili's hand in hers and turning it over; she gave it a short, sharp, painful smack on the back.

"Ouch!" Vili cried in surprise. "That hurt."

"Ha, ha, ha, serves you right." Ve mocked, laughing nervously.

SLAP!

"Ouch! What was that for?" Ve cried, rubbing his face. Frigg had slapped this considerably harder.

"For laughing at your brother's misfortune," she scolded him. "Honestly, sometimes you two idiots make me glad I married Odin and not one of you."

"Oh, don't be like that, please," the two brothers begged in unison as they stared crestfallenly at the sand. They had only been trying to help.

"Look at this mess!" she continued, chastising them as she began to massage the sloppy, streaks of suntan cream properly into their patient's face. As she did so, the merest flicker of a smile twitched at the corner of his lips. His sunken eyes, too, popped wide open.

Picking up a bowl of stewed apples, which she had brought with her, she carefully mashed these with the back of a spoon before slowly feeding their charge the puréed fruit. Choking a little, the man just managed to swallow the tiny mouthfuls Frigg gave him.

"There you go, that's how you do it," she cooed lovingly, caressing greasy strands of matted, grey hair from his forehead. "Boys, I don't think you ought to keep him out here too much longer," she cautioned, glancing at Odin's brothers once more. "It's awfully hot."

"Hey, Vili look, look!" Ve cried abruptly, pointing to one of their patient's fingers. "Look, it just twitched; I swear I saw him move his finger."

Both Frigg and Vili bent forward and examined the man's hand more closely. Taking his hand in hers, Frigg gently stroked the back of it. Sure enough, a finger quivered and then twitched.

"Good boy, good boy," she purred, smiling as she replaced his hand in his lap. "You're doing awfully well. You'll soon be up and running about in no time; oh, and by the way, your scar's healing nicely, too." She added, tracing her finger along the outline of a wound, which ran all the way round the patient's neck. "It's a lovely, neat job," she murmured, letting her finger slip to loiter lazily on his collar bone. Frigg was about to say more when she suddenly froze; and motioned for the brothers to do likewise.

Someone was watching them.

Unknown eyes were burning holes in her, and she could sense the presence of a mind not very far from where they were sitting. The intruder was straining to eavesdrop on their conversation—and there was something else. Something about the intruder felt familiar, but without being able to see who it was, who was spying on them, Frigg couldn't be sure.

It felt like, it felt like...

"Oh, do shush, boys!" she exclaimed crossly as the brothers latched on to her troubled expression. They were whispering nervously as they looked around them like a pair of startled hares. This spooked their spy—and interrupted Frigg's chain of thought. The prowler took flight;

and a rustle in the undergrowth some fifty metres from where they were sitting betrayed where he'd been hiding. The person she ought to have recognised disappeared quickly out of range.

Frigg was furious. A few more seconds and she would have identified their stalker. His presence so close to them was troubling, very troubling. Crescent Cay had been built like a fortress. No one should be able to get to the island, let alone move around it undetected. Frigg determined she would have a word with security to beef things up a bit. Spying on her was an annoyance.

Spying on other, more sensitive, secrets could be catastrophic.

Unfortunately, before she could chastise Odin's brothers for breaking her concentration, there was another even more disturbing interruption.

"Oh, my lady, my lady!" it was Fulla this time who came charging down the path and into view. She was extremely flustered. "You need to get back to Asgard right away and—oh, I'm so sorry to interrupt you, my lords." she ended abruptly, bobbing a small curtsy to Vili and Ve. She hadn't realised that her mistress had been talking to Odin's brothers.

Getting up from her crouched position, Frigg took Fulla by the arm, and the two women wandered out of earshot to huddle close together, talking in hushed whispers. Their conversation was strictly confidential, and try as Vili and Ve might; they couldn't catch a word they said. When at last Frigg returned to the trio, her jocular mood had changed. Fulla was right; she really did have to leave immediately.

"I'm so sorry, boys," she began sadly. "But I have to go. Something important has cropped up, and I have to get back to Asgard straight away." Frigg tried to retain her composure, but the cheery smile had faded from her face and tears glistened in her eyes.

"Would you like us to come with you?" Vili volunteered sympathetically.

"No, you must stay here and look after him," Frigg pointed to their patient. "And another thing, if neither Odin nor I are back in two days time, one of you must take the phone call from Captain Halcombe. Do you understand? That's very important."

"Yes, of course, we haven't forgotten," Ve replied, nodding his head. Odin had reminded them of the same thing only a few days ago.

"And what are you going to say to the captain?" Frigg decided to quiz the pair, just to be sure.

"To proceed as planned and give captain, captain, oh, captain whatever his name is; give him the coordinates." Vili finished with a smug expression on his face. He should get a nice kiss from Frigg for remembering that.

"And where has Odin put the slip of paper with the coordinates?" Frigg enquired once more. She wasn't finished with the two of them just yet, and she had to be certain that they weren't going to make any mistakes.

"It's in the black box on Odin's desk. Honestly Frigg, we're not stupid; do grant us a little bit of intelligence," Ve exclaimed indignantly.

"I know you're not stupid, it's just you're absent minded, that's all," Frigg chastised as she gave each of them a gentle, goodbye peck of a kiss on the cheek. Bending forwards, she stroked the grey-haired gentleman's head once more as she planted a much more loving kiss upon his forehead.

"Hey, that's not fair!" Vili exclaimed sulkily. "Why does he get a proper kiss and not us?"

"Because, dear brothers-in-law, he's not very well, and he hasn't been naughty." Frigg waggled her finger humorously at the two men. "Any slipups and you will be in big trouble, okay?" she warned, patting their faces lightly with the palm of her hand. Her gesture was both a tease and a threat. She loved them dearly but my; they could be so scatterbrained sometimes. Planting a kiss on her finger tips, Frigg pressed this against their patient's forehead.

"I will see you again soon, my dearest Mimir," she whispered affectionately before setting off down the gravel path.

Fulla fell in quickly behind and as she did so, she handed Frigg her handbag. Hastily, Frigg opened the golden clasp and checked inside. A sachet filled with white powder was clearly visible amongst the contents.

"Will this be enough?" she enquired, and Fulla nodded that it would. "Good, thank you so much for arranging this," she continued as the two ladies approached the mansion's capacious terrace.

Fulla, Gna, and Lin, her three ladies in waiting, were like sparkling diamonds; gems she would be lost without. Glancing anxiously at her watch, Frigg headed quickly inside the building. She was on her way to Asgard to bury her son, but Frigg's thoughts didn't dwell on that painful task, Mimir's recovery or indeed their unwelcomed intruder.

Her mind was focused on a much more pressing matter.

With a gateway now open for Hel to return to Asgard, it was time for her to get on with her part of their plan.

It was time for Frigg to bury her husband.

20

No Hard Feelings

For the first time since Loki had seen Carmel canoodling with Thor, a smile formed on his lips. It was a good feeling, and he had to thank his daughter for cheering him up; even though it had been unintentional.

Standing in the middle of the Berserker Hall, Loki pulled a crumpled letter from his pocket and read it one more time. It certainly helped to explain the extraordinary sight that lay in front of him…

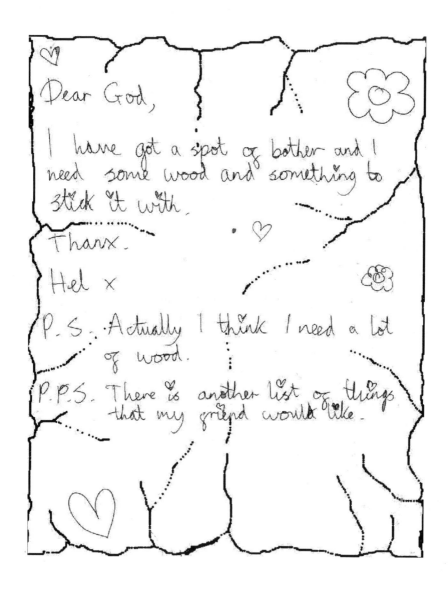

Dear God,

I have got a spot of bother and I need some wood and something to stick it with.

Thanx.

Hel x

P.S. Actually I think I need a lot of wood.

P.P.S. There is another list of things that my friend would like.

Wood was very much in short supply in Niflheim, and quite clearly Hel had requested some from one of her deities via the White Room. Unfortunately for the god who had been so kind as to send her this gift, the lack of clarity in her letter explained the two bizarre structures that now stood before him.

Two towers had been erected on either side of the sleeping dragons.

Not knowing what Hel intended to do with the wood must have given the god something of a dilemma. Hedging his bets, he had sent a sublime assortment of planks, driftwood, boughs, and saplings. With these, Hel and her Fallen Angels had constructed her masterpieces; cobbling the bits and pieces together with string, nails, and sticky tape.

Their resulting works of art made for an eye-watering display.

Two twisted, lopsided edifices had been constructed, and these had been joined at the top by a buckled walkway that by some miracle actually managed to pass over the heads of Surt and Nidhogg. Balancing precariously in the middle of this flimsy gantry was a large, iron cauldron, pilfered from Hel's kitchens. A team of slaves under Hel's instructions were currently busy emptying buckets of water into this vessel. Provided the whole chaotic mess didn't collapse before their task was completed, Hel's intentions were clear. A potent cocktail of freezing, cold water and falling timber might just be sufficient to wake the dragons from their slumbers.

"Daddy!" Hel cried excitedly when she eventually caught sight of her father. Skipping merrily over, she flung her arms around his neck and gave him a big, sloppy kiss. "What do you think, Daddy, do you like it?" she squealed breathlessly.

"It's um, um," Loki paused, searching for the right word. He didn't want to ruin Hel's enthusiasm, but he certainly wouldn't be asking her to put up shelves any time soon. "It's, um—unusual," he chuckled, settling on a word that just about summed up her glorious creation.

"You're just in time," Hel continued cheerily, lifting a piece of twine from the sandy floor. "When the cauldron's full, I'm going to give this a tug and tah-dah! No more sleeping dragons cluttering up my hall."

Loki smiled and kissed her forehead. He didn't want to rain on her parade, but he suspected Hel hadn't thought her plan through properly. For example; what might two startled, wet, and most probably furious dragons do after being so rudely awakened?

He decided not to mention this minor detail to her; it was all part of the fun of seeing his daughter and why she could always make him smile. Besides, anything that relieved the icy pain gripping his heart made for a welcome break. It stopped him thinking about Carmel and Thor, Carmel and Thor; Carmel and Thor.

Of all the people in Asgard, why did the woman he love have to have an affair with his best friend?

How could she do that to him?

"Daddy, what's wrong?" Hel enquired, lifting Loki's chin up with her finger. She could sense he wasn't his usual, jaunty self. "What's that maggot Odin done to you this time?" she continued crossly. It had to be him who had upset her father.

Hel had good reason to suspect that Odin was at the root of her father's problems. She was already aware of Balder's funeral and the fact that she hadn't been invited. This was a deliberate snub, and the reason behind it was all too obvious. Odin was trying to provoke her, trying to force her to unleash the Guardians and have them lay waste to Asgard. This had to be his plan, and she could see right through it. Get her to start Ragnarok and then blame her for the end of the world—not him.

Well, she wasn't going to fall for it.

She might have idolised Balder once, but there was no way she was starting a war over his funeral snub; even if it meant not joining those mourning the ex love of her life as he burned into a pile of ash. This was her resolve; this was the line in the sand that she wouldn't cross. Besides; now that she had a portal to his realm, there might be a less dramatic way to take the god of gods down. Crossing her fingers, Hel whispered a prayer for Frigg's plan to succeed.

"Come on daddy; tell me, what's wrong?" Hel pouted as she posed the same question again. Her father was avoiding this and avoiding her gaze, too.

"Nothing, darling, really nothing at all," Loki finally replied with a voice that sounded strained. He hoped she wouldn't push the question and make him crack. Hel had enough problems of her own to deal with, without adding his to her burden.

Fortunately for Loki, his daughter didn't get the opportunity to verbally twist his arm. A commotion by the entrance that led to the royal quarters interrupted their conversation.

"You nasty, evil, spiteful bitch!" Hod screamed as he dragged a limping Hermod across the hall toward them. "I can't believe you could do such a thing to…to…to a god." He stuttered, spitting disgustedly on the floor.

"Why? What have I done?" Hel yelled back indignantly.

"You know exactly what you've done, you poisonous snake," Hod hissed as he and Hermod drew near. He wasn't going to spell her actions out for fear of upsetting his friend, but the direction of his gaze left Hel in little doubt that her mischief had been sprung.

"Hey, that wasn't my fault," she retorted. "It's Kat's. She told me to do it."

"Don't be so daft, Hel! Kat would never say such a thing; she's not like you." Hod was furious and rightly so.

"Oh, yes she did. She told me to relieve his pain, and that's exactly what I did." Sticking her tongue, Hel folded her arms defiantly across her chest. That was her excuse and she was sticking by it.

Hod looked at her in amazement. "I can't believe you can say that. Blame your evil wickedness on your best friend. I guess I should have expected as much. Fine friend you turned out to be," he ended with a contemptuous snort.

Hel blushed.

Damn you Hod! He'd found the chink in her armour. He was right; she couldn't let her sister take the rap.

"Well, I was upset," she pleaded. "Sucky was being all nasty to me, Hermod was getting uppity, and Kat, well, she was going away. What do you expect a girl to do? Just sit back and take it on the chin? Sweet Niflheim! I am the flipping Queen of the Damned, you know. I'm supposed to do wicked things!" she ended angrily with a naughty, guilty, smirk written across her face.

"So that's it, is it?" Hod fumed. He was livid. Hermod was not only his stepbrother but also a good friend. Hel had been bang out of order treating him the way she had. "No apology, no tears of regret, no nothing. Typical Hel, that's just bloody typical of you."

Looking down shiftily at her feet, Hel ran the tip of her boot through the sand. They'd all grown up together, and when Hod put it that way; she supposed she really oughtn't to have done such a thing. "I'm sorry," she began coyly, trying to suppress a silly smirk as she held her hand out to Hermod. "No hard feelings, hey?"

"Oh, that's good," Loki tittered, trying hard not to burst into laughter. He had got Hel's double entendre—even if she hadn't.

"What?" Hel enquired, staring in bewilderment at her father. Pausing for a moment, she replayed what she had said in her head—and then suddenly got the joke. "Hey, Hermod, that's a good one, what do you reckon?" she guffawed, cackling loudly.

Hermod looked away and said nothing. He certainly wasn't going to shake hands with the vicious, teenaged viper who'd taken his manhood. "Come on, Hod," he mumbled bitterly. "Let's get out of here before she starts on you."

"Hey, that's not very nice," Hel chortled cruelly as Hermod limped beside Hod toward the swirling, blackness of the wormhole. "I've said sorry, haven't I, what more can I do? Besides, I don't see why you're making such a big deal over such a little thing," she continued with a sneer.

Neither Hod nor Hermod bothered to reply. What was there to say?

Hermod might still be a god, but he was no longer a man. Hel had seen to that, and she obviously couldn't care less. Hod had hoped she'd changed, but she hadn't. That was why he was leaving.

Hel truly was the Queen of the Damned and deserved to remain so.

"You know, you should be thanking me," she taunted the pair as they neared the gateway. "I've lightened your load, and you'll be able to run faster," she cackled sarcastically before adding gleefully as an afterthought. "And you won't get any chaffing, either."

As the two gods disappeared into the vortex, Hel blew a loud raspberry and then turned and hugged her father warmly. "Pathetic fools," she muttered under her breath. "Hermod had it coming, that's for sure. I only wish it had been Odin."

Loki patted her on the back as he breathed a sigh of relief. He'd been worrying about his daughter lately, and this outburst had put his mind at ease. Since the arrival of Kat and Henry, Hel seemed to have been going soft, and that really bothered him. With the final battle so close at hand, she was going to need all her vengeful hatred to bring their nemesis to his knees.

"I thought you'd be busy assembling another army," Loki suggested tactfully when at last Hel let him go. "You're going to need a whopper to have any chance of thrashing Odin's heroes."

"I might not need an army at all," Hel winked mischievously at her father. "There may be other ways to bring down the lying, cheating, braggart," she added with a grin.

She wasn't going to let Loki in on Frigg's plan just yet.

Loki had a mouth on him, and his tongue had a habit of wagging too freely, especially when he'd been drinking. She loved her father and trusted him completely; but it would only take one drunken, boastful taunt at the feasting tables, and Frigg's scheme would be undone. She couldn't take that risk. Not now, not when she was so close to seizing Asgard in a bloodless coup.

"Hey! Come on, Foxy!"

Catching sight of Henry in the distance, Hel decided to change the subject. "Have you got the camera?" she yelled. "And what in Niflheim are those things doing attached to the bottom of your legs?" Giggling hysterically, Hel nudged her father as she pointed to Henry's feet.

"My new slippers, Taz the Tasmanian, what do you reckon; aren't they cool?" Henry exclaimed, trying to do a little twirl and stumbling as he did so. The slippers were enormous, flopping all over the place.

"They're mad, but so are you, my dearest, darling Foxy." Cooing lovingly, Hel hugged and squeezed him tightly when Henry arrived by her side. Loki raised his eyebrows and looked away. Quite what his daughter saw in this awkward, geeky, eccentric idiot was more than he could fathom.

Greetings over, Hel raised her fingers to her lips and whistled loudly at the slaves on the scaffolding. There must surely be enough water in the cauldron by now, and she was itching to pull the string.

Hastily, the slaves leapt from the structure and fled as fast as they could away from the sleeping dragons.

"On the count of three!" she yelled.

"One…two…THREE!"

Hel yanked at the rope with all her might, and the cauldron wobbled dizzily before toppling over sideways and crashing through the walkway.

"TIMBER!"

Henry yelled as a cascade of cauldron, timber, and water descended upon the heads of the two, sleeping dragons.

FLASH!

His camera captured the moment.

21

The Last Goodbye

The day of Balder's funeral began early for the gods and guests at Noatun; and it began in a most unusual way. Just before dawn, a massive electrical storm erupted over Middle Sea.

Giant peals of thunder echoed around the mountains as violent tongues of forked lightening lit up the sky; flickering angrily from horizon to horizon as they lashed the world with a vengeful wrath. A brief but heavy hailstorm whipped its way along the coastline before fading as abruptly as it had started. By the time the first lazy fingers of sunlight had crept over the hilltops—the storm had gone. Quite where it had come from or where it went to was a mystery; but many believed that the heavens had vented their anguish.

They too mourned the loss of Asgard's most cherished son.

Along with the other Valkyries, Carmel woke early and after a chilly wash with a bucket of tepid, soapy water; she put on her white leather tunic and stepped outside her tent. Shivering in a freshening breeze, she pulled her feathered cloak tightly around her neck and crept over the shingle in the direction of last night's mysterious arrival. To her surprise, Thor was already there; pacing irritably beside the intriguing, black box; kicking at its iron clad wheels as he did so.

"I missed you last night," Carmel whispered quietly in his ear and, after a furtive look around, she wrapped her arms lovingly around his waist and kissed him tenderly. It was the first night for some time that they hadn't slept together, and she had missed his warmth beside her. Thor put his arm around her shoulders and gave her a half-hearted kiss upon the forehead. He was distracted and irritable; and not in a good mood. "What's wrong, darling?" she cooed, stroking his stubbled cheek with the back of her hand.

"It's these evil devils inside here, that's what's wrong," he muttered grumpily, kicking a wheel angrily once more. The whole cart shook with the force of his blow.

"Are you saying that you know what's inside?" Carmel enquired with an air of genuine surprise.

"Know what's in there? I not only know who's in there and why they're here as well." He retorted miserably before stumping off angrily along the shore. Whoever or whatever it was that was inside the box, Thor obviously wasn't keen to let on.

Undeterred and spurred on by a sense of growing curiosity, Carmel trotted up beside him and with a little, sensual, womanly persuasion; she gradual teased the shocking truth from him.

The guests inside the heavy, black box were dark elves, or more precisely, Alvis with most probably one or two travelling companions. Using hindsight, the presence of these strangers inside the sealed black box should have come as no surprise; its dark colour and lack of windows being something of a giveaway. Perhaps, however, the reason why no one had thought of this was the mythical status of these shadowy beings.

Some believed that their kind was long dead and gone; while others considered them to be the ghosts of Elf Lords who had fallen in the Elf Wars. Others denied that they had ever existed at all. According to Thor, however; not only were dark elves real and alive; they were very much here and amongst them now.

This was a shock, and Carmel begged her lover to tell her more.

Just like regular elves, dark elves were eternal, childlike inhabitants of Asgard. They had been created at the dawn of time and were destined to perish at its end. Unlike their surface-dwelling relatives, the dark elves lived in fear of the sun; a single ray being sufficient to turn their bodies to stone. This was their reason for their bleak and claustrophobic form of transport. They lived almost all their lives buried deep within the rocks beneath Nidavellir; the dwarf kingdom.

Carmel thought at first that she had heard this wrongly until Thor repeated his words.

In the absence of light, the dark elves could lose their physical form and move within solid objects as freely as though they were walking across a field of corn. Dark elves only took bodily form at dusk or dawn, or on the cloudiest of days; and it was only on these occasions when they had taken physical form, that they could they be seen for what they were; ghostly, ghoulish demons. Their cart had been driven by two dwarves who were their slaves, and this fact revealed an even uglier side to their nature.

Dark elves were carnivores; living upon the flesh of dwarves whom they captured and entombed. They were vicious, predatory killers, and if the sun should ever fail, they could—and most probably would—seize Odin's realm.

Dark elves were bad news. The darkest shadows of an eternal night.

As Carmel's relentless cajoling continued; Thor revealed another bleak secret of these unpleasant inhabitants of Asgard. The main purpose of their visit wasn't to mourn at Balder's funeral; they were here to claim their prize; a prize that chilled him to the bone.

Many years ago in the Aesir-Vanir civil war, Odin and the Aesir people had struck a bargain with the dark elves. In return for mining the strongest iron for their weapons from deep within the heart of Asgard; Odin had promised Alvis the hand of his first, full-blooded granddaughter when she came of age. That day had now come, and the betrothed child was none other than Thor's daughter, Thrud.

Thrud had only just turned sixteen and was coming to the funeral today with Sif. This was why Thor believed it had to be Alvis inside the box; and why he was so glum. Alvis had come to claim his daughter for his bride.

"I don't understand!" Carmel cried when Thor revealed this bizarre agreement. "Just smash Alvis with your hammer and he'll be gone; it's easy."

"I'm afraid I can't," he replied glumly. "Even if I could kill Alvis, the deal would be broken, and my daughter would be forfeit to the next dark elf who took his place."

"So protect her, then!" she exclaimed. "Shield your daughter from them; lock her away in the castle or Valhalla or somewhere. She would be safe by day at least, anyway." Carmel couldn't see why he was worrying; with sunlight being so deadly to these nasty, vicious creatures, they could pose little threat above ground.

"That's more easily said than done," Thor sighed. "If they can pass through the solid rock of Asgard, then the walls of the castle will give little protection. They are thieves of the night, and under the cover of darkness they would seize her as easily as if the castle's gates had been left open wide. There is nothing I can do, save pray for a miracle."

"Oh, come on, honey," Carmel smiled, giving him a tight hug. "There has to be a way out of this problem. Remember how we got your hammer back? That seemed impossible, but we did it, just the two of us." Taking his hand in hers, she squeezed it reassuringly. "Why don't we take another walk along the shore, and by the time we're back outside your tent, I'll bet I'll have come up with a nice, juicy, sneaky little plan."

Skipping off merrily beside her crestfallen lover, Carmel didn't notice Kat stretching and yawning outside Njord's hut. Kat, however, had seen her, and she rubbed her eyes in astonishment. Thor and Carmel were quite a long way from where she was standing, but she could clearly see that they were holding hands.

Their secret was out.

Something was going on, and the gossip grapevine would soon be sizzling with innuendo.

Beside the arrival of the dark elves, another unpleasant event took place during the night. Hyrokkin's wolves had been slain, and the finger of suspicion pointed toward the Valkyries.

With this shocking discovery, a wave of bellowing and chest beating erupted from the giants' encampment. They couldn't be pacified no matter how hard the gods tried to appease them. Reparations would have to be made, but a price could only be agreed when Odin arrived.

While Hyrrokin ranted and raved, the Valkyries speculated as to who might be the true culprit. No one would admit to the killings, which was rather unusual; giant baiting being a sport Valkyries would normally boast about. Eventually, however, after much wheeling and dealing; word got round that Tyr, assisted by Vali, had done the deed. Having lost an arm to Fenrir, Tyr's hatred for wolves was well known. The shoe certainly seemed to fit his godly foot.

Shortly before noon, when the hullabaloo over the dead wolves had finally died down, a mighty longboat driven by a blustery wind sped into the cove and beached itself with a loud crunch upon the shore. The boat was enormous and far bigger than any other the warriors had ever seen before. Leaping from its prow before offering his hand to assist a female companion was the equally enormous captain of the vessel—Aegir.

His companion was his wife, Ran.

Aegir was a rotund and ebullient god, a larger than life, jovial character who was almost the equal of Odin in stature. He was tall and heavily muscled with wild, curly grey hair, which descended in a chaotic scramble to below his shoulders. His beard was equally unkempt, being of equal length and matted with salt and seaweed. His voice boomed like thunder, and his hands were the largest Kat had ever seen. When she shook his, she felt both of hers could have fitted twice over in his palm.

Despite his great girth and bluster, Aegir was a kindly god who presided over all the creatures that lived in the sea. His hall—or *palace,* as he preferred to call it—lay several kilometres to the south; just off the Isle of Hlesey. According to stories the warriors had been told, this place was magnificent and lay upon the ocean floor. Everybody was delighted when Aegir announced that he would be holding a special feast there this evening and that they were all invited. Not even Ruby had visited his underwater kingdom; and excitement spread like wildfire amongst the girls. To dine beneath the ocean's waves seemed an impossible dream.

Today looked set to be a day of wonder.

By noon, a horn was heard blowing from the mountain pass high above the bay. Looking up, the warriors and other guests could see sunlight dancing from the glittering procession of Balder's funeral cortège. This travelled slowly down the winding trail such that it was almost an hour before Odin and the accompanying gods arrived in Noatun.

Odin led the party, riding his stallion Sleipnir while Frigg and Freyja rode beautiful, dapple grey mares on either side of him. Both goddesses wore white, as did all the other gods and goddesses. Gungnir was in Odin's hand, and this potent weapon coupled with Thor's mighty hammer should ensure that any hostilities between their fractious guests were kept firmly at bay.

Today was going to be a day for peaceful mourning, and Odin was determined it stayed that way.

With a last, baleful, fanfare of horns, Balder's body was gently removed from a gilded carriage and lain between the bodies of Mist and Prima on Ringhorn. Balder's sword was placed in his hand, and a wreath of exquisite oak leaves spun from purest gold was laid upon his cold and silent chest.

Amongst the goddesses who arrived with Odin, Carmel spied Thor's daughter Thrud.

Although they had never met before, Carmel was absolutely certain it was her. Slim, shy, and with a shock of curly, ginger hair that fell in tight ringlets to the middle of her back; her beautiful, rounded face and sky blue eyes were the very reflection of Thor's. She rode a small chestnut mare next to her mother Sif; who looked her usual magnificent self; dressed in white with her golden wig shimmering in the pale, winter's sun. For a brief moment, Carmel felt a pang of jealousy and guilt; jealousy that she wasn't Thor's wife and guilt that her affair might wreck their brittle marriage. Should she be the cause of their separation, it would be Thrud who would suffer most. That thought caused Carmel angst.

What she and Thor were doing was wrong, so very wrong; but how could they stop their desire?

Thrud looked so terribly young and innocent astride her horse, and Carmel knew instinctively that she was unaware of the horrific fate that lay in store for her today. What Alvis and the dark elves had in mind was sickening; and Carmel redoubled her efforts to come up with a plan to save Thor's daughter. As she mused and deliberated on that nightmare, Thrud's mare reared and whinnied in protest. Something had startled her. For a brief moment, Thrud fought to control her steed and as she did so, her wild and colourful hair sparkled in the sunshine.

This was it; a 'Eureka' moment.

Carmel had had an idea. Clapping her hands gleefully, she slipped away from the throng to begin her preparations.

Whilst Carmel busied herself with her plan; for the next several hours, each god, goddess, Valkyrie, dwarf, elf, and giant filed solemnly past the body of Balder.

Each one placed a small gift inside the boat and offered a silent prayer for his soul. It was a moving ceremony, and everyone was thankful that Silk wasn't present.

She and Heimdall were the only notable absences from the funeral.

Heimdall hated crowds, and Silk feared that she wouldn't be able to control her emotions. It was better that she mourned his parting in private and didn't shed tears for all to see. Silk couldn't handle such an indignity.

As the last few guests offered their gifts and prayers, attention focused briefly on Balder's horse. He was prancing anxiously along the shore, sweating profusely as great white flecks of foam dribbled from his mouth. He too was mourning the loss of his master. In a moment of great compassion, one of Balder's faithful servants comforted the stallion before plunging a dagger through his heart—killing him instantly. With a fanfare of horns and loud beating of drums, his body too was placed inside Ringhorn.

The time had come at last to bid farewell.

Picking up the heavy, plaited ropes that were attached to the magnificent longboat; Thor and the other gods took up the strain. It was time to launch Ringhorn into the sea.

To their mortification, no matter how hard they huffed and puffed and tugged at the vessel; it wouldn't budge. Weighed down by all the gifts and corpses inside it; Ringhorn appeared to be stuck fast on its wooden rollers.

It was a moment of great embarrassment, but Odin was spared more blushes by a most unexpected and helping hand.

"OUT OF MY WAY, WIMPS!"

It was the giantess Hyrrokin who had hollered these words, wading angrily into the freezing waters to snatch the ropes from Thor's hands.

"You and your Valkyrie whores think yourselves so strong and powerful," she fumed. "But all of you together are no match for a daughter of a mighty Frost King." Digging her heels into the loose shingles and passing the ropes around her waist, she twisted these into a bundle and then grabbed them securely in her powerful hands.

With a single piercing yell that reverberated back from the mountainside, she hauled on the ropes with all her might.

To gasps of astonishment and admiration, the longboat lurched forward and hurtled across the rollers faster than a man could walk. Reaching the point where the shingle bank curved gracefully down to the shore, Ringhorn plummeted forward and crashed into the water with a mighty splash.

All the guests were soaked.

No one had seen such a display of strength before, and everybody cheered and clapped Hyrrokin when she eventually waded from the waters. Thor smiled as he pointed toward the wooden rollers that had been left behind. The force of the giantess's tug had set some of these alight, and they were now crackling and smoking merrily.

"My great lord Odin!"

Everybody had been so busy marvelling at Hyrrokin's feat that nobody had noticed the activities of Balder's wife, Nanna.

She too had waded into the waters and had hauled herself into the longboat. She was standing there now, erect and noble before its mast;

shivering with the chill of the icy waters that drenched her clothes—and with the knowledge of what was to come.

"My great lord Odin," Nanna began again. "I have loved your son with all my heart since the dawn of time. Without Balder in my life, this world no longer fills my soul with joy. I feel cold and empty inside, and my heart now breaks with sorrow. It is my wish to give myself to my dear husband; it is my wish to join him in his afterlife." Pausing briefly, Nanna glared defiantly at the silent Valkyries. Silk had been the cause of much of her pain, and her words were aimed as a message for her.

"This is how a goddess honours her husband," she declared with a passion blazing inside her heart. "This is how a goddess chooses to die." Seizing the top of her dress with both hands, she tore it open; exposing her heaving chest for all to see.

"Is there anyone brave enough to send me to my afterlife?" Nanna cried. "Will anyone spare me the torment of the funeral pyre?" She beseeched loudly, casting her eyes along the shore.

No one moved. No god or Valkyrie could raise their bow and send an arrow to pierce her aching heart.

Moments ticked by as Odin struggled with this nightmare.

Nanna was too proud and heartbroken to back down; and he knew that she wasn't going to leave Balder's side. He couldn't order anyone to kill her, and yet he couldn't bear to listen to her screams as the roaring flames consumed her living flesh. Both options were unspeakable, and as Odin struggled with his decision, Ringhorn began to drift further from the shore.

Something had to be done—and done now.

Seeing Odin wavering, an Elf Lord stepped forward and raised his bow. With an eagle eye, he unleashed a single dart that sped across the stretch of water and buried itself deep within her heart. Nanna slumped backward without making a sound. Her wish had been granted, and she embraced her husband as the last rays of life bade her body farewell.

Nanna and Balder were together again; now and for all eternity.

With Nanna's death, a great silence fell upon the gathering. Her courage and devotion left many close to tears and speechless with emotion. Slowly Odin raised Gungnir and the Valkyries lit their arrows and prepared to unleash the volley that would set the funeral pyre ablaze.

"HAIL ODIN!" Thor led the tributes, and the crowd responded.

"HAIL VALOUR!" Thor bellowed once more, and the crowd cried out their response.

"HAIL BALDER!" Thor bellowed with a final, audible tremor to his powerful but breaking voice.

Odin brought Gungnir down upon the shingle, and the warriors unleashed their deadly hail. The dry, kindling faggots began to splutter and spit and in the brief moments before Ringhorn became consumed with flames; Thor raised his hammer above his head. His intention had been to deliver a small speech, but to his intense annoyance, an irritating dwarf called Lit stumbled in front of him giggling and laughing.

Lit had been making a nuisance of himself all afternoon, messing around and not paying attention to any of the proceedings. This final act of disrespect was the last straw. Leaping forward, Thor let out an almighty, vengeful roar and kicked the tiny dwarf as hard as he could. Lit howled loudly as he flew through the air—and then howled louder still when he landed in the middle of the blazing pyre. In an instant, the dry timbers had ignited, and the dwarf perished amidst the inferno.

Nobody wept at his demise.

His dreadful behaviour had earned a just reward.

Ringhorn creaked and groaned as the flames leapt higher until the whole boat was engulfed in a seething cauldron of fire and smoke. Whooping mournfully, a single, black swan swooped low across the fishing village and sped out across the waters in the direction of the fading vessel. Banking heavily, the graceful bird circled Ringhorn twice before returning to the shore. Heading directly toward the gathered gods and guests, Odin was forced to duck and step sideways as the bird passed within a whisker of his head.

A large dropping splattered on the pebbles where he had stood.

Few doubted the identity of the beautiful swan as they watched her fade into the shadows of the mountainside. Hel, The Black Valkyire, had paid her last respects to her childhood sweetheart.

With a final, spluttered gasp of despair, Ringhorn broke apart and disappeared into the ocean depths.

Balder was gone; and Asgard was left a bleaker place for his parting.

As the guests began to drift away, Odin called Thor toward him. Arm in arm, father and son wandered slowly away along the shore together. They were locked in deep conversation for what seemed an age, and upon their return; Thor beckoned for Carmel to join them.

As the three of them talked together, each in turn cast a glance toward the ominous, black box.

The dark elves had watched the funeral from its interior.

A tiny hole no thicker than the shaft of a bird's feather had been made on the side of the box, which faced the sea. Sitting beneath this, the elves had been able to watch a projected image of the funeral in much the same way as a box camera works. This simple but ingenious idea had kept them safe from the sun's deadly rays.

Now Alvis and his friends were ready to claim their prize.

Nodding in agreement, Odin beckoned Sif and Thrud over and after a heated but hushed debate; Carmel's plan was finally agreed. Smiling broadly, she mounted Sleipnir and, with a single dig of her heels, spurred the horse into a gallop. Pebbles spattered in all directions as the stallion sped across the banks of shingle and headed out of the village and then up the single mountain trail.

Intriguingly; Carmel hugged a large, flattened parcel beneath one arm.

"Gods, goddesses, and my beautiful Valkyries," Aegir boomed loudly and theatrically to the remaining guests. "Step right up for the trip of a lifetime."

Holding out his hand, he helped each warrior aboard his longboat. It was time to lighten the atmosphere, and Aegir was determined to throw a wake that would rival the splendour and majesty of Balder's funeral.

Tingling with excitement, Kat wobbled up the narrow gangplank and found a seat beside Jess. Following the heartache of the cremation, the exhilaration of this trip to Aegir's underwater palace was a welcomed relief; and the girls chattered eagerly amongst themselves.

Despite the large number of invited guests, Aegir's longboat was enormous; easily big enough to accommodate all the Valkyries, their maids, the gods and goddesses of Asgard; and still have room for its crew and a huge haul of bars of gold which littered the vessel's floor. These bars were unlike any the warriors had ever seen; each burning with the fiery passion of the midday sun.

When the last passenger, Odin, set foot on the vessel; the ropes were cast on board and its mighty sail unfurled. Aegir took the helm and after bellowing instructions to his crew, the vessel slowly turned about and headed out in the direction of the setting sun.

Their destination was Hlesey, but Aegir had one last surprise for his captive audience.

"Now, my dear friends, how would you like to arrive at my magnificent palace?" He enquired mischievously; looking around the excited faces of the gods and warriors with a teasing twinkle in his eye.

"By land or by sea?"

22

Reunited

Silk stood in front of her balcony and watched as the sun slowly set behind the distant mountains of Jotunheim. In her hand she held a large horn of mead, and in her eyes she held large tears. These trickled in an endless, painful river down her salt-stained cheeks.

Hidden behind closed doors, this was how Silk faced the end of the god she loved.

With shaking hands, she raised her horn once more, and with a tremulous voice she whispered "Hail Balder" before downing her mead in one almighty gulp. Reaching for the pitcher beside her, she refilled her horn and started the same ritual over again.

Too drunk to think and too heartbroken to move; Silk stood at her window and cried her heart out.

Had she gone to the funeral at Noatun, she would have joined Nanna on Ringhorn in a heartbeat. There could never be another man like Balder, and just like Nanna; Silk too felt her life was at an end. The realm was in the grip of winter and so was her heart, but any similarity between the two ended there.

Odin willing, spring would eventually come to Asgard. The frozen fields and pastures would thaw, and a warm sun would breathe new life into plants and animals. For Silk, however, spring could never come. The sun had gone from her skies, and her world was filled with the darkest, deepest, blackest shade of despair.

Silk sobbed loudly and then stared down at her dress. Made from the sheerest white silk, it was heavily embroidered with silver thread.

This beautiful, strapless, figure-hugging gown had been Balder's favourite, and she was wearing it today in his honour. She smiled briefly at the memory of the times he had held her tightly in it; showering her neck and shoulders with passionate kisses.

Throughout the morning, Silk had busied herself getting ready for her party for one. She had asked her maids to tie her hair up in the style that Balder loved; and she was wearing a pair of large, silver earrings, which dripped with countless tiny diamonds. Balder had bought her these when she first became a warrior—the Valkyrie Gunnr.

Raising her hand, she toyed with the thick, closely linked pendant around her neck.

This too was made from solid silver and had a large central effigy of a pair of swans swimming side by side; heads turned down in a shy dance of courtship. These too sparkled with the diamonds that festooned their wings and a pair of larger gems that lit up their eyes.

Silk smiled again.

Balder had given her this when she captured Fenrir.

How she regretted gloating at her victory over him. It now seemed such a pointless, stupid, selfish act; and one that brought fresh tears rolling lazily down her cheeks before dripping from her jaw onto her neck and chest.

Sweet Odin! How could she live another day without him?

Asgard was so cold and desolate without her god by her side.

Sniffing back tears that stifled her nose, Silk toyed with a heavy, solid silver bangle she was wearing on her left wrist. This was her sword arm, her arm of vengeance as Balder had called it when she battered him to the ground.

This bangle too was filled with memories.

Balder had given it to her after her first kill; the one she had made as a fresh faced maiden when she first arrived in Asgard. This was the first time she had felt his love, and that memory made her smile once more.

What a relief Asgard had been all those years ago. Leaving wartorn Midguard and the shattered isles of the Western Pacific far behind her.

This was where she had fought and died; loyal to the last as one of Emperor Hirohito's elite Kamikaze bombers. Cropping her hair short and binding her breasts tightly, she had masqueraded as a man and flown as courageously as any of the other pilots. Memories of her death suddenly flooded back; the maelstrom of the 'ack ack' as she had locked on to her target; and the terrible impact of her plane as it smashed into the shattered deck of the warship.

Miraculously, her bomb had failed to explode.

Undeterred but badly injured, Silk had struggled free from her plane's blazing cockpit, Samurai sword in hand and wearing the band of martyrdom wrapped tightly around her head. Hell was erupting all around her, but she hadn't cared—throwing herself at the waiting nest of machine guns and dying as she had lived her life; in an impassioned blaze of glory. Silk had fulfilled her pledge to her Emperor, ending her life with a fearless spirit.

This had inspired her comrades then as it did her sisters now. This was why she couldn't let anyone see her today; emotions stripped bare and her heart torn and bleeding.

"HAIL BALDER!"

Silk raised her horn of mead once more and took a long, deep, satisfying draught. Lost in her thoughts, she didn't hear the door creak quietly open nor sense the silent footsteps as a shadow glided across the floor to stand behind her.

"Hello, my dearest sweetheart."

She felt strong arms around her waist and the familiar warmth of a man drawing her next to him.

"Have you missed me, my darling?"

The voice was kind and gentle, whispering in her ear as warm lips caressed her neck.

"Mmmm," Silk murmured, closing her eyes and turning to pull him close to her. "So very, very much," she cried, pulling Balder's head toward her and pressing her lips against his.

Silk didn't care if this vision of her love was an alcohol-fuelled illusion or if she had simply gone insane. The touch of his hands; the scent of his body; and the passion of his lips just felt too real. The comfort of his hallucinated embrace was worth more than life itself.

Waltzing slowly in elegant spirals across the room; Silk led Balder towards her bed. She couldn't let go, she wouldn't let go, and she wasn't going to open her eyes. This was her perfect dream; one that would allow her a final night of happiness.

Reaching the bed, Silk pulled Balder down on top of her; tingling as his weight crushed her aching body deep into the mattress. Usually she preferred to be on top, the warrior in control of making love; but tonight was different. Tonight would be Balder's night, and she could already feel the strength of his passion between them.

Nervously, Silk parted her legs a fraction and gasped with joy as she felt his hands reach beneath the folds of her dress. They were warm and sensitive, just as they had always been; firm yet caring as they massaged their way up the delicate softness of her inner thighs. Parting her legs a little further, Silk trembled at the thrill of what was to come. The pleasure of his touch caressing her sweetness; a pleasure she had sworn she would never know again.

Silk could bear it no more.

She had to have Balder.

Biting his neck with the hunger of her desire, she dug her nails deeply into his back. Spreading her thighs wide, she wrapped these tightly around Balder and with a single joyful moan; she begged his manhood to ignite her heart and soul.

Gasping with ecstasy, the broken-hearted warrior made love more exquisitely than she had ever done before.

23
Alvis

Thor heard the gentle 'hiss,' the creaking groan, and then a heavy 'thud' as the seal to the dark elves carriage was broken and the two dwarf slaves forced its ancient door open.

Just as he had hoped, Alvis was emerging from the black box as soon as the last rays of sun had dipped below the horizon. The dark elf was every bit as excited to claim his new bride as Carmel had predicted he would be. Her scheme, to save Thrud from a fate worse than death, had begun exactly as planned.

"You must promise me one thing, darling," Thor asked, hugging his daughter close as the opening door creaked to a halt. "Don't be scared. No matter what happens, don't be scared. I swear by all the gods in Valhalla that no harm will come to you, no matter what. Remember, you are a goddess, and you must be strong. Honour your mother, okay?" Squeezing her tightly, he planted a tender kiss on the top of her head.

Thrud nodded. So far, she was more curious than afraid about the inhabitants of the black box; the innocence of youth sparing her the horror of reflecting upon what might happen if Carmel's plan failed.

"Good girl."

Thor kissed her head once more before glancing anxiously toward the mountains beyond the village. The crimson wall of sunset was beating its daily retreat, fleeing reluctantly before the relentless march of darkness. This groped and fingered its way from rock to tree to bush; claiming each in victory as day surrendered the realm to night.

Somewhere, hidden on the mountainside was Carmel; the key to his daughter's salvation.

Thor muttered a silent prayer for success.

"Daddy," Thrud murmured, nudging Thor to bring his attention and gaze firmly back to Noatun. "Look, they're coming."

Like a trio of evil ghosts, Alvis and his two travelling companions glided down a loose bank of shingle without making a sound. Not a single pebble moved beneath their feet as they made their way eerily toward Thor and his daughter. All three elves were wearing charcoal grey capotes with hoods raised such that their faces were shrouded from view.

Arriving in front of Thor, Alvis stopped and extended a hand in greeting.

He didn't shake it.

"Greetings, mighty Thor," Alvis croaked in a hiss like rasp, pulling back his hood to reveal his hideous face. "I believe that," he continued, pointing a long, spindly finger in the direction of Thrud, "belongs to me."

Catching sight of his face, Thrud gasped loudly, flung her arms around her father, and then buried her head in his protective chest. It was all she could do not to scream and collapse onto the shingles at her feet. Now she understood the full horror of their predicament; now she knew why death would be preferable to even one night with Alvis.

Perhaps, if you were a lady dark elf buried somewhere deep within the bowls of Asgard, you might have considered Alvis's appearance quite appealing. Indeed, some dark lady elves might have gone so far as to say that Alvis could be considered handsome. Unfortunately, to a mortal or godly eye; his features were more revolting than the maggot-infested skull of a rotting pig.

Alvis, like all dark elves, had a sideways squashed, elongated head which was completely white; not a nice, warm, healthy, living white; but the pallid, deathly, winter's mask of deeply frozen snow. His head was bald, and his unblinking eyes were tiny and the palest shade of pink. Unlike regular elves, who had beautifully rounded, smooth, cherubic faces; those of the dark elves were rough, angular and heavily jowled. Their noses were long and sharply hooked, and their chins jutted out into a narrow, tapering point.

Adapted for a life spent in total darkness, the sides of their cheeks bristled with long whiskers that wouldn't have looked out of place on the face of a mole or a rat. Their ears, too, were unusual; being large, delicate, and cup shaped; and heavily laced with an intricate pattern of dark blue veins.

Undoubtedly, however, the single most repellent feature about the face of a dark elf—was his mouth. Thin lipped and with a row of tiny, dagger-shaped teeth; Alvis's forked, reptilian tongue flickered in and out as he joyously scented his new bride.

"My, she is a wondrous creature," Alvis exclaimed gleefully as he circled Thor and his daughter, taking stock of his beautiful, new possession.

Thrud was beginning to tremble, but she didn't cry. She was a goddess and determined to stand her ground.

"That she is," Thor agreed with a sigh. "And it will break my heart to give her to you, but the gods always honour their word. A deal is a deal, and a bargain is a bargain. However, my daughter must come with a warning."

Alvis stopped abruptly. "Oh, and what might that be?" he sneered sarcastically. He knew full well that Thor was heartbroken and silently he rejoiced at the anguish he was causing the mightiest of the gods. Revenge was sweet and definitely a dish best served cold.

Like all the other inhabitants of Asgard, Odin had fostered great hatred amongst the dark elves. They too had suffered badly in the First Elf Wars, and Odin's devastation had yet to be avenged. Taking Thrud as his consort was but one step on the staircase to the god's ruin.

"Do you see my daughter's beautiful tresses?" Thor enquired, and Alvis replied that he did so. His voice was almost as hideous as his face. With each rasp and croak he made, Alvis' mouth and lips never moved. His utterances came from his throat; making each word slither into the next such that every sentence became one continuous slur. His voice hissed like that of a snake.

"Her locks could prove fatal to you and your kin," Thor continued gravely. "My daughter's hair has been blessed with the sun's fire, and you had best never touch it."

"What?" Alvis stepped back abruptly. He had been on the verge of running his fingers through her beautiful, ginger locks. "You're lying. Not even Odin's magic can trap the power of the sun. What you're saying is impossible." Choking with disbelief, Alvis scratched his chin with the tip of a curved and sharply pointed, claw like finger nail. For the moment he was flummoxed.

What use was a bride if he couldn't take her to his bed?

"I know what this is about," Alvis finally spoke after he had given thought to the problem. "You're trying to wriggle out of our agreement, aren't you, Thor? You don't want me to take your daughter as my bride, do you?" The angles of Alvis's mouth curled cruelly upwards in a sinister smile. "Tell me Thor; are the gods about to break their word?"

"No, no, not a bit of it," he retorted hastily. "A god's word is his bond. You may have my daughter and be blessed with many, many children; but mark my warning well. Her hair can outshine the splendour of the sun and will put you in great peril."

Thor stood back when he had finished and gently peeled his daughter's arms from around his waist. The next part of the plan was going to be tough for Thrud; very tough indeed. Nudging her toward Alvis, Thor raised both his arms in the air as a sign of surrender.

This was the signal.

"Take her, Alvis, she's yours. Take her and feel the beauty of her hair, but don't you dare say that you haven't been warned."

With a loud and lecherous hiss, Alvis stepped forward and stretched out an arm toward Thrud. She flinched, sobbed quietly, but stood firm. She had to stick to the plan; she had to be brave. She was a goddess and would honour her royal blood.

Alvis's hand drew closer still.

Thrud shut her eyes and winced—this was it.

A fingertip touched her hair and, in that instant, a brilliant spark of sunlight erupted in her locks. Stunned with amazement, Alvis could only gaze in awe as this flickering ray of death flashed along his arm to his shoulder and onward to his head; scorching the skin of his face as it sizzled and crackled.

"AAAarghhh...!"

Alvis screamed, but his final breath died like a sigh from a pair of deflating bellows. He had turned to stone in an instant.

Hissing loudly with fear and anger, his companions turned tail and fled back to the safety of their black box. The deal with the gods was off. No dark elf could wed Thor's daughter and live to tell the tale.

"Come here, you!" Thor bellowed elatedly, opening his arms as Thrud flew into them, sobbing loudly with relief. "You were so good, so brave, and so strong; your mother will be so proud of you."

Thor cuddled her hard.

"Bravo, bravo!"

Njord, who had been watching the proceedings from his hut, clapped loudly as he trudged across the waves of shingle banks. He paused briefly in his journey to admire the stony, new addition to his village.

"I don't know how you did it," he continued. "But what a brilliant plan! Those dark elves are bad news, and all of Asgard would have wept if Alvis had taken your lovely daughter." Arriving by their side, Njord joined Thor in taking turns in hugging and kissing Thrud.

High up on the mountainside, Carmel breathed a heavy sigh of relief. Bundling up the polished, silver platter, she leapt upon Sleipnir and began to trot back down toward the shore. It had been a close shave, but her plan had been successful, and she thanked Odin for Thrud's salvation.

Like so many plans, the best ones were often the simplest.

What Alvis and his colleagues had failed to consider when they leapt from their carriage was the fact that, although the sun had set from the seashore; it was still radiant high up on the slopes surrounding the bay. Armed with a large, polished mirror—the silver platter— it had been simplicity itself to reflect the sun's rays back toward Thrud and Alvis. It had been a close call, however. If Thor's gesture had come a moment later, Carmel would have been engulfed by twilight's gloom, and the plan would have failed.

Arriving on the beach, Carmel leapt from Sleipnir's back and stumbled across a narrow strip of shingle to the waiting group. Both Thor and Thrud threw their arms around her, and the three of them embraced for what seemed an eternity.

"Thank you, thank you so much," Thrud cried when she eventually released Carmel from her embrace. "You're so wonderful, you've saved my life."

"Oh, it was nothing. You should thank your dad, he's the best," Carmel joked, trying to hold back a tear as she tenderly stroked the girl's forehead.

"Are you all right?" Thor enquired anxiously, using his fingers to wipe away a tear that trickled from the corner of her eye.

"Yes, yes, I'm fine, really; just overcome with joy at our success." Carmel turned away quickly as she wiped her eyes with the back of her hand. Happiness was part of the truth behind her tears, but sadness, too, played its role. Thrud was such a beautiful girl that, for a moment, Carmel wished that she was hers.

Her tears were a painful reminder. She could never carry a child.

This was the price she paid for being a Valkyrie.

"Now everybody," Njord announced as he cleared his throat loudly. He needed to get their attention. "Have you all had enough excitement for the day, or would you like to come with me and join the party in Aegir's palace?"

Thrud and Carmel held hands and jumped up and down as they danced excitedly around each other.

As if Njord didn't already know their answer.

24
The Fire of Aegir

Approximately one kilometre from the towering cliffs of the Isle of Hlesey, the sailors stopped rowing and shipped their oars.

Quietness descended upon Aegir's guests as they wondered what was going to happen next.

The sun had already set, and the grey twilight that is neither day nor night was slowly fading into darkness. A chill breeze blew in leisurely gusts across the longboat and a long, slow, ocean swell rocked the vessel gently in its arms. Taut ropes creaked and groaned as the sullen slap, slap, slap of murky waters against the gunnels sang the sweetest of lullabies.

As the boat drifted lazily, a sense of anticipation grew among the guests.

AHOO—HOO!

Aegir blew two notes from his gilded horn. These rang out loud and clear across Middle Sea. Cupping his hand to his eyes, Aegir squinted and searched ahead for the recipient of his signal.

"There she blows!" he boomed suddenly and excitedly, pointing his arm in the direction of a disturbance on the surface of the sea.

Turning quickly, the warriors and gods were just in time to see the head of Jormungard rise from the water. Even from this distance, everyone could see that the mighty serpent was enormous. Opening his mouth wide, Kat was convinced that the beast could swallow their longboat whole, even with its sail unfurled. Rearing higher still before letting out a low-pitched, booming noise, Jormungard arched his neck and then dived beneath the waves.

Lost from view, the inhabitants of the boat felt, rather than saw, him next.

With a tremendous swirl of ripples, Jormungard passed close underneath the vessel before swinging his huge body around. Slowly he began to swim in a large circle that captured their vessel within its circumference. Other, lesser serpents took up his lead, and soon the water began to boil and stir around them.

Slowly, as Aegir's longboat picked up eddies of their motion; it began to follow the circling pattern of the beasts.

Faster and faster the serpents swam, and swifter and swifter the sea began to spin round and around. Jormungard's intent was soon apparent; he and his fellow monsters were creating a giant whirlpool, one that would suck the longboat down into its depths.

Holding both her breath and Jess tightly, Kat shut her eyes and prayed. She could feel the vessel lurch and then tilt sideways as it began to slide down a steepening bank of water. Pitching and yawing wildly, the longboat drew ever tighter and faster circles as she plunged down toward the ocean's floor.

"Look!" Jess yelled excitedly in Kat's ear. "I can see the seabed."

The roar of the seething water around them was deafening.

Kat opened one eye a fraction and then promptly closed it again. The motion was nauseating, and she prayed she wouldn't be sick. She didn't need eyes to see where they were headed; she could feel the bumping, churning motion as the vessel skidded and skittered ever closer to the whirlpool's apex.

AHOO—HOO!

Aegir blew his horn once more and, bearing down hard upon the rudder, he expertly steered the bucking ship toward an opening which had appeared close to the ocean floor. With a tremendous whooshing roar, the vessel shot into the blackness of a subterranean cavern.

Freed from the current of the swirling whirlpool, the longboat slowed rapidly and began to pitch and vibrate far less violently. Kat opened her eyes once more and was rewarded with a kaleidoscope of red, blue, and green lights that flickered and shimmered from the surface of the churning water. Slowing further still, the longboat eventually ground to a halt at the bottom of a large, vaulted cavern. Far above them, a doorway gleamed invitingly at the end of a short pier.

With a sudden, tremendous gurgling sound, the waters around them began to foam and froth once more. Tossed around like a cork, the longboat bounced and spun as the waters rose around it to fill the cavern. With surprising swiftness, their vessel rose until it drew level with the wooden pier.

"HAIL ODIN!" Aegir bellowed triumphantly.

"HAIL VALOUR!" the warriors replied excitedly.

"HAIL AEGIR!" the gods responded appreciatively.

The funeral party had arrived at the palace beneath the waves.

Aegir and his wife Ran were the first to disembark from the ship, and a gangplank was quickly positioned. Donning thick gloves and using iron tongs, the sailors picked up the heavy bars of gold and placed them on large carts that had been positioned next to the vessel. The golden bars not only glowed brightly, but they had become extremely hot; a warmth which Kat had appreciated during their chilly journey across the open sea.

"What are they?" Kat whispered loudly to Jess, who shook her head in reply. The metal looked like gold, but it obviously wasn't. She didn't know what it was, either.

"Aegir's fire," Frigg interrupted confidently. She had somehow managed to pick her way across the crowded boat and had overheard Kat and Jess's conversation. "It's a form of gold, but one only found on the ocean floor. Each day Aegir brings the bars to the surface, and they soak up the energy of the sun. Each evening, when he returns them to his palace, they fill the place with their warmth and light. Don't they look beautiful?" she purred, hugging and kissing both warriors tightly.

It was good to see them again; especially Kat.

Once the sailors had departed, Aegir held out his hand and helped each guest from the boat. He embraced them one by one and welcomed each warmly to his private Xanadu. He was incredibly proud of his magnificent palace, which was why he had insisted on the sailors disembarking first with the gold. He wanted the bars properly positioned before his guests set eyes upon his feasting hall.

Kat looked anxiously around her. To her immense relief, she wasn't the only one looking a little worse for wear. Jameela and Elijah were both looking a bit bilious, and they returned Kat's look of relief. The journey had been an incredible experience, and Kat chuckled wryly as she swore a special vow. Should she ever return to Midgard, she would never again flush a spider down the toilet.

She now knew exactly how that felt.

Joining up in pairs, Kat linked arms with Jess (there were more ladies than gentlemen in the party), and they followed the other guests along a short corridor that opened into Aegir's feasting hall. As each couple emerged into the chamber, Kat could hear involuntary gasps of admiration, and when their turn came; she and Jess were no exception.

The sight was magnificent beyond compare.

The vast chamber was as large as a Midgard football pitch and at least ten metres tall. Once upon a time, it had been an underground cavern until, somehow, Aegir had managed to remove its rocky roof and replace this with a flattened dome of thick, solid glass. Now, instead of rock above them, the inky ocean depths stared silently back. Kat wished they had arrived in daylight; perhaps then she could have seen the weird and wonderful creatures that lurked beneath the ocean waves.

The centre of Aegir's feasting hall was dominated by a large rock pool. This was filled with salty water and connected to the sea by a secret, subterranean tunnel. Some of the bars of gold had been placed by the sailors on tables and in the waters of the pool. These bathed the room in a rich, yellow warmth that rivalled the candlelit splendour of Asgard's feasting hall. Dotted around the walls were bowls of seawater, and these twinkled with reds, greens, and blues as countless plankton and algae sparkled and fluoresced. The whole display was magical and reminiscent of fairy lights on a Midgard Christmas tree.

"Wow!"

Everybody gasped in unison as four sailors suddenly appeared in the water above the dome. Each was carrying a bar of gold, and they placed these around the edges of the dome, illuminating the water around them. Kat wasn't sure if the rest of the guests were gasping in admiration at the fish, lobsters, octopuses, starfish, and other creatures that had suddenly emerged from the darkness—or the revelation of the true identity of Aegir's crew.

They were all Mermen, now resplendent with their fishlike tails and an extended ruff of gills that sprang from their necks like plumes of peacock feathers.

Kat stared at the rock pool once more.

How could she not have noticed its occupants sooner?

The beautiful women sitting and singing so sweetly among the rounded stones were Mermaids. Their silver, fishy tails were now obvious and sparkled in the light. These women would be their hostesses; tails becoming legs once they were out of the water.

To Kat's disappointment, the Mermaids—like Mermen—couldn't speak. They were only able to sing or converse when they were at least partially submerged in water. It was such a shame; she could have listened for hours to tales about the marvels of their lives on the ocean floor.

Slowly, after greeting and chatting amongst themselves, the guests took their seats at the tables, which formed a horseshoe shape around the rock pool.

AHOO—HOO!

Aegir blew his horn once more, and the hall fell silent. For the last time, Jormungard made an appearance, slithering gracefully through the waters above them. His body seemed to go on forever, and Kat guessed that he must be over one hundred metres long.

"My lord, ladies and gentlemen, welcome to my humble home." Raising his horn, Aegir led the salutation that would mark the start of the evening's festivities.

Sitting down excitedly, the whole hall erupted into a hubbub of chatter as the guests picked their way in wonder over the countless, fabulous dishes spread before them. Lobster, bass, eel, swordfish, crab, giant prawns, and numerous other weird and wonderful dishes that Kat didn't have a clue about. Each one seemed to taste more delicious than the last, although Kat's favourite was perhaps a simple broth. Made with marinated fish, seaweed, ginger, black peppers and coriander, the taste was sublime.

Jameela and Ruby agreed; between them they would have loved to take a whole cauldron of it back to Asgard.

Midway through the second course, Thor, Carmel and Thrud arrived. They had come by the land route, which was a long and bumpy walk along a tunnel from the Isle of Hlesey. They seemed in excellent spirits, if a little flushed, after their hurried scamper along its uneven floor.

Thor quickly filled Odin in on the success of their mission, and he then announced the wonderful news to a rapturous reception. Everybody toasted Carmel for her brilliant plan and Thrud for her exceptional bravery. The poor girl blushed violently as she hid her head in her mother's dress. She was quite overcome by the attention.

As the other guests became seated once more, Sif indicated for Carmel to come and receive her thanks. Drawing close, Carmel bobbed a quick curtsy.

"I really must thank you personally for taking such good care of my daughter," Sif offered with an overly sweet smile upon her lips. "Come; let me embrace you."

Carmel stepped forward, and Sif hugged her close.

"If I find that you've been fooling around with my husband, I'll rip your throat out," Sif hissed angrily, smiling as she whispered her threat into Carmel's ear. Slapping the Valkyrie a little too heartily on the back for comfort, Sif released her from her embrace. Carmel stood back; shocked, and blushing hard.

How did she know?

"Oh, and my darling husband," Sif continued, kissing Thor passionately (and deliberately) on the lips before hugging him too in a similar manner. She must have hissed the same warning in his ear, because when she released him; his face had turned the colour of beetroot.

Sif may not have known the full depth of Carmel and Thor's affair, but the looks on both their faces screamed its truth.

Guilt, guilt, GUILT!

Luckily for the pair, any further discomfort was spared by another, much more unpleasant interruption. With an almighty thud, the massive wooden doors to the hall flew open as Loki forced his entrance.

Like Hel, he hadn't been invited to the feast.

Unlike Hel; he was damned if he wasn't going to turn up.

Two Mermen went to seize him, but Aegir waved for them to stop. Provided Loki didn't make trouble, he was welcome to stay.

"Greetings my lords, ladiessssh and gentleman," Loki began, slurring as he attempted to make a flamboyant bow. Swaying and lurching from side to side, he belched loudly before righting himself. He was obviously as drunk as a skunk.

"Oh," he continued with a belated, sarcastic sneer. "And greetings too to my lovely lady Valkyriessssh. Yesssh, essshpecsshially to the lovely, lady Valkyriessssh."

Staggering once more, Loki drew his sword and brandished it above his head. Slowly but surely, he cast his gaze around the now silent room. He swayed as he did so; his eyes flashing malevolently—purple, red, violent, and blue.

"PAHHH!" He hawked loudly, spitting a huge wad of phlegm contemptuously on the floor.

"What a disgusting load of filthy, lying, thieving, cheating BAAH-HHSHSHTARDS!"

Loki had come to make trouble—and he was just about to get started.

25

An Entangled Slipper

"**W**hat!" Hel hollered. "What do you mean he just got up and walked out of here? That's impossible!"

The Queen of the Damned had collared Henry in the corridor outside her room and was wearing a familiar expression; the look of disbelief and shock, mixed with a sprinkling of horror.

"He did, I swear, honestly he did," Henry bleated fearfully. "Rhett just got up, walked out of his room, and left."

"Rhett? You do mean Balder, don't you?" Hel enquired, just to be certain. Her lover could be so silly sometimes. She had already noticed the box of clothes, computer games, and CDs he was carrying in his arms and would ask him about these later. For now, however, confirmation that Balder was alive and well was the single, most important question.

"Yes, of course I mean Balder, that's obvious," Henry replied with a nervous grin.

"But that's not possible," Hel continued. "I only left here for a couple of seconds and what happens? Incompetence, that's what happens." she shook her head in disbelief; she was struggling to come to terms with what she was hearing.

How could Balder just get up and leave?

"Actually, darling, you were gone for quite a bit longer," Henry volunteered. "Several hours at least by my reckoning." He was trying to be helpful, but his idiotic grin wasn't doing him any favours. This was winding Hel up—and she knew it.

"Oh, do shut up Foxy," she huffed. "How do you know how long I was away for anyway? There aren't any clocks. Besides, as I was saying, how can Balder just get up and leave? Odin's incinerated his corpse! It's impossible, there has to be an explanation." She was struggling badly with this paradox.

"Entanglement," Henry replied confidently. "That's the answer; entanglement."

"Foxy, what in Niflheim are you going on about?" Sometimes her genius lover spoke in riddles that even she couldn't understand.

"It's easy really. You said yourself that your dad made a mess of bringing Balder here didn't you?" Henry began, putting the box down as his arms were starting to get tired.

"Yes. So?"

"Well," he continued. "Somehow Balder's consciousness, soul, or whatever you want to call it; must have got stuck between the two bodies, entangling their minds. With the dead body in Asgard being the original Balder, his consciousness assumed the dead Balder's state; all whacked out and zombie-like. Once this body was burnt, the entanglement was broken and hey presto; the Balder down here comes alive and wakes up. It's easy, really," Henry ended dismissively with a shrug.

He really was a genius, so why pretend to be modest?

Hel rubbed her chin thoughtfully as she began to pace up and down, puckering her eyebrows. She hadn't really understood what he was saying, but after replaying his words several times slowly through her mind, they did make some sort of sense in a weird kind of way. This was actually very annoying. She would now have to congratulate her irritating lover, and she hated doing that, especially when he was behaving so smuggly.

"All right, smarty pants," Hel suggested as she stopped pacing up and down. "Tell me this, how did he know how to get out of here?"

"Oh, that's the easy part," Henry replied innocently. "I showed him the way."

"You did what? Henry! You blithering idiot!" she really couldn't believe her ears. "Are you telling me that you helped my meal ticket out of this dump to leave? You...you...you—" she flustered, struggling hard to find a suitable insult for her lover. "—You complete muppet!"

"Well, he was extremely charming and seemed so terribly confused; what else was I supposed to do?" Henry replied indignantly, deciding to defend his actions. "You told me he was a god and could go anywhere he liked when he woke up. I thought he wanted to go and find you; I...I...I thought he loved you," he ended lamely.

"Oh, Foxy," Hel slumped back against the tunnel wall and sighed deeply. "You can be such a silly boy sometimes. I said I loved him, not the other way round. He's only gone running back to Sucky and daddy; that's all."

"Well that's his loss then; isn't it? If the stupid god can't see a good thing when he's got it, then good riddance to him." Henry retorted huffily, and he meant it; every last word. Hel was gorgeous—she just didn't know that yet.

"Oh, darling," Hel gushed, throwing her arms around his neck and giving him a great, big, loving kiss on the lips. "Sometimes you say all the right things," she murmured contentedly. She couldn't help but love him.

"Does that mean you love me?" Henry enquired cheekily with a smirk; she still hadn't used the 'L' word, and he was determined to make her say it.

"No, of course it doesn't!" Hel rebuked, slapping his arm playfully as she decided to change the subject. "And where are you going with that box?"

"Well, I thought with Rhett all alive and up and about and stuff; you would want to spend some time with him." Henry shuffled awkwardly, "I was moving my things out to give you some room, if you know what I mean."

"What?" Hel stood back, eying him mischievously up and down. She was no longer angry and intent on having some fun with her lover. "Are you saying that you're leaving me? *Me?* The Queen of the Damned? The most powerful and feared ruler in all the Multiverse? You, Henry, dumb-arsed, half-wit Fox, is dumping—*moi?*" she teased. "Since when did I give you permission to do that, anyway? Oh, and by the way, that's not your stuff; it's mine." Hel pointed to the box as Henry giggled. He sort of guessed that she was messing with him now.

"Well, what would you like me to do with *your* stuff?" he asked, beaming broadly.

"Put it back where it belongs, that's what," she commanded, waving a finger in mock anger toward her chamber. Picking up the box, Henry let out a nervous snigger.

"Oh, so you think it's funny do you?" Hel scolded, warming to her task. Pretending to be angry with Henry was almost as much fun as the real thing. He just played along so perfectly. "Showing the one-time love of my life the way out of here and then dumping me; you find that funny do you?" she continued, stifling a giggle.

Henry shook his head. "Sorry," he mumbled, before bursting into a fit of laughter. He loved playing games with Hel.

"Sorry, I'll give you sorry my lad." Grabbing him sharply by the ear, Hel dragged him back toward her chamber. "You're going to find me a nice, firm slipper when we get inside," she sniggered impishly.

"Why? Are you feet cold?" Henry replied with a loud guffaw.

"No, you stupid boy, and neither will your bottom be."

Cackling wickedly, Hel kicked the door open.

"It's about to become entangled with that slipper."

26

The Reckoning

"**I** really think that it's about time you went to your bedroom dear," Sif whispered plaintively in her daughter's ear; praying that her voice didn't betray her desperation. She had to get Thrud out of the feasting hall before things went pear shaped.

"Oh, mummy," Thrud moaned. "Can't I stay and listen to Uncle Loki? He's so funny when he tells stories."

"Um, not this time my darling. I don't think Uncle Loki is going to be very funny tonight."

Sif's words had to be the understatement of the century. Loki was reeling around the rock pool waving his sword, roaring "Hail Odin" sarcastically while laughing at the top of his voice. He wasn't a pretty sight.

"Oh, Mummy!" Thrud pouted sulkily. *It just wasn't fair, why did grown-ups get to have all the fun?*

"Now darling, be a good girl and give daddy a kiss, and then I'll get one of these nice Mermaid ladies to show you to your room."

Sif waved anxiously with her hand, and a Mermaid hurried across the floor; gracefully sidestepping Loki as she came over. After Thrud had kissed her father goodnight, the Mermaid took hold of her hand and whisked her swiftly from the room. Thankfully, the woman could see her mother's anxiety.

In truth, nobody really wanted to watch the spectacle that was about to unfold.

When Loki eventually stopped shouting and had busied himself with taking large swigs from a bottle of spirits; Bragi decided to chance his hand. "I think Loki, you have had far too much to drink, and it's best for all of us if you leave this hall and go home."

Bragi tried to speak in a tone that was as helpful and polite as possible.

"You think I should go, do you?" Loki sneered as his eyes flashed a violent crimson colour. "Bragi the Bragger wants me to leave the room. Oh dear, I'm so scared; look everybody, I've shit my pants." Loki belched loudly in his direction. "Come on then, make me, you faggot. Everybody knows Bragi can talk the talk but can't walk the walk. When the arrows start flying, Bragi the Brave takes flight; cowering behind his shield or some Valkyrie's tresses."

"Why you filthy little—" Bragi went to leap over the table, but much to his relief, Tyr held him back. His bluster had almost been called.

"Loki, you should go, before you upset someone bigger than yourself," Tyr shouted angrily as he bundled the god of poetry back into his seat.

Taking a final swig from his bottle, Loki hurled it in Tyr's direction. It was way off target but still exploded angrily, shattering itself against the cavern's wall.

"Brave, armless Tyr to the rescue," Loki sniggered as he swayed. "Do you get it—armless, harmless, armless, hey, hey?"

Tyr's face began to turn red; he wasn't used to this sort of abuse.

"Good old Tyr," Loki continued. "Strong in the arm and thick in the head. What a clever god you were to ram your fist down my wolf's throat and tickle his tonsils. What in Asgard were you thinking of? Fenrir would just suck on your arm like it was some kind of a lollipop? What a stupid, ignorant, brainless twat."

Loki broke wind loudly; he was having a ball.

"By the way," he goaded. "Fenrir can't wait to chow down on your other arm, but do him a favour; put a bit of meat on it first, there's a love. Otherwise, it's hardly worth his trouble in ripping it off."

"You're so dead, you disgusting piece of shit!" Tyr fumed, reaching for his sword.

"Boys, boys, please!" Freyja pleaded, rising to her feet. "We're Aegir's guests, please, for his sake; show our host a little respect."

"Oh, that's rich coming from you, Freyja," Loki sneered venomously as he turned to face her. "Respect hey? What? Like the respect you showed when you won the Necklace of the Brisings? They've still got a nickname for you in Nidavellir, you know; the dwarves have a foul, dirty little nickname especially for you. Do you want to hear it? Do you all want to hear it? Do you, do you?" Loki shouted as he waved his arms up and down in an attempt to whip the guests into a chorus of saying "yes."

Nobody did so.

They knew he was going to tell them anyway.

"The Whore of Asgard, that's what they call you; the filthy, dirty Whore of Asgard. You're a standing joke down there. Freyja, the tramp, Freyja, I'll-spread-my-legs-for-a-crock-of-gold; you dirty, stinking trollop!"

Loki spat in her direction. He wasn't holding anything back. Tonight, his alcohol-fuelled pain had given him the rage to curse every god in Asgard.

"Loki, how dare you insult my sister like that!" Freyr yelled, beating Odin and the Valkyries into defending Freyja's honour. "Get out of here now; you foul- mouthed bastard. Get out before I rub your face in your own shit."

"Oh no, I'm so scared! Look everybody, my knees are knocking." Loki wobbled his knees and strummed at his lips with his fingers in a display of mock terror.

"Why don't you come over here Freyr and fight me like a man," he sneered. "Oh wait; let me see; you can't, I forgot. You've sold your sword. I guess you'll have to just fight me with your great, big, enormous, fat cock then, won't you."

"PAH!" Freyr snorted. "At least I've got one, unlike you; you dickless piece of garbage."

Everybody laughed; at last one of the guests was winning the war of insults.

"Ha, bloody ha." Loki yelled angrily in disgust. Perhaps mocking him wasn't the most tactful thing the god could have done. It was a bit like pouring oil on a bonfire; it could only make things worse. "I've had nearly as many women as you, Freyr, but at least I've never bedded my own sister."

Uproar followed this vicious insult; with a loud chorus of boo's and jeers being followed by a hail of food. This insult was a taunt too far.

"Loki, please," Njord began, standing up and waving for the rest of the gods to calm down. Being one of the more senior statesmen, everyone decided to show him their respect and returned to their seats. Perhaps he could pull off a miracle and restore some dignity to the evening.

"I swear someone has mixed venom with your ale tonight Loki," he continued hopefully. "You're not only drunk, you're hissing like an asp. If you beg Odin for his mercy right now, then I'm sure he'll let you walk free. If not, then I for one cannot vouch for your safety."

"Well said Njord, here, here." Loki stomped around the rock pool once more, clapping his hands loudly and mockingly as he spoke. "Good old Njord. Njord the sensible, Njord the peace lover—Njord the pussy-whipped more like. We all know why your marriage failed, don't we, Njord? You weren't man enough for a magnificent giantess like Skadi, were you?"

"Don't talk such rubbish, Loki; that insult is beneath even you. Everybody knows she couldn't stand the sea." Njord was trying to stay calm, but it was difficult even for him.

Loki's insults had teeth.

"Oh yeh, believe that and you'd believe anything," Loki gibed. "Word on the old jungle drums has it that Skadi put you in a frock and made you wear lipstick. You were the woman in that marriage, not her. She used to screw you by night and piss on you by day."

"AAARGH!"

Njord yelled and leapt up like an enraged boar. It took all the strength of Thor to prevent him from jumping over the table and starting a brawl.

"You have a dirty, foul, evil mouth Loki; I can't believe I ever called you my friend." Thor growled furiously. Some of the things Loki had said were funny; but insulting a noble and respected god like Njord definitely wasn't one of them.

"Yeh, I used to call you friend, too, Thor; but that was before you shagged my one true love." Loki waved his sword passionately in Carmel's direction. "How could you do that to me Thor how could you? Why her? Out of all the women in Agard, why did you have to FUCK her?"

This was it; this was the excruciating pain behind Loki's horrific outburst tonight. His heart was battered and bleeding, and he yearned for revenge.

"Did you do that, husband?" Sif cried, leaping to her feet and giving Thor a dagger stare. "Have you been off whoring with that Valkyrie tart?" she shrieked, waving a finger accusatively in the direction of the warriors.

Thor said nothing; just turned a deeper shade of puce.

"Oh, like you're all holier than thou, Sif the little Miss Innocent." Loki goaded, deciding to take a swipe at her, too. "I don't remember you being all that faithful when you were first married, do you Sif? It was all—*Oh, Loki, uh, I love you, Loki, uh, give it to me, Lok—uh, uh.*"

Loki made obscene sexual thrusts with his hips as he mimicked Sif climaxing. Stopping abruptly, he undid the belt to his trousers. "Hey Thor, guess what? I've just found a ginger pube! Do you reckon Thrud could be my daughter, hey, hey?"

Loki had pulled his trousers down and was holding his genitals up for all to see.

That was it. Thor's hammer was out and he made ready to beat the living daylights out of Loki.

"No, Thor, don't please; I beseech you!" Frigg screamed, throwing herself in front of her son in a desperate attempt to stop him killing Loki. "Please, not here, I beg of you. Not today, not when we're mourning the death of your brother."

"Ha, ha, ha!" Loki burst out laughing as he clapped his hands together. He was delighted that Frigg, of all the gods, had chosen to join the fray.

"Ah yes, here we have Odin's bitch of a wife, the traitorous queen of Hel's Angels. How nice of you to defend the gods you hate; to defend your wonderful, darling son; the fabulous, the one and only Balder. What a god he was, hey? The fairest, the kindest and most loved of all the gods in Asgard. What a fabulous god—what a bloody fool more like! I made the dart that killed him, and do you remember that poor little old lady Thokk who simply refused to cry?" For a brief moment, Loki shape shifted into the form of the old hag and then back again. "That was me!"

Throwing back his head, Loki howled with laughter.

"Kill him!" Frigg screamed hysterically. "Kill the lying, scumbag murderer."

"STOP!"

Odin had risen to his feet, and Gungnir was in his hand. "Nobody is killing anybody today. Sit down Thor, sit down all of you and show our host some respect."

One by one, the furious gods sat down.

Loki had insulted them all.

The atmosphere in the hall was electric. One spark and their fury could erupt once more.

"Loki, go. You have sealed your doom, and I will deal with you tomorrow." Odin commanded sternly, staring unblinkingly at the drunken god. By his own words, Loki had hanged himself. This was it, the opportunity he had been waiting for; the moment to push Hel over the edge.

"Oh, I'll go all right, my lord," Loki spat furiously. "But only when I'm well and truly done. I'll be walking safe and sound out of this hall, and do you know why that is? Do you? Because I survive Ragnarok; that's why; it's just one of Mimir's many, many prophesies built out of sand—the lying, cheating toad." Loki turned and gazed slowly around the room.

Everybody had gone quiet. The mention of Ragnarok had chilled their blood.

"Why don't you tell your warriors the truth about Ragnarok, hey Odin?" Loki quizzed in a voice that was now hushed and filled with menace. "Why don't you tell your precious, little Valkyries the lie that is Ragnarok? They've done your dirty work; so don't you think they deserve to know the truth about their fate and that of Asgard? Don't you think they need to hear this rather than the bottomless pit of lies you've spewed year after year after year."

Nobody spoke; you could have heard a pin drop.

What foul slurs was the trickster going to vomit next?

"Lambda."

Kat's voice suddenly echoed loudly above the silence. She couldn't stop herself. Something in what Loki had said just made sense. Lambda had been the word that Mimir croaked when Hel had nearly killed him; Lambda was important, Lambda was somehow connected to Ragnarok.

"Lambda, flamda, damda," Loki played with the word. "I don't know what it means, but your god of gods does. You're all going to die because of flamda, because of his screwup and because he isn't man enough to tell you why. Instead, he gives you Ragnarok; the great big, bogus, final hurrah that's his excuse for condemning you to your doom."

"Loki," Odin muttered furiously. "You can lie as much as you want about me, but when it comes to taking Mimir's name in vain and blaspheming about Ragnarok, then you've gone too far."

Odin slammed Gungnir down into the floor.

"Valkyries, seize him!"

With an ear-piercing chorus of battle cries, the tables in front of the Valkyries were upturned as the warriors leapt over them. Within an instant, Loki was surrounded by a dozen swords pressed tightly against his throat.

He was a heartbeat from death.

"STOP!"

Aegir's voice bellowed furiously across the hall such that the whole cavern trembled and quaked.

"This is MY hall, and this is MY feast. How dare you desecrate my home! If anybody, god or Valkyrie, dares to draw blood; then I will personally feed them to Jormungard." Aegir glared angrily, baring the whites of his eyes. "And that isn't a threat—it's a promise," he hissed furiously through clenched teeth.

"Thank you, thank you my excellent host," Loki sniggered with more than a little relief. Taking his sword, he stepped back and then rattled its tip along the cluster of those in front of him. "You stupid bitches," he scoffed. "You wouldn't be half so brave if you weren't all drugged up on Odin's mead. I can't wait to see your faces when you find out what's it's made of and what it does to you. When were you intending to tell them that priceless little gem, hey Odin? When are you going to tell your precious little band of harlots that you're no better than a drug-peddling pimp?"

With a final guffaw and a gob of spittle that was aimed at Carmel, Loki strode toward the great, wooden doors.

Warriors' hands twitched ominously on their swords.

"Let him go, Valkyries!" Aegir bellowed. "I'm warning you; let him leave this room unharmed." He could see their hands itching to strike the first blow.

"Oh, yeh, that's right, I forgot. God forbid anyone dares to draw blood tonight." Loki sneered as Fimafeng, Aegir's most trusted servant, dragged the heavy door open. "Cheers mate!" he chortled sarcastically before stabbing his sword deep into the man's chest.

The blow killed Fimafeng instantly.

"Oh dearie me, just look at what I've done!" he exclaimed mockingly. "I've only gone and killed your stupid servant. Now what are you gonna do about it hey—*cry?*"

Turning around, Loki made a final, defiant 'fuck you' gesture with his fist and after blowing a loud raspberry, he swaggered cockily from the hall.

He'd managed to piss everybody off—and guess what?

He didn't give a damn.

It took Odin a long time to bring some sort of order to Aegir's hall. Loki had turned the party in paradise into the nightmare from Niflheim. Everybody, with two exceptions, was baying for his blood.

Those exceptions were Kat and Carmel; who exchanged brief but empathetic glances.

Carmel's sympathy for Loki was driven by a sense of guilt. She had always believed she was just another one of his dalliances; but now she knew otherwise. She could feel his pain. Perhaps if only he had shared his feelings sooner, then Thor wouldn't have happened.

Then again, perhaps he would. She could never have been content with just one love in her life. Duplicity was her nature now, as it always had been. She needed and craved both her godly lovers.

Kat's sympathies for Loki were for a completely different reason, a mutual distrust of Odin. What Loki had said about Ragnarok and his limited understanding of lambda hinted at a deeper truth; and one she had long suspected. Kat was certain that Odin was the true enemy of Asgard, not Hel. The problem was; what could she do about it?

How could she get her sisters to see his darker side?

Tuning in to the conversations buzzing around her only emphasised this point. Had Njord really worn a frock? Had Loki slept with Sif? Why was Freyja the Whore of Asgard, and the single, hottest question of all—was the mighty Thor really that mighty where it mattered most?

Not one Valkyrie seemed to care two toots about what had been said about Ragnarok. There was only one villain now in Asgard, and that was Loki: Loki the arrogant; Loki the blasphemer. His attempted exposé on Ragnarok had to be lies—damn lies and the warriors were having none of it.

"My fellow gods and dear Valkyries."

Odin gestured with his hands for everyone to settle down and stop talking. It took some time, but eventually, after clearing his throat a couple of times, he was able to speak.

"I am sure you will all join me in extending my deepest sympathies to Aegir for the unpleasantness that has happened tonight. We all feel for his loss of such a loyal and trusted servant."

Odin paused whilst a loud round of clapping, foot stamping, and whistling acknowledged what a splendid evening they had all been having. Aegir had been an exceptionally generous host.

"Now, I would ask my beloved Valkyries if they would kindly excuse themselves so that we gods may discuss what to do with Loki.

He is a god, and as such his punishment must be decided by his peers."

"My lord." It was Ruby who stood up to offer a response on behalf of the Valkyries. "If there is anything we can do, then we are at your service. We have all loved Loki, but this time he has gone too far. We live to serve you, my lord—hail Odin."

"HAIL ODIN!"

The warriors cheered their salutation and, after a prolonged round of hugging and kissing goodbye, they reluctantly left the hall. The doors were closed and securely bolted behind them. Everybody wanted to stay and listen, but Odin's stern expression had told them otherwise.

Loki's fate would be a decision for the gods alone.

Odin paused for several minutes before he spoke again. He had to be certain that the warriors were safely out of earshot.

"Right, now that we are alone we must discuss preparations," Odin began, looking carefully around the room. To his relief, he could see that everyone knew what this private chat was really going to be about. "Loki's taunts are a trifling annoyance and of little consequence," he continued. "Thor, Tyr; you will help me sort him out. We won't kill him; that would disturb the prophesies. However, I promise you we will punish him in a manner that will make him rue the day he ever was born."

With Loki's fate determined; Odin paused to allow a rousing chorus of "Hail Odin" and foot stamping to subside. Loki had insulted almost every god at the feast, and they were as mad as hornets. Death would be too kind a fate for him; and they seemed reassured that Loki would receive a far worse punishment.

"Now, you all need to see this," Odin continued solemnly, withdrawing the plastic disk from his pocket. Passing it to Freyja, she studied it intently before handing it on. Her expression as she did so said it all. Things weren't looking good.

The disk had been completely orange in colour and was now flecked with a spattering of scarlet dots. These were enlarging and coalescing. It wouldn't be too long before the disk became completely red.

Odin waited patiently until the object was back in his hands before he spoke again. "I'm afraid, my friends, it's time for us to go. You must all make your preparations and say your goodbyes. You should have sorted out what you wish to take by now, so when you see the sign, you must depart quickly and discretely. I don't want anyone left behind, okay?"

A gentle ripple of murmured agreement echoed around the room.

"What's the sign again, please?" Tyr asked awkwardly before ducking. The reward for his question was being pelted with food; he really should have known this detail by now.

"Will somebody please remind him?" Odin tutted irritably, drumming his finger tips on the table. There always had to be one.

"When the sun is gobbled by the moon and all of Asgard quakes," chanted Bragi, pulling a silly face as he did so. Tyr could be so dumb. Loki had been right—the god really was a stupid, ignorant twat.

"Good, thank you, Bragi. Now, I think it's time to call an end to the evening's festivities. Good luck everyone, and if fortune favours us, we will all meet again soon." Odin stood up and raised his horn of mead.

"HAIL AEGIR!" he cried, and the gods responded.

"HAIL ODIN!" Aegir cried, and the gods responded.

"HAIL RAGNAROK!" Odin cried as the hall erupted into wild jubilation.

"Hello, my darling husband," Frigg called out sarcastically as she pushed the door open to Odin and Freyja's chambers. Glancing quickly round the room, she was relieved to find that her husband was all alone.

That was just what she needed.

"What do you want, wifey?" Odin muttered angrily. He was tired and really didn't want to trade insults with the 'love of his life' right now.

"Now is that any way to greet a loyal and faithful wife who has brought you a lovely, hot, soothing nightcap," she cooed, placing a tray with two horns of mulled wine down on a table.

"What are you up to, Frigg? You never brought me drinks even when we shared the same bed," Odin retorted crossly as he stomped across the room and picked up one of the horns. On reflection, a nice warm toddy could be just what he fancied.

"Just trying to be nice my darling; is that a crime?" Frigg mocked with a pout.

Odin raised the horn to his lips and made ready to enjoy a long, soothing draught.

"Cheers!" Frigg volunteered, raising her horn as well. The slightest hint of a smirk twitched nervously at the corners of her mouth.

"Cheers," Odin replied—before freezing abruptly. His mouth was wide open, and the delicious wine lapped tantalisingly close to his lips.

Something wasn't right.

After peering closely at the horn, Odin sniffed the contents cautiously. Still not satisfied, he carried the vessel over to a candelabrum and took a closer look. "Hmmmm," he mused with a wry smile after finishing his inspection. "There are interesting traces of a white powder on the rim of this horn, don't you think, my darling?"

"Just a little sugar my love; something sweet for my sweet," Frigg flustered with an anxious smile. She knew she'd been busted.

Damn him—the cautious old crow.

Relieving Frigg of the other horn, Odin replaced the two vessels on the tray and then beckoned for a servant to take them outside. He whispered something into his ear; words that Frigg couldn't hear.

"Darling," Odin started with a grin, taking both Frigg's hands in his. "I know you hate me, and you know that I hate you, too."

"Yes, my sweetness," Frigg nodded slowly in reply. "It's called a hate-hate relationship and has been so for many a year." Smiling sarcastically, she blew him a kiss.

"Hmmm, exactly," Odin replied as a delicate, cautiously tapped knock emanated from the door. Striding over, Odin relieved the servant of the tray of drinks before carrying them back into the room.

"I asked my servant to give your sugar a little stir," Odin began coyly as he offered both horns for Frigg to hold. "As you can see, he's done a splendid job. Frankly, I can't tell which one now has the sweetener in it, can you; my dearest?"

Frigg gulped nervously before raising each horn to her nose and sniffing them in turn. *Damn!* The poison was odourless, and even she couldn't see a difference between the two vessels.

She had to think fast.

"Perhaps a nightcap wasn't such a good idea after all," she suggested hastily as she began to make her way toward the door.

"Oh, on the contrary, my angel," Odin interrupted, tactfully blocking her exit. "I think it's an excellent idea. Help us to, shall we say, bury the hatchet, in a manner of speaking." Chuckling wickedly, he pointed to the horns that were still in her hands. "You choose—my dearest cupcake."

Frigg hesitated. Odin had her good and hard—and she could never read his mind. *Damn it! Which horn had Fulla's poison in it?*

She really couldn't tell.

"No rush," Odin sneered revelling in her discomfort. Reaching out to take the horn from her left hand, Frigg pulled it away, before offering him the horn in her right hand, and then pulling that one away, too.

Damn! Which wretched horn was poisoned?

Was her vile husband bluffing, double bluffing—or what? She couldn't tell.

"Come on, my love, do hurry up and choose. The wine is beginning to chill." Odin was growing impatient. He wanted to get this over with, once and for all.

"Here, take this." Frigg held out the horn in her left hand before, at the last moment, swapping it with the one in her right.

Odin took it. Their fates were sealed.

"Cheers!" he exclaimed, holding the horn up high and after toasting Frigg; he downed the contents in one long, satisfying draught. "Aaaah, absolutely delicious," he sighed, returning the empty vessel to the platter. "Well drink up, my angel, or should that be Hel's Angel." He added with a sarcastic chuckle.

Frigg raised her horn and then hesitated.

How in Asgard did Odin know which horn had been poisoned?

"Come on now, don't be bashful," Odin began as he swayed slightly and then staggered sideways. "Oh dear, I...don't...feel...terribly..."

Odin collapsed onto the bed as saliva dribbled from his mouth. He shook violently for a few moments, exhaled loudly, and then after another final, violent paroxysm—lay still. Frigg couldn't tell if he was still breathing or not, but his eyes seemed fixed and were open wide.

She tapped cautiously at a dangling foot. It swung limply.

She kicked it harder—still no response.

Maybe the fool hadn't known after all?

"Cheers, darling," Frigg relaxed, breaking into a broad grin as she offered a relieved, farewell toast to her prostrate husband. "You miserable, scheming, sly old bastard," she added contemptuously, gratefully downing the contents of her horn. She'd won.

Victory belonged to Hel at last.

"May you rot in Niflheim for all eternity," Frigg cursed loudly as she swaggered triumphantly over to the platter and placed her horn down beside his. Removing her hand, she noticed a slight residue in its bottom. There was none in Odin's horn. Spinning round in alarm, Frigg stared hard at her husband.

She jumped.

Odin's eye had swivelled upward and was staring back. A wicked grin was beginning to form on his lips.

NO! Surely not?

"Oops! So sorry, my darling," Odin tittered as he uprighted himself.

27

The Smoking Gun

"ONE WORLD!"

"ONE NATION!"

"ONE MOVEMENT!"

"YOU!"

Marcus yelled each round of chanted slogans with the same fervour as the rest of the crowd around him. The hall was packed to capacity, and with each impassioned salute, the jubilant crowd pressed forward, punching their fists in the air as one. The atmosphere was electric, and Marcus thanked god for the opportunity of being there.

Not being a member of the New Youth Movement, his presence at one of Thirle's private speeches was a rare honour. It was also a glowing testament to the power of the butterfly effect.

Following his meeting with Herr Flöda where, for lack of anything better to say, Marcus had flapped his butterfly wings and suggested extra security within the audience; a memo had been posted at the police station asking for volunteers. Marcus had been the first, and after assisting in the reception area screening attendees for guns and other assorted weaponry, he had made his way into the hall to mingle with the heaving throng.

With good fortune and a little elbow grease, Marcus had managed to work his way toward the front, which is where he was standing now—three rows back and to one side of the great man.

Wow! What an evening it had been. Who would have thought that mere words could be so powerful, so passionate, and so moving?

On stage, the diminutive figure of Thirle Flöda had at first seemed completely lost, standing almost hidden behind the vast lectern before him. The crowd had bayed incessantly for him to begin, but he just stood there silently, arms folded; expressionless; waiting for the crowd to quieten.

It hadn't.

Growing impatient, Herr Flöda had begun his talk, speaking so softly that even the people in the front rows had difficulty hearing his voice. This was his intended affect, to cow the audience into submission; imposing his iron will upon his followers. Within seconds, the whole hall had fallen silent; enveloped in a hush so deathly you could have heard a ghost whisper.

Thirle's speech hadn't lasted long, perhaps an hour, maybe an hour and ten minutes tops; but it wasn't length that counted—it was quality. Thirle's message had been so simple, so elegant, and so sublime that it amazed Marcus as to why he refused to have his speeches recorded. The wider world would beg to hear his eloquence, and their need to hear was so much greater.

His refusal to embrace the wider audience was a peculiarity; a quirk of eccentricity from which Thirle wouldn't be budged. No one was allowed to record his speeches, and his loyal followers respected this edict absolutely. His beautiful diction was intended for them the party faithful; and if you wanted to hear it—you had to sign up.

It was that simple.

The man had a genius that extended far beyond his prose and linguistic skill.

It was the whole presentation, the total package, that made him so uniquely talented. On its own, the content of Thirle's speech was brilliant. On its own, his presentation was flawless. Put the two together and there you had it: a spellbinding hour of mesmeric magic.

Quite why Thirle had never chosen to run for government office was another one of life's imponderable mysteries. His oratorical skill alone could have made him a President as easily as falling off a log. Thirle was undeniably the finest living orator of his generation.

As the crowd continued to roar their support, Marcus took a moment to reflect upon the message in his speech and the profound impact it had had upon his followers.

Starting quietly, impassively, and gently; Thirle had carefully unravelled the problems that faced the modern world. He had done this in a way that was so easy to understand that a child of five could remember its simplicity.

Pollution; war; overcrowding, inequality.

Taking these building blocks as his starting point, Thirle had elegantly woven a single, compelling solution that was both inspirational and obvious.

Why was the world so blind to his genius?

Why could no leader of any country see the answer that was staring them in the face?

Thirle had posed these questions as his speech gathered in its intensity and passion; his voice rising in volume and pace as his gestures became increasingly animated. He was a man on a mission, and he loathed the lack of clarity and foresight displayed by presidents around the world. He was contemptuous of their narrow vision, their limited ambition, and their total failure to grasp the magnitude of the task at hand.

How could they fail their children and their children's children so miserably?

How could they sit on their hands while humanity choked?

Thirle's answer to civilisation's problems was as simple as it was laudable. Pausing in his speech, Thirle allowed the audience to calm before sharing the brilliance of what he was about to say.

His solution came in just two words.

Reduction and redistribution.

In response to a redistribution of wealth, technology, and aid from the richer nations; the poorer countries would give an irrevocable and binding agreement to cut their population sizes. Fewer people would mean less pollution; and a redistribution of wealth would eliminate poverty, famine, and the resentments that led to war.

This was it, the blindingly obvious yet impossible solution for any one nation to aspire to. This was where Thirle Flöda came in; this was where he and the globalised might of his New Youth Movement hurtled to the fore. That was his message, and the message that propelled his disciples into the stratosphere.

Rising abruptly in volume, tempo, and emotion; Herr Flöda strafed the audience with his words as efficiently as though he were using a machine gun. Each climactic sentence was hammered out with a resounding thump of one fist in the palm of the other; and each word was delivered in a clipped, staccatoed assault that sent flecks of spittle flying from his lips.

Thirle was a man on fire, and his message was dynamite.

"One world, one nation, one movement—you!" He exhorted his adoring disciples as they screamed their devotion back.

His movement and his movement alone could unite humanity into one healthy and harmonious body. The modern plagues of war, poverty, and pollution could be wiped out within a generation. To Marcus, as to the rest of the audience, this vision of a global hegemony was lacking in only one, final, triumphant flourish. It had to be orchestrated by a single, brilliant, and inspired leader.

You—Herr Flöda; you, you, YOU!

Cheering loudly once more, Marcus pushed forward with the crush. The man was a genius, his speech was poetic, and his vision was that of a god.

It was such a pity that he had to die.

Marcus didn't know why, but he couldn't question that unshakeable belief; his tattooed poppy tingling violently as its hidden power forced him to act. He was the death maker; the assassin in the night; the blood-crazed stalker that Thirle so desperately feared—and he was here tonight.

Pulling a revolver from his pocket, Marcus raised the gun and took aim.

BANG!

His first shot missed, smashing a hole in the lectern. No one had twigged to the presence of an assassin as yet; their roars having drowned the blast of his gun.

BANG!

His second shot hit Thirle in the shoulder, and the man staggered back, dazed with shock. His security guards looked startled as they raced to form a protective cordon around him.

BANG!

His third shot hit Thirle in the stomach, and he collapsed to the floor. Hundreds of eyes were now frantically searching the hall for the wannabe killer.

There was time for one last shot—maybe.

BANG!

Marcus's arm was jostled as his gun was wrestled from his hand. His final shot flew wild. This was it, the end of his quest. Hands tore at him as they dragged him down to the floor in a welter of punches and kicks.

Marcus saw stars, and his body exploded in an orgy of pain. Blackness would come soon; the relief of unconsciousness masking whatever future fate had planned for him.

Had he fulfilled his duty, the one demanded by his queen?

Marcus didn't know, but he hoped so.

The Contessa would be pleased, so very pleased, if a bullet had found its deadly mark.

28

Loki's Flyting

The Fimbulvetr, the winter of all winters, hit Asgard shortly after the gods and Valkyries had returned from the coast.

Leaden clouds rolled down from the mountains of Jotunheim, and a howling gale brought freezing temperatures and a mighty blizzard. This engulfed Asgard for two days and two nights. A snowstorm raged all around as sheets of icy pellets swept horizontally across the castle's courtyard. Massive drifts piled up high, one on top of another; some reaching almost halfway toward the castle's battlements.

Nobody had ever seen such a storm, and its portent was ominous. Ragnarok had Asgard in its icy grip.

Cooped up inside the castle's walls, tensions and tempers became frayed. Everybody wanted to do something, and the frustration of inactivity was almost impossible to bear.

The one glittering ray of sunshine in this air of irritability was the blissful return of Balder. He lit up the castle like the summer sun, and everybody expressed alternate joy, amazement, shock, and bewilderment that he had returned safely. Balder could remember nothing about his stay in Niflheim, not that that mattered. He hadn't changed; and he forgave Hod for firing the deathly dart as easily as if his brother had merely trodden on his toe.

Silk's behaviour, however, was completely different.

She was transformed, beaming from ear to ear as she pranced along the castle's passages, grinning as though all her birthdays had arrived at once. Gone was the sullen, hard-as-nails warrior to be replaced by an adoring, loveable kitten. She became so inseparable from Balder that some suspected they were bound by a piece of thread. Silk was happy beyond her wildest dreams, and she no longer cared to hide her love for her dashingly handsome god. She would have shouted as such from the rooftops—if only she could get outside.

Carmel and Thor's relationship was as stark a contrast to Silk and Balder's as could be imagined. Following the feast, they both felt a tremendous guilt and awkwardness; and did their best to avoid each other. Thor locked himself in his forge, and the muffled, rhythmic bang, bang, bang of his hammer on metal could be heard through even the loudest of wintry squalls.

It was a tough break.

Neither enjoyed the spotlight on their affair, nor the fact that it was the number one topic on everybody's lips. What made their dilemma so murderously painful was a bitter, underlying truth; a truth that neither would admit in public nor to each other.

Their passion was still growing.

Denying their hearts cut deeper than the sharpest sword.

After the events of Aegir's fateful speech, Sif and Thrud had headed back to Valhalla, Sif needing room to breathe. Frigg's sudden disappearance was also noted, but dismissed by Odin as being "just another one of her Midgard shopping trips." Although it seemed odd that she hadn't stayed on to greet her beloved son; it wasn't so desperately out of character as to cause concern. Frigg lived to shop and shopped to live; that was the goddess all over; Asgard's one and only 'shopping Shelley.'

After an initial display of frostiness, Hod forgave Kat for her part in Hermod's misfortune. He couldn't stay mad at her for long, and besides, he knew in his heart that she wasn't to blame. Hel still had a demon locked inside her, and no amount of love from Henry or friendship from Kat would change that. Devilry was like a canker buried deep within her soul; no matter how hard you tried to destroy it, Hel's inner wickedness would always prevail. Evil and Hel were one and the same; and it would only be a matter of time before the vicious, inner beast reared its ugly head again. As far as Hod was concerned, the Queen of the Damned was a lost cause.

After two long days and two even longer nights, the terrible storm finally abated. The winds dropped and black clouds still pregnant with snow lifted their petticoats just far enough to allow a delicate shard of sunshine through. This wandered shyly amongst the woods and fields of Asgard; its tender rays flitting coyly from bush to shrub to hedge to tree.

Whooping with relief, the gods and warriors would soon be able to leave the castle walls.

The hunt for Loki could begin.

For a fugitive on the run, Asgard could be a small place.

Donning their cloaks of swans' feathers, the warriors joined Odin's trackers as they fanned out across the realm looking for clues. Loki could, of course, have used his ring and gone straight to Niflheim, but Odin dismissed this out of hand.

That wasn't the flamboyant trickster's style.

The most likely route he would have taken would be to head toward Jotunheim. Here he could raise a host of angry giants. Loki was no coward, and the prospect of attacking Odin with an army at his back would be too great a temptation to ignore. Using Odin's hunch as their guide, the Valkyries and trackers concentrated their search in the most isolated reaches of Vanaheim. These were the rugged, rural foothills that rose in gentle swells before erupting into the fortressed walls of Jotunheim.

Their efforts were soon rewarded.

Several shepherds had spotted a 'stranger' heading in the direction of Franang's falls. This was as lonely and desolate a spot as you could find anywhere in the realm. Nestling in a small hollow that sloped gently down toward an icy pool at the bottom of the falls, lay an invisible crofter's cabin. Built entirely from local rocks and boulders, the dwelling merged into its surroundings. The building had four doors, and these offered any fugitive a bird's eye view in all directions. This had to be the perfect location for a god on the run. A place to lay low and weather out the storm before continuing on his journey.

Confident that the stranger in question was Loki; Thor, Tyr, Aegir, Bragi, and Vali headed out at dawn to seize the foul-mouthed rascal. Odin himself headed off in an entirely different direction.

He had to finalize his plans for Loki's punishment.

No Valkyries were invited to join the avenging posse, and none requested to swell their numbers. Whatever the gods' plans were, it was going to be a particularly unpleasant affair. Loki's punishment was for the gods of Asgard only.

As the band of bloodthirsty gods drew near to the falls shortly before noon, Loki saw them and stopped what he was doing. He didn't turn tail and bolt because he had already anticipated their arrival.

Wading through the thick snow, he quickly broke a hole in the ice that covered the surface of the pool. Then, after a final cautious look around, he plunged into the freezing waters and headed toward the bottom. Loki had shape shifted into an enormous salmon. In this disguise, he felt certain he would be concealed and beyond the reach of the vengeful gods.

At first, when the gods arrived at the cabin, Loki's confidence in his deception seemed to have hit the mark. The gods were flummoxed, and they hunted around wildly, cursing and muttering. It looked as though he had given them the slip.

Unfortunately, the heavy snow gave the gods a crucial advantage.

Loki's floundering trail to the water's edge was clearly visible, and intuition told them that their quarry must now lurk beneath its frozen surface. Taking his hammer from his belt, Thor gleefully set about smashing the ice until the entire surface of the pool was exposed.

Loki was trapped and at their mercy.

From the bottom of the icy waters, Loki could see the gods above him, but he felt no fear. He was well hidden in the inky waters, and a thick layer of blubber was keeping his fishy body blissfully warm. There wasn't much to eat, but he knew the gods would freeze and give up their vigil long before he succumbed to cold or boredom. If it came to a waiting game, he was going to win hands down. Fishy fins permitting, he could have quite happily flicked two fingers at the posse and wished them good riddance.

Loki was safe and secure—and he wasn't going to budge.

Realising their predicament, the gods lit a fire inside the cabin and settled down to discuss what to do next. None of them had seen Loki hiding at the bottom of the pool, but they were absolutely certain he was there. Looking around the hut, it was Aegir who spotted the object that would ultimately lead to Loki's undoing. There, sitting in tatters in a corner, was a large, old fishing net. Setting to work with a needle and thread, Aegir expertly mended the frayed and twisted muddle.

Within the hour, they had a sturdy net with which to capture their elusive prey.

Taking one end in his hands and giving the other to the remaining gods, Thor sent them over to the far side of the pool. With some difficulty, and with a lot of slipping and sliding around, the gods began to slowly dredge the waters. Loki was a goner for sure.

Loki heard the splash of the net as it hit the waters, and he darted down to the deepest depths of the pool. Taking shelter between two slimy boulders, he waggled his fins in delight as the net passed harmlessly over his back. If fish could laugh, Loki's salmon head would have fallen right off.

It was Loki—one; cold, wet, stupid gods—nil.

"Damnation!"

Thor cursed loudly when at last the gods returned their empty net to the shore. There were a few small stickle backs, weeds, twigs, and other creepy crawlies lurking in its tangled weave; but not the nice, fat, juicy fish they desired. Stamping their hands and feet in the biting cold, the gods returned to the shelter of the cabin for a powwow. Vali was getting particularly fed up. He was a tracker and unused to such cold and energetic work.

Undeterred, Aegir put forward a suggestion that might just wipe the smile of Loki's fishy face. Grinning broadly, the gods set about the task of preparing plan 'B.'

When the gods eventually emerged from the cabin, they were greeted by an almighty splash. Loki had been loitering near the surface of the water and couldn't resist taunting the gods with a display of his leaping skills.

"I'll soon wipe the grin off his wretched face," Thor muttered grimly as the gods took up their positions on either bank once more. Slipping, sliding, and cursing vehemently, they set about dredging the pool again.

Loki heard, rather than saw, the net coming toward him this time as Aegir's cunning scheme quickly became apparent. The gods had added weights to the bottom of the net, and this was bouncing and skidding along the bottom of the pool, scooping up everything in its path.

This time, there could be no escape for a fish hiding amongst the boulders.

Irritated at being disturbed from his cosy retreat, Loki flicked his tail angrily and powered his way toward the surface. With a final, satisfying twirl, Loki leapt high into the air and flew clean over the top of the net. Silver scales sparkled in the afternoon sun as the gods looked on in anguish. Loki had sprung their trap once more.

He was proving to be a very slippery customer indeed.

"I've had enough of this," Thor fumed angrily as the gods hauled the net out of the water once more and began to pick the slimy detritus from its mesh. Loki was thumbing his nose at them, and the agony of their failure was becoming unbearable. Scowling furiously, Thor pulled the others into a huddle and outlined his idea for plan 'C.'

This would be it, their final attempt to capture their slippery foe.

Satisfied that everybody understood his idea, the gods 'high fived' to a chorus of "Hail Odin" and headed back toward the pool. This time, Aegir and Vali took one side of the net, and Tyr and Bragi took the other. Grumbling angrily, Thor waded into the freezing waters as far as he dared and took up his position near the centre of the net. If Loki tried to leap this time, he would be there to catch him.

Loki heard the net coming once more and muttered something in fishy bubbles that probably would have translated into "Oh, no, here we go again." Flicking his tail, he made ready to dance over its top once more.

This third attempt to catch him came as something of a surprise to Loki. He was amazed that the dumb gods hadn't given up already; they must be getting awfully tired and fed up with their miserably impossible task. After blowing a few bubbles, he smirked a fishy smirk. The only thing the dummies were going to catch today was their death of colds, and of that they could be certain. As far as he was concerned, he could go on leaping and twirling all day and night if that was what it took to get these dimwits off his back.

Settling on performing a double back somersault with a half pike for the gods' entertainment, Loki spiralled quickly up toward the surface of the pool, gathering speed with each powerful beat of his muscular tail.

Breaking surface, Loki flew into the air and pirouetted majestically before the waiting gods. Caught up in the smugness of his arrogant display, he didn't notice Thor's waiting arms until it was too late.

THUD!

Smashing into Thor's chest, Loki floundered wildly as the mighty god struggled to catch hold of the massive, writhing fish. He had both hands around Loki's waist, but he couldn't get a proper purchase. Loki, now furious and terrified; flipped and flapped and wriggled and squirmed as he struggled to break free.

For a brief moment, it looked as though the salmon would prove the victor. His shimmering, slimy scales were far too slippery for Thor to catch hold of.

With a final, grizzled yell of determination, the god dug deep and clenched his iron grasp around the tail of the salmon. Thor's hands held firm, and Loki flapped wildly in a last, desperate bid for freedom.

Loki was stuck fast and he knew it.

With a mighty heave, Thor hurled the massive fish onto the bank and, after a crunching thud as bone hit rock, Loki returned to human form. He was badly winded but otherwise unharmed by his fall. Chuckling loudly, Thor splashed his way out of the pool and into the delighted arms of his fellow gods.

"Hello, Loki," Aegir boomed loudly when at last the rogue had staggered to his feet. It was going to take Loki some time to get his land legs back again. "Odin's got some guests who are dying to meeting you," he continued with a fiendish grin. Stepping forward, Aegir unleashed a powerful blow, punching Loki squarely in the face.

He collapsed unconscious to the floor. He was out cold.

"That's for Fimafeng," Aegir growled with a chilling sneer.[*]

---

[*] Author's Note: The interesting saga at the heart of this chapter was intended to explain why a salmon's body tapers toward its tail before fanning out into a large fin. In my opinion, it's a rather beautiful explanation.

29

Proceed as Planned

"**G**ive it to me, it's my turn."

"No it isn't, it's mine. Besides, I'm the oldest."

"Only by ten minutes. Hey—ouch! That hurt. Give it to me."

"No. Get lost."

"That's not fair, you're such a bully."

Vili and Ve had been squabbling in the mansion's conference room for at least ten minutes. The clock was counting down the seconds, and it was almost eleven. Captain Halcombe would be calling precisely on the hour, so the gods' argument was about to become academic. Vili, the slightly older of the duo, currently had the headset, so it looked as though he was going to be the winner.

Furious at losing again, Ve plonked himself down hard on the table and folded his arms angrily across his chest. He was going to have the sulks for the rest of the day.

"Putting the call through to you now, sir," came the lilting Caribbean voice of one of the Dragza Corporation's receptionists. Vili put the headset on and smirked smugly. Just like Ve, he had been dying to play with this toy.

"Hail Odin!" came the distorted voice of Captain Halcombe over the loudspeaker. The brothers had turned the volume on the conference call up way too high.

"Hail Odin!" Vili replied loudly and jubilantly, sticking two thumbs up toward his brother. It was a total success; the voice synthesiser making him sound just like Odin.

219

"My lord, I await your instruction," Captain Halcombe enquired politely.

"Ah yes. Carry on as planned," Vili beamed ecstatically. It was so peculiar to hear Odin's voice as he spoke. What a cool, Midgard gadget.

"Sire, may I have the coordinates?" Captain Halcombe continued. This was the purpose of his phone call, to receive the target for his mission.

"Of course, of course. Just one moment, please—"

Vili began to fluster.

The brothers had been so busy fighting over who was going to be Odin, they had completely forgotten the point of the call. Gesturing frantically with his hands, Vili raced around the large, circular table until he came to Odin's seat. Scrabbling madly with the black box, he eventually tore its lid off and spilt its contents across the table.

Now they really were in a mess.

"Sire?" the captain enquired hopefully. He didn't want to be kept waiting with such an important and clandestine call.

"One moment, uh; my good man," Vili replied in a tizz as he struggled to sound all dignified and Odin-like. He beckoned frantically for Ve to come and help him sort through the jumbled papers. Odin would be livid if they didn't deliver his message.

Moments ticked by and, with a reluctant sneer, Ve joined in the hunt for the missing slip. Finding it, he waved it victoriously aloft before prancing off, sticking his tongue out defiantly at his brother. Finders keepers—losers weepers. There was no way Vili was going to have it—no way at all.

Vili raced over and tried to snatch it from Ve's grasp.

"Nah, nah, na—na—nah; you can't have it," Ve chanted childishly as Vili grabbed hold of him and wrestled him onto the table.

Things were getting sillier by the second.

"Is everything all right, sire?" Captain Halcombe enquired anxiously. The extraordinary noises from the brothers' struggle sounded extremely bizarre.

"Ouch!" Ve exclaimed loudly as Vili pinched him hard on the arm.

That was it, the younger brother had had enough. Screwing the piece of paper up in a tantrum, he hurled it as hard as he could across the room and then flounced off in a huff.

It just wasn't fair; Vili always won.

"Just one moment, please, captain," Vili replied breathlessly, picking up the paper up and hastily unfolding it. "I have the coordinates for you now."

With some relief, Vili read these off, and after a final round of "Hail Odins," Captain Halcombe hung up. Quite what he had made of their call was impossible to say, but it didn't matter. The brothers had successfully delivered Odin's message, and Vili was cock-a-hoop. Dancing enthusiastically, he skipped round the table until he arrived at Mimir's wheelchair. "What do you reckon, hey?" he enquired, kissing his friend warmly on the forehead. "Didn't I do well?"

Mimir didn't reply; but he did nod his head ever so slightly and wiggled a finger slowly up and down. The golden apples were doing their job; he was beginning to look so much better.

Someone had very kindly cut his hair, and his beard had been groomed into a much more flattering shape. Gone too were the ill-fitting pyjamas; replaced by tanned Bermuda shorts and a slightly garish Hawaiian shirt, which had been chosen by Odin's brothers. With wraparound, tinted sunglasses and flip-flops to complete his ensemble; Mimir was barely recognisable from the man—or should that be the head—that had arrived on the Isle less than a week ago.

His new body was linking up fast; with nerves growing and connecting muscles and joints to his brain. He was still as weak as a kitten and unable to walk; but he could swallow, smile, and even wiggle his fingers and toes now. It was excellent progress but tarnished by one small but significant failure.

His mind remained a shambles.

Mimir's utterings were random and chaotic, with only occasional words making any sense. Whatever damage had been done to his brain by the countless eons locked inside the cask, it looked like it was going to be permanent, which was unfortunate. Odin needed Mimir sound in both body and mind for what would come to pass.

Releasing the brake, Vili began to wheel Mimir slowly out of the room. As the two of them stepped into the hall, Vili spotted Ve locked in conversation with two security guards. This wouldn't have been particularly unusual were it not for the presence of a third person hanging limply between them. It was a man, twitching, dishevelled, handcuffed, and stinking to high heaven.

Vili hurried forward. Something was going on.

"So, are you telling me that we're now in charge?" Ve asked the guard eagerly, before turning and beaming cheerily at Vili. All resentment over their recent argument had been forgotten by this exceptionally exciting piece of news.

"Yes, my lords," the guard nodded and bowed politely. "Both Odin and Frigg are away, and we cannot raise any of the Contessa's personal secretaries."

"Do you hear that, Vili? Nobody's around; Fulla, Gna, and Lin, they're all missing. We're the only ones here. We," Ve emphasised with a grand flourish of his hand, "are in charge."

"Wow! Cool," Vili murmured and then pointed to the collapsed body dangling between the two guards. "Who's that?"

"I don't know," Ve replied. "The security guards caught him in the orchard stealing apples. They want to know what to do with him," he continued.

"Kill him," Vili responded without hesitation or emotion. "Isn't that what we always do with intruders?"

"Yes, but they felt they ought to double-check with Odin first. Apparently, he knows the Contessa." Ve waved a finger in the direction of the fugitive.

"Oh really?" Vili enquired in surprise. "Well, in that case I suppose we'd better take a look at him, shouldn't we?" Moving a little closer, he screwed his nose up. The prisoner smelt like a dead rat.

"Guards, why don't you lift his head up so we can get a better look?" he suggested. He really didn't want to touch the revolting creature.

"Yes, my lord." Grabbing hold of the prisoner's hair, one of the guards jerked his head up.

Vili and Ve leant forward and peered enthusiastically. This was turning into a very exciting day for them.

"Hey, Vili, I recognise this fellow," Ve exclaimed loudly after a short pause. "Isn't he that agent thingy, you know; the one we met when we rescued Brynhildr and Herja?"

"Gosh, bro, I think you could be right." Vili replied, echoing Ve's observation. Despite the foul odour, the lank, matted hair and the thick, blood stained stubble; Agent Woods' features were unmistakable.

"What in Midgard is he doing here?" Vili mused.

Looking up through sunken, half-shut eyes, Woods let out a feeble, croaked rasp. His parched lips were swollen and blistered; and his mouth was as dry as a bone. Despite his miserable state, he, too, had recognised the brothers.

"Wow!" murmured Ve. "What should we do? We can't kill him, because we know him."

"Yeh, that would be murder, right?" Vili added, and the brothers both nodded their heads in agreement.

"Still, we can't have him running about the island, can we?" Ve continued.

"And we can't lock him up either; because he's a friend of Frigg's," Vili added in a voice that sounded even more perplexed. One thing the brothers definitely didn't want to do was to upset her further. They would be slapped for sure if they did. "What should we do?" he continued anxiously.

"What do you think Odin would do?" Ve offered as a smile began to light up his face. He'd got it; he had the solution to their dilemma.

Looking at his brother, he could see a smile beginning to form on Vili's lips, too. Clapping their hands together gleefully, the brothers turned toward the guards and yelled their command in unison.

"Process him!"

After putting the phone down, Captain Halcombe turned to the small gathering of senior officers who had joined him on the main deck. He handed the slip of paper with the coordinates to the helmsman, who issued the order for the vessel to adjust course.

After synchronising their watches, and to a rousing chorus of "Hail Odin," the men separated and went about their individual tasks.

By six thirty in the evening, the USS Harry S. Truman supercarrier and its associated battle group dropped anchor and hove to. They were at their designated launch site.

At twenty two hundred hours precisely, a thunderous roar and sheet of flames heralded the departure of a single cruise missile. This had been programmed with Odin's coordinates.

Its ordinance was a low-yield nuclear warhead, and this was fully armed.

Twenty minutes later; weaving erratically and flying low, the missile crossed the Florida coastline just south of Miami and continued inland; passing unnoticed by both civilian and military radar installations. Their test of homeland security had been a success. The missile had passed US defence systems undetected.

Twenty six minutes later, a large mushroom cloud erupted from a nuclear explosion. The detonation had occurred in the Everglades National Park.

Odin's conquest of paradise had begun—right on schedule.

30

The Binding of Loki

"**W**ell hello, Loki, my old mate," Odin sneered sarcastically, using one of the trickster's favourite greetings. "Would you like to have a look at your lovely new home?" he offered as he assisted him down from the creaking, wooden oxcart.

Loki didn't reply.

What was there to say?

He had spent a warm but uncomfortable night gagged and bound on the floor of the crofter's cabin at Franang falls. After Thor had caught him, it had been too late for the gods to make it to their rendezvous with Odin before nightfall; the inclement weather and the deep snow drifts making this journey too arduous and dangerous to risk in the dark. Vali had flown back to the castle with the news of their delay while Thor, Aegir, and Tyr had passed a very pleasurable evening toasting their success with storytelling and heavy drinking. As a consequence of this, the three gods looked nearly as trashed as Loki did; although only he was sporting a black eye.

Stumbling as Loki landed on the slippery ground, Odin led him by the arm to his new home. It was a cave; but one with a very low and well concealed entrance. A huge snow drift draped itself lovingly around one side of this while a cluster of elongated icicles hung dagger like from its opening. These sparkled excitedly in the mid-morning sun.

Loki eyed the void suspiciously and shivered loudly.

"Feeling a bit chilly, are we?" Fryeja enquired caustically. She had joined Odin on their journey and was looking forward to the horror they had planned for their enemy. Over the years, she, more than any of the other gods, had suffered most at Loki's expense; the 'whore of Asgard' slur being but one of many, many, countless insults. "Don't worry," she continued. "We have some friends of yours who can warm you up. Would you like to meet them?"

Snapping her fingers, two frozen looking slaves pulled three hooded bodies from the back of their oxcart. All three prisoners were bound and staggered in a blind panic as they struggled to find their footing on the icy slope. None of them was properly dressed for the freezing weather.

Loki gulped hard as his face fell. Three was a very significant number for him.

Praying hard, he just hoped that his trio of companions weren't who he thought they might be.

"Come on, then, let's go inside and get this party started." Grabbing Loki by the arm, Odin half dragged, half carried him through the narrow entrance. Both men had to bend almost double to get under the low ceiling, and Loki could hear thuds and howls from the hooded prisoners as each in turn banged his head on the craggy roof.

Fortunately, the tunnel rose quickly in height, and after a short distance and two small, winding twists, it opened out into a large and well lit chamber. Loki surveyed this studiously while Odin held up a piece of twine against his body and made some quick, rule-of-thumb measurements. He chuckled as he did so; he was having such fun.

"What's that for?" Loki slurred grumpily as he wriggled to push Odin away. "Measuring me up for my grave?"

"Oh, good gracious me, no," he exclaimed gleefully. "No such luck, I'm afraid. Death would be way too good for you. No; I'm just measuring you up for a lovely, comfortable bed we're going to make. You see, Loki; I'm sparing absolutely no expense for such a bloody nice chap like you." Grinning malevolently and with measurements completed; Odin drew three approximate lines on the gravel floor with the heel of his foot and then instructed the slaves to start digging. They set to work enthusiastically; the exercise helping to warm their frozen bodies.

By now, the other gods, Freyja, and the three prisoners had assembled inside the chamber.

Loki looked around once more. There was a slight breeze blowing from a vent hidden somewhere above him, but the cave still smelt dank and musty. Its roof was high and vaulted and festooned with clusters of stalactites. These twisted and turned as they spiralled down from the darkness. Freezing drops of water dripped endlessly from them as they fell monotonously into myriad puddles at their feet. Their constant, rhythmic drip-splash, drip-splash, drip-splash would be like a clock; drumming out the eternity of his punishment.

The walls of the cavern were damp, smooth, and worn; and a leathery fluttering of wings heralded the only other permanent occupants of the cave. Along with the stalactites; the ceiling was laced with a bustling carpet of irritable bats. The bright lights from two candelabras had disturbed their winter's slumber, and they weren't impressed.

Loki ducked low as one swooped over his head.

"Would you like to meet your companions?" Odin suggested with a wave of his hand as Tyr and Vali set about unmasking the three prisoners. "I would offer to introduce you, but I suspect you already know their names."

Loki did. His three cell mates were indeed his worst nightmare.

He spat at Odin in disgust.

How could he?

How could Odin drag his wife and kids to this hellhole?

"You're a piece of shit, Odin," he snarled. "What have Sigyn, Vardi,[*] and Narvi done to deserve this fate, hey? Punish me by all means, but not them; not my family. They're innocent."

Thor looked quizzically at Odin as Loki pleaded his case. Images of Sif and Thrud flashed through his mind. Loki was right. This dreadful hellhole really was no place for a woman and two teenaged sons.

"Well, I'd like to send them home," Odin offered mockingly. "I really would; but I'm afraid, Loki, they all have their roles to play in your suffering." Rubbing his hands with glee, Odin walked slowly behind the bedraggled prisoners. "Let's start with these two here, shall we; your sons." Odin gestured toward Vardi and Narvi. "Now I need their help in finishing your bed. Would you like me to explain why?" Odin offered with a sinister grin.

Loki didn't reply, merely fixed Odin with a stare that could have burnt a hole in their sun.

The slaves had finished digging the holes and were straining and heaving at three huge slabs of slate. These were slowly being

---

[*] Author's note: I have deliberately changed the name of one of Loki's sons from Vali to Vardi. This is to avoid confusion with Odin's son Vali, who was also a shape shifter.

manoeuvred into their positions. Half completed; the slabs formed an intriguing shape, quite unlike any bed Loki had ever seen before.

With ghoulish relish, Odin set about explaining his one-of-a-kind creation.

All three pieces of slate were approximately a metre tall and roughly hewn into the shape of tombstones. The tops of each had been flattened and then curved into a slight concave. All three slabs had now been upended, one in each of the holes such that they stood erect and tall, like a row of dominos; one in front of another. Toward the top of each slab a single, peculiar, large circular hole had been bored.

With great delight, Odin explained the reasons behind his measurements.

The curved top of the first slab would support Loki's shoulders, the second would sit under his hips; and the third would support the backs of his thighs just above the knees. The holes were for the ropes that would bind Loki to his 'bed.'

This was where his sons came in.

"Now, boys," Odin began, turning toward the two teenage youths as he spoke. They were shivering violently; both with fear and cold. "As you can see, we haven't brought enough twine to bind your father; nor have we brought any chains. In the good old days, in situations like this; we used to resort to using catgut; but unfortunately, I can't see any cats around here, can you?"

Odin looked deliberately around him as Freyja, Aegir, Tyr, and Vali joined in. They chuckled ghoulishly as wicked grins betrayed their sinister plot.

Thor stayed silent. Thrud's smiling face filled his head, and he really didn't like where this was going. Something was wrong; badly wrong.

"So what do you reckon, hey boys? There definitely aren't any cats." Odin smiled and stated the obvious as the gods finally grew bored of their farcical search. "Now, here's the deal," he continued smarmily. "One of you is a shape shifter like your father—and the other one isn't; but I don't know who is whom. One of you is therefore going to kill the other to provide the guts to bind your dad. This is up to you. If you don't fight, then I'm afraid I'm going to have to kill the both of you, and then we'll have too much gut. Now I'm sure your mother wouldn't want that, would she?" he ended with mocking sympathy.

"Odin, how could you stoop so low? They're children; think about it; they're just two innocent boys."

It was Sigyn who had uttered these words, speaking for the first time with a voice filled with pain. Loki's wife was a plain and retiring woman; the complete opposite of her flamboyant and showy husband. As married couples go, there could never have been a bigger mismatch.

"Yeh," Odin sneered, as he rounded on her like a coiled tiger. "They're just boys, Loki's boys; and they'll grow up to be just like their father—twisted, evil, and rotten to the core. Just be grateful I am giving one of them a chance to live. That's more than either of your foul offspring deserves."

"Father," Thor interrupted Sigyn before she could reply. "May I have a word with you in private?" he enquired, placing a hand heavily on Odin's shoulder suggesting that his question wasn't really a request.

"Please, my lord," Freyja stepped forward, grinning maliciously. "Do step outside and have a chat with your son. The whore of Asgard would dearly like to have a little word with her tormentor before you truss him up." She thumped a fist ominously into her hand as she spoke.

The gesture spoke for itself.

"Of course, my dearest," Odin replied sweetly, kissing her tenderly on her cheek. As he made to leave the cavern, he turned for one last, irresistible quip. "Oh, but please, don't do anything I wouldn't do; there's a love."

"My lord," Thor began cautiously when he and Odin were just a few metres from the entrance to the cave. "Do we really have to harm Loki's sons? They're just kids, and Sigyn is right. They can't be held responsible for their father's crimes."

Odin turned to face Thor. Unfortunately, his expression was not what Thor had hoped it would be. "Son, this is no time for my mighty giant slayer to go all soft on me," he began soberly. "This is it; this is Ragnarok. This is the moment we've all been waiting for. There can be no half measures, no sitting on the fence, and no compromises. You know Mimir's prophesies as well as I do. Hel must unleash the Guardians and finish Ragnarok. Only she has the power to do that.

Without them, Asgard cannot be cleansed, and if Asgard isn't cleansed; paradise cannot be reborn."

"I know, I know," Thor retorted gruffly. "But do we really have to shed the blood of an innocent boy?" He felt sick. He couldn't get Thrud's face out of his head. Vardi and Narvi were her playmates.

"We have to provoke Hel, and the death of one of her stepbrothers will guarantee this." Odin was adamant, his mind was made up. "I don't want to shed anyone's blood, least of all mine," he continued. "But you know the prophesies. To save the gods and start anew, sacrifices have to be made. Both you and I will fall in the final battle. That is our sacrifice; that is the price we pay to purge Asgard of its curse. Without our deaths, lambda's spectre cannot be cleansed from the realm." Putting his hand on his son's shoulder, he squeezed it empathetically. "Sometimes we have to do things, terrible things, for the greater good. You, I, and one of Loki's sons must die so that the gods can live."

Thor placed his hand on top of Odin's and held it firm. "Yes, I know father and I'm more than willing to pay that price; but must a child die as well?"

"I'm afraid he must son, I'm afraid he must. I'm so sorry." Odin removed his hand and with a sigh he turned back toward the entrance. "Are you coming?"

"If it's all the same to you; I'd rather not."

Thor wasn't going to stop Odin; because he understood what he was saying. However, he couldn't be a party to it. For Thrud's sake, he couldn't be.

"Very well," Odin nodded understandingly before ducking as he disappeared back inside the cave. He smiled grimly. Raucous laughter and thuds were coming from inside; Freyja must be having fun.

"Oh, darling, back so soon?" Freyja quipped as Odin reappeared inside the cavern. She punched Loki hard in the stomach. "I was just getting started, what a shame," she continued, landing another crunching blow to the side of his face. Loki crashed to the ground on his knees.

He looked a right state.

While Odin and Thor had been outside, the whore of Asgard had set to work. After Aegir and Tyr had untied Loki, Freyja's justice held court. In an unfettered and remorseless display of hatred, she had given the trickster a brutal and merciless beating.

Blood was pouring from one of Loki's eyebrows, and his nose was bleeding. His lips were swollen and split, and the rest of his body had been used as a punching bag. He was smothered in cuts and bruises from head to toe. A placid Queen of the Valkyries made for a formidable foe; but once enraged, the Queen of the Valkyries was an unstoppable force. In many ways, Loki was lucky for Odin's return. Another five minutes and Freyja would have surely killed him.

"Well, boys," Odin clapped his hands gleefully as he got straight down to the task at hand. "What's it to be?"

Vardi didn't hesitate.

Transforming into a large, snarling wolf, he leapt at his brother, and in a single, flailing bite; he ripped his throat out. Narvi died instantly. Weaving his head left and right and growling angrily, Vardi backed slowly toward the tunnel. He didn't trust Odin, and he eyed the other gods suspiciously.

Who would strike first?

No one raised their swords. Odin remained true to his word; his life would be spared.

Howling loudly, Vardi bounded down the tunnel and out into the snow. Thor watched as he hared away; leaping and crashing through the deep, powdery drifts.

"Come on, let's get this over with," Odin ordered, signalling for Tyr and Vali to seize Loki and lay him on the slabs. While they did this, Freyja held Sigyn back from the body of her dead son.

Withdrawing his sword, Aegir skilfully gutted Narvi's corpse, and Odin himself wound the intestines around their prisoner. Standing back, Odin taped Gungnir lightly on the ground as he chanted a strange and guttural incantation. This was an enchantment; and the still steaming tissues that bound Loki shrank and tightened as they turned swiftly to stone.

"There we go, Loki, how does that feel? Nice and comfy?" Odin quipped as he cleaned the blood from his hands. "But I'm sure I've forgotten something," he mused, looking quizzically around the cave. "Ah yes; a little party trick I picked up from your daughter. I really ought to thank her for it someday." Cackling coarsely, Odin whispered in the ear of one of the slaves. The man raced outside and came back soon after with a small, sealed, Hessian bag. He held it at arms length.

Whatever was inside the sack was clearly alive, because the bag wriggled and writhed alarmingly.

Chuckling loudly, Odin asked the slave to go back outside and bring Thor in. Bowing deeply, the slave turned and made off again. A few moments later, he reappeared with Thor close behind.

"Here, Thor, we're going to need your iron gloves for this part."
Odin pointed toward the bag.

Putting these on, Thor carefully untied the neck of the bag and
placed one hand inside. As he did so, he glanced briefly at the
remains of Narvi—and then wished he hadn't. Thrud's face flashed
once more in his head. He shivered; he could have saved the boy's
life, and that thought pained him. "Sweet Odin!" he bellowed loudly
as he pulled the bag's contents into view.

"Splendid!" Odin clapped gleefully and the remaining gods followed suite.

There, in Thor's hands and held securely by its tail; was an enraged
cobra, twisting and spitting. This struck repeatedly as Thor struggled
to keep the serpent's venom from his eyes.

"Isn't he a darling?" Odin mocked sarcastically as Thor set about
securing the creature to a stalactite hanging above Loki's head. "Now
let me see; I think that position is just about perfect." Stepping back,
Odin eyed his handiwork with some admiration.

Loki's punishment was complete. Bound securely to his bed, a
venomous snake had been placed above his head. This would drip
poison onto his face.

"Now, Loki," Odin chuckled as he beckoned for the slaves and
other gods to leave the chamber. "Unlike your vile daughter, I'm not a
god without mercy. For year after year after year you have slighted
me; pouring vitriol on my friends and family. I should take no pity on
you; and yet I do. Here, Sigyn; this is for you." Picking up a small,
wooden bowl he threw it at Loki's wife.

"This is your role in Loki's punishment," he continued glibly. "You
can catch the dripping poison if you like and spare your dashing husband's face; although personally, I wouldn't bother. He's an evil,
backstabbing, two-faced liar and cheat, but hey; what do I know?
You're his wife; so I'll let you decide."

"This isn't over Odin!" Loki yelled as the god made to leave.
"We'll meet again, and when we do, you will suffer, I swear, you'll
suffer."

Odin paused and turned. A wicked glint twinkled in his eye.
"Sticks and stones may break my bones but words will never harm
me," he chanted. "Goodbye Loki, and yes: yes, it is over."

To blood curdling taunts of abuse, Odin departed from the cave.
Stepping out from the end of the tunnel; he turned and tapped its
entrance lightly with the tip of Gungnir.

The ground shivered and shook.

With a thunderous roar; an avalanche of rocks, ice, and snow obliterated the entrance. Loki's tomb was sealed.

Picking up the reins to Sleipnir, Odin turned to Thor. He had one last question on his mind. "Which direction did Vardi head off in?" he enquired casually.

"That way," Thor gestured with his hand toward the trail in the snow. "He was heading in the direction of Muspellheim and the volcano."

"Excellent, son, that's excellent news." Odin ended with a smile. It was exactly what he had hoped for.

Rather than heading toward Jotunheim and Loki's fellow giants; Vardi was racing with his horrific news toward his stepsister Hel.

This was it: checkmate.

This was the beginning of the end.

31

Valkyries

Surprisingly, both Thirle and Marcus survived the assassination attempt; and in an extraordinarily perverse twist of fate, they ended up in the same hospital.

Thirle's bed was on the Intensive Care Unit. He was wheeled there following emergency surgery to remove the bullet from his bowels. Marcus's bed was on the observation unit. He was taken there hand-cuffed and unconscious. He had suffered severe facial wounds, concussion, and had a suspected hairline fracture to his skull.

He would survive, but he had been lucky.

In some ways, it was perhaps more of a miracle that Marcus survived the shooting than Thirle; his saving grace being the sheer size of the mob eager to lynch him. The mêlée to avenge his gunshots had been so great that there simply wasn't enough room to throw a lethal punch or kick. Dragged from the baying throng by embarrassed security guards, he had been bundled safely into police custody.

In a further twist of irony, both Marcus's and Thirle's hospital beds were equally heavily guarded. Thirle's guards were there to keep press, fans, and potential assassins out; while Marcus's guards were there to keep him in. Not that he was going anywhere. Drifting in and out of consciousness, he was barely aware of what he had done and the media storm that had been created. Safe in his secluded hospital bed, Marcus lay sleeping, lulled by the reassuring beep, beep, beep of a cardio monitor; oblivious to the furore encircling the globe.

Bizarrely, Anna's repercussions for his crime were far more brutal.

At 02:00 AM precisely, a well organised and heavily armed SWAT team hit their flat. The violent, explosive battering ram that smashed the locks from their front door was followed by searing canisters of tear gas and the blinding cracks of 'flash-bangs.' The assault squad scattered these like confetti as they raced through the apartment, hastily checking and securing each room in turn. Dragged half naked and screaming from her bed, Anna had been thrown face down to the floor before being bound and hooded. As she struggled and tried to protest her innocence—she was tazed.

The squad weren't taking any chances.

Trussed up like a turkey, she was taken by armoured van to the local police station—Marcus's station—for interrogation. Dazed and confused, her senses reeled as terrorist officers lambasted her with a blizzard of bewildering questions about the plot to kill Herr Flöda. Why, what, when, who, and how. It wasn't until her third hour of interrogation that the reason behind her arrest was explained to Anna; and it wasn't until the sixth hour of interrogation that the officers realised they were shooting blanks.

Anna knew nothing about her husband's crime.

Slowly, little by little, the fog of ignorance lifted, and by mid morning the shocking truth behind the shooting was naked and obvious for all to see. Far from being part of an organised and sophisticated plot, Marcus's actions were those of a loner; a spur-of-the-moment fame seeker. He had attacked Thirle in a fantasist, Chapmanesque, "I killed John Lennon" style shooting.

His presumed motive—immortality through infamy.

This seemed a particularly sad and sickening end for a New York cop and his pretty young wife.

The rigorous search of Marcus and Anna's flat produced no clues and seemed to support the conclusions from Anna's interrogation. Marcus had to be a wacko. With some reluctance, she was eventually released without charge a little after noon.

Before stepping outside into freedom and the warmth of a sunny June sky, Anna glanced briefly at the news headlines that were streaming across the television screens in the station. To her surprise, the shooting of Herr Flöda had already been eclipsed by another, even more extraordinary event. Details of 'a nuclear incident' in Florida screamed for her shocked attention. Two huge, disparate events, and yet to Anna's perverse sense of female logic; there could only be one possible conclusion.

Somehow, somewhere the Valkyries were involved.

There was not one shred of evidence, not one single shard of suspicion to link these cursed women to either event; yet in her heart Anna knew instinctively that they were. It was a feeling, an inkling; an unshakeable, intuitive certainty when you absolutely know that you have to be right.

As Anna walked slowly home, she mulled this feeling over in her mind.

Marcus had sworn he had cut his ties to the Contessa, the Dragza Corporation, and to Jess; so how could they have dragged him down and involved him in the shooting? More confusing still; why on earth would the Valkyries want to see Herr Flöda dead?

The man was a visionary and leader of a powerful youth movement; but nothing more. He was harmless. And what about the 'nuclear accident'; what on earth was that all about? How could the cursed cult have anything remotely to do with that?

Arriving at last at their flat, Anna had to admit that all she had was a string of random questions—and no answers. However, she knew that she was right. Valkyries were somehow buried in the mire, and somebody, somewhere, would be able join up the random dots of her suspicions.

They had to. Her husband's life depended on it.

Marcus was innocent of his crime, even though he had fired the gun. It was the evil Valkyrie bitches who had brainwashed him; they were the true culprits, the true hands that had pulled the trigger. They had to be brought to book. Find them and you had your answer.

The trouble was; where to start?

Where could Anna find *The Someone* who could link them to these atrocities?

Taking a deep breath in, and after brushing aside the police tape, Anna pushed open the shattered door to their flat. To her eyes, the nuclear accident must surely have occurred there.

The place had been ransacked beyond the point of no return.

Not one single book, cushion, plate, or piece of furniture had been left untouched. The scale of devastation was horrific, and Anna stood there; rooted to the spot. Mouth wide open and hands pressed firmly against her cheeks, slowly turning her head left and right, she drank in the aftermath of the conflagration. Tears welled in her eyes, and these began to trickle slowly down her cheeks. This was it, the end of her cosy dream; the fantasy of a long and happy marriage—screwed.

Marcus was behind bars, and their home had been reduced to tatters. The whole affair was beyond comprehension.

Their lives had been destroyed in a single night of madness.

Anna wept.

RING-RING, RING-RING

This was ridiculous, a sound that bordered on farcical.

The muffled tone of Marcus's mobile phone was echoing from somewhere in the flat. He must have forgotten to take it with him last night, and the 'eagle-eyed' SWAT team had missed it as they blitzed the place. Anna followed the noise frantically; it was coming from the bathroom. Entering this on the run, she raced to a pile of dirty clothes upturned from their laundry basket.

RING-RING, RING-RING

Don't hang up! Anna begged silently, fumbling her way through the discarded and crumpled garments. To her great relief, it was there, Marcus's phone; still stuffed in the bottom of a trouser pocket.

The idiot!

Trembling as she grabbed hold of it, Anna pressed the answer button and held it tightly against her ear.

"Hello, is that Marcus?" a woman's voice enquired. Anna didn't recognise her, but the accent was Eastern European. The woman sounded scared. "It's me, Lia. Remember? I'm one of the Contessa's hostesses at the island."

Anna kept quiet. She didn't want to speak in case the frightened girl hung up. To her relief, the hostess Lia didn't. She continued to talk.

"I'm scared Marcus, really scared. They're all dead," her child-like voice trembled. "All the angels—Christina, Olga, Vika—they're all dead, every one. They're killing all of them, and they won't stop there. They'll be coming after me next, and then they'll be coming after you, too. You've got to help me, please, Marcus; I beg of you. Please, please save me."

Anna remained silent, although a tiny smile had began to curl around her lips. Her instincts were right; her sixth sense had been vindicated.

Those fucking Valkyries were involved, and better still, she'd just found *The Someone* who might help her join up the dots.

If she could save Lia—Lia would save Marcus.

32

Angels and Demons

Such was Hel's horror at Vardi's tale; the echoes of her screams were felt throughout Asgard.

The volcano around the gateway to Niflheim blasted smoke and cinders into the twilit sky while the ground beneath it heaved and shook with a terrible force. Fresh cracks appeared around its jagged edges and streams of molten lava poured freely down its slopes. Sizzling and crackling violently, these flowed inexorably through the drifting piles of snow who screamed belligerently as they vaporised into hissing clouds of scalding steam.

Fire and ice were locked once more in a deadly combat.

The stage was set.

This was the terrifyingly beautiful scene that lit the skies the eve before Ragnarok.

Odin, Freyja, and the rest of gods returned from the cave shortly after Hel received her news. The shaking of the ground and plumes of smoke confirmed what Odin already knew. The final battle of Ragnarok had begun, and it was no coincidence that its climax would be tomorrow—the twenty-first day of December.

This was the winter solstice; the shortest and coldest day of the year.

Aegir didn't dally long in Asgard. He said his brief goodbyes and set off swiftly toward the coast. Along with Njord, he had much work to do in defending Noatun from the threat of invasion. Naglfar, the ship of the dead, was destined to break free from its moorings in the final war to end all wars. This terrifying vessel held the bodies of countless giants and undead Berserkers; and was believed to have been built from the nails of corpses.

It would be the greatest longboat ever to set sail on Middle Sea.

Vali didn't return from the cave. He had flown straight to the watchtower to alert Heimdall. From there, he travelled on to Valhalla. The heroes would be made ready, as would the rest of the gods.

This thought comforted the warriors as they sat soberly at the feasting tables that evening. Their numbers were few and the Aesir soldiers were still weak from their battle with Hel's Berserkers. Like it or not, the best hope for Asgard's salvation lay with the monstrous, metal machines of Odin's heroes.

As the warriors dined, they could hear the distant ringing of Gjall. Heimdall was already on his way from the watchtower, and his horn beckoned the Aesir to take up arms once more.

During the discussions over the feasting, the warriors agreed to allow both Ben and Elijah to join them in the battle. Ben was back to full health, and Ruby was confident that Elijah would stand firm against his former queen. His flare for tactics might prove invaluable against the unknown host that Hel had promised to unleash. This threat, the pledge of nameless monsters, dampened the spirits of all those present at the tables. Rumours of Demon Angels and the power of the Guardians swept around the hall like a tornado. Whatever the truth might be, one question was uppermost in everybody's mind.

Could Odin's heroes defeat her monstrous army of evil?

Picking rather than eating heartily, the warriors left the feasting hall in twos and threes. Conversations were hushed and brief as the women came to terms with their destinies. Tonight would be the last night before Ragnarok, and beyond its dawn—their futures were blank. Its outcome was unknown.

Hod spent his last night alone in his bed. Kat had chosen to spend her time with Jess, and he knew the futility of begging her to do otherwise. He knew his place, and secretly, he was grateful for her decision. Freyr had joined the small gathering of gods at the castle. He would be taking part in the battle tomorrow, and Hod was delighted that Kat hadn't chosen to spend the night with him. She could have, and would have; had carnal pleasure been uppermost in her mind.

Freyr was the god Kat hungered for when the bloodlust held her in its grip, and she had made that known on many an occasion. To have Kat's friendship—and any crumbs of love—he had to endure this torment. It wounded him deeply, but in his heart he knew that he was winning the battle for her affection. He had come this far, and he wasn't for turning.

Kat was the love of his life, even if all life ended tomorrow on the battlefields of Vigrid.

Fortunately for Hod, anxiety, and not lust, was the emotion of the hour; with each warrior and god making their individual preparations to confront their destinies. He too felt this fear, but it wasn't for himself. He would stand shoulder to shoulder with the Valkyries and play his part in the conflict. His prowess as an archer would be in demand, and he would fight beside Balder and Tyr in the thick of the fray. Hod was confident in his skills and sure of success; but his heart still twitched with fear. He hadn't heard from his mother since the celebrations in Aegir's hall; and her silence troubled him.

It was unusual for Frigg not to wish him well or to get Fulla, Gna, or Lin to check up on him. These women, her ladies in waiting; they too, had been conspicuous by their absence. Of course they could all be in Midgard together on some ridiculous shopping spree; but surely even his mother wouldn't be so callous at this hour? This was Ragnarok; and Hod knew that if she were able, she would have joined the gods assembling in Valhalla.

Something was wrong; he could feel it in his bones.

Where was Frigg?

As Hod mused away the hours; Kat stood beside Jess and gazed out through her window. The sombre feast had finished a long time ago, and tunics and armour had already been polished. Swords, too, had been sharpened and oiled until their edges shone. Preparations complete, all that remained was the tedium of waiting; whiling away the long hours of darkness with futile attempts at sleep. This was a thankless task. None of the Valkyries were tired, and they flitted like nervous butterflies from room to room; gossiping and discussing Mimir's prophesies for the morrow.

So much was known—and yet so much remained unknown.

Kat and Jess had given up on this rumour mill some time ago. They stood now silent and contented; side by side; arm in arm; gazing intently at the scene before them.

It was a clear, moonlit night, and an eerie, red glow flickered and danced from the volcanic skyline away to the east. Jagged rivers of lava poured from the volcano's mouth and occasional tremors still rippled angrily across the land. No torch-lit army had descended from the volcano's rim, and this confirmed the warriors' darkest nightmare. The final battle of Ragnarok wouldn't pitch man against man or the dead against the living.

Tomorrow's fight would be man against evil; the living against the supernatural; the darkest and most cursed souls in all of Niflheim.

As the girls watched, sporadic bursts of orange and yellow flames flickered amongst the fields and woods. The dragons had taken to the skies again as they had done every night since their awakening. They were busy snatching sheep and cattle, torching barns and cottages, and spreading misery and suffering throughout the realm. Few people had been killed, but the nightly fear of death was a heavy burden to bear. Nerves were frayed beyond breaking point, and many Aesir now secretly welcomed Ragnarok; the end of days. At least this would bring an end to their nightly torment—even though it might spell an end to life itself.

The townsfolk and villagers were beyond caring.

Death now seemed preferable to famine, fear, and frostbite.

Odin, too, gazed out across the land.

He was standing in his citadel and taking stock one last time. Despite the growing chaos all around, it was still the most beautiful world he had ever laid his eye upon. It would definitely break his heart to go.

Turning around, he made his way from the window toward the middle of the chamber. The room was bare, save for a few chairs and a depleted cluster of telescopes. He had removed almost all his belongings, although he had made one significant addition to the room. This was what he was standing over now; this was where he would bid his last farewell.

Pulling a short, stubby instrument from his pocket, he pressed its two, sharp prongs into the large, coarse, hessian sack and pulled the trigger. A violent blue bolt of lightening flickered between its teeth, and the lumpy mass trapped inside the sack convulsed and moaned briefly—before lying still once more.

Odin had tazed its contents, just to be sure. He could never be too safe.

Carefully he untied the thick rope knot that bound the neck of the sack firmly shut. "Hello, my dear," he sneered, peering inside. "Comfortable?" he enquired as he kicked a response from the body still twitching in its depths.

This groaned once more.

"Look, I'm spoiling you," he teased as he tossed a flask of water and several of Idun's apples into the sack. "Can't have you starving to death, can we? I wouldn't want you miss all the fun; that wouldn't be fair now, would it?"

The body didn't reply.

"Oh well, be ungrateful, don't say thank you; just see if I care. Anyway, it's time to say goodbye, my sweetness," he chortled, pressing his fingers to his lips as he blew a kiss into the bag. "Have fun while it lasts; wifey dearest," he muttered as a final retort before sealing the neck of the sack tightly shut.

Odin sighed as he took one last, longing look around his citadel.

Yes; he would definitely miss this place.

Much later on the same evening, Carmel slunk into Thor's forge and tiptoed quietly up behind him. She ran her arms around his waist and squeezed him tightly.

She was glad he was still awake.

"I've missed you so much," she whispered in his ear, and to her surprise, he turned around and kissed her tenderly on the forehead. His face looked drawn and long; and even in the dim, yellow furnace light she could tell that he was troubled. His forehead was deeply furrowed.

This had been her excuse for coming; her excuse for breaking the brittle wall of silence that had stood between them since Loki's outburst. Thor needed cheering up, and that was what she intended to do. She needed to show their passion remained and expel the demons of Ragnarok from his mind.

To Carmel's great relief, Thor didn't resist her advances, and he wrapped his mighty arms around her, holding her tightly. The warmth of his body thrilled her, and she wriggled up snugly as she sought out the most comfortable spot. Like Kat and Jess, neither of them spoke. It was sufficient to be close again.

After a long while, Thor broke their silence.

"I've missed you," he began, kissing the top of her head once more. "And I'm sorry I've been so distant and standoffish. Sif can be so vengeful sometimes."

"Shush," Carmel whispered, pressing a finger tightly to his lips. There was no need for words, she understood. "You're here with me now; that's all that matters," she cooed.

They cuddled silently for some minutes longer until Thor broke their silence again. "I feel so ashamed," he began, glumly and awkwardly.

"Why, what have you done?"

"It was Loki; what we did; it was wrong, so terribly wrong."

Thor turned away, he couldn't face her.

"No, it wasn't," Carmel retorted defensively. "What you did was right. Loki deserved his punishment. What he did to all of us was beyond evil. He had it coming, and you mustn't blame yourself." Carmel pulled him close once more.

What was the silly god on about?

Thor tried to return her cuddle, but couldn't. The image of Narvi's corpse blazed across his mind. "I could have stopped them, but I didn't. There's no excuse; I'm more to blame than they are," he muttered angrily to himself.

"I can punish you, if that would help," Carmel quipped jokingly. She wished he would snap out of whatever was on her mind.

"If I don't perish tomorrow, then that would be in order, my lady," Thor murmured apologetically, hanging his head. He felt wretched inside.

He was a god, a warrior, a giant killer. He lived to protect the lives of women and children—not to take them. This crime tortured his soul as he faced his last night alive. His death was assured at Ragnarok; it had been one of Mimir's first prophesies; a necessity to purge the realm of evil.

"Don't be so silly," Carmel retorted, slapping his arm playfully. "I was only jesting." Thor's misery was now beginning to trouble her, too. "You will survive the battlefield, of that I swear. Odin's heroes will defeat any evil Hel might throw at us, and besides, I'll be by your side. I won't let you out of my sight, I promise."

Thor looked up, shrugged, and then smiled a weak but loving smile. His eyes twinkled warmly. Carmel was a wonderful woman, a true Valkyrie. He was so proud to be with her in his hour of need.

"Thank you," he whispered softly pulling her close. "I needed to hear that."

"Good," Carmel giggled as she removed his arms and walked over to the door. Reaching it, she closed it tightly and then turned the lock. "Now," she smiled slyly, pushing its key deep into the cleavage of her bosom. "Are we really going to waste the eve before Ragnarok indulging in idle chitchat and self pity?"

Running back to Thor, she grabbed his hand and dragged him giggling down into the hay.

The realm may be teetering on the very brink of oblivion, but for now, that was Odin's problem.

Tonight, Carmel was determined to have some fun.

Odin's heroes would save the day, they had to.

After all, wasn't that what they'd been training for?

Hel's screams weren't because she loved her stepbrothers. In truth; she didn't even really like them. Her screams were for the anguish of her father, the pain he must have suffered as he watched his son die. This thought haunted her soul and scorched a rage more blinding than any she had ever known.

Odin had been right. This last, horrific act was too deep a blow.

She couldn't hold back.

He would have his wish; she would unleash the Guardians and lay waste to Asgard, just as he desired. If she had to inherit a blackened, smoking, cinder of a realm, one that was filled with the ghosts of the tormented dead; then so be it. It would be his doing and not hers.

Victory belonged to her—that was her destiny.

Saying a tearful goodbye to Henry, Hel locked him inside her chambers. A guard was posted at the door; for his safety. The guard wasn't to keep him in; it was to keep her out. She didn't want him to see what she would become, the terrible monster unleashed from inside her soul.

Changing into her garish scarlet, figure-hugging, leather catsuit; Hel painted her lips and nails vermilion before applying henna to her hair. She let this dry wild and loose.

Powdering her face and arms to a ghostly white pallor, she blackened her eyes with a thick layer of kohl. This would be her victory salute, the deathly mask that would triumph over life. With eyes blazing like blood red rubies from deep within their darkened sockets; Hel's gaze would burn with hatred and rage.

She was ready to wage war.

Sending slaves on ahead to round up horses, Hel's first stop was at her kennels and her beloved hounds. Throwing its doors wide open, she rallied her babies. Barking and yelping loudly, the ecstatic dogs leapt over one another in their haste to be the first to reach the Berserker Hall. The hounds of Hel would lead the advance on Odin's forces; a ferocious wall of muscle, fur, and slashing teeth.

Hel's second call was to the VIP chambers. Eternal damnation had just been cancelled—eternally.

Tearing up the roster of punishments, she summoned her Fallen Angels and commanded them to assemble in the Berserker Hall. Their terrible might would be the back bone of her assault.

Stops completed, Hel continued on her march and soon arrived in the Berserker Hall. To a mixture of delight and sorrow, she could see that her servants were already sitting astride their mounts. Four horses had been brought from the slopes of the volcano; two black and two gray in colour. These pranced and twitched nervously as the Guardians sat impatient to be off.

Their time was almost upon them, and they were lacking only one thing; the queen of Niflheim's command to set them free. The four servants nodded expectantly toward Hel as they began to chant in a dark and guttural tongue. These incantations grew in pace and volume as they trotted round and round. Their time was nigh and lengthening tongues of white and blue sparks flickered eagerly from their fingertips as their horses trotted nose to tail, nose to tail, in an ever-tightening circle.

The horsemen were impatient for their freedom.

Hel acknowledged their agitation before marching over to her Angels. They were already lined up, standing in neat rows and numbering some one hundred in all. Hel had one last duty to perform, and she was grateful that Modgul had made the necessary arrangements.

Standing on a rough-hewn block of black marble was a large, jewel-encrusted chalice made from purest gold. This sparkled in the candlelight with all the colours of the rainbow.

Picking the chalice up, Hel stared down briefly at the thick, black liquid inside. It was crushed poppy concentrate—bitter and deadly in its potency.

This was the moment of no return. Once drunk, there could be no going back. The die would be cast for all eternity.

Her Angels were ready.

One by one, each of her privileged guards stepped forward and knelt at her feet. Placing a hand on their foreheads, she blessed them in turn as they sipped the bitter liquid. Rising once more, Hel embraced her Angels. These were her elite, the chosen few; the Angels who had served her faithfully in life and in death.

This was the moment of their reward, the moment of their triumph.

Standing back, Hel raised her arms and began to chant an ancient spell. Her words sounded coarse and ugly; her voice crackling in the same foul tongue as that of the Guardians.

Before her eyes, her faithful followers made their final sacrifice to their Queen.

The Angels were no more.

Demons would now lay waste to the battlefield of Ragnarok.

33

Woods—Redux

gent Woods awoke from a light sedative with a splitting headache and a sensation of numbness at the base of his spine. Squinting painfully in the harsh, artificial light, he tried to get his bearings. He didn't recognise where he was, but that shouldn't really have come as any surprise. He was underground; hidden within the catacomb that lay buried deep beneath the surface of Crescent Cay.

With senses slowly coming into focus, Woods tested the strength of his restraints. To his intense disappointment, they didn't budge. He was secured to some sort of sophisticated dental chair in a manner that would have made Houdini weep. There could be no way out of his new prison.

"Hey!"

Woods tried to call out but the best his parched throat could manage was a coarse whisper. A week or so on the run had taken its toll.

He felt as weak as a kitten and in many ways relieved to finally come in from the cold. His life had been going nowhere; an existence left on hold as he ducked and dived and dodged and weaved his way around the island's security systems. It had been a hellish nonexistence, and he was glad that it was over. So long as they didn't kill him, then at least he would suffer a better deal than the one that bitch Christina had offered him.

Briefly, Woods turned his mind back to that fateful day.

As soon as Christina had turned the speedboat about and cranked up the motors, he had instinctively guessed what was on her mind. If women laid claim to the sixth sense, then men must have the seventh—self-preservation.

Waiting until the very last possible moment, the instant when he disappeared from his killer's view; Woods turned his body sideways and took the full force of the boat's impact on his right shoulder. This had also been slashed by the swirling propeller—hence the ominous slick of bright red blood.

Submerged, dazed, and wounded, Woods blessed his parents for forcing him to become a strong swimmer. Remembering that the steering wheel was on the right-hand side of the boat, he dived deep and followed the boat's movements from three metres down—rising to the surface only when it came around and was passing slowly overhead. Grabbing hold of the port gunnel, he hung on grimly as Christina circled the location of his 'accident.'

Had she bothered to swap sides of the boat, his cover would have been blown, and he would now be feeding the fish. As it was, she stuck religiously to peering over the right gunnel—and his life had been saved. Eventually, sensing his hostess throttling up the engines and preparing to leave, he released his hold and dived to the bottom once more.

Free from Christina's murderous glare, Woods half swam, half floated toward the distant shore. Bleeding heavily, he had made the sanctuary of the shallow coral reef moments before the larger sharks had tracked his scent. Negotiating this prickly obstacle course more by good luck than judgement, he had headed toward the rocky southern extremity of the Isle.

There he'd struck gold; a sheltered cove concealed from both sea and shore.

This had been his home for the last two miserable weeks; living a life that teetered daily on the verge of discovery. Hiding by day and foraging by night; he had subsisted on a diet of golden apples and sprinkler water. Surprisingly, the apples had rejuvenated him in an unexpected but welcomed manner. His arm had healed quickly without infection, and his desperate craving for the mead had all but disappeared. Perhaps he had been wrong; perhaps the apples were the elixir of youth—not the mead. This was an interesting question and one he mulled over often as he struggled to find a way off the Isle.

With a secure, rocky hideaway; stealthy, nocturnal habits, and a Spartan diet; he could have survived on the run almost indefinitely. However, it wasn't a life. Whichever way he looked at it, he was still a captive.

Growing increasingly frustrated, bored, and careless; he had begun to venture out by day; making notes of guard patrols and spying on the Contessa. This had been his undoing and what had led to his eventual capture.

"Hello, Agent Woods, does your head hurt?" Vili enquired sympathetically.

The arrival of the two brothers caught Woods by surprise, and frustratingly, he couldn't see them. The door they had come through was behind his head, and this was immobilised in some sort of a tight-fitting helmet. Woods tried to mumble "yes," but neither brother heard him.

"I'm so sorry if it does," Vili continued. "Your headache is really our fault. I'm afraid we took a little too much of this out of your body."

Moving into view, Ve held up a large syringe filled with a straw-coloured fluid. It had obviously had come from somewhere inside him, but he couldn't tell where. He needn't have worried; the boys were eager to enlighten him.

"Your brain," Vili announced proudly, "floats in this stuff."

"Yeh," Ve added. "And we took it from down here," he continued, pointing to the base of Woods' spine.

"Hey, boys, I though you two were special agents. I didn't know you were doctors." Woods chuckled, trying unsuccessfully to crack a joke. His parched throat had killed its intended, barbed sarcasm.

"Oh, no, we're not doctors," Vili replied earnestly, taking his quip seriously.

"We're scientists," said Ve, lifting up a can of air freshener and spraying its contents liberally in the air. The fragrance was pungent, but not unpleasant. Ve was glad he had remembered to do this. It was important; an insurance policy—if he remembered Odin's words rightly—just in case.

"Yes, we're scientists and very good ones, too," Vili agreed smugly. "That's why we're going to replace that fluid around your brain with some of our own. Would you like to take a look?" he enquired enthusiastically.

Woods didn't reply; the question was rhetorical.

Beaming broadly, Vili held up a glass vial and gave it a little shake. The grey, oily goop shimmered as though it was filled with glitter. God only knew what the stuff was; but it looked disgusting.

Woods took a deep breath in. This was going to be unpleasant and would definitely hurt.

"Here we go, say cheese!" Upending the vial, Ve sucked its contents into a syringe and, after connecting this to a slender, plastic catheter; he injected the substance.

Woods closed his eyes. This was it; death by lethal injection.

Concentrating on his senses, Woods first felt a coldness at the base of his spine and then a tingling sensation. This travelled down his legs to his feet before ricocheting back up again. The liquid must have entered his spinal column, like an epidural anaesthetic.

Spreading swiftly, the wave of tingling coldness swept up his body to his neck—before disappearing; as did his headache. At first this seemed to be good news, until an icy chill enveloped his head and a pressure, like an iron vice, pulsed inside his skull.

Countless nerves jangled, and muscles twitched as a zillion, tiny nanobots bored rapidly through the thick, protective, fibrous sheet (the Dura Mater) that covered his brain. These tiny, miniature robots then hacked deep into the nerves beneath.

His mind was on fire.

These tiny, microscopic machines were the sparkling glitter he'd seen in the goop. Their role was simple—to make connections with his nerves and then with each other.

Their purpose was as unambiguous as it was ominous.

The nanobots were linking up to create a communications network that covered the outside of his brain. This would form a permanent, silvery mesh no thicker than a spider's web; tuned to Odin's specification; tuned to Odin's control.

As the tingling, twitching, and sensation of pressure began to ease, the brothers flicked a switch. The helmet around Woods head had been activated, and a myriad images, sounds, flavours, smells, and movements besieged his brain.

It was sensory overload.

Woods blacked out; fitting spasmodically as he tumbled into unconsciousness.

Firing precise electromagnetic impulses at the speed of light, the helmet's sensors swiftly identified the functions of each and every nerve in his brain. Having determined these, it set about its primary task; forging and reinforcing a synthetic network that imposed Odin's will on top of his own.

When Woods eventually awoke and asked blearily where he was, the brothers proudly told him his precise location without fear or compromise. Woods was no longer a threat. He could roam the island just like any other guest.

Glancing down at his wrists, Woods noted the small, 'v'-shaped tattoo on the inside of his right arm. He had been marked; and was now part of Odin's fold. In Marcus speak, he was a "have"; one of the privileged few who could eat a golden apple each day. This was his reward, access to their eternal secret.

It was a cherished prize, but one that came at a terrible cost.

Over the next few days, to all intents and purpose, Woods felt normal. Actually, he felt better than normal. His senses were heightened as the silvery halo set to work; hyping communications inside his head. The process was painless; the surface of the brain having no pain receptors.

At first, there seemed no downside to these super senses; until Woods tried to delve a little deeper. This was where the blackness began; this was where his ownership of his mind now ended—and Odin's began.

Some memories were blocked while others had been altered. His thoughts were changed in a way he wasn't allowed to understand. His head was in a straitjacket; imprisoned and beyond his control. Woods no longer had 'access all areas' to his mind.

He could only think the thoughts that Odin's silvery network allowed him to; and nothing more. He was blinkered; able to focus with crystal clarity on the road ahead—but banned from looking left or right.

Woods should have been terrified by this discovery—but he wasn't.

Access denied.

The silver halo wouldn't permit such fear. Woods controlled his body, but Odin controlled his mind. The agent had been processed, just like all of Valhalla's heroes.

This was the terrible truth behind the Einherjar; the nightmare imposed by their god of gods.

Odin had control—complete and utter—over each and every soul in his army.

34

Thy Kingdom Come

The inhabitants of the castle were up many hours before dawn on the day of Ragnarok. With heaviness in their hearts; tunics and armour were carefully fastened, swords checked and then rechecked for sharpness; and breakfasts eaten in a tense and gloomy atmosphere. Odin was there to greet the warriors, but he did little to raise their spirits.

"Do your best; honour Asgard," wasn't exactly the finest speech for their darkest hour.

Words, however, mattered little.

Stepping outside into the winter's bitter chill, horses were mounted, and after lining up behind Odin; the party left the castle—quite possibly for the last time. As each Valkyrie passed through the open gates, no one could resist the temptation of looking back and bidding a silent farewell to their happy home. It felt as though they were riding to their doom; not a battlefield that would be steeped in glory.

Setting out across the fields, stars twinkled brightly, and the air felt crisp and whisper still. Moving quietly and in single file, the procession of gods and Valkyries wound their way around and between the deepest snowdrifts in a delicate, torchlit ribbon. The warriors were mostly silent; lost in their thoughts.

Minds wandered between visions of the day ahead and memories of days gone by.

In the distance, an owl hooted and, other than his lonely cry, the night remained silent, save for the muffled, steady footfalls of their horses. Occasionally, one of their mounts would rear and offer a frisky snort or an impatient whinny. Prancing and bucking irritably; the bitter chill and the excitement of war urged their powerful steeds to break into a canter. The girls welcomed this distraction. Controlling their troubled horses helped while away the hours and stole their attention from what lay ahead.

As the sands of time ran out, the burning slopes of Muspellheim grew ever nearer.

Ahead, the volcano continued to erupt; the ground quivering in nervous spasms as explosive blasts of soot, cinders, and incandescent lava lit up the sky. Ragnarok seemed already lost—the fires of Niflheim having overwhelmed the land while they were sleeping.

The sight of this blazing nightmare scorched their souls.

Could this burning, lifeless horror really be Asgard's fate?

Odin rode on Sleipnir at the head of their column, and behind him came Freyja, riding on Gold Mane. Behind her came Balder, Tyr, and the rest of the gods. The Valkyrie warriors rode next and were followed by their maids. Behind all of these, and trailing by some distance; was Thor. He disliked riding, and the snow was too deep for his beloved goats. Trudging along on foot, Carmel rode patiently by his side. Just as she had promised, she wasn't going to leave him, not even for an instant.

From time to time, when the trail permitted, Silk would trot forward to be beside Balder. Kat would do the same with Jess. During these brief periods, whispered exchanges took place and cold hands sought warm embraces. The need for silent contemplation ran neck and neck with the desire for love. The icy, leaden air matched the frosted, stillness of the Valkyries' hearts.

The battlefield for Ragnarok—the plain of Vigrid—was a place no one hankered to stand upon.

Dawn eventually broke, and a leisurely sun eased its way into a crisp, ice blue sky. Shafts of golden sunlight yawned and stretched lazily before spreading slowly across the frozen realm; embracing each and every glistening snowdrift with a glittering, golden kiss.

Ragnarok looked set to be a beautiful day.

By mid morning, the party had arrived at the plain of Vigrid. The volcano now filled the horizon in front of them; its summit barely half an hour's walk from where they were standing. On either side of the warriors, strangling lines of loyal Aesir soldiers came to a stuttering halt.

They made for a sorry sight.

Fewer than a thousand men had come to the battlefront, and these were mere shadows of the force that had once stood its ground against the Berserkers. Never before had the need for Odin's heroes been so great; and all eyes turned to him in hopeful expectation. His heroes would come, they had his word; but only after Hel's mighty host had taken to the battlefield.

Looking furtively around them, for now at least; the slopes of the shattered cone stood bleak and empty. Hissing flows of lava slurped and belched as they flowed noisily down its slopes, but as for the war—cries of demonic soldiers and ghoulish monsters—there were none. The deathly black portal from which these beasts would pour was hidden behind a broken shoulder of rock. This craggy outcrop was clearly visible, lying high above them.

For now at least, the Valkyries held the battlefield.

Heimdall, who had arrived moments before, raised Gjall to his lips and let out a piercing blast. Fanning out, the gods, Valkyries, and Aesir took up their positions.

Odin, Freyja, Balder, and Thor would hold the left flank while Heimdall, Tyr, Freyr, and Hod would hold the right. The Valkyries and their maids would mingle with the Aesir soldiers and hold the centre of the field. Ben and Elijah would join them there. Elijah was already busying himself; issuing orders and arranging the men in a defensive formation.

Odin smiled weakly. Should his force prevail, Elijah would make a great commander of this army.

AARGH! AARGH! AARGH!

First one scream, then another and another erupted from the soldiers as terror swept through their ranks. Fear turned quickly to panic, each man shielding his eyes as they looked toward the sun.

Following their gaze, the warriors raised their hands and squinted hard. Confronted by such an improbable spectre, it was almost impossible for the girls not to join them in their screams.

Their sun was dying.

Minute by minute, just as the prophesies had foretold; a dark shadow was eating its face. Passing beyond the halfway mark, the light around them began to fade. The soldiers cowered, and some made ready to run. This was too much; the end was nigh. They needed to be with their families.

Spurring her horse into a canter, Kat decided to take charge. She had to do something; she had to steady the soldiers' nerves.

"Calm down, it's all right!" She yelled frantically, galloping up and down before their lines as she waved an arm in the air. "It's an eclipse, that's all. It will pass, the sun won't die, I promise you. Stand firm, this darkness means nothing; it won't harm you."

Calling out to each warrior and maid in turn, she begged them to spread the word. They did so; and offered toddies of mulled wine and warm mead to sooth the soldiers' shattered nerves. Gradually, their shouts and screams subsided to be replaced by a low and disgruntled rumbling. The men would hold firm for now, but they were far from convinced. None had ever seen an eclipse before, and for all they knew, the sun was truly gone forever.

With a final, brilliant flash of light, the tiny sliver of sun collapsed into a diamond ring before vanishing completely. It now lay hidden behind Asgard's moon. The eclipse had reached totality; and the realm was plunged into a sudden and eerie twilit gloom.

The battle of Ragnarok had begun.

With a violent fluttering of leathery wings, a mighty host of dragons spewed from the volcano and headed high into the skies above them. Banking smoothly, the massive creatures began to glide slowly round and round; swooping lower with every turn.

KABOOM!

The ground shook so violently that the soldiers fell to the ground, and the knees of horses buckled; throwing their riders. A massive earthquake had struck the realm and the Isle of Lyngvi—the Isle where Fenrir had once been bound—disappeared into Middle Sea. Such was the force of this collapse; a giant tidal wave erupted; one stirred from the very deepest of the ocean's depths. Turning swiftly into a massive Tsunami, this deadly swell hurtled toward the shores of Noatun; smothering it in a foaming wall of death. There would be no survivors, save for the occupants of Naglfar, the ship of the dead. Its undead warriors and beasts rode high and victorious on the crest of this monstrous wave.

Hel's invasion was underway.

Soundly shaken by the earthquake's force, the fragile slopes of the volcano split, and furious bursts of lava erupted around its rim. Through billowing clouds of choking smoke, a solitary figure came into view, her silhouette etched against the faded skyline.

Illuminated by red-hot pools of lava seething all around her, Hel looked magnificent; the incandescent, living, beating, heart of evil. Clothed entirely in red, she sat astride a stallion soaked in blood.

Hel smouldered like a newborn star.

Slowly, step by step, her mount descended the slope. As the horse did so, a ferocious clamouring broke out behind her. Barking, baying, and whining; Hel's hounds emerged, straining wildly at their leashes. Each brace of dogs was restrained by a monster, an evil that had never set foot in Asgard before.

Hel's Demon Angels had taken to the battlefield.

Half human, half snake, these terrifying creatures slithered and writhed as they slipped down the slopes behind their Queen.

Howling with jubilation, Fenrir was the next to emerge, accompanied by a pack of hungry-eyed wolves. Somewhere in their number was Vardi, Loki's son. He too thirsted for revenge. Zig-zagging wildly, the beasts cascaded down the hillside to surround their Queen as she arrived upon the battlefield.

Hel raised a horn and blew three, short, sharp blasts. The dogs and wolves fell silent. The final, terrible act of her master plan was about to take the field.

Emerging silently as four ghostly shadows, Hel's servants, the Guardians of Niflheim, rode slowly into view.

Clad in black with hoods raised high around their heads and hands folded in their laps, their faces were hidden from view. Descending a mere fifty metres from the summit, they came to an unexpectedly and abrupt halt. Sitting upon their mounts as still as statues and silent as the grave; their horses forming a small semi-circle with heads radiating out toward Asgard.

Their riders sat sullen and impassive, an arm span apart.

Hel continued to trot forward. Reaching the battlefield, she continued onward until drawing to a halt before Odin. She was barely thirty metres from him and well within the range of a skilled archer.

Odin raised his hand.

He didn't want her killed; at least not just yet.

"Is this the best you can muster to fight me?" he mocked as he urged Sleipnir a few paces forward. "A gross of mange infested dogs, a pack of cowardly wolves, and a few dozen brain dead demons. Pah! Hel; you waste my time." Thumping Gungnir on the ground, a yellow light glowed brightly over the Great Sea.

"You see that?" he continued smugly. "That's my heroes. They're coming, but I don't know why. The children of Asgard could defeat your insult for an army."

Hearing his slur, the Aesir soldiers tried to raise a cheer; but it sounded limp and half hearted, and so much less assured than Odin's confident words.

Hel looked up but didn't smile; her eyes blazing like embers from their darkened sockets. "You forget one small detail, great God of Gods and King of Kings. Have you not seen my Guardians?"

"What, all four of them? Where are their friends?" Odin snorted contemptuously. "You've tasted the power of my heroes; they will destroy your army in an instant. Go back to Hel, Hel. Go home whilst you and your demonic friends still have legs to carry you."

"Odin, your display of arrogance and ignorance does you no favours," Hel continued quietly and confidently. "Your heroes and their cowardly machines may slay flesh and blood, but can they kill shadows, too? Answer me that. Can they really stop the Guardians, the Ghosts of Niflheim?" Raising the chalice she was holding in her right hand, Hel pressed it to her lips. "This is your last chance Odin. Surrender now or feel my wrath."

Odin said nothing. He stared resolutely ahead, his helmet laced with Aegir's gold shimmering in the grey half light of the eclipse.

It was a stalemate and one that seemed to stretch for all eternity.

It was Hel who finally broke the silence.

"Very well, if you will not surrender, then so be it. Your will, will be done. Asgard will be destroyed."

Tilting the golden chalice, she took a small sip of the liquid and then stared at Odin for the last time. Raising her arms high above her head, she closed her eyes and let the vessel slip slowly through her fingers. It clattered noisily to the ground.

This was the sign; the deed was done.

There could be no turning back now.

"Kill everything," she whispered mournfully. The kingdom she would inherit would be one of never-ending darkness.

A disturbance on the slopes above them suddenly distracted the gathering. The gods, Valkyries, and Aesir soldiers looked up expectantly.

The Guardians had dismounted and were now standing side by side; their arms outstretched with sleeves rolled up. Fingertip touched fingertip as sparks of blue and white lightening flickered from hand to hand.

Behind them, their horses fell to the ground like stones. They died instantly; their proud bodies turning immediately into parched, stretched and splitting skin. These crumbled before giving way to bleached, ivory skeletons that crackled as they fell apart and dissolved into dust.

The guardians had begun their conquest, and they glided motion-lessly down the slopes of Muspellheim; leaving no footprints in the snow.

This was it; their dance of death. Behind them, the seething lava hissed violently before fading to a silent, stony grey. Straggling plants withered, died, and then crumbled to ash. Even the snow faded to black.

Colour, life, heat; the Guardians consumed everything.

"Oh, sweet Odin!" Kat breathed in terror. At last she understood Hel's servants, at last she knew what Henry had tried to say to her—his warning screaming inside her head.

FOUR!

The clue to their secret identity was four.

The deathly silhouettes advancing toward them weren't Hel's servants; nor were they Guardians. These names were as meaningless as all the other terms used down the ages to describe their hideous forms. Hel was Victory—dressed in red—and her four, ghostly companions were now unmasked. The Four Horsemen of the Apocalypse had taken to the battlefield, and Asgard was surely doomed.

"We must surrender now, it's our only hope!" Kat cried before confusion seized her mind. Her poppy tattoo, which had been itching since dawn, now burned with the fire of Niflheim.

Hello, Sis, don't be afraid.

Hel was inside her mind—or was that vice versa? Kat couldn't be sure. She was Hel, and Hel was she. The sensation was impossible to describe.

Don't hurt my sisters, she pleaded silently.

Don't worry, they will be unharmed. I have come to kill the gods and the Aesir, not the Valkyries.

Please spare Hod, too; he's innocent.

If that is your wish, so be it. Stay close to me Kat, when the hour comes, you alone can save Asgard.

"Kat, draw your sword, the Demon Angels, they're coming!" Jess's cry stirred Kat's consciousness.

"I can't, they won't hurt you. You must surrender," Kat murmured in a daze as reality and nightmares blended into one.

"Never!" yelled Silk, who had overheard her. "What in Asgard is she blathering about, Brynhildr?"

"I don't know, she can't fight," Jess replied, crouching low and forming a protective shield in front of Kat. "It's the poppy. Hel's controlling her through it; her mind has gone."

"Oh, sweet Odin!" Silk cursed in exasperation. "That's all we need."

"VALKYRIES!" Ruby's voice rose high above the battlefield. "Prepare for war. No retreat, no surrender. Today will be a good day to die."

To a chorus of blood-curdling battle cries, the warriors and maids took up their positions. The fight was on.

Hel's army struck first.

Bounding through their ranks, Fenrir raced toward Odin as the god raised Gungnir and made ready to stand his ground. Eyes blazing yellow and red and with deadly white fangs drooling saliva, Fenrir took flight, leaping at Odin's neck.

Odin hurled Gungnir at the swirling wall of fur and muscle.

Fenrir span and twisted in mid air.

Gungnir, the enchanted, unmissing, magical spear—missed.

With a terrifying howl of delight, Fenrir crashed into Odin, throwing him from his horse. Tumbling over and over together, the two disappeared in a flurry of snow down a small slope and into a thicket. The pack of wolves followed close behind.

"Balder! We must help your father!" Freyja screamed, leaping from Gold Mane. "Not you, Thor!" she hollered. "Stay here and hold the line. You know the prophesy. Don't follow us."

Flailing wildly as they struggled through the snow, Freyja and Balder followed the path of the wolves down into the small depression. They were quickly lost from view. Carmel drew her sword and moved closer to Thor. She wouldn't let him die, she couldn't.

Can you feel them Kat, can you feel my Angels?

Kat nodded. She understood the ultimate power of the poppies. A dozen spears and arrows had taken flight toward Hel, but each had passed harmlessly through her.

She was everyone—and no one, all at the same time.

Eyes tightly shut and sitting motionless, Hel was like an octopus with each of her Demon Angels forming a tentacle. Through them she could see, hear, feel, touch—and fight.

Hel was every Angel, and every Angel was Hel. It was her sword, her fangs, and her whip-like tail that was slaughtering the Aesir soldiers; their blood flowing like wine upon the silken napkin of snow. The tattoo on Hel's arm burned like a furnace, bathing her arm in a deathly, reddish glow. Her poppy was alive and growing in strength.

The Demon Angels were terrifying.

Slithering like snakes on their bellies with human arms and legs tucked flush against their bodies, they could rise at will to fight with sword and shield. Arrows and spears struggled to pierce their armoured skin, and only decapitation could kill the ungodly beasts. Their heads were vaguely humanoid but devoid of hair and with enlarged eyes splayed like tear drops upon their brows. With tiny pits for ears, forked tongues and hollow fangs that spat a deadly poison; the creatures were unstoppable. Slashing, spitting, and flicking their venomous scorpion tails, they decimated Odin's ranks as Hel kept her word. Not one Valkyrie was harmed.

The hounds now joined the fray, picking the gods off, one by one.

Tyr was the first to fall, drowned in a sea of fur. He fought ferociously, but it was Garm, the leader of the pack, who eventually dragged him down. Snarling ferociously, the dogs leapt upon him.

He wasn't seen again.

Freyr fell next, much to Kat's dismay. Surrounded by Demon Angels, it was Surt who struck the decisive blow. Swooping down low, he slashed at Freyr with his talons, wounding him in the chest and stomach. Freyr collapsed to the floor as the Angels huddled around him. He too became lost from view.

His death was assured.

Heimdall's turn followed. Standing beside Hod, the pair fought valiantly, Hod unleashing arrow after arrow into the swirling mass of hounds that surrounded them. Heimdall cut and slashed as a pile of bodies mounted swiftly. It was carnage; and at first it looked as though they were winning.

Striking at the pair with their tails, a dozen Demons joined the fray. Spitting poison, Heimdall was soon blinded. Floundering forward, he tripped and fell amongst the corpses. Hod tried to save him but was pushed back; a flurry of barbed tails lashing a deadly warning against his shield. His life would be spared, but only if he retreated.

"ODIN IS DEAD!"

A terrified cry went up as all eyes turned to the thicket where he and Fenrir had tumbled. Prancing into view with head raised high, Fenrir held aloft a severed arm.

Passing totality, a ray of sunshine flashed from the emergent sliver of sun. This flickered its brilliance across the battlefield, igniting the diamonds in the jewelled ring that sparkled from a finger on the severed arm.

Nine diamonds glittered the ugliest of truths.

The hand was Odin's.

Their lord of lords, the king of kings was dead.

"FENRIR!" Thor yelled furiously as he struggled desperately forward through the snow to catch the wicked beast. Mjollnir was in his hand.

Dropping his prize; Fenrir turned and crouched low; making ready to spring.

"NO, THOR!" Carmel yelled in desperation as she tried to reach him. This was the prophesy, his life was doomed. She had to stop him.

Fenrir pounced as Thor swung his hammer. Fangs slashed at his neck as Thor's hammer crushed the beast's skull.

Fenrir fell to the ground, dead.

Thor, too, fell to the ground, dying; great arterial spurts of blood gushing from a gaping wound in his neck.

"Oh, Thor, Thor! What have you done my dearest darling," Carmel begged hysterically as she collapsed into the snow beside him. Lifting his head into her lap, hot tears of pain streamed from her eyes and splashed upon his face. Mika and Zara raised their shields to shield the pair. Carmel was grief stricken, barely able to utter a word. Her god, her hero, and the joy in her heart lay dying in her arms; his lifeblood forming a scarlet shawl around his head.

How could this be?

Fate mustn't take him, she wouldn't allow it.

"Hod!" Jameela yelled as she raced across the battlefield to stand beside him. "Where are the heroes?"

"They're coming, look, look! Can't you see, the gateway's opening?"

Jameela turned and shielded her eyes. The yellow glow in the sky had indeed enlarged, but it still wasn't wide enough yet to allow an army through. "You must go and get them, Hod. You must open the gates and bring the heroes, now!" She hollered in his ear. Demon Angels had begun to surround them; hissing and spitting in fury.

"I can't, Odin wouldn't allow it," he bleated nervously.

Jameela slapped him hard. She had to, their lives depended on it. "Odin's dead, Thor's dying, and Freyja and Balder are missing. You're the only god left. You have to get the Einherjar." She was furious. Every second lost would cost yet more lives. They needed the heroes now.

"I, I—" Hod stuttered and dithered. His mind was frozen. Trapped between death and duty, he couldn't move.

Jameela slapped him again, harder; drawing blood. The corner of his mouth had split wide open. "Do you want another?" She threatened furiously, raising her arm ready to strike. He had to snap out of it, now.

"No, please; I'm so sorry," Hod's head was reeling; but the force of her blows had brought him to his senses. He was back in the room.

"Please, Hod, get them, now. I beg of you," she pleaded. "It's all up to you. Save Asgard Hod. Open the gates of Valhalla and save Asgard."

"Yes, my lady." Bowing low, Hod waved his hand over his ring. Jameela was right. To hell with Odin's rules. He had to unleash the Einherjar.

Gasping for breath, Jameela crouched low and raised her shield. Seconds ticked by. The Demons hissed and circled but wouldn't attack. She was cornered; down—but not out.

With a sudden flash of light, Hod returned. He was empty handed and ashen.

"Where are they Hod, where are the heroes?" Jameela demanded.

"They're not coming, any of them," he breathed, his eyes wide open in terror.

"What? How? Why?" Jameela couldn't believe her ears. This couldn't be happening.

"Because there's no one there!" he cried despairingly. "Valhalla is empty. The heroes and gods are gone."

Collapsing to the ground in a heap, Hod began to cry. He couldn't save Asgard; nobody could without Odin's Einherjar.

The gods, the Valkyries, and the Aesir; they were all defeated.

Victory belonged to Hel.

35

Destiny's Hand

*Y*ou have to get them to surrender, Kat. Now Odin's dead, I can stop Ragnarok, we can stop Ragnarok, together.

"Prudr, Gunnr, we have to surrender, it's our only hope," Kat cried in a daze, reflecting the words that were echoing inside her head. Hel's voice was calling her, but it felt so confused. Was it Hel or was it she who was begging her sisters to surrender?

"Never!" Ruby and Silk yelled defiantly in unison.

"We fight to the death. Valkyries never retreat; Valkyries never surrender." Silk screamed furiously; lunging and slashing at Demon Angels as they crowded around her.

Tell them about the Guardians, Kat. Look at the Guardians; they're drawing closer. Tell them to look at their tide of death. Do they really want to die at their hands? Where's the honour in that; where's the glory?

"Please, I beg of you; look at the Guardians," Kat begged, repeating Hel's plea. "They're coming and they're killing everything," she yelled coarsely, struggling to focus. Her head was spinning, and she couldn't control her words.

Who was she? Kat? Hel? Kat? And did it even really matter anymore?

They were one now, together inside each other's minds.

"Brynhildr, do shut Kat up for Odin's sake," Ruby fumed. "It's bad enough she isn't fighting, without having to listen to her nonsensical babble. We really don't need her defeatist drivel." Of course she could see the Guardians—*who couldn't?*

Like some rotting wall of death, the four horsemen had arrived on the plain and were now fanning out, floating effortlessly across the ground; creeping forward, inexorably, inch by deadly inch. Behind them lay darkness; no light, no heat, no life—nothing.

They consumed everything and were unstoppable.

Arrows and spears had been fired at them, but these all passed straight through their ghostly shadows; turning black and crumbling to ash before they hit the ground. The Guardians were hungry, and their hunger knew no bounds. They would consume all of Asgard, its realms, and its sun; and still thirst for more.

That was their purpose; that was their joy; that was the reason for their existence. They were the bringers of absolute death. They were the ultimate killing machines, the end of days; the end of time itself.

Please, Kat, I won't stop the Guardians if our sisters don't surrender.

"We must surrender," Kat pleaded once more.

"Shut up, Kat, please." Jess, too, had had enough. Not only was she fighting for her life, but she was shielding Kat and the small group of Aesir soldiers who had joined them. "If it is our destiny that we die today," she continued, "then we do so with honour. We are warriors; we are Valkyries; that is our way." Raising her sword, she screamed a defiant cheer. "HAIL ODIN!"

"HAIL ODIN!"

Came a faltering reply from the struggling and besieged Aesir. They had needed to hear her battle cry, and they rallied to her call. It was like a tonic. Raising their swords and shields; they redoubled their efforts to repulse the seething tide of hounds, dragons, and demons.

It was an impossible task.

With no gods, no heroes, and their ranks reduced by half, the remains of Odin's army were fighting in dwindling clusters. They hadn't given ground, but each group of soldiers had become isolated and surrounded. Dogs slashed at them, demons spat poison, and dragons swooped low overhead; clawing with their talons as they scorching great trenches of fire. Many soldiers had been burnt to death while others were stumbling around in the snow, blinded by venom with hounds tearing at their bodies, dragging the weak and injured down to their doom.

It was a hideous sight.

The once-beautiful, virgin blanket of whiteness now lay bloodied and churned; pockmarked and spattered with blood, flesh, and mangled corpses.

Vigrid, the final, horrific battlefield of Ragnarok, lay littered with the detritus of war.

"Thor, please, I beg of you don't die." Carmel knelt in the snow as she cradled the god's head in her lap. The battle still raged, but she didn't care. Her life didn't matter; saving Thor's did.

"Don't cry, my darling," he choked as blood gurgled in his throat. His face was ashen and greying fast. A pool of blood lay all around, and the gash in his neck was spurting less furiously now.

He had practically bled out. His end was nigh, and he was content.

"This is my destiny and my sacrifice," he gasped. "Asgard will be purged and life will spring anew." His eyelids began to flutter.

"Thor! For Odin's sake, it doesn't have to be like this," Carmel wailed, pulling his head closer as she caressed his face with her hand. "Wave your hand over your ring, I beg of you. Take me to Yggdrasill, to Odin's garden. The apples can save you."

"I can't, my sweetness." Thor was fading faster now. His head was beginning to spin, and colours were bleeding from his sight. He didn't mind. To die in Carmel's arms was a beautiful way to go. "Kiss me, please, one last time," he whispered hoarsely as Carmel did so.

"I love you, Thor. Please, please let me save you; for my sake if not your own. I beg of you, I love you," Carmel wept as she sobbed into his ear.

Somehow, somewhere, from the depths of his dying mind, Carmel's words struck a chord. Overwhelmed by grief; Carmel watched as Thor raised a trembling hand and passed it slowly over his ring.

In a heartbeat they were in Odin's garden.

The place was dead; but Carmel paid no attention. Leaping up, she made a beeline for the basket of apples.

Odin be praised!

Mercifully, there were still some left. Some looked old, some looked tired, and some were heavily wrinkled; but they were apples; Idun's apples—and they promised life.

Grabbing two, she raced back to Thor and collapsed down beside him. It was a race against time. He was now too weak to bite or chew.

Carmel took a huge chunk in her mouth and hastily chewed the sweet fruit. Placing her hand on Thor's chin, she pulled it gently open before dribbling the mashed pulp into his mouth. She was feeding him like a baby bird.

"Swallow, please, Thor, I beg of you, please swallow."

Choking and spluttering, Thor gulped and did as she asked. The apple stayed down.

He could be saved.

Slowly, chunk by chunk; Carmel bit, chewed, dribbled, and spat the life-giving fruit into his mouth. She stroked his forehead, kissed his lips and cheeks; and sang the sweetest of lullabies as she cradled his head in her lap.

Little by little, she coaxed life back into him.

After what seemed an age, she cautiously removed her hand from the rent in his neck. The severed artery had already healed, and the loss of blood had stemmed to a tiny ooze. Colour was returned to Thor's cheeks and although his eyes remained shut; the waxy, grey pallor of death had gone.

Her lover would live.

Carmel was elated and stuck to her task. The ground was freezing and covered in several inches of snow. The once bubbling stream now lay frozen solid, and Yggdrasill, the mighty ash tree, was blackened and stripped bare. Not one creature could be heard, and the Norn had disappeared. The sight was bleak and heartbreaking, but it couldn't dampen Carmel's spirits. She sang loudly and triumphantly. She had saved her hero's life, and she felt ecstatic.

Mimir was wrong. Thor didn't die at Ragnarok.

Fate must be rewritten.

Who cared if Asgard stayed cursed and their future paradise remained unborn; Carmel had saved her godly hero, and that was all that mattered. The remaining gods, wherever they might be, they could all go hang themselves.

Thor was alive, and her heart felt fit to burst.

Carmel had no idea how long she knelt in the snow beside her godly hero, cuddling and nurturing the life back into his soul. All she knew, and all that she needed to know, was that when they returned to Ragnarok, he would live.

When the two of them eventually vanished from the garden, a tiny shaft of sunlight broke through its wintry sky. A delicate breeze swept through the grounds as the tiniest and tenderest of green shoots burst from Yggdrasill's loftiest bough.

Carmel had indeed changed fate.

Paradise had been reborn.

They must surrender, Kat, now, NOW!

"They won't Hel, they can't. They're Valkyries; our sisters are too proud." Kat muttered as she staggered from side to side.

The Guardians are almost upon us, this is their last chance.

"No retreat, no surrender. No retreat, no surrender," she chanted, both inside her head and out loud. Her Valkyrie sisters they would never back down. Hel might, she might; but their sisters wouldn't. Hel would have to change her plans.

Sitting motionless on her steed, Hel deliberated Kat's words.

The Guardians were barely fifty metres away, and already she could feel the icy blackness of death. The gods were dead or dying, and the Aesir soldiers had been destroyed. She had won, Asgard was hers—but she couldn't kill her sisters; and she didn't want to inherit a lifeless, blackened cinder.

She had sworn an oath that she wouldn't stop the battle until the Valkyries had surrendered; but that would have to change. Her soul now had a conscience—thanks to Henry and Kat.

She couldn't kill the ones whom her sister loved; and she couldn't bear the sadness in Henry's eyes as he gazed upon their new home; lifeless, barren, and choked with endless mounds of charred and smoking ash.

That was not how it should be; that was not how it was going to be.

She had to act. She had to stop Ragnarok, and she had to do so now.

Come to me Kat and take my dagger. I will tell you what to do.

Stumbling as she wielded her sword left and right, Jess watched helplessly as the demons cleared a path for Kat. The Queen of the Damned was stealing her sister's body, as if taking her mind hadn't been enough.

This was too much; she couldn't let Hel claim the love of her life.

"AAARGH!"

Screaming loudly, Jess hurled herself at the wall of Demon Angels. They had closed ranks behind Kat and now formed an impenetrable barrier. All Jess could do was to watch and fume as Hel took her love.

It took only a few minutes for Kat to reach the vantage point where Hel was sitting, but in that time, the Guardians had advanced another twenty metres. They were perilously close and almost upon the struggling forces.

Taking Kat's hands in hers, Hel pressed the handle of her dagger into them.

Kat, you alone can save Ragnarok. Plunge this into my tattoo.

"I can't do it, Hel, I can't hurt you," Kat cried despairingly.

You must, it's our only chance. Kill the poppy Kat, kill its power. Do it Kat, do it now!

Hel's voice raged inside Kat's head as she raised the dagger high.

Do it Kat, kill the poppy.

"Aargh!" Kat yelled in anguish as she plunged the dagger deep into Hel's arm, ripping through the tattoo to strike at the bone below.

"AAARGH!"

Kat, Hel, and all the Demon Angels screamed as one.

The enchantment had been broken. The poppy was no more.

Both Kat and Hel collapsed into the snow; their tattoos bleeding heavily. The Demon Angels collapsed, too; but their fate was very different from their queen's. Shrivelling and fading to ash, they died were they fell. They were Hel, and Hel was them. Without the Queen of the Damned inside them, their bodies were empty shells. There could be no life without their mistress.

Hel gasped and then opened her eyes. She was back; and she pulled Kat toward her and kissed her hard. Kat had saved all their lives.

Turning her head, she glanced furtively at The Guardians. They had advanced another ten metres. She shivered violently; her life was being sucked toward them. Staggering to her feet, Hel snatched a horn from her saddle and held it to her lips. One long, loud blast rang out across the battlefield.

It was a message—and the dragons responded to her call.

Swooping down as one, the mighty creatures landed heavily behind her and spread their wings. These formed a leathery shield, a barrier between the dead and the living. The Guardians march of death ground to a halt.

The ghostly horsemen were untouchable by any mortal being from Asgard; but the dragons weren't from the realm. They hadn't sprung from Asgard's soil or from any other soil in its universe. The shadowy shapes of the Guardians, so ephemeral to the peoples of Asgard; were like solid rocks to the dragons. Holding their ground and then pressing forward; the mighty creatures forced the darkest, deadliest evil into retreat—a surrender that pained the horsemen greatly. Howling mournfully with their despair, the anguished ghouls were shepherded back through the portal.

Asgard had been saved, and its destiny was changed.

The realm wouldn't die.

With her usual businesslike efficiency, Hel quickly set about clearing the battlefield. Raising her fingers to her lips, she let out a long, shrill, high-pitched whistle and, hearing their mistress's command; the hounds stopped their attacks and bounded back toward her—heads held high and tails wagging furiously.

Surrounded by a sea of fur, both Hel and Kat knelt and hugged the beasts. Their job was done, and the dogs would all find new homes in the castle's many kennels.

Surt waddled toward Hel, and their eyes met. Kat wasn't a party to this conversation, but a contingent of dragons took off immediately and headed south toward Middle Sea.

This was at Hel's request.

They would destroy the army of giants and Berserkers cast ashore by Naglfar; the ship of the dead. There could be no home in Asgard now for these cursed souls.

Jobs completed, Hel watched and waited patiently as the exhausted Valkyries stumbled toward her. Whistling once more to her hounds, they obediently cleared a path to let them through.

Eventually, all the warriors and maids stood before the two Sangrids. It was time to talk turkey.

"Why didn't you surrender?" Hel asked in bewilderment. She was standing beside Kat, and the two of them were in a sorry state.

Kat was mentally shattered, and Hel looked like some beat up, gothic princess; one who'd been dragged through a bush on her way to a bad taste Halloween party. Her hair was tangled and matted, blood streamed from her arm; and charcoal-coloured rivulets of kohl streaked her ashen cheeks.

"You should know that answer better than I," Silk spat angrily. "Valkyries never surrender." She still hadn't forgiven Hel for Balder; or for calling her Sucky.

"Thank you Sangrid," Ruby offered suddenly and generously, stepping forward, bowing, and then holding her hand out toward Hel. "Thank you for sparing Asgard."

To everyone's great surprise, Hel too stepped forward and hugged Ruby tightly. When they parted, her cheeks were stained with tears.

Their embrace had made her cry. "It was my pleasure, honestly," she gulped, sniffing back tears as she spoke. Ruby's gracious gesture had moved her profoundly. "My fight was never with you, my dearest sisters," she continued. "My fight was only with that maggot Odin and his pack of evil gods."

"Please, be respectful, Sangrid," Jameela begged, stepping forward as she spoke. "Many of us still love Odin; and both Thor and Hod are still alive."

Hel nodded. She would try to be more polite about her bastard, hated nemesis.

"I suppose you'll be heading back there, then?" Jess enquired pointedly; waving her hand in the direction of the smoking, volcanic summit. "You've won Sangrid, and you needn't have spared us. Thank you; thank you so very much."

Hel thanked Jess for her kind words and then shook her head. She wasn't going to be returning to Niflheim; she couldn't.

"Why not?" Silk asked in amazement.

"That was my deal with the dragons," Hel retorted. "They would stop the Guardians when I won the battle, but only if I gave them Niflheim," she sighed resignedly. "A realm for a realm: that was our deal."

"But Sangrid, you didn't win Ragnarok; we didn't surrender; remember?" Ruby interrupted, taking her hand. She too had been moved by Hel's hug and the sincerity of her tears.

"I know," Hel replied mournfully, gazing down at her boots.

"So what are you going to do then, hey, now that you're homeless?" Silk goaded cruelly. She was completely unmoved by all the hugging and crocodile tears. Seeing Hel destitute was poetic justice; an eye for an eye and a tooth for a tooth. Let the spoilt bitch live like a penniless beggar, grubbing for roots with a frozen ditch for a home.

Pausing for a moments thought, a cheeky smirk crept slowly across Hel's face. "I don't suppose there'd be any room in the castle for an ex-Queen of the Damned?" she giggled nervously, glancing at each of the Valkyries in turn.

The warriors turned and looked at each other in amazement. It was a mad request, but one they couldn't ignore. Hel really was homeless, and they dissolved into a fit of nervy laughter. The situation was farcical.

"Come on, you," Ruby sighed reluctantly, shrugging as she stepped forward to give Hel another hug. She didn't need to ask her sisters for their decision; their laughter had said it all.

The ex-Queen of the Damned could stay.

"What would you like for supper?" she chuckled loudly.

36

Whydya Do, Whadya Did?

"**S**o come on, Finch; whydya do it?"

Marcus sat back in the uncomfortable, moulded plastic seat and took a deep breath in. He'd lost track of how many times he'd been asked that question already this afternoon, and yes; he'd heard quite a few fists smashed on tables as well. The interrogating officers were irritated and getting nowhere. It was a case now of clock watching and waiting; waiting patiently until the next, frustrated, double act took over and went through the same old miserable routine again.

The officers changed like clockwork; every hour, on the hour; but the questions remained the same.

Marcus didn't blame the detectives for being bad tempered. In a funny sort of way, he actually felt quite sorry for them. He'd been there, read the book, and got the T-shirt, too. He'd played the good cop/bad cop routine himself and all the variations in between. He'd lost count of how many times he'd sat, or stood, where they were now; verbally mind-fucking a criminal. If he had to make an educated guess; judging by the number of shift changes, they'd been at it now for a little over four hours.

Fuck! No wonder they were so pissed off.

He'd been bamboozled with simultaneous questions, had snarling faces shoved so close that he could practically tickle tonsils with his tongue; and he'd been threatened with impossibly grotesque acts of obscene sexual abuse.

Oh yes; and he was getting tired and thirsty, too.

Sleep and fluid deprivation were par for the course. It was a tough experience being on the wrong side of the law, but that's what you got for being a dumb-arsed criminal. Marcus had no excuses. He'd broken the law and had to face the consequences; getting fucked to buggery.

Thank god he hadn't actually killed Thirle.

Of course, the cops would eventually get their confession; they always did. It was just a question of when, not if, he'd crack. Marcus reckoned in about another four hours he'd be singing like a canary; reciting line for line any one of the myriad suggestions they'd given him for pulling the trigger.

"I was high on crack cocaine, officer," or "the man in the moon told me to do it," or "look officer; I'm a teapot," or "I'm a card-carrying terrorist—all hail Bin Laden."

Whatever reason they wanted, the police would get it; because that's what they always did. What hurt the most, as Marcus stared dolefully at his shoes, was the real truth behind the shooting; the simple, honest, blinding truth that nobody could believe. He actually didn't have a clue.

Marcus had absolutely no idea why he had tried to kill Herr Flöda.

He wished he knew; he really did. It would certainly make his life one hell of a lot easier. *For fucks sake, why had he done it?* He practically worshipped the man.

What in god's name had he been thinking of?

The whole ludicrous shooting was a mystery—and Marcus hated mysteries. He wanted to know the reason "why?" as much as the officers yelling at him did. After all, he had so much more to lose. They weren't going to be banged up for the rest of their lives. He was.

If he could only understand, just catch a glimpse of his motive. Why had he drawn his gun and squeezed the trigger? Why, why, why?

This thought bugged him; it really, really, fucking bugged him.

Anna raised her hand and shouted loudly at the teenage girl who had just stepped off a greyhound bus. It was just after noon, and the day looked set to be a scorcher.

Thank goodness Lia had come prepared for it.

Micro, denim hot pants, a paper-thin, cotton blouse tied up high above her navel, strapless high-heeled sandals, and of course; no bra. With honey blond hair pulled viciously back into a tight ponytail; designer sunglasses, upturned nose, and pursed, sullen lips; Lia looked every inch the killer bitch. She was perfection in every detail; a drop-dead gorgeous, wannabe Valkyrie-in-waiting.

Okay, okay; Anna shook her head as she tried to get a grip on her emotions. Perhaps she was overreacting and being a little harsh on the girl. Perhaps she shouldn't be too hasty in judging her book by its slutty cover—or jumping to conclusions. Then again—perhaps she should.

She hated the Valkyries; I mean she really, really hated them; them and their fucking cursed cult. Marcus was going to spend the rest of his life behind bars thanks to those bitches. *Christ!* She fumed as she hurried across the road; it was all she could do to stop herself from tearing this vixen's face off.

She already hated the girl so much.

"Hi, you must be Lia, how lovely to meet you." Anna extended her hand and, with a sickeningly insincere smile on her face, she shook that of the bewildered child. "Can I help you with your luggage?" she offered politely.

Lia flashed Anna a nervous smile before replying that the small holdall she was carrying was all she had.

That figured.

Lia had left Miami penniless and in a hurry. Hitching, blagging, and using every seductive means at her disposal: she had somehow managed to cadge her way north to New York. Anna didn't press her for details of her journey; she shuddered to think what powers the little prick teaser had used to get her way.

The thought of Lia hitchhiking made for a terrifying prospect.

She was a woman of male destruction; a lean, mean, ball-breaking machine. Anna pitied the poor guys who must have begged to give Lolita a lift. The soulless minx would have eaten them alive.

Hailing a yellow cab, Anna bundled the girl into the taxi, and they set off in the direction of home, if that was what she could call her bombed-out-shell-of-flat these days.

Two days had passed since the shooting, and Marcus had been discharged from the hospital and back into police custody. To Anna's relief, the identity of the would-be assassin in Herr Flöda's shooting was being kept a closely guarded secret. *"The suspect was a terrorist, and it would be against national interest to release further details yet,"* to quote a spokesman for the case.

The truth behind this mealy-mouthed smokescreen was unfortunately much less pleasant. The government was embarrassed—as were the NYPD. How could one of their officers be responsible for this act?

It got worse.

Without a motive, the state had to swallow an even more unpleasant pill. One of their own was a nutter.

Marcus had to be some sort of a sicko; a whacked-up, motherfucker of a psycho; so how the hell had he fallen through the system? Why hadn't he been picked up earlier?

Ex-detective Finch really was an embarrassment.

Anna smiled ruefully at this thought. She bet right now the top brass wished her husband had been lynched. That would have made their lives so much easier. As she toyed with this idea, she shuffled uncomfortably. From what Marcus had told her in previously conversations, arranging 'accidents' in custody was only too easy.

Now wouldn't that be a convenient end to their problem?

Anna shuddered at this thought before forcing her attention back to her conversation with Lia. Unfortunately, this was becoming as unpalatable as her daydreaming.

When Lia had phoned Marcus the other day, she hadn't hung up; even after Anna had broken her silence and explained that her husband wasn't available. Luckily to Lia's mind, all she wanted was sanctuary, and Marcus's wife would make as good a provider as the man himself.

Marcus was her only contact in America, and self-preservation was her game.

At the time of her call, Anna had decided not to mention that Marcus was in police custody; just in case this frightened her away. Lia was desperate to be saved, and Anna was desperate to save her. The girl had to have some useful knowledge about the Dragza Corporation—and the Valkyries.

As they travelled through the crowded streets; Lia chattered away in her broken, childlike, Eastern European accent; giving Anna a chilling insight into what might lie ahead; and why the girl was so afraid.

Over the years, Crescent Cay had been a bustling tropical oasis; a seething hotbed of people coming and going; all day, every day, without exception.

When Anna pressed her for names or numbers, the results were quite startling. Lia had been a hostess there for nearly two years, and during that time, she would estimate not hundreds but thousands of guests had passed through the Isle. Names were always first name only, and occupations were never mentioned. However, being a cocky, money-grasping little so and so, Lia had feathered her nest with some interesting titbits.

Broadly speaking, she could divide the guests into two groups; young, military types and 'people of importance.'

This latter group was a bit vague and extended from the obvious— politicians, company presidents, and judges—to the less so. Pop stars, senior police officers, doctors, and even members of the clergy. All of these had come and passed their time as guests of the Count and Contessa. It was a curious, eclectic mix and one that was truly international in its aspirations. People came to the Isle from all corners of the globe so long as they fulfilled the Dragza criteria. They had to be rich and powerful; or preferably both.

What Lia said next, however, was what made Anna's hair stand up on end. It quite literally shook her world.

Lia, along with the other hostesses, had been recruited by the Contessa. She ran the entertainments side of the island and did so with great efficiency and flare. All the girls were beautiful and very highly paid. However, rewards for the hostesses didn't just stop at money.

The lucky few, the chosen ones, those who had proved their courage and loyalty; they received a far greater reward; one that wasn't counted in cash. What Lia and the other girls hankered for was to join this privileged elite. What Lia wanted, what all the girls wanted; was to wear the poppy tattoo.

This was why she had made a note of Marcus's cell phone and why she had tried to contact him. Marcus was one of the chosen few, he too had been branded. Marcus bore this tattoo.

Anna was gobsmacked.

Jesus Christ! She hadn't even noticed it.

Sitting back in her seat, Anna caught her breath. Admittedly, Marcus hadn't been back long, and he had complained about a soreness in his arm, but she still couldn't see how she could have missed it. This oversight was extraordinary; but the matter didn't end there.

The whole poppy issue was about to take a sickening turn for the worse; and Lia was terrified because of what had happened next. All the girls who had been tattooed had disappeared.

Here today—gone tomorrow.

No goodbyes, no forwarding addresses, nothing. The Contessa, too, was also missing. Something was going on, and a cold change had swept the island. Word was out that the hostesses had to go—permanently.

That's why Lia had fled.

The rumour on everybody's lips was that the girls were being murdered, one by one. Lia didn't have a tattoo, but she had been there too long and knew too much. She had to be on the hit list—and Marcus would be, too. Of that fact, she was certain: he had the tattoo—so he had to be.

Now came the killer blow.

When Anna mentioned that Marcus was in police custody safely behind bars; Lia visibly blanched; shocked into a state of silence. It was a silence that had taken Anna some time to coax her out of. Speaking slowly and in hushed tones, the former hostess had told her that Marcus was in danger; terrible danger.

At liberty, the three of them could vanish. With any luck, they could disappear off the radar; become invisible and hidden from view. In jail; Marcus, however, was a sitting duck.

The Dragza Corporation owned men everywhere.

In Lia's opinion, it wasn't a question of if; it was rather a question of when—when would somebody come for him; a hired gun to bump him off.

In her naive, teenaged, have-no-fear eyes; the solution to this problem was simple and obvious. They had to break him out.

She and Anna would have to free Marcus.

Five and a bit hours in, Marcus was getting bored of his interrogation. Actually, when he came to think of it, it wasn't so much bored as frustrated and confused.

These sensations had been growing inside his head for some time now. His arm, too, was hurting. It had started with an itch in his tattoo, and this had developed into a pain—which had suddenly increased dramatically.

It reminded him of the time in the church—but with an added dimension. This time he was struggling to think straight.

Blurred images were crowding his mind.

He could hear shouting, feel a sword pressed in his hand, and he could see strange, snake-like monsters on either side of him. He was one of these, too; he was a snake, a monster, and he was serving their Queen—*His Queen.*

"Why did you do it Finch? Come on, you're going to have to tell us sooner or later. Whydya do it?"

Marcus looked up. He felt angry; a terrible, furious, all-consuming rage.

"I had to do it," he muttered aggressively. "I had to serve my queen. He was evil, they're all evil. They all have to die; all of them. My queen needs me, she's calling me. I have to serve her, I have to help her." Marcus clenched his fists tightly. He had to get out of there.

The two tired detectives exchanged glances. This was different.

"Um, who exactly is this queen?" one of them enquired sardonically. Reaching forward, the other detective turned the tape recorder back on. Things were about to get interesting.

"She's my queen, the Contessa's queen. I have to serve her," he snarled.

Marcus could take no more. A white hot poker scorched his arm. Leaping up, he threw the table over and hurled himself at one the detectives. Grabbing the man by the throat, he pinned him against the wall; throttling the life out of him. The other detective tried to pull him off. Turning abruptly, Marcus lashed out with his handcuffed fists.

The man spun across the floor.

This was it, the moment of escape. Marcus lunged for the door—it was locked.

Hammering and kicking at it with all his might, the door suddenly gave way. *Wow!* He felt so strong, so powerful, so invincible.

He had to fight for his queen.

Gasping for air, one of the detectives hit the panic button. The station was placed in lockdown.

Beating off one, two, three police officers; Marcus's war eventually ground to a halt not far from the building's entrance. He was cornered, and tranquilliser darts had been issued. The order was out. Marcus was to be put down, but not killed.

The detectives had got their confession—and their answer. Detective Marcus Finch was a loony. A bona fide, certifiable fruitcake.

After shouting a brief warning, an officer took aim and squeezed his trigger. As a dart sped through the air, Marcus let out a terrifying scream and collapsed to the floor, clutching his arm.

Kat had stabbed Hel's tattoo—and he had felt it. Blood poured from his arm; bright red blood that pooled all around him.

Marcus had been released from Hel's servitude.

He was freed from her nightmare—but was about to join another.

37

Bollocks!

"Foxy!" Hel shrieked elatedly as she flew into his arms, hugging and kissing him enthusiastically. "Are you all right?" she continued in a voice now filled with concern. She started to check him over, just to be sure.

The other warriors looked on in amazement.

Arriving back at the castle just after dark, they had thought that the day couldn't get any stranger. Apparently, it just had. How could this goofy, eccentric oddball possibly be Hel's boyfriend?

This beggared belief.

Shivering in the cold, Henry made for a comical sight. The dragons had kept their side of the bargain and released him almost as soon as they vanished through the portal into Niflheim. Henry had obviously been evicted in a hurry and had grabbed the things that mattered most to him. These items, unfortunately; didn't include clothes. Dressed in a luminous, pink, bobble hat, fur-lined three-quarter length ladies coat (he obviously couldn't find a man's), pyjama bottoms and with 'things' stuck on to his sockless feet—he was a sight for sore eyes and then some.

"Would you like some help getting your belongings into the castle?" Ruby volunteered with a guffaw.

"Oh, and what are those?" Silk added sarcastically, pointing to his feet.

"They're my Taz the Tazmanian slippers. Why, do you like them?" Henry enquired excitedly, giving the girls a little twirl. He had never seen so many beautiful women in one place before, and he was lapping up their attention.

"They need shooting," Silk replied with a haughty snort. She wasn't going to laugh, even though she desperately wanted to. He was Hel's boyfriend, and she still had a score to settle with his evil bitch of a girlfriend.

After the battle of Ragnarok had finished, Hod and Thor were the only gods to leave the battlefield alive with the warriors. All the others were missing, presumed dead.

To Silk's great relief, Balder's body hadn't been found, so he could still be alive, somewhere. Curiously, other than Odin's arm, no body parts had been found for any of the gods who had fallen. Clearly, Hel's hounds and demons had done a good job butchering and devouring their corpses; a brutality that shocked the Valkyries to the core. Injury and death was to be expected—*but cannibalism?*

That broke new ground for horror.

The very thought of it made them sick.

All the warriors and maids were exhausted. Along with the fighting, the journey to and from the battlefield through the heavy snow had taken its toll. They were too tired and numb to think about the consequences of the battle—the terrible losses; and the remaining, unanswered questions this posed.

All these matters would have to wait until tomorrow. For now, they were content to haul Henry's 'possessions' off the back of the ox cart and into the castle.

Kat sniggered as they did so.

The plasma screen, his X box, PS3, CDs and DVDs; she simply didn't have the heart to tell him that there was no electricity in Asgard. She couldn't ruin his enthusiasm; he was going to be so disappointed when he eventually found out.

Mission accomplished, the warriors bid each other goodnight and headed for their beds. At least tonight they could sleep in peace.

Ragnarok was over, and the battle had been a draw—well sort of.

The following morning dawned clear and sunny, with a hint of a thaw in the air. It was almost as though the realm knew that it had been saved from destruction and was dancing a little jig in celebration. Songbirds could be heard singing, and slushy streams of water trickled cheerily in small rivulets across the castle's courtyard.

Winter was on the wane.

Breakfast started late.

It wasn't until mid morning that the bedraggled warriors finally surfaced and made their way down to the feasting hall. Bleary eyed and tousled hair; they gratefully helped themselves to large chunks of bread, butter, and honey; and brimming bowls of porridge piled high with dried fruits. Today they were going to chill and fill. No battles needed to be fought, and chores in the arenas could be put on hold. Today was a day for serious relaxation—and poignant contemplation.

Awkward questions still needed to be answered.

In spite of his terrible injuries, Thor was one of the first to arrive in the feasting hall. Sitting close to Carmel, he held court; loudly discussing his concerns about the battle.

"I shouldn't be alive," he muttered gruffly.

"It's my fault, I'm so sorry," Carmel replied, wrapping an arm around his slumped shoulders. With Sif and the other gods gone, she no longer cared to hide her feelings for her mighty hero.

"I don't blame you, my lady," Thor continued, patting her hand sympathetically. "It's my fault entirely. It was the wave of my hand that took us to Yggdrasill. I'm afraid I've rewritten history; Asgard remains doomed. My apologies to you all, my dearest Valkyries."

"Don't apologise," Jameela perked up. "We're alive, thanks to you. Who cares about the prophesies. Asgard lives—hail Odin!"

"HAIL ODIN!" The warriors replied in a rousing chorus. As the sound echoed noisily around the room, it gave them cheer; a reassurance that they all needed to hear. Asgard had survived the terrible onslaught, and it felt good, really good to still be alive.

"Yeh, hail Odin," Thor muttered miserably when the cheering eventually subsided. "He's dead and yet I still live. All his dreams for a new paradise have been ruined by my selfishness. Lambda's curse hasn't been defeated; our realm is doomed."

"Bollocks!"

"What!" Thor turned around angrily. "What did you say?" he bellowed such that the hall shook.

"I said bollocks; you're talking bollocks."

It was Henry who had uttered the profanity, and he remained as cool as a cucumber, standing at the serving table with his back toward the enraged god. His life was at stake, and what was he doing—only helping himself to a portion of *Cocopops;* his favourite breakfast cereal. He had rescued this along with the other toys.

"How dare you speak to me like that, you impudent puppy!" Thor hollered, rising to his feet as his face turned puce. Mjollnir was in his hand, and he was getting ready to smash some skulls—Henry's to be precise.

"Henry!" Hel scolded him angrily. "Apologise to Thor at once. That's no way to talk to a god, you stupid boy."

"Oh, I'm sorry." Henry turned round with an innocent smile upon his face. "I didn't mean to upset you, it's just that what you were saying was rubbish."

"How so?" Ruby chipped up. She was sitting at the same table as Thor and beckoned for Henry to come and join them. She was intrigued. Hel's gangling lover had balls, she'd give him that.

"Lambda isn't a curse, it's a number," he replied nonchalantly as he sat down opposite her and began tucking into his breakfast.

"What?" Kat enquired in amazement. "Are you telling us that you know what lambda means?"

"Yeh, of course," Henry mumbled as he chewed on a large mouthful. "Doesn't everybody?" he looked around hopefully.

The room had gone deathly silent. Here, sitting amongst them, was the answer to their prayers.

"Henry, you've got to stop eating, now please," Kat whispered breathlessly. "What you've just said, it's important, it's very, very important."

Henry put his spoon down and swallowed hard. He nodded for Kat to continue.

"Lambda is the reason for Ragnarok," she began soberly. "The reason why the realm should have been destroyed and why Odin sacrificed his life. Please, if you know the answer to this puzzle please, please tell us what it means?"

Henry took a deep breath in and looked around him. A spark twinkled excitedly in his eyes. He was a freak no more. Suddenly, he was important and the centre of attention. He had status and authority; and he intended to have some fun with it.

"I can probably best explain lambda with a little demonstration," he continued with a cheeky smile. "Ruby, would you care to arm wrestle?"

Ruby chuckled. *He was joking,* right?

Reaching forward, she took his hand firmly in hers. "Tell me when you're ready," she scoffed.

Henry took up the strain, and his arm began to shake. Veins bulged and popped out in his neck. Ruby's arm hadn't budged.

"Have you started yet?" she quipped—making everybody laugh. With a single powerful push, she forced his arm over and battered his knuckles into the table.

The idiot!

What a humiliation, being beaten by a woman.

"Did you all see that?" Henry enquired enthusiastically. "Wow! You really kicked my arse, as could the rest of you most probably," he continued, glancing around as the girls nodded. They were transfixed. What was the geek on about?

"You see, your strength lies here, in your muscles," Henry acknowledged, holding Ruby's arm up and squeezing a bicep. It was as hard as iron. "Mine, however lies here; inside my head." Henry tapped his skull playfully with a finger. He was enjoying this. "You may be able kick my physical arse from here to Niflheim but I—I can kick your mental arses far, far further. My brain is my muscle, and it can eat all of yours for breakfast."

"Oh, Foxy, you're such a clever-clogs; that's why I love you," Hel exclaimed excitedly, squeezing him hard and kissing him firmly on the lips.

Henry blushed.

"My little Henry, he's a genius," she continued with a smirk, basking in his glory.

"Okay, okay, but you haven't explained lambda yet, smarty pants; or what it has to do with Ragnarok." Silk interrupted viciously; deliberately raining on his parade; she wasn't buying into this nonsense. As far as she was concerned, Hel was an evil bitch, and Henry was a stupid prat. "So what if lambda is a number, it doesn't tell us anything," she added with a sarcastic sneer. Suck on that—buffoon.

"Actually, it does. It tells us everything." Henry retorted smugly.

Leaning forward expectantly, Kat joined the rest of the girls who were eagerly gathering around the table. Henry's explanation was likely to be complicated, but Kat hoped she could understand it— somebody had to; for all their sakes.

Lambda, as Henry explained, was the 'cosmological constant'; a mathematical number used to describe the balance between energy and gravity in a universe.

Most of the warriors and maids were already confused, but Kat and a few others seemed to understand, and they urged Henry to continue. Perhaps his explanation would become clearer to everyone else later.

It did.

Every universe, as he explained, begins with a big bang; but not all big bangs are the same. Some universes start with a really, really, enormous bang with lots and lots of energy. To demonstrate this, Henry picked up a bowl of oats and chucked the contents in the air.

These scattered in all directions.

This sort of universe had so much energy that the figure for lambda would be a very large number. Energy would defeat gravity, and the universe would blow apart, ending almost as quickly as it started in a great, big, enormous rip; scattering matter—like the oats—everywhere.

Other universes, however, started with much smaller amounts of energy. Their big bangs were really quite pitiful. The force of gravity, the attraction between matter in these universes, would quickly triumph over energy.

To demonstrate this, Henry found a small, dried blue berry and squashed it beneath his thumb.

These universes would collapse soon after they started, with everything getting squashed back together and ending in a big crunch. These universes curiously had a very large number, too, but their number was negative, having a minus sign in front of it.

The trick, as Henry concluded, was to have a universe with a number close to zero. In these universes, the starting energy perfectly balanced the force of gravity. This harmony meant the universe could go on gently expanding forever. Apparently, the Midgard universe had a figure very close to zero, which was good news for its inhabitants.

Explanation over, Henry sat back and waited for applause and kisses. They didn't come. Even the warriors who had understood his explanation were baffled by its significance.

"So, what does that mean for us and Asgard?" Kat enquired; posing the question that hung on all their lips.

"Isn't it obvious?" Henry responded, looked around him in bewilderment.

Surely the answer was black and white?

"Odin created this universe, but when he did so, he got the amount of energy in it's big bang wrong. Either he put too much energy into it, or too little; I don't, however, know which. Either way, the universe won't last forever. I'm so sorry."

The warriors looked around them. Everybody had got this bit. Thor had been right, Asgard really was doomed. Their world was either going to get blown to pieces or squashed to the size of a pinhead. Whichever way you looked at it, neither sounded very nice.

"Do you know how long we've got?" Hel enquired. She'd only just returned from Niflheim, so his explanation was a bit of a bummer. She'd been planning on enjoying herself, not getting squashed or blown to smithereens.

"I haven't got a clue," Henry replied emphatically. Without a wealth of sophisticated instruments, how could he possible measure lambda?

"Is there any way you could find out sweetie; there's a love?" Hel asked hopefully. He was genius, there had to be a way.

Henry paused and rubbed his chin thoughtfully. He was silent for a good few minutes, buried deep in concentration. Measuring lambda would be an interesting challenge; that was for sure. "Well," he finally spoke. "A telescope would be useful."

"Any particular colour?" Kat enquired mischievously as she planted a big kiss on his cheek.

"You've got to be joking!" he gasped in amazement. It was his turn now to look surprised.

"No, I'm not. Odin's got loads of them, up in his citadel. Why don't we go and take a look?" she suggested, grabbing hold of his hand.

"Hang on a minute, brain box," Silk interrupted, putting her arm out to stop the pair from leaving. "You're missing one tiny detail. Odin's dead, and we don't have a key to his tower. Even if we did, the citadel doesn't have any stairs. We always get whisked up to the top. So what if there are loads of telescopes in his chamber? We can't get there, so we can't use them."

Kat sat back down. She had a point. "Any suggestions?" she enquired glumly.

"The chamber at the top has got windows," Jess volunteered. "He may have left one open."

"Or we could smash one," Hel added excitedly.

"You two are geniuses!" Kat hugged and kissed the pair. "Come on Henry, it's time to put that brain of yours to use."

Grabbing him, mugs of tea, cloaks, and anything else that they thought they might need; the warriors stumbled excitedly out into the courtyard. Looking up, Henry could see the spire of Odin's citadel. It shone with a blinding brilliance in the harsh winter sunlight.

"Bet you haven't seen this trick before." Ruby grunted as she put on her cloak. Chanting quietly under her breath and following a brilliant flash of light, she was transformed.

"Wow!" Henry gasped in astonishment as an elegant swan honking noisily in front of him.

"Hey Henry! I can do that, too," Hel whispered anxiously, eager not to be upstaged by another Valkyrie. Henry was her boyfriend to impress—not Ruby's.

Taking flight, the girls watched as Ruby rose high into the air, banked, and then swooped in tightening spirals around the citadel. Unfortunately, being such a large bird, it was impossible for her to hover or land on any of the window ledges. With a final, loud hoop, Ruby flapped her wings and headed swiftly back down to the courtyard.

When she emerged from the flash of light, she looked troubled.

"All the windows are shut," she gasped, waving her hands to indicate to the girls that she wasn't finished. "The telescopes are still there, but there's something else, something new."

Bending forward, Ruby placed her hands on her knees. She was feeling a bit puffed. It had been some time since she'd flown so swiftly. After taking a few deep gulps of air, she stood up once more and pointed dramatically toward the chamber.

"There's a great, big sack on the floor up there," she breathed. "And it's alive!"

"Something or someone is trapped in Odin's chamber."

38

A Family Affair

aah, this is the life.

And life, it seemed, had turned full circle.

Woods sighed contentedly at this thought as he relaxed a little deeper into his poolside recliner. He had an ice-cold beer in his hand, a straw hat on his head, and a deliciously hot Caribbean sun beating down fiercely upon his chest. A soothing breeze added to his delight, merrily twisting and twirling to a Calypso beat as it meandered slowly across the pool.

Aaah, it was good to be alive.

It was also good to be on the inside, a member of 'The Dragza Club' as he liked to call it.

Woods looked down at the small, 'v' shaped tattoo on his wrist and smiled. Now that he was getting used to it, the halo of silvery goop surrounding his brain wasn't so bad. He was getting used to the peculiar sensation of having his thoughts restricted; and when you set this minor, inconvenient 'con' against the formidable 'pros' of joining The Dragza Club; the contest was a no-brainer.

A 'processed' life was a good life: period.

Immortality.

The word spun crazily in his head.

It had been his dream for so long, ever since he had first come across the murderous Valkyries; and now it was his for the taking. Just one delicious, succulent, apple a day—and that was it, bingo; no

291

more wrinkles, no sagging bum, and goodbye to withered limbs. He felt refreshed, completely refreshed, and in a way he had never felt before.

Wow! Life was good; life was really, really good.

It was late morning, and Woods let his gaze drift leisurely around the pool. Apart from the usual, odd macho, military type the patio was empty—so very different from the scenes of yesterday. Woods casually wondered when the party revellers would get up and what sort of state they might be in. They would definitely be suffering that morning-after-the-night-before feeling; apples or no apples. What a night—and what a mother of a party.

Yesterday had been one hell of a day.

Shortly after dawn, a small, air ambulance had arrived early and noisily on the island's runway. Woods had been up and taking a pre-breakfast stroll when he saw it touch down. Being reasonably close to the terminal complex, he had upped his pace and hastened to get a better look.

The halo around his brain might have limited his thoughts, but not his curiosity.

Drawing closer, Woods was surprised when he was stopped by two guards. He had thought that his 'v' tattoo gave him access all areas; but clearly it didn't. Only the youthful, big 'V,' military types were allowed near the plane. Craning his neck, Woods had managed to catch a brief glimpse of the new arrival as he was wheeled hastily across the tarmac and into the shadow of an aircraft hanger. In spite of the intravenous drip, oxygen mask, and blankets pulled up around his chin; the features of the patient were those of a middle-aged man— one with greying and receding blond hair. He was wearing distinctive glasses, circular and gold rimmed; and Woods knew he ought to have recognised him. Without the inhibition of his halo, he probably would have. Unfortunately, this memory was stamped 'access denied'— which was a pity.

Loitering for a period of time that didn't look too obvious or arouse suspicions; Woods waited and watched hopefully. He was certain that the patient would reappear and head toward the mansion complex. He didn't; which was also peculiar. The doctors and nurses must have taken him downstairs into the shadowy underground complex; the area that Woods had had such a brief—and unpleasant—introduction to.

Woods didn't attempt to follow the path of the stretcher underground. With or without his halo, he knew that the complex beneath the Isle was strictly out of bounds. It was one of those unwritten rules. Only the military types again—the ones with the large 'V' shaped scars on their chests—had access to that mysterious subterranean world.

Returning poolside, and after refreshing himself with a leisurely swim, Woods settled down for an energetic day in the pursuit of leisure. Unfortunately, for once, blissful relaxation wasn't going to be the order of the day.

Within a couple of hours of the arrival of the air ambulance, the ground had begun to shake and quake. In itself, this wasn't at all unusual; minor tremors being a daily occurrence on Crescent Cay, and Woods was already familiar with them. They never lasted long and caused no damage. He didn't have a clue as to their cause—and his halo prevented him from digging deeper. It was yet another topic that had been placed off limits.

Anyway, the tremors had been far stronger and more prolonged than any he had experienced previously. They weren't continuous but kept recurring every hour or so pretty much throughout the day. It may have been a coincidence, but about half an hour after each tremor a new guest, or guests, would arrive at the mansion. Each new visitor sparked a flurry of frenzied activity as they were whisked inside to join a growing throng gathering in the large conference room. As the day progressed, the noise from this room grew steadily louder; and with the hubbub came the distinctive sound of champagne corks popping. A party was going on, and to Woods intense frustration; he hadn't been invited.

Once again, the big, burly, 'V' scarred, army types were on the do-come-and-join-our-fun list, but he wasn't. Woods did, however, draw some comfort from the fact that no other pinpricked softie with a small 'v' on their wrists had been invited, either.

Here lay an important and unambiguous divide. The little 'v' members of the Dragza Club were inferior. Their membership gave them access to a point; and then it stopped. Woods had joined the club, but he wasn't a member of the inner sanctum. This was the privileged domain of the big 'V' military types.

It was an interesting divide—but thinking about this was also off limits and made his head hurt.

By mid afternoon, the gathering had grown so large that a couple of guards had politely suggested for Woods to vacate the patio area and spend the rest of his day down by the beach. It was a request he wasn't expected to refuse, although he had been able to inquire as to the reason why.

Apparently, the sudden influx of guests was due to a reunion; a get-together for the extended family of the Count and Contessa. Peering nosily from the beach, Woods had managed to catch a glimpse of some of the guests through the swathe of palm trees.

They were an excited and eclectic-looking bunch.

The two brothers—Woods couldn't remember their names—were there of course; prancing about enthusiastically while plying the guests with copious amounts of alcohol. There was a tall and slender man with teeth that flashed alarmingly in the sun; and another swarthy gentleman who had lost half an arm. A particularly beautiful woman was also present. She stood out from the crowd by virtue of the fact that she was wearing a wig. Not some boring, pedestrian, off-the-shelf, fancy dress costume wig; but one that shone like gold in the late afternoon sun. Several teenagers were also present, including a pale-skinned girl with a violent shock of curly, ginger hair. He also remembered a large and ebullient man with a booming voice. His hair and matted beard were greying, and he wore a ring upon a finger. This sparkled with a cluster of radiant diamonds.

When he came to think about it, most of the guests had been sporting diamond-encrusted rings, too.

Curiously for a family reunion, one person was conspicuous by her absence: The Contessa. Whether or not the Count was there Woods wouldn't know; they hadn't yet met, so it was impossible to say. Certainly Woods couldn't see anyone sporting the Count's distinctive eye patch.

Growing tired with guest watching and with the party showing no signs of letting up; Woods had made his way to bed in the small hours. Music, laughter, and the splashing of guests as they ended up falling or being chucked into the pool continued until long after he had drifted into sleep.

What a day—and what a party.

"Sir, excuse me, sir."

Woods' daydreaming came to an abrupt end as a shy but persistent servant invaded his contemplation.

"I'm so sorry to disturb you sir; but your presence is requested in the conference room."

Putting his beer down, Woods stood up slowly and stretched. After thanking the servant and reassuring him that it wasn't an inconvenient time, Woods followed the man back across the patio and toward the mansion steps. Tingling with anticipation, he followed the servant inside.

This was it, the debit side of joining the Dragza club; the price all members had to pay for the privilege of eternal youth.

A request to the conference room could only mean one thing.

The Corporation had a job for him.

After an initial euphoria with the information Lia supplied, Anna's happiness quickly turned to dismay. Far from being a treasure trove of insider knowledge, the girl's mind was reminiscent of a small child's piggy bank; one rattling with paltry pennies—but precious little else.

Yes, Lia had heard of the Valkyries, but no; she had never met one.

Yes, she had seen the news about the nuclear accident; but what did that have to do with the Dragza Corporation?

Self-preservation and greed were her only guiding principles, and unless information helped Lia in either of these directions; knowledge was discarded like so many empty sweet wrappers. She didn't give a damn.

Despite her lack of usefulness, Lia seemed a bright and cheerful soul who had an arrogant and infectious personality. With Marcus gone, she made for an entertaining companion, and the two of them set about the task of tidying up the flat with gusto.

Shaking her head mournfully, Anna decided to make a painful, watershed decision. Despite so many happy memories; the tattered, old, corduroy settee had to go. In Lia's words; it was "disgusting."

Lia was a snob and a man hater; both attributes acquired from a cosseted and privileged life on the island. She had become accustomed to luxury; a lifestyle bought with the currency of her body. Acquiescing to the sexual demands of the Dragza's guests had bought her affluence and privilege, but it had come at a cost. She was contemptuous of men. To Anna, that price was too high, and she felt a deep sense of pity for the girl.

How could Lia fall in love as Anna had done; and how could she ever experience the joys of motherhood?

High-class whoring, prostitution, or whatever name you chose to call it; had destroyed her. It had raped her womanhood and plundered her soul. Stripped of the trappings of privilege, the exquisite child had nothing.

Lia was a plaything; a pretty toy for the billionaire jet set—until they grew bored with her. Her treatment had been criminal; but it was probably one of the lesser crimes perpetrated by the many guests of the Dragza Corporation.

As the two of them set about their day of frenetic cleaning, Anna took a disturbing phone call from the police. Marcus had been transferred to a secure mental unit. The officers were sketchy about the details, but he had suffered some sort of nervous breakdown and had required sedating. To Anna's cynical mind, if you substituted the words 'extreme physical violence' for 'sedation,' then you would probably be closer to the mark.

This news alarmed her and brought back the morbid thoughts of yesterday.

Marcus was on a slippery slope and sliding ever closer to the 'accident' that lay in store for him. Lia's crazy suggestion may have been naïve, but it was one Anna needed to give some serious consideration. If there was any way at all that she could spring her husband from jail, then she would have to give it a go.

She didn't care if she failed. *So what if she went to prison?*

Without Marcus, her life was meaningless anyway. Physical detention behind bars would be little different from the suffering she was experiencing behind the mental bars that had shuttered her life since his arrest.

Trying to rescue her husband was a risk worth taking.

"Hey, Mrs. Finch, I mean Anna, come over here and take a look. Wow! It's amazing."

Lia was standing at an open window and leaning excitedly out of it. Anna hurried over and joined her. To her surprise, the girl wasn't pointing at a disturbance on the bustling pavement but rather to something on the roof of the building opposite.

Following the line of her arm, Anna had to agree; the sight was certainly spectacular—and most unusual.

Perched high on a ledge and clearly visible was a large bird of prey. A crowd of hostile feathered 'friends' were flapping angrily around him; mobbing and squawking their fear at his intrusion. The presence of so large a predator was definitely unwelcome.

Growing increasingly irritated by their noise, and after about five minutes of suffering, the majestic bird unfurled his wings and took flight. To Anna and Lia's delight, his path brought him within a whisker of their window.

Passing barely an arm span away from where they stood, Anna was convinced that the fabulous creature had turned his head and studied them intently. The moment lasted but an instant, and then the mighty bird was gone.

Excitement over, the two women returned their heads inside of the flat and, after securing the window carefully behind them, they got on with their work.

There was still much tidying to do.

Vali flapped his wings lazily as he took flight. Fed up with the annoying gaggle of squawking birds, he had decided he didn't need to suffer their taunts and heckling any longer. The first part of his mission was over—and it had been an unqualified success.

In an arrogant display of self-confidence, he decided to fly as close to his target as he possibly could.

Inhaling her scent as he memorised every blemish on her comely face; Vali took stock of Mrs. Marcus Samuel Finch.

He would be seeing her again—real soon.

39

Gods No More

Rescuing Frigg from Odin's citadel was a lot trickier than most of the warriors had anticipated. It took three attempts by Thor to smash one of the windows with his hammer. Still desperately weak from losing so much blood, his first throw was too soft, and his second missed the target; making a big crack in the wall. Cursing angrily at his incompetence, Thor threw his hammer for a third and final time. Luckily, this was bang on target.

Silk took charge for the next part of the operation.

Flying up and smashing her swan's body through the remnants of the shattered glass; she liberated a tired, cold, dehydrated, and extremely dishevelled Frigg from the sack.

Her presence inside the bag came as something of a shock.

There had been considerable speculation by the girls as to who the captive might be, but no one had considered Odin's wife might be the prisoner.

Freed at last, Mika fired an arrow through the window with a length of slender thread attached to it. Thicker rope was then hauled up and a crude winch constructed using the remaining chairs in the room. After approximately an hour or so, Frigg was slowly, but surely, lowered to the ground. While she dusted herself down and went inside the castle to get freshened up, two telescopes were lowered for Henry to have a look at. He tried to be picky, but Silk had had enough. After stupidly asking for a third instrument, he was forced to duck sideways. Silk had hurled the rope down, and it had nearly landed on him, much to everyone's amusement.

Drama over, the party returned to the warmth inside the castle. After a brief rest and some mulled wine, the seats in the feasting hall were quickly rearranged. When Frigg was ready, they were going to have the mother of all meetings.

Asgard lay in tatters.

The earthquake and dragons had either burnt or demolished a third of the buildings in the small town. Even Gladsheim, the great judgement hall of Odin, lay in pieces. Not content with just torching the flagpole, the dragons had returned and set fire to its thatched roof. The place was gutted; collapsed and charred rafters lying smouldering in piles beneath an open sky. It would take months to rebuild the heart of Asgard.

With her usual attention to detail, Frigg took at least three hours to get bathed, find some clothes that she could consider wearing; and then have her hair styled in a manner to her liking. All of these things would have happened a lot quicker if only she could have waved her hand over her ring and gone to Fensalir. Unfortunately, while she'd been drugged; Odin had taken this. She was now powerless and at the mercy of the warriors; not that anybody would have known. Barking orders left, right, and centre; Frigg held court; regally recruiting every servant and maid in the castle to assist her in her preparations. Serfs were running around in a terrible lather as the process of Frigg's beautification gathered a head of steam. Every other matter was put on hold until the goddess had been suitably pampered and coiffured.

Like some grand operatic diva, Frigg wasn't going to accept second best. She would either arrive at the meeting as the belle of the ball—or she wouldn't be arriving at all.

Minutes ticked into hours, and it was to a chorus of muttered discontent that Frigg eventually made her entrance to the meeting. Despite the hostilities between her and Odin; and her well known dislike for his Valkyries; their annoyance at her tardiness quickly turned to rapture. Everybody got to their feet and clapped and cheered. Three hours of prinking and preening had done their job.

Frigg looked magnificent.

Taking her place on a chair that had been hastily seconded into the role of a throne; the first order of the day was easily decided. With Odin dead, Frigg graciously accepted the title of Queen of Asgard. She would become the new ruler of the realm.

Initially, there had been some controversy as to who might succeed Odin. Many of the Valkyries (particularly Silk, Ruby, and Carmel) believed that Thor was the natural successor, but on asking; he had flatly refused the invitation. He enjoyed being who he was and where he was, and besides; how could he boss his mother around?

Most of the warriors accepted his decision and the reasons behind it. Carmel, however, didn't; and she had a fit of the sulks. Her aspirations of becoming Astrid 'The Powerful Queen' who would sit beside Thor had been dashed; and she was none too pleased with his lack of ambition.

They would be having words—later.

Succession sorted, the next important issue was the restoration of the power of nine. There were currently only eight Valkyries, and two eager contenders had already staked their claims to being the ninth; Hel and the maid Lara. Neither was willing to back down, and both had staunch and vociferous supporters.

In Lara's corner stood Silk, Carmel, Ruby, Mika, and Jameela. Silk hated Hel with a vengeance and made it clear that she wouldn't tolerate Hel as a warrior; although quite what she would do if Hel became one was anybody's guess. Ruby had issues as regards Hel's former Valkyrie persona. The Black Valkyrie mustn't be allowed to rise again—and safeguards would have to be put in place to ensure that she didn't. Hel's horrific past was chilling, and that nightmare couldn't be unleashed again.

In the former Queen of the Damned's corner were Kat, Jess, Zara, and of course Frigg. Frigg felt particularly strongly about this point. It was going to be awkward being the Queen of Asgard and having power over Hel when only a few days earlier the roles had been reversed; she serving her as the Queen of Niflheim. Having raised this delicate issue, Hel was extremely gracious as regards her fall in stature. Her only desire, now as it always had been, was to be a Valkyrie.

This had been the joy of her life until Odin had shattered her dreams.

With battle lines drawn, the meeting quickly descended into chaos with mud being slung by both sides. It was a stalemate; and one that was rapidly becoming ugly. Neither side would back down, nor was there any room for compromise. It was either Hel or Lara, black verses white—or vice versa; depending on your point of view.

Remarkably, it wasn't a Valkyrie or a god who ended the deadlock.

Stepping forward into the middle of the hall, it was Elijah who suggested the perfect compromise.

Along with the Valkyries and the remaining gods; only Henry, Elijah, and Ben had been invited to the meeting. Once Frigg had arrived, the doors to the feasting hall had been securely locked and bolted; and a guard posted outside. Things were going to be said that could damage the confidence and loyalty of the Aesir.

Their casualties at Ragnarok had been heavy.

Less than half the thousand-strong army of men had returned from the battlefield, and many of these had been severely injured. Couple these losses with those sustained in the earlier battle against Hel's Berserkers, and a clearer picture of the realm came alarmingly into view.

Asgard was teetering on the verge of collapse.

With Odin's death and the deaths of the other gods so well witnessed and documented; word of Asgard's weakness would spread fast. Giants, dwarves, and dark elves were all eager to conquer the realm and lay claim to its fertile hunting grounds. All around Asgard, axes were being ground and swords were being sharpened.

It would soon be time for their enemies to declare open season.

With this somber truth weighing heavily on their minds, the meeting today between the gods and the Valkyries was going to be so much more than just petty bickering about who would be doing what job. It was the last chance saloon to restore order before the realm descended into chaos. Fear of invasion would provoke rioting and looting; and this could be but a moment of indecision away. If the Aesir so much as smelt a whiff of dissent among their ruling elite; that would be it—game over. A civil war would ensue, and everybody would lose.

The warriors' victory in saving Asgard might yet prove to be premature; hence the need for secrecy to this meeting. Eventually, when matters were settled and the doors flung open wide; the gods and Valkyries had to be united. Anything less could spell trouble: deep, dark, sinister trouble.

Elijah's solution to the ninth Valkyrie impasse was therefore like a breath of fresh air—and also rather elegant. Make Ruby their queen so that both Lara and Hel could become Valkyries.

The solution was so breathtakingly simple that it was passed in a heartbeat—and to a chorus of furious cheers and stamping of feet. It was the perfect outcome, and the warriors and maids quickly formed a line and swore their allegiance to their new queen. Each in turn knelt and kissed her hand; as did Hod, Thor, Henry, Ben, and a much embarrassed Elijah. He hated being in the limelight.

Without Mimir (the absence of his cask from Odin's citadel having been noted), Frigg decided to choose Lara's warrior name. Probing deep inside her mind, her eventual choice came as a very pleasant surprise.

The fair Lara would become the Valkyrie Eir; her name meaning 'peace' or 'clemency.' Although the rather bullish Lara was neither peaceful nor merciful by nature, she accepted her warrior name with pride. As Frigg explained; she had chosen this name looking forward rather than back.

Eir was both a declaration of hope and a statement of intent.

Asgard needed to become a happier, safer, and more peaceful realm if it was going to live long and prosper. Every effort would be made to dampen hostilities with other kingdoms, defusing the many ticking time bombs left by Odin's bigotry. With the realm so badly devastated, contrition and respect for Asgard's neighbours might be their only hope for salvation.

After the hiccup of choosing the next Valkyrie, the meeting seemed to get nicely back on track. Several further decisions were passed unanimously and without undue acrimony or argument.

What had happened to the heroes?

It was decided that Frigg would accompany Ben and Jameela to Valhalla and see if they could find any clues as to their disappearance. This issue was troubling, but not nearly as disturbing as the next bombshell Frigg exploded inside their heads.

"The gods are still alive," she announced calmly and in a matter-of-fact way of speaking. The hall hushed immediately as the importance of her statement sank slowly in.

"Well, if they are; where are they?" Silk eventually responded. She had been certain that Balder was alive; she could feel it in her bones.

"I'm not exactly sure. Do you know?" Frigg enquired looking toward Hod and Thor. They both shook their heads.

"Excuse me," Ruby interrupted indignantly. "Are you trying to tell us that the gods we saw perish on the battlefield are not only alive, but that the three of you knew this all along?"

"I'm sorry," Thor muttered as he nodded his head apologetically. "We should have said something sooner."

"Should have said something sooner?" Silk fumed. "How dare you! We have suffered and wept tears for their deaths, and that's all you can come up with—*I'm sorry, we should have said something sooner!* How could you!" She was livid, as were the other warriors.

Pandemonium erupted.

Hands twitched on swords as the warriors swiftly surrounded the gods who had retreated into a huddle by the throne. The trio looked embarrassed, as well they should be. This news was horrific. The Valkyries had sweated blood, defending the realm and for what?

Absolutely nothing.

This couldn't be happening. How could the gods have just got up and left? The thought was impossible; they had all seen them fall— Heimdall, Tyr, and Freyr. Frigg must be lying, she had to be.

Not so, she cried as she tried to calm the furious girls. Look at the evidence. Other than Odin's arm and ring; what other body parts had been found? Bits of the dead Aesir soldiers lay strewn throughout the battlefield but not one single piece of any of the gods. Yes, the warriors had seen them fall—*but had they seen them die?*

A simple wave over their rings and that would be it; they would be gone, spirited away to safety; wherever that might be.

The warriors' angry denial slowly crumbled into acceptance; and from acceptance rose a fresh and even fiercer rage. This was directed at Thor and Hod rather than Frigg. She had been trussed up in Odin's citadel throughout the battle and couldn't have raised the alarm. Thor and Hod on the other hand, could have and most certainly should have done so.

Swords were drawn, and it looked as though blood would be spilt. Thor might still be the mightiest warrior in the realm, but with the Valkyries baying like a pack of hungry wolves; in his weakened state even he could be defeated.

"Banish them!" Came a cry from one of the girls. This was rapidly followed by louder and more passionate demands for whipping and castration. The Valkyries wouldn't kill the gods, but they intended to punish them severely for their betrayal.

One thing was for certain. The warriors could no longer accept the gods' leadership and omnipotence. A price would have to be paid for their lies. The warriors' hearts were bleeding, and that bitter flow had to be stemmed. Harsh retribution was the order of the day, and the girls were determined to reap a bloody vengeance.

It was Hod who surprisingly took up their challenge and offered a flag of surrender. Stepping forward, he got to his knees and knelt before Kat. Raising his hands, he begged the angry warriors for silence. After some minutes, a semblance of peace descended.

Hod would get his chance to sing for his manhood.

"I fully understand why you are so angry, and I'm sorry, truly sorry, from the bottom of my heart," he began, ruefully. "I alone chose to stay with you all in Asgard. I could have left, but I didn't. I love Asgard—and I love you, my lady Sangrid."

A brief murmur of approval rippled around the room. This public apology and declaration of love was appreciated—but it still wasn't enough to save him from a public flogging.

"Please don't blame Thor," he continued pleadingly. "He expected to die beside Odin. His sacrifice was the most noble of sacrifices; to give his life for the realm. Please, I beg of you, don't discard the love and respect you have always had for him."

"That is all well and good, Hod, but it doesn't exactly help you, does it?" Ruby hissed menacingly as she stood over him. "Your partner in crime may be innocent, but you most certainly aren't." She prodded him harshly with the tip of her sword.

"Hey, wait a minute," Thor stepped forward and pushed Ruby roughly out of the way. "That's my brother you're talking about. If any of you want to pick a fight with him, then you will have to get through me first." Placing his hand on Mjollnir, he pulled his hammer from his belt.

This was it. The moment of meltdown.

"Please, Thor, wait," Kat implored, stepping forward and putting her hand on his arm. "Hod hasn't finished. Why don't we all just calm down for a moment and let him speak."

Thor nodded grumpily and released his grip. What Hod had to say had better be good, for all their sakes.

"Here, my lady Sangrid," Hod offered. "Take this; I entrust you with its care. This is my sacrifice; this is my peace offering to you all." Placing one hand over the other, he pulled his ring from his finger and offered it to Kat. The room fell silent as she held it briefly in her hands before slipping it onto a finger. It was a surprisingly snug fit, and she felt a tingle of excitement and power as the ring settled into place.

It sparkled magnificently.

She was a goddess!

Hod's gesture was as humbling as it was bold. He was no longer a god.

Without his ring, he was as powerless as any mortal and completely at the mercy of the Valkyries. They would now decide when, or if, he received Idun's apples; the apples upon which his very life depended. In a very real sense, this now lay in Kat's hands.

"What about you, Thor, what sacrifice are you going to make?" Silk goaded. Hod had surrendered his omnipotence—but would his brother follow suit?

"My lady Astrid; please accept my ring as a token of my sincerity. I too wish to remain in Asgard; defending our beautiful realm against its enemies."

To everybody's surprise, Thor had knelt before Carmel and offered her his ring. With a great squeal of delight, she accepted it and tried to put it on. Unfortunately, being so big it didn't fit, not even on her thumb. She scowled angrily at him. She, too, wanted to become a goddess.

"Don't worry," Thor added wryly, noting her annoyance. "I can always sort the band out for you."

Taking his hand enthusiastically in hers, Carmel helped Thor back to his feet and turned to face her sisters. "I say we accept Thor and Hod's apologies and reparations. Hail Odin!"

"HAIL ODIN!" Came the rousing reply.

Their betrayal had been appeased.

Chuckling and smiling broadly, Thor hugged and kissed each warrior in turn. Hod did likewise, although he blushed rather more than chuckled. For once, he had saved the day, and Frigg thanked him warmly for his selflessness when it was her turn to congratulate him. She had reservations about the power her sons had given the warriors, but that could wait for another day. Peace had been restored, and that was what mattered most.

As the room settled down once more, Henry decided to deliver another unintentional but equally profound bombshell.

"Odin is alive," he announced cheerily and unexpectedly.

"What!" Ruby exclaimed loudly. "Henry, you weren't even at the battle, how can you make such an outrageous statement?"

"I can and I will," he retorted calmly with typical disregard for his safety. His outlandish suggestion really was playing with fire.

"Before I take you outside and thrash you for this blasphemy," Ruby raged in a manner that left nobody in any doubt that she intended to do just that. "Would your fabulous, genius mind please kindly explain how it could have arrived at such a ludicrous conclusion? We all saw Odin's severed arm in Fenrir's mouth. Trust me when I say it: Odin is dead, dead, dead."

"No he's not," Henry retorted with a boyish grin. "It's a classic case of Occam's razor."

"What in Asgard are you talking about? Stop speaking in riddles you idiot," Silk snarled, clipping him soundly around the back of the head. She too felt insulted.

Odin had been slain, and the next item they had intended to discuss was how to honour his noble sacrifice. The last thing they needed was a silly debate as to whether this had actually happened or not. They had half an arm and his ring; surely that was proof enough?

"When there are several possible answers to a problem, then the simplest solution is usually correct," he began confidently. "That's Occam's razor, and it applies in this case." Henry folded his arms across his chest. Silk and Ruby may well be fuming with rage, but their power and fury were nothing compared to Hel's—and he'd survived that. "If all the other gods have survived Ragnarok," he continued, "then you can be certain Odin would have done so, too. There's no way he would sacrifice himself, he's far too selfish to do that."

"Prove your blasphemy," Ruby seethed. "Because if you don't—you die."

"Yes, I will prove it and no; no I won't die. You won't kill me; because you can't," he snorted arrogantly. "None of you can kill me. You need me. Without my help, you will never sort out the mystery behind lambda."

Ruby made to strike Henry for his insolence—before thinking better of it. The impudent puppy was right, more's the pity.

"Can one of you get me Odin's ring?" Henry enquired politely. "Preferably without a rotting hand attached to it," he added with a titter. He really was pushing his luck.

After a brief delay, the ring was brought to the room. It sparkled and gleamed majestically in the fading, afternoon light.

"Please, my lady. Would you be so kind as to put it on?" He asked Frigg, and she did so. "Now, why don't you wave your hand over it and get some apples from Odin's garden."

Pausing briefly as she looked around the room, Frigg tried to do as Henry had suggested. Nothing happened. There was no flash of light and no instant appearance of a basket filled with apples. Frigg tried again—still nothing.

The ring had to be a fake.

"You're such a clever boy," she enthused, smiling warmly at Henry.

"This proves nothing," Ruby retorted loudly, raising her voice above the erupting hubbub. "Why would Odin's ring work on Frigg?"

This question silenced the girls. Prudr had a point.

"Well, it should," Frigg volunteered. "Just as Thor and Hod's rings should work for Sangrid and Astrid. They're not specific to the wearer. Odin was never very good about security."

"I can't accept that," Ruby stormed defensively. "Even if their rings do work on Sangrid and Astrid, it doesn't mean that Odin's ring has to do so as well. This proves nothing. Our noble lord is dead; I'd wager my life on it."

"Please, your majesty," Henry butted in, deciding to up the stakes. "If I may borrow the ring for one moment, I may be able to prove my case conclusively."

Frigg took the ring off her finger and gave it back to Henry. She was intrigued. She would have loved to read his mind and spoil the surprise, but in the end she decided not to. Sometimes, even she enjoyed a good punch line.

Kneeling on the floor, Henry placed the ring on one of the flagstones. "May I borrow your hammer?" he asked Thor cautiously.

Scratching his head with curiosity, Thor handed it to him.

Raising the hammer high above his head, Henry made to strike the ring.

"Sweet Odin!" Silk exclaimed, thrusting her sword deep into Henry's neck such that it made him jump. "What in Asgard do you think you're doing, you idiot?"

"If this genuinely is Odin's ring, then it should be made of diamonds, right?" Henry enquired, and the warriors nodded. "If I hit it, the ring will be damaged, but the diamonds should remain intact. If, however, the ring is fake; then the gems will shatter," he continued.

Silk lowered her sword. "I think, rather a lot rides on this act of treason," she muttered grimly, looking toward Ruby. "If you break Odin's ring and the diamonds remain intact, I will take your head. Think about it. Is smashing it really worth the risk?"

Henry gulped hard. For the first time nerves got the better of him. Looking up, he glanced anxiously around the gathering. The warriors were nodding their agreement to Silk's suggestion: it seemed fair. Henry would lose his head if the ring was genuine.

It was his call. Prove his case—or die. It couldn't be simpler.

"Oh, do go on, darling," Hel enthused provocatively, pushing forward and ruffling his hair. "Prove that that filthy, evil lying scum bag was a cheat. Show these doting idiots how big a bastard their beloved master really was."

Hel startled abruptly when she'd finished speaking. The sudden coldness of Ruby's sword was now resting firmly against her neck.

"I think, my dearest Gunnr," Ruby growled, staring hard in Silk's direction. "Two heads should role if Henry is proved wrong."

It was the former Queen of the Damned's turn now to gulp and pale. Dissing Odin in front of his loyal Valkyries hadn't been the brightest of moves. Still; there was no turning back now.

"Go on, Foxy," she urged with a prod. "Smash the bastard's ring."

Raising Thor's hammer high above his head, Henry brought it down with all his might.

40

Dispersal

$\mathcal{M}$uch to Woods' delight, a technical hitch with his mission meant that his departure from the island was delayed for twenty-four hours. Settling back into his recliner once more, he looked forward to another day of tanning and another day of marinating his liver in alcohol. It was divine, and just when he thought things couldn't get better—they did.

New hostesses had arrived and, with the VIP guests still very much the worse for wear, Woods had the pick of the crop. In one way he missed Christina and the other girls; but in another he didn't. A certain, bitchy snobbery had been replaced by fresh and innocent faces; girls willing to impress and eager to please. Woods didn't bother making a mental note of the name of the hottie he bagged for the day—and night; she was young, beautiful, and good in bed; and at least she didn't intend to kill him.

That was all he really needed to know.

Surprisingly, the new hostesses seemed to be taking orders from an equally new boss. This was a tall, somewhat severe-looking woman who appeared about the same age as the Contessa. Woods wasn't introduced to her, and he didn't struggle to get acquainted. Something in the steely stare of her blue eyes, her arrogant, Roman nose, and the harsh, wedge-shaped, bob of her jet-black hair screamed an emphatic "No!"

This was a woman he definitely shouldn't mess with.

311

Eating a cheery supper at the beach bar with his new companion, Woods retired for the night. The family reunion held centre stage once more, but this time it was in a much more subdued and civilized manner. The patio once again had been placed off limits, but the guests didn't dally. By the time Woods headed toward his bed, the area was already deserted.

Clearly, the Count's VIPs had plans for an early start, too.

Rising early, Woods was taken by surprise when he arrived at the island's airstrip. It was a hubbub of activity, with three jets waiting with engines running and each plane already full of passengers. The party goers were returning home, and Woods was going to share his flight to Washington with four of them.

Just before they took off, a black sedan car emerged from one of the hangers and sped off at high speed across the tarmac in the direction of the mansion. All the windows to the vehicle were blackened, and it was clear that the occupant or occupants wanted to remain hidden from view. For the briefest of moments, Woods mused if the person in the car was the patient from yesterday.

With a sudden, muffled roar and with a heavy pressure in his back, the jet sped down the runway before climbing steeply into a cloudless Caribbean sky. Banking tightly, the plane turned north to follow the contours of the coastline. It was going to be a picturesque journey home.

Glancing around him, Woods recognised all four of the other occupants. The excessively beautiful woman with the golden wig was there, minus her wig, and the shy, ginger-haired, teenage girl was sitting opposite her. Woods guessed intuitively that she must be her daughter. Sitting opposite him was the tall gentleman with the gold capped teeth; and behind him sat an extremely handsome man with dark, curly hair. The plane had one empty seat.

The party guests were in a jovial mood as they chatted excitedly amongst themselves. Woods tried to join their conversation, but his attempts to forge links with this inner sanctum were politely turned down. He was a member of the club, not the family.

In a manner very reminiscent of the snubs he had received from the Contessa, his friendly overtures were rejected with generous—but faked—smiles.

Knowing when to fold, Woods beat a gracious retreat and turned his attention to enjoying the view from the window. Slights from the Dragza Corporation didn't hurt anymore. He had got his reward, and he tapped the contents of his hand luggage reassuringly.

He had the golden apples; he would live forever.

Touching down at Dulles airport, the tall man disembarked with Woods. He hugged and kissed his travelling companions goodbye and then sped away in a waiting limousine without offering Woods as much as a handshake. The other three passengers stayed on board and, by some fluke, Woods discovered their destinations. He had accidentally overheard the flight plans as they were being discussed in the cockpit. The plane was going to be refuelled and heading off across the Atlantic. Two stops were planned before its return flight to New York tomorrow. One was for London Heathrow, and the other was for Charles de Gaulle in Paris.

Flagging down a taxi, Woods headed for the centre of Washington, and within two hours, he was sitting comfortably behind his old desk in his old office—munching an apple. He was back, but he wouldn't be staying, thank goodness. Tonight was to be but a brief stopover, that's all.

Paperwork had already been put in place, and this was what he was scrutinising now. He would be heading off early tomorrow morning to New York, and he didn't want any last-minute administrative foul-ups to delay his progress. He was only too aware of the catastrophic consequences of the wrong form being stamped or names and dates not tallying.

With any luck, he would be back in paradise before sunset tomorrow with his mission accomplished and his target to hand.

The person he was destined to collect had something the Dragza Corporation wanted—and what the corporation wanted, it always got.

41

Naked Hearts

$\mathfrak{H}$enry shattered the hearts of the Valkyries far more effectively than he did the baubles of Odin's ring. The diamonds were made of glass and smashed instantly into a million tiny pieces.

The ring had been a fake.

Odin was alive.

Hel shrieked loudly with joy before falling silent.

In the moments following the hammer's cataclysmic blow, the walls of Asgard came crumbling down. Large tears began to roll down the cheeks of the silent warriors as they reflected on an apocalyptic truth.

Odin had deceived them.

While the warriors wept, Carmel slipped quietly out of the hall for a few minutes and then returned. She too was now crying. She had the final proof of Odin's callous treachery. A fake ring, Mimir's cask missing from the citadel, Gungnir vanished from the battlefield, and now this; Odin's eye taken from the Chamber of the Valkyries. Short of leaving the girls a *Dear John* letter and a forwarding address, the evidence was overwhelming. Occam's razor had been vindicated.

Odin lived—and therein lay their anguish.

The Valkyries had been living a lie.

The warriors cried and hugged each other as the bitter truth stabbed deep into their hearts. All the terrible wars they had fought, all the heroes they had rescued, and all the evil souls they had tortured and killed; had been for nothing.

They had been duped and used.

Odin had taken them all for a ride, and when he had no further use for them; he'd abandoned them—leaving them to die on the battlefield; fighting for him and his duplicitous lackeys. The gods hadn't even bothered to say thank you for the warriors' efforts. No flowers and certainly no slap up, thank-you-for-saving-our-arses feast goodbye. They'd been dumped; and left to perish in pools of their own blood. They had been used and abused.

The warriors felt humiliated.

Thor joined them in their grief, and a wave of sympathy spread round the room. He too had been duped; conned into sacrificing his life by a father who couldn't care less. Odin had saved his own hide while flicking two fingers at Thor's. Thor wept for the mighty Valkyries, and Carmel offered him back his ring. He waved her away. He didn't want it; it made him feel physically sick to even look at it, let alone put it on his finger. She and the Valkyries were its new deserving owners; and they were worthy of its awesome power. The Valkyries were the true gods of Asgard, the defenders of the weak. They alone had stood firm while the lying, cheating pack of sycophantic gods had followed their Pied Piper to paradise.

Odin and his ilk weren't worthy to kiss the girls' feet.

A fresh wave of anger grew toward Hod. He was now the visible face of treachery and stood alone before the vengeful women. Seeing their fury rising, Kat acted quickly and decisively. She was upset by their lord's betrayal, but not completely devastated.

It hadn't really come as a surprise.

She had suspected a hidden darkness to Odin's soul some time ago. Forcing Hod to his knees, she spelt out his fate. Not only was he no longer a god, he would now be her servant. Slapping him hard across the face, she sent him scurrying from the room. His escape came just in time. In a matter of moments, a fresh chorus of anger gave way to calls for his blood. If Hod was lucky and Kat treated him harshly enough; his life might just be spared. Without Frigg and her support; Hod's life was forfeit. He was public enemy number one—and there was nowhere left for him to run or hide.

After Henry's horrific revelation, it took a long time for order to return to the hall. Everyone was in a state of shock, and other decisions were passed numbly and on the nod. No one really wanted to talk. Any enthusiasm the warriors had had for the meeting had disappeared.

Odin's betrayal had left them wretched.

It was quickly decided that the gods must have gone to Midgard. Carmel and Thor hadn't seen them in Odin's garden, and Frigg confirmed that destination as likely; describing the countless orchards of apples on Odin's island as the damning proof. Midgard and not Yggdrasill had been the chosen lifeboat for the cowardly gods; the safe haven from which the despots could weather Asgard's fatal storm.

After some deliberation, it was agreed to send a reconnaissance party through the well. Its role would be strictly a fact-finding mission; and not vengeance. With the gods still very much alive, a key question screamed to be answered.

Did they intend to return to Asgard?

Kat and Jess were chosen for this mission. They knew the lay of the land and also had a secret house to shelter in. Marcus was one of Hel's Angels and he would surely assist them. Other warriors begged to join the posse, but Frigg held firm with one exception. Hel would be going along, too.

This was a calculated gamble, weighing Frigg's sense of obligation to her former queen against Hel's desire to kill Odin. Hel was volatile and hated the self-appointed god of gods more than anyone; but she also had an instinctive cunning and tremendous strength; both qualities that might just come in handy. Sending her to Midgard would be a high-risk gamble, but it was one Frigg decided to take.

She owed her former queen a debt of gratitude, and this would repay it.

Apart from sending Jameela with Ben and Henry to Valhalla, two further expeditions were planned to depart from the castle tomorrow. Ruby, Silk, and Elijah would head toward the watchtower and secure the Bifrost Bridge against invasion. The giants would surely take advantage of their weakened state, and the presence of Valkyries at the outpost might just dissuade them from attacking.

Thor and Carmel would also depart on a mission; a mission to undo the wicked slur that shamed the name of Asgard. They would liberate Loki and his wife Sigyn; if they were still alive.

This matter was dear to Thor's heart. His failure to save Loki's son still troubled his conscience, so freeing Loki might just assuage that guilt. He was anxious to make this trip alone, but Carmel insisted otherwise. She held his ring, so she was going and that was that. Besides, she was still intrigued by their conversation on the eve of Ragnarok.

Whatever crime Odin had committed, the truth must be exposed and not covered up. If the gods had done wrong, then she would personally punish Thor. Carmel had given her word on that, and she wasn't going to break it; not even for her godly lover.

Exhausted from a day of high drama, the meeting drew to its eventual close, and food was brought in by serfs and laid upon the tables. The meal looked delicious, but little was eaten. The Valkyries had lost their appetites.

Exhausted, depressed, and thirsting for revenge; the warriors headed toward their beds with one thought on their minds.

The gods must pay for their crimes.

TAP—TAP—TAP

"Ouch!"

"Oops, sorry, Hod," Kat apologised, tripping over the straw mattress she had laid for him at the foot of her bed.

"What's going on?" he enquired sleepily.

"Shush! Nothing; go back to sleep, I'll deal with it." Stumbling blindly over to the door, Kat fumbled with the lock and then opened it. Henry was hopping about outside in a state of agitation. "Do you have any idea what time it is?" she muttered crossly; it had to be late because it felt like she'd been asleep for hours.

"Late, very, very late," Henry mumbled apologetically. "I'm sorry, but I need you to come and have a look at something; to confirm something for me. It's very important."

"Is it to do with lambda?" Kat enquired with a loud yawn. Henry nodded.

"Okay. Just hang on a minute."

Grabbing a cloak and some shoes, Kat set off down the corridor and followed Henry to Hel's chambers. To her surprise, Frigg was already there. She was standing in front of the open window next to Hel, and beside them stood a telescope pointed toward the stars.

Henry had obviously been hard at work.

Kat shivered. A log fire was burning fiercely in the hearth but with the window wide open, the room was still freezing. *Why in Asgard did they need her, too?*

Gesturing with his hand, Henry beckoned for Kat to come over, and after adjusting the eyepiece to the telescope, he got her to take a look.

It took a good few minutes for Kat to get her bearings and for her groggy eyesight to focus properly, but when it did; she took her time and stared thoughtfully through the telescope. After a few minutes, she stood up.

"You're absolutely right, Henry," she scoffed wearily. "I can see stars, lots and lots of stars."

"OH hah, hah, Kat. Very funny—not. Look, this is serious; can you describe how the stars look to you?"

Kat studied Henry's face. He really was being serious.

Taking a deep breath in, Kat tried to compose her thoughts. "Well, there were a lot of stars; all very bright and quite a few looked blurry," she began.

"What colour were they?" Henry interrupted excitedly.

"White, twinkling," Kat was struggling for descriptive words. "White—but more like a sort of a bluey, white colour, actually, if you get my meaning."

"Absolutely," Henry enthused with a smile, "my finding exactly. Did you see any red stars?"

"No," Kat hadn't, she was sure of that.

"And the blurry stars," Henry continued. "Would you say that they were stars or could they be galaxies?"

Kat muttered something rude under her breath and then took another look through the eyepiece. After a few minutes she stood up again. *Curse him;* it was infuriating having him being so clever so late into the night.

"You're right, Henry, they're galaxies," she confirmed. "Lots and lots of great, big, spirally galaxies."

"You see!" Henry exclaimed triumphantly as he turned to Frigg and Hel with a grin upon his face. "Kat agrees with me, so I must be right."

"Right about what?" Kat enquired; he was talking in riddles again.

"The number for lambda," Hel interrupted as she leant forward and gave her clever boy a big hug. "He's worked it out, isn't Foxy a genius?"

"Okay, so come on, spill the beans already," Kat pleaded. "I'm tired and I want to get back to bed." She wasn't in a mood to watch Henry wallowing in his victory. If he really did have the answer—he should tell her now.

Taking a deep breath in, Henry repeated the explanation he had already given the others. It really was rather clever but unfortunately made the problem with lambda more confusing rather than less.

The sky at night in Asgard was much brighter than that in Midgard because there were many more stars visible. Importantly, many of these stars were fuzzy and blurred even to the naked eye. Just as Kat had confirmed, these blurry stars were in fact galaxies; and lots of them. All of these, just like almost all the stars, were a bluish white in colour.

Importantly, none of them had a reddish colour.

Taking these two observations into account, Henry could draw an elegant conclusion as to what the number for lambda, the Cosmological Constant, for their universe would be.

It was a negative number; and a large one, too.

Kat couldn't remember what this meant, so Henry explained its significance once more.

A negative number for the Cosmological Constant meant that there was too little start-up energy in the universe. Its big bang simply hadn't been big enough. Gravity would win over the energy of the initial explosion, and their universe would eventually collapse back upon itself to end in a big crunch; with everything becoming squashed to the size of a pinhead. The presence of so many galaxies close by suggested that the universe was already in an advanced state of collapse and hurtling in upon itself; the blue colour to the galaxies and stars confirmed this fact.

Light coming from stars behaves just like the siren of a fire engine, changing in frequency depending on whether it is coming toward you or going away. Light appears bluer from stars and galaxies coming toward you and redder (as in the Midgard universe) from stars and galaxies flying away from you.

The conclusion was therefore irrefutable. Their universe was collapsing and near to the end of its existence.

"So," Kat enquired nervously, deciding to ask the million-dollar question. "How long do you think we've got?"

"Well," Henry began, scratching his head and looking a bit perplexed. "That's the odd part. I'd say at least another one to two billion years or so."

"Oh, so no need to panic just now," Kat retorted sarcastically and with more than a little relief. "So can I go back to bed and not worry about being squashed to the size of a pea while I'm asleep? Honestly, Henry, I don't know why this couldn't have waited until the morning."

"Look, I'm really sorry to have woken you," Henry sighed apologetically. "But I needed someone who had a vague idea of what they are looking at and could confirm my findings," he continued. "No offence meant, ladies," he added hastily, turning and nodding apologetically toward Frigg and his lover.

"None taken, dear Henry," their queen enthused as she rubbed his arm. "It does leave us though with a bit of a headache, wouldn't you agree Kat?"

Kat nodded and hoped that she wouldn't be asked as to what she thought the headache might be. Her brain felt like mush.

"If Asgard has still got about two billion years left," Frigg volunteered, "then why was Odin in such a hurry to abandon the place right now?"

Pausing for a moment's silent contemplation, she decided to pose an even stickier and more pertinent question.

"What does Odin know about the Cosmological Constant that we don't?"

42

Carrots and Sticks

"Cheers!"

Odin clinked his glass against that of Mimir's and then, much to his delight, he watched as his friend shakily lifted the vessel to his lips and took a sip. It was only orange juice, but Mimir was making splendid progress. He could nod his head, move his arms and even stand unaided for a few moments. Physically, things were looking good but unfortunately, mentally, his friend remained a train wreck. Mimir could speak, but the words came out in random strings. It was as though his mind was desperately reaching out to the world; but hadn't quite made it there, yet.

Odin hoped he would do so soon; he missed and needed his friend.

It was ten to eleven, and the two of them were sitting in Odin's conference room. The windows had been opened, and a stiffening breeze was teasing the net curtains; tickling them in short gusts before retreating, waiting, and then tickling some more. The air was hot and humid, but not outrageously so; and Odin was in a cheerful—if somewhat reflective—mood.

They had all come so very far in the last forty-eight hours.

Looking back, he was secretly delighted that, with the exception of Hod, all the gods had made it safely to Midgard. A few were injured—notably Heimdall and Freyr, who had tried to play the role of heroes—but other than that, they were all present and accounted for.

Leaving Hod behind was a pity; but then again, Hod was a fool.

The boy had been warned, and he'd made his choice. If the love-sick dote wanted to stay with the treacherous Kat, then Odin wouldn't stop him. Sure, Hod believed he could make a difference, but then again; so had the attendant rearranging the deck chairs on the Titanic—and look what good that had done him. His youngest son was an idiot, but Odin hoped he would die happy. He deserved that much at least.

Odin had only one regret.

Why, oh why had he thrown Gungnir at Fenrir?

He had intended to miss the wretched beast anyway, so why bother to throw his spear in the first place? He shook his head in bewilderment; it was such a dumb thing to do, but a force of habit, he supposed. The loss of Gungnir was extremely annoying, and he could have done with this powerful weapon in Midgard; conjuring up the odd earthquake now and again to impress the natives.

Taking the plastic disk from his pocket, Odin smiled broadly. This was another annoying habit that was refusing to die; his constant glancing at the wretched thing. Tossing it in the air like a coin, Odin caught it and fondled the disk lovingly in his hand. It was beautiful; a lovely, healthy shade of forest green again; just as it had once been in Asgard. He really should throw the thing away, now that he had no need for it. However, just like some lucky penny, he put it back safely into his pocket.

It was a keepsake; a reminder of their narrow escape.

After checking his watch once more, he still had a few minutes, Odin mused over how Asgard might look right now. The planet still existed, its signature pattern was still registering on his well under the island; but how did it look?

How deep had been the damage inflicted by the Guardians?

No one from the realm had yet tried to use the well, so it was safe to assume that they must all be dead; toasted to cinders by Hel's apocalyptic nightmare. He was almost tempted to pop back and take a peek—but not quite tempted enough.

It would be foolish to take such an unnecessary risk.

Still, he would leave the well's connection open for another few days just in case someone popped up. They could yet surprise him. His cunning Valkyries were a resourceful bunch; he'd give them that.

Somebody might just have come up with a scheme to stop the unstoppable; halting the Gaurdians as they laid waste to Asgard.

However, all things considered, Ragnarok had gone extremely well.

It had been the perfect smoke screen; the monstrous, cataclysmic ending to all those bogus prophesies. The final, fatal battle must have been a wonder to behold; a tragically doomed struggle that had allowed the gods to slip away quietly; 'dying' like heroes with their reputations intact. What a delightful sight it must have been, he mused; to watch his Valkyries and the Aesir weeping over the deaths of their dear, beloved gods. The great bard himself couldn't have penned a more melodramatic—and fraudulent—ending.

Shouldn't he feel some shame at his deceit?

No. Unfortunately, he didn't.

The foul-up with lambda had been bad luck, not intentional. Maybe if Mimir had been whole, he might have been able to come up with a solution to its intractable flaw; who knew? But the problem had certainly defeated him and his brothers. Lambda couldn't be fixed, and the unavoidable consequence of that fact was sadly as plain as it was simple.

People had to die.

He couldn't save everybody, so some just had to accept their fate and perish, gracefully. His Valkyries and the Aesir had been the unlucky losers in that particular lottery, not his kith and kin. His fellow gods, they were his priority, and they'd been first to the lifeboats. There were always going to be casualties in war—and there were going to be a whole lot more in Midgard before he'd be done with the place.

When he put numbers to these figures; Asgard had actually got off lightly; very lightly indeed.

"Comfy?" Odin enquired with a chuckle as he opened the lid to the cask on the desk and poured a glass of water over the head inside. It was Mimir's cask, and it had seemed such a pity to leave the beautiful box empty. Waste not, want not; that was a good motto to live by, and by some ghoulish quirk of fate, he had found an eminently suitable head to replace that of Mimir.

A clock on the wall chimed the hour. It was eleven o'clock, and a bank of plasma screens on the wall before him flickered into life.

Odin closed the box quickly.

His video conference was about to start.

With customary politeness, Odin took his time in greeting each of the nine heads of state he had requested to call this morning. He knew some of them already, and those he didn't; he had made meticulous notes on. He enquired about the monsoon in India, the career of the French president's wife, the fitness of the Russian premier and, of course, the welfare of the American President's new puppy. This latter dignitary was particularly disgruntled, and Odin apologised profusely.

How dare Count Dragza explode a nuclear missile on American soil? This was an outrage and one the president was still smarting over. He had also had great difficulties covering the 'accident' up.

Odin smiled self-consciously before arguing his corner. He had at least detonated the bomb where it would cause minimum loss of life; and besides, would he really have got the attention of nine heads of state if all he had done was to send them a letter of invitation?

He thought not.

He needed to get their attention, and he'd done just that. The nuke had been a wake-up call; an alarm bell for Midgard. The gods were coming, and they weren't here to play tic-tac-toe.

Apologies over; Odin quickly got down to business. He had a lot to offer, and his asking price he felt was exceedingly generous. For just ten billion dollars a state—and a little culling of their populations— he would fix the world's problems. No more wars, disease, global warming, or famine; a world united in harmony under one rule—his rule.

There was an angry chorus of dissent at this point, which Odin did his best to calm. No, he wasn't seeking personal fame and glory; far from it. In fact; his place in a new world order could happily stay hidden from view. He was content to merely be the force behind the power, guiding the assembled, esteemed gentlemen toward a greater enlightenment. They should consider him perhaps as a kindly benefactor rather than some "money-grabbing despot" as one of those gathered had so unkindly put it.

Still not convinced?

Odin could offer more.

Lifting a basket of apples onto the table, Odin took a bite. For their peaceful co-operation, he was prepared to offer each and every leader the gift of immortality. They could rule forever—as long as they played by his rules.

At this point, just as Odin had predicted, the nine heads of state rounded on him.

Count Dragza was insane, a crazed empire builder who had let too much sun get to his head. They knew where his island was, so what did he think was stopping them from wiping the place from the face of the planet?

"That would be unfortunate," Odin retorted with a merry grin. He had anticipated this rather obvious move. Pulling a vial of fluorescent, pink-coloured fluid from his pocket, he waggled it tantilisingly before his camera.

"What's that?" enquired the British premier, voicing the dignitaries' collective thoughts.

"An insurance policy," he replied solemnly. "A deadly virus I will release if you try to destroy me." It was difficult not to laugh out loud as he made his threat. His ploy was laughable and reminiscent of the worst 'B movies' he could ever remember seeing. Remarkably, however, his crazy ultimatum worked. The assembled heads of state quietened down.

"What about your boast of immortality. Where's our proof?"

Odin could tell from this question and by the body language of the presidents of China, Brazil, and Japan; that at least some of the leaders were wavering; clearly tempted by his outlandish offer. Only the German premier remained silent; listening intently and without passing comment. Perhaps history troubled his conscience.

Odin decided to play his trump card.

Pressing his hand on a button under the table, the door to the conference room opened slowly, and a man shrouded in a blanket was led inside. Helped by one of his security guards, the mystery 'guest' was brought to stand beside him.

"Please allow me to introduce a very dear friend of mine," Odin offered with a smile, removing the blanket in a triumphant flourish. He felt just like a magician pulling a rabbit out of a hat. These puffed up, arrogant, Midgard leaders were all alike; so predictable and easy to manipulate. If proof of his godly powers was what they wanted, then proof they'd have.

Odin's magical bunny had the desired effect.

A shockwave of recognition blasted from screen to screen as each premier struggled to come to terms with the horror of the man standing before them. Of course, it could be a trick; the Count's friend might be an actor; but what if he wasn't? What if the person standing before them really was *that man?*

This thought was beyond imaginable horror. It was unthinkable.

Odin smiled once more.

"Gentlemen; I'm sure you need no introductions to our mutual friend and, of course, I will allow a small team of scientists to come and take genetic samples just to prove my claim. You too could live forever; just as my dear colleague here will do."

There was a long silence as the dignitaries digested Odin's offer.

"You mentioned a cull, Count Dragza. Perhaps you could be a little more specific?" Finally the German premier had spoken; and at such an interesting point in their negotiations.

"Oh, it's hard to be precise," Odin mulled nonchalantly, scratching his head. "Look, the world is overpopulated, we all know that. For us all to enjoy a happy, healthy lifestyle, then we need to shed, say, three or four billion, or thereabouts."

"Did you say million or billion? I didn't quite catch that," enquired a mystified Chinese president.

"Billion, of course; we need to leave about three billion people alive. That's a nice, sensible figure," Odin replied casually but emphatically.

"You're mad!" the President of the United States blustered angrily. "You and that ridiculous actor beside you! I'd laugh if the two of you weren't such a sorry sight." Leaning forward, he indicated that he was about to pull the plug on his part in the conference call. "You'll soon be history, Count," the President warned. "You and all your crackpot friends." He'd had enough. As soon as he got off the videophone he was going to authorise an air strike—napalm or something; anything to wipe the obnoxious, arrogant, jumped-up nobody from existence.

"I'm sorry you feel that way," Odin apologised politely. "Same goes for anyone else I may have offended. I am only here offering my help, that's all. My ambition is to guide you to a better world, one beyond your wildest dreams. That is my offer; that is my gift to you all."

Odin paused.

The President stayed on line, and no one else pulled their plug. They already knew Odin had clout, so he decided to up the ante—just a little bit.

"Here's the deal," he began. "I'll give each of you two weeks to deposit the ten billion dollars in my Swiss account as a gesture of good will. I'll also give you a further month to draw up the lists of those you want to save. I think that's being pretty reasonable, don't you?"

Odin paused once more; still no one had left the conference.

"Of course you can always decline my offer," he suggested wickedly, waggling the vial once more between his fingers. "But that, in my humble opinion, would be unfortunate. I will, of course, be in touch."

Pressing a button under the table, the screens went blank.

Odin turned to his friend, and after shaking his hand warmly, he threw an arm around the fellow; hugging him tightly. "I think that went down pretty well, what do you reckon?" he beamed excitedly. "Would you care to join me in a little celebratory toast?"

Thirle nodded as Odin made his way over to the drinks cabinet.

"Just an orange juice for you?" he remarked as he helped himself to a large, malt whisky. Old habits, as in his friend's case, were hard to break.

Drinks poured, he passed the juice to Thirle and then placed a reassuring hand on his arm. "Look, I'm so sorry I had to change you back to how you used to look; but you do understand my reasons for doing so, don't you?"

Thirle nodded that he did. It had been a necessary evil but one he hated nevertheless. Apart from being so dated, his old persona made him feel uncomfortable and vulnerable. The face was too well known; too hated and reviled.

"Once the scientists have had their little play, I'll change you back again, I promise," Odin winked as he raised his glass. "One of the many miracles of my well, don't you think?"

Thirle smiled as he raised his glass, too. "Here's to you, my dear friend," he exclaimed. "Hail Odin!"

The pair clinked glasses and after raised them to the ceiling, they each took a small sip.

"Please, may I propose another toast?" Odin inquired hopefully with a mischievous twinkle in his eye. He hadn't made this particular one in over sixty years, and yet he still remembered it with such affection. The fevered, spine tingling, excitement it used to cause. Oh, how he missed that sudden, exhilarating burst of fervour.

Thirle smiled and nodded. He wasn't going to stop Odin, and besides, it would be rather nostalgic. The salutation brought back such happy memories; memories of days long faded into history.

Odin put his glass down.

"To your very excellent health, Mein Fuhrer."

Clicking his heels sharply together, Odin extended his arm as he stood stiffly to attention.

"HEIL HITLER!"

43

A New World

"Thank you for looking after Hod," Frigg whispered quietly as she tiptoed with Kat down the corridor away from Hel's bedroom. "Saving his hide seems to be coming a bit of a habit for you," she added with a nervous giggle.

"Please, don't thank me yet," Kat cautioned earnestly. "It may be premature. My sisters are furious at the gods, and I may have to be nasty to Hod, just to keep them happy. I may have to really hurt him; whip him or something to satisfy their anger."

"I understand," Frigg nodded thoughtfully. "Just do what you have to do to keep him alive; that's all I ask."

Kat stopped dead in her tracks.

"Are you sure? Who knows where their rage will end? I won't be able to refuse their demands; they're my sisters." She was deadly serious. The warriors were baying for blood; Hod's blood.

Frigg turned and took both Kat's hands in hers.

"My dearest Kat; I fully understand your situation and yes, you have my blessing to do whatever needs to be done to save his life. In an ideal world, I wouldn't want any harm to come to my son. But the Asgard we once knew is no more. This is a new world, one in which the Valkyries rule. Hod chose to stay, and he has to live by your rules, just as I do. I won't stand in your way, I can't. I need the support of the sisterhood if I'm to be your Queen. If Hod has to be punished, then I would rather it was by you than by the others. At least you'll show him some compassion. Besides, hurting Hod mightn't be such a bad thing; it might just persuade him to leave. My son only stayed because of his obsession with you."

"I know," Kat sighed in resignation. "I do care for Hod, it's just; it's just, well, you know—complicated." She hung her head. She didn't know what else to say. She loved Jess, and Jess would always come first in her heart.

Frigg nodded empathetically.

"Hod's hurting really badly, as are you. I know, because I've read both your minds. He's madly in love with you but can't understand your needs, your desires; and that in turn hurts you. You're both caught in a vicious circle, and it has to end. Being cruel to my son might be a kindness; end his stupid infatuation once and for all. It's not safe for him here anymore, and that really scares me."

Kat hugged Frigg. "I wish I could explain how I feel; I do care so very much for Hod, but not in the same way as he feels for me."

"You don't need to explain," Frigg replied as she tenderly stroked her face. "I understand your Valkyrie needs; men don't. It's the blood-lust, the bond between a warrior and her maid; it never dies. This passion brings great joy and great torment; it's both a blessing and a curse. Your love for Brynhildr is tearing him apart, but he won't give in and allow you to quench your thirst. Unfortunately, knowing Hod; I suspect he never will."

The two women continued to talk and walk until they reached Kat's room. They embraced warmly. "Please, I beg you; help him to let go. You owe him that," Frigg whispered as they kissed goodnight. "Make him leave you, it's his only hope. I can't bear to see the foolishness of his heart get him killed."

Kat nodded and, after kissing Frigg goodnight, she closed her door behind her. Creeping quietly over to her bed, she paused beside Hod's mattress. He was asleep and snoring gently.

Kat smiled as she listened to its peaceful rhythm.

What Frigg had said made sense in a twisted sort of way; and it would solve their problems. Keeping her son here, safe in her room, day after day, was going to be a terrible obligation. How could she enjoy spending time with Jess while worrying all the while about him?

Kat shrugged as she climbed into bed.

Frigg was right; but her strange request caused great pain. She wasn't sure if she could be cruel to Hod, and even if she was; that cruelty posed a far more disturbing question.

How far would it have to go?

At breakfast the following morning, Frigg's words had an eerie, prophetic ring to them.

Henry was desperate to explain to the warriors his findings from the telescope, but they weren't in the slightest bit interested. Vengeance was in the air, and Hod was in their sights.

As soon as the former god arrived in the hall, he had been greeted by a chorus of boos and jeers that turned swiftly to food being hurled at him. This was followed by angry prods and pushes. The mood soon became uglier still; and with Frigg upstairs and Thor down at his forge fixing the band of his ring for Carmel, Hod was a sitting duck: completely at their mercy.

Kat had to act quickly to save his life.

Shouting angrily at him, she sent him packing to her room—and safety. Fists were about to be thrown, and worse would have followed. It was another close call, and she worried over what would happen when she left for Midgard. The god would be alone and defenceless: his life would be in jeopardy.

Explaining her concerns to Frigg, their new queen thankfully acted decisively.

Shuffling plans around, Frigg managed to persuade Elijah to take Hod with him to Noatun on a special mission. Their task was to assess the damage to the coastal settlement and help rebuild the village if the tidal wave had subsided. Outside the castle, the Aesir still loved the gods, and Hod would be safe amongst them. Only the Valkyries knew of Odin's betrayal. The rest of the realm still grieved the loss of their hallowed leader.

This decision to leave the Aesir in ignorance of the truth had been an extremely shrewd move by Frigg.

The Valkyries were Odin's handmaidens, and if the people found out about his treachery, they would naturally assume that the warriors had been in on his devilish plan. Just as the Valkyries had turned on the gods, the Aesir would have turned on the warriors; creating a bloody civil war for the control of the realm.

That prospect was an unthinkable nightmare.

For now, until they had gotten to the bottom of the mystery surrounding lambda; it was best that the Aesir be left to mourn the passing of the gods.

Too much knowledge could be a dangerous thing.

"So how do you like my new ring?" Carmel purred ecstatically as she waggled her fingers excitedly under Thor's nose. It fitted perfectly, and she tingled with the same exhilaration that Kat had felt yesterday.

The ring promised such power it was intoxicating.

"Would you like to kiss the hand of your new Queen?" she crowed as she extended it toward Thor.

To her surprise, he did just that; although he didn't look happy. Secretly, he wished he'd smashed it along with Odin's. The ring would only bring trouble; to both Asgard and its wearer. Still, if it made Carmel happy—and she looked elated—he would play along with her for now.

"Hey, will it work for me?" she enquired eagerly as she examined the three sparkling diamonds intently.

"I don't see why not," Thor replied gruffly. "All you have to do is think of the realm you want to visit and wave your hand over it. The ring does the rest."

"Where can I go?" she pleaded. It was a new toy, and she desperately wanted to play with it straight away.

"It can take you to Odin's garden, Valhalla, and Midgard; although that diamond hasn't worked for many years."

"All right, here goes." Beaming broadly, Carmel waved her hand over the ring, and in the very same instant she returned. A golden apple was in her hand. "Here, this is for you," she smiled holding it out for Thor.

"Thank you, my lady," he muttered expectantly as he made to accept her gift.

Unfortunately, Carmel was in a playful mood. Snatching the fruit away at the last moment, she waved it high above her head. "Ah-ah, not so fast, my naughty macho god," she teased. "Apples have to be earned first. Now, let me see, what can I get you to do?"

"Spank you?" he suggested roguishly as he started to chase her round the forge. Laughing loudly, he eventually pinned her against a gnarled, oak support. He pressed himself against her; she smelt beautiful. "I can see my little goddess is going to be a handful," he chuckled as he watched her take a large bite from the apple before letting him have a tiny nibble. "Are you going to give me trouble today?" he enquired, kissing her neck affectionately. He could feel his passion rising, and it felt good.

"No, not if you don't misbehave," Carmel teased before pushing him away. "That reward," she promised, patting his swelling manhood suggestively, "has to be doubly earned." Prancing provocatively, Carmel headed toward the door. He would have his wicked way later; but for now, she was going to enjoy being a mighty queen; his queen.

"I'm going to need my cloak and my flask of mead," she ordered, smiling slyly as she turned around. "And you're going to have to be very obedient if you want an apple today. So come along," she jested, snapping her fingers impatiently. "We haven't got all day."

Laughing loudly, she strutted off toward his waiting chariot.

"Your wish is my command, oh queen," Thor bowed mockingly before heading back toward the castle. He pretended to huff in anger, but in truth, he was enjoying every minute. Opening the cave where Loki had been imprisoned was going to be unpleasant, and the horror that might lie inside didn't bear thinking about. Carmel had always been bossy, and he loved her arrogant streak. Pampering to her airs and graces would keep his mind from other things, like Narvi's rotting corpse.

This sudden recollection made him shudder.

What in Asgard would Carmel do when she discovered the gods' depravity?

Her wrath would know no bounds.

The beauty of Valhalla exceeded every dream Jameela had ever had. It was exactly as Ben had described it—only better. She hugged him excitedly as they stood before its gates and took in the view.

The magnificent, golden hall was bigger, the sky was bluer, and the sun was warmer; even the air smelt fresher and cleaner than any she had ever breathed before. Heidrun, the goat, was there, bleating quietly as she nibbled at the tender shoots of Lerad; and myriad insects buzzed and hummed as they went about their daily tasks. Birds sung in a never-ending chorus, and butterflies danced lazily as they flirted coyly with iridescent flowers.

Jameela was in love and she wished they could stay forever—only they couldn't. That wasn't their mission and, after looking around them, it was only too easy to understand why.

Valhalla was deserted.

Not a single soul remained.

The doors to the mighty feasting hall hung hauntingly open and creaked quietly as they stirred. The place was a ghost town; the kind where cacti thrived and balls of tumbleweed drifted lazily under cloudless, rainless skies.

Valhalla felt empty—and sinister.

"HELLO!"

Ben yelled out loudly, and Henry echoed his calls; their voices fading swiftly into silence. There was no reply. After agreeing to a quick plan of action, the three of them set about their task; hunting for clues, anything that might explain the mysterious human vacuum.

For a full two hours the trio searched.

They checked room after room around the deserted hall; and building after building in the modern, military city that had engulfed the ancient building. Vast, steel aircraft hangers and concrete bunkers spread out in every direction as far as the eye could see. Valhalla had been turned into a huge military complex, complete with miles of tarmaced runways and gravelled paths. If they had stayed for a month, they still wouldn't have been able to search every part; although in truth, they didn't need to.

Every vista and every shout returned the same, eerie message: a muffled, empty, silent stillness.

No one was there.

"So, what do we do now?" Jameela enquired as she sank a draft of mead from her flask and wiped her glistening brow. Her voice felt hoarse, and she was perspiring hard in the fierce, midday heat. There was barely a breath of wind, and the air felt like a leaden weight; hot and sticky against her skin.

Both Ben and Henry were sweating, too. The sudden change from winter to high summer had caught them all unawares. Their bodies could barely cope; the heat was stifling.

"Why don't we go inside," Ben suggested hopefully as he gestured toward the entrance to the hall. "Let's take a look in the chamber, the one where the initiation ceremony took place."

To a chorus of agreement, Ben led the way inside. The shade was a welcome treat, and the three sat down on a bench and fanned themselves for a while.

Wow! It really was baking hot.

"So where's the room?" Henry enquired eagerly. Curiosity had got the better of him, and he was itching to take a look.

"It's over there, in the middle," Ben motioned with his hand. Standing up, he and Jameela followed Henry toward the narrow flight of steps that led down to the chamber.

"Hey, why don't you boys go on ahead," Jameela suggested nervously. "I'm not needed, and I'd much rather not go down there."

"Are you sure?" Ben asked.

"Positive," she replied adamantly.

Watching with an expression of relief, Jameela smiled and waved reassuringly as Henry and Ben disappeared from view. The narrow stairway leading down into darkness had stirred unpleasant memories—flashes of her time in Afghanistan and a horror long before.

Jameela sat down on a bench and hung her head between her knees. Suddenly she felt faint. Sucking in a couple of long, slow, deep breaths, she hoped the memories would fade.

They didn't.

It was August 1947, and she was back in Rawalpindi. She and her family had been caught on the wrong side of the Radcliffe Line; the new border that would separate Pakistan from India. Partition was in full swing, and they were trapped; a Hindu family caught inside a hostile, angry, Muslim nation.

Cornered by a mob consumed with nationalistic pride, her father had been killed instantly while she, her mother, and her four brothers and sisters had been captured. They had been thrown down a steep and narrow flight of stone steps into a crowded, airless cellar. There, along with twenty others, they had been left to rot in the sweltering heat.

With no food or water for two days, many perished, and the few who survived wished they hadn't. After being dragged in turn from the dungeon, the lucky were beaten, raped, and put out of their misery by a bullet in the back of their heads.

The less fortunate received a much more ugly death. Using a rubber tyre wrapped around their necks as a necklace; the captives were doused in petrol. This was then set alight for the amusement of the gathered mob. The prisoners died screaming; a slow and gruesome death.

Jameela had watched as one by one those around her met their doom.

When her family's turn came, she snapped. Seizing one of their captor's machetes, she discovered her Berserker fury. Forcing her way up the steps to the street, she had slaughtered dozens of men before she'd been eventually gunned down. This was why she had been chosen as a Valkyrie; and this was why she found the chamber at the bottom of the narrow stairway so creepy.

Its stench screamed of evil.

"Hey Jameela!" Ben's muffled voice cried from somewhere underneath the hall. "You really should come down here and take a look. I was right about this place. The heroes were altered; experimented on or something."

Jameela said nothing and didn't move. Let the boys have their fun. She was grateful, however, for Ben's call; it had broken her spell. Taking another swig from her flask, the memories of a distant past faded swiftly into the gloom; buried once more in the darkest recesses of her mind.

"Hey Ben, look at this stuff," Henry exclaimed excitedly shaking a vial of the same glittering, grey goop that Vili and Ve had used on Crescent Cay. "I think we've got something here."

Looking around him, it wasn't hard for Henry to come up with a theory as to what might have gone on. The sophisticated dental chair—complete with restraints; the helmet, the needles and syringes, and now this; the vial he held in his hands. It wasn't some ancient, mystical, religious rite that had changed the heroes; it was science.

Cold, hard, naked science.

Henry didn't know what exactly he was holding in his hands, but that didn't really matter. The stuff was clearly meant to be injected, and it probably hurt like crazy. The belts and ties on the chair definitely hadn't been put there as ornaments. Looking at the intriguing helmet and the bank of dials and buttons beyond, he deduced that some sort of mind manipulation must have taken place; presumably aided by the silvery goop. He would have loved to take a closer look at the stuff, but without a microscope he was stuck. Grabbing a few more bits and pieces as evidence, the two retraced their steps and ended up back with Jameela.

Ben gave her a tight squeeze. She looked pale and welcomed his hug. Valhalla now gave her the creeps.

Getting the two boys to grasp their coins in their hands as she did, the trio recited the ancient words. In a dazzling instant of blinding brightness, three flashes of light signalled they were gone.

Valhalla could return to its silent, lonely vigil.

The exalted home of the gods had been abandoned and would remain so; now and for all eternity. Its army of heroes had moved on, and it didn't take a genius to guess where they'd been heading.

Only one question now remained.

Why?

Why had Odin's Einherjar returned to Midgard?

44

Dead Men Walking

"**S**o, what does it feel like to have two eyes again?" Thirle enquired casually, relaxing back into a chair as he took another sip of his orange juice.

"More peculiar than you might imagine," Odin replied, contorting his face as he took it in turns to cover first one eye and then the other. "Still, it means I can start playing ping-pong again," he chuckled. "Although I was never really any good at it."

Thirle joined in the laughter and then took another sip of juice. For a few moments, the two men sat in silence; reflecting on the success—or otherwise—of their video conference. Thirle had certainly found it interesting, although he felt anxious for their future. The cat was out of the bag, and he really wasn't sure if his trusted friend was properly prepared. Humiliating memories of 1945 still haunted his mind.

"What's in the vial?" he decided to ask, pointing to the luminous, pink ampoule sitting on the table.

Picking it up, Odin tossed it from hand to hand as he laughed once more. "I don't really know, and I don't really care. Most probably, it's just some coloured water my brothers knocked up."

"What?" Thirle exclaimed sounding shocked. "I thought this was the deterrent, the ultimate weapon; some sort of biological 'kill all' if they didn't accept your demands?"

Chuckling loudly, Odin tossed the vial toward him.

"'Fraid not," he continued. "It's just a bit of razzmatazz, some eye candy to grab their attention. They're so gullible, those Midgard politicians, and so easy to con. You just have to give them a bit of a headline grabber, a visual cue, and off they go, imaginations running in overdrive. It's a bit like that nuclear explosion; which was really uncivilised and so totally unnecessary. Still, I suppose it gives them something to get their teeth into, helps them focus their tiny, little minds…" Odin drifted off; the vial really was of trifling importance.

"But my dear fellow," Thirle interrupted impatiently; his voice sounding strained. "Such an ultimatum is way too important to back with a bluff. That seems a very risky strategy, in my opinion."

Odin sat up and put a hand inside the draw of the table in front of him. Pulling out a can of air freshener, he sprayed it liberally in the air. "Who said anything about bluffing," he winked, knowingly. "They're all dead men walking; they just don't know it yet."

"Well, I hope you're right," Thirle retorted with a sigh. "I really don't want to get involved in another debacle like the one I started." Shoulders sagging, he slumped back resignedly into his chair. Count Dragza—Lord Odin—was a weird fellow and always had been. He had never been easy to keep up with and impossible to pin down. He was always the player with an ace up his sleeve; the smartest guy in the room. Thirle's one regret was that he hadn't listened to Odin sixty years ago. The Count had been spot on. He'd told him that he was going to lose the war—and he had.

"Do you like the smell?" Odin enquired as he sprayed more freshener in the air.

"Yes, I suppose so. It's pleasant enough, I guess," Thirle replied absent-mindedly.

"It says on the label 'apple blossom with a hint of citrus,'" Odin read out loud, raising his eyebrows as he broke into a sneaky smile. "But I really think it should be branded death."

"What?" Thirle sat up, curiosity piqued.

"Death." Odin repeated as he banged the tin resolutely on the table. "This and various other brands of air freshener, deodorant, perfume, and polish; one whiff and you're a dead man."

Thirle didn't say anything; he couldn't. His mouth just hung there, opening and closing slowly in disbelief. "So, why aren't we all dead then?" he gasped eventually, when he could get his head around the obvious question. "Is it a poison?"

"Yes, sort off; but not in the same way as a poisonous gas. It's much slower acting; more like a time bomb," Odin admitted before pausing; he could see he was losing his friend. "Would you like me to explain how it works?" he offered enthusiastically. "It really is awfully clever."

Thirle nodded his head. He just hoped he would be able to understand, because the Count didn't always give the easiest of explanations. "So go on then," he prompted. "Tell me how these tins of air freshener, polish, and the like can conquer the world?"

"I will, but first—" he paused. "My brothers cooked up some slides about it somewhere." Muttering absently, Odin fiddled with a mouse and keyboard on the desk. "If I can just get them up on the screens, they might help you understand better what I'm about to say."

After a few more minutes of mumbling, cursing, and blank screens; a display eventually lit up with the images Odin wanted.

Thirle studied these intently.

"Binary nanospores," Odin began with a flourish, stabbing a finger at one of the displays. "That's what we call them; binary nanospores. The deadliest biological weapon ever created."

Leaning forward, Thirle tried as best he could to follow the ensuing mini-lecture. Odin tried to keep it simple, but Thirle's understanding of biology was quite limited and horribly out of date.

The nanospores were tiny artificial capsules that were smaller than the size of a bacterium. Through Odin's various companies, trillions of these particles had been manufactured and packaged into various sprays and aerosols that were sold around the globe. Millions of people used these products every day; and if that wasn't enough, Odin had also installed sprayers into office air conditioning systems and under the bodies of his fleet of cargo planes. These released their deadly aerosol over cities when they came into land or when they took off.

According to his brothers' estimates, over the last five years, at least half the world's population had been contaminated, and this figure was rising monthly as their program intensified. Their target was to spray two thirds of humanity before they entered the second phase of their plan.

At this point, Thirle nodded his head. He now understood the delivery mechanism, but getting to terms with how each tiny nanospore worked looked considerably more confusing. However, the images on the screen were helping, so he decided to try to keep up.

Each nanospore was shaped like an oval capsule and had two different types of receptors poking out of it. There were spiky ones—

that made it look a bit like a hedgehog—and there were other, flatter ones with heads that resembled a cluster of grapes.

People who used the spray could either inhale these tiny particles or swallow them if the particles happened to land on their hands or food. Either way, one of the receptors allowed the nanospores to penetrate their lungs or bowels and get inside the body; and the other helped the nanospores to enter cells in its victim's liver.

This second receptor was unique, and Odin was especially proud of it. The nanospores would only infect human livers and nothing else. The weapon was completely harmless to animals and birds.

Once safely ensconced inside the liver cells, the nanospore would just sit there and wait...and wait...and wait; until Odin decided to activate it. That was why he called it a binary nanospore. There were two stages to its life cycle.

Invasion followed by activation.

Activation was the second, lethal phase.

In the middle of each nanospore was a small sac of fluid. This looked similar to the nucleus in the middle of a cell, or the yolk of a fried egg. Inside this sac was an enzyme that worked a bit like an acid. The sac was quite delicate and tuned to burst in response to a signal sent by Odin. This signal could be focused and targeted on only one person at a time; or sent globally to everybody, or to endless permutations in between. This was why Odin considered the weapon to be so perfect. He could use it when, where, and on whomever he liked.

Once burst, the enzymes in the sac would melt away the outer wall of the capsule, liberating its deadly payload—the killer blow.

The nanospores contained a lethal protein that damaged other proteins in liver cells. These then hijacked the machinery of the cell to make yet more damaged proteins. The technical term for this type of disease was a 'prion' infection; and Odin had got the inspiration for his weapon from a disease that infected the brains of cattle—*Mad Cow Disease.*

Thirle didn't dwell on these details, they were far too complicated. What he did remember and what he needed to remember was that each liver cell would get so stuffed with the damaged proteins that it would eventually burst, spilling its contents into the bloodstream. These damaged proteins then went on to infect other liver cells.

Once initiated, the process was irreversible.

What had started out as a small trickle of damaged cells quickly turned into an avalanche; each infected cell churning out thousands of proteins that would damage hundreds more cells. Within a week of the infection starting, its victim would turn yellow with jaundice; and by the end of a further week—they would be dead. Their livers would have failed. The disease was incurable and horrific; an unstoppable human holocaust that Odin alone controlled.

It was the ultimate madman's weapon: a despot's dream.

Thirle decided to interrupt his friend here. He sort of understood what he'd been saying, but he had a question; and it was a good one.

"Are we also infected with the spores?" he enquired tensely. He didn't relish the prospect of dying such a hideous death.

"Yes, but don't worry," Odin smiled reassuringly. "You and I, my heroes, and all the members of your New Youth Movement, we've all been vaccinated. Even if the nanospores are accidentally activated, we won't get sick. The damaged proteins will be mopped up and won't infect other liver cells."

Feeling more relieved, Thirle relaxed. "Just one more thing," he enquired as Odin nodded for him to continue. "If you can make a vaccine, can't others do so as well?"

"Yes, of course," Odin beamed confidently. "But it would take time, lots of time; and that's something Midgard scientists won't have. When they finally realise what's going on, it will already be too late. In a very real sense, their war will have been lost even before it's started."

Thirle got to his feet and raised his glass in a toast. He was impressed. "Bravo, my dear Count. Bravo indeed."

Clinking their glasses together, the two old friends downed their drinks in one.

"You see," Odin began once more when they were seated. "History won't be repeating itself. This time we can realise our dreams without a single shot being fired. No fuss, no unnecessary deaths, and no setbacks; just a nice, clean, clinical takeover. The world will be under new management before anyone knows it has happened. At last, dear friend, we can have our dream. One world, one ruler, and one supreme, race of warriors—and that's just the beginning. Believe me; I have such dreams, such ambition. There are millions of worlds out there to conquer and rule, and we can have them all!"

Standing up, Odin raised his glass once more. The thought of all that power was electrifying.

"Are you really going to let the world leaders chose who they want to save?" Thirle asked, remembering what his friend had said earlier during the conference.

"Of course not," Odin chuckled mischievously. "We've made our own lists and we will compare ours with theirs. It's just a smoke-screen, a distraction that gives them something to think about while we get on with the master plan. Once my fellow gods have settled in, we can start the show. Your New Youth Movement is well organised, and my heroes are already inserted in all the top jobs around the world."

Odin paused; and then disclosed a tiny niggle he had had on his mind for some time. "You know, if only you'd just listened to me back then, we could have done all this seventy odd years ago. Goodness knows what you were thinking of when you opened up that Russian second front. And what about Hirohito? What in Midgard's name was he thinking of with Pearl Harbor? Honestly, I did warn you; we've wasted so much time."

"I'm sorry," Thirle replied apologetically. "Thank you for giving me a second chance. I won't let you down, I promise."

"I know you won't and besides; I'm going to keep a tight eye on things this time," Odin warned. "No more distractions, I promise. Asgard is no more. Midgard is now my permanent home."

"By the way," Thirle enquired. "Do you think any of those world leaders will try to attack us? We're quite vulnerable, being such a small island and so close to America."

Odin laughed loudly. "They can try," he chortled. "But they won't get very far."

"Oh, and why not?" Thirle quizzed.

"Because I control their forces."

TAP–TAP–TAP

A gentle knock at the door interrupted their conversation—and sent Herr Flöda into something of a spin.

"Please, is there somewhere I can hide?" he enquired anxiously, looking around him as he tried to cover his face with his hands. "I really don't want people to see me looking like this."

"Oh, don't worry about that, I'll take care of whoever it is," Odin reassured, patting Mimir on the head as he walked past his wheelchair and then slipped outside. A few minutes later, he returned with a puzzled expression on his face.

"Is something up?" Thirle quizzed. He could see something was wrong.

"There's been a bit of a…a surprise," Odin murmured slowly as he returned to his seat, sat down, and then rested his chin thoughtfully on clasped hands. He was lost momentarily in deep concentration.

"Penny for your thoughts?" Thirle asked hesitantly after an awkward silence.

"Oh, it's nothing really," Odin replied absently. "It's just the well has been activated. Apparently three visitors have arrived from Asgard; which is rather unexpected."

"Are they here, right now, on the island?" his friend enquired eagerly. It had been a long time since he'd met a Valkyrie, and the thought of another such encounter excited him. Odin's warrior women were superb; true Aryans through and through.

"No, not yet: but I think I know where they are," Odin muttered, speaking as though he were in a bit of a daze. "It's funny," he continued, musing out loud as he stroked his beard.

"By now they should all be dead."

45

Tremors

Without Elijah to slow them down, Ruby and Silk travelled swiftly, Valkyrie style, to Heimdall's watchtower. Before they set off, both girls expressed concerns about their trip. Something didn't feel right.

Bad vibes were emanating from the foothills of Jotunheim.

Spreading their wings in a graceful, harmonic flight; the warriors gossiped as they flew wing tip to wing tip over the rippled waves of drifted snow. These covered fields and tracks in a powdered coat of seamless white. Laced with the tracks of deer, foxes, wolves, badgers, and hares; they made for a wondrous sight.

Silk was convinced that Balder had left Asgard under duress. There could be no other explanation for his disappearance, and she refused to believe otherwise. He loved her and would never leave her. Somehow Odin or Freyja must have tricked him into going. This added to her fury. When they had secured the watchtower, Silk was determined to travel to Midgard with or without Frigg's permission. She would rescue Balder and kill Odin if she could find him.

Ruby chose to be more cautious with her vengeance.

Odin was a slippery fish. He would be hard to find and harder still to kill. She wanted his head as much as Silk did, but they would need a plan if they were going to succeed. For now, Ruby's anger was directed more toward Hel. She was having serious misgivings about her reinstatement as a Valkyrie and vowed to shadow her every move.

Somewhere along the line, she was certain that The Black Valkyrie would surface again—and when the cursed warrior did, she would be there waiting. The former Queen of the Damned looked set to be an unpredictable troublemaker, and her boyfriend didn't seem to be any better. He behaved like jumped-up, pompous nobody; and he needed to be brought down a peg or two.

The two warriors were in agreement on other issues as well.

Kat had done well in making Hod a servant, although even that lowly post was still too good for a rotten, lying, scumbag of a god. They hoped she would be merciless and not let her soft spot for Odin's geeky son get in her way. He needed to be made an example of; brutalised and humiliated; before being sent packing to Midgard with his tail between his legs. He had to be a lesson to the other conceited gods.

Asgard belonged to the Valkyries—return at your peril.

Both warriors were also miffed that Kat and Carmel had been given the gods' rings. These should have gone to the most senior Valkyries and not their 'girlfriends,' as Silk disparagingly referred to them. This had been a mistake and one that couldn't be easily undone. Neither Valkyrie would surrender their ring without a fuss, and this was cause for concern. The rings were very powerful, too powerful for mortals to control. Carmel's arrogance was well known, and Hel's acerbic influence over Kat was growing. Delusions of grandeur and goddess aspirations could give their sisters ideas above their station; fragmenting the delicate bonds that held the sisterhood together.

This could lead to disastrous consequences.

Lara, Frigg, Thor, and the problems with lambda were also discussed; but neither girl really understood the last matter. Cosmological Constants and gazillions of galaxies hurtling together to collide in some big crunch were but meaningless words to them. As far as they were concerned, Asgard had been saved, and it was time to rebuild the realm.

At last the Valkyries were in charge, and they needed to flex their authority; show the Aesir who were the new mistresses in town. Although they would miss the gods—and Balder in particular—it was a thrill to finally be in control; to have divine and absolute power over the realm.

Drawing close to the watchtower, alarm bells began to jangle inside the warriors. Their instincts had been right.

The watchtower was in ruins.

Landing messily in a snowdrift, both girls quickly dusted themselves down before drawing closer to its shattered remains. The building had been completely destroyed, collapsing into a jumbled pile of scattered rocks and timbers, which lay half buried under a thick blanket of snow. It was a sad sight and a sorrowful end to the once proud fortress. The Aesir could rebuild it, but that would take months, and the process couldn't even begin before the last snowfalls had melted.

Two further features about the shattered tower gave the girls cause for concern.

The first was perplexing.

The watchtower was easily as strong as the castle in Asgard, and this had survived Ragnarok's earthquake relatively unscathed. Why, therefore, had the fortress been so utterly devastated?

The second concern was more urgent.

From the air, the warriors had spotted trouble. Four, sturdy yurts—used for overwintering—lay clustered on the far side of the Bifrost Bridge. From these tents, delicate fronds of smoke could be seen snaking gracefully into the sullen sky. Giants were home and they were unlikely to be welcoming.

Squinting hard, the girls tried to ascertain the strength of their number, although they needn't have bothered.

Silhouetted against the frosted background of snow; a man, escorted by two large men from Jotunheim, was making his way precariously across the swaying rope bridges toward them. From this distance, they couldn't make out who he was; but in one hand he was carrying a long, thin, shiny object.

This glistened with a strangely familiar hue.

It wasn't until late afternoon that Carmel and Thor eventually reached the entrance to the cave where Loki had been buried. They were exhausted; worn out by the constant need to keep stopping and digging the goats out of the snowdrifts. The animals had struggled magnificently; but lacking the height of horses, they had been overwhelmed by its sheer depth in places. It had been a long and taxing journey, but they were almost there. With mounting trepidation, they rounded the last corner, and the cave slipped into view.

"'Pon my beard!" Thor exclaimed in astonishment. "It's been opened."

Spurring his goats into one last effort, he exhorted the pair into their fastest trot, and the chariot sped up the hill to the entrance.

Thor's first impression was right.

The landslide Odin had created to bury the cave had definitely been disturbed such that a small, black tunnel now wound its way awkwardly between the jagged boulders and into the mountainside. The passageway wasn't very big, but easily wide enough for a man to crawl through.

"Please, my lady," Thor begged with considerable alarm to his voice. "Allow me to go in alone. There could be things—" he paused, deliberating as to what to say, "—that might upset you."

"Thor, you promised you wouldn't hide anything." Carmel replied, tapped the butt of her whip authoritatively. "You aren't going to go back on your word, are you?"

"No, my lady," he muttered apologetically; but he was worried, very worried.

"Good, so come on; lead the way," she commanded, waving her hand bossily toward the tunnel. "Did you bring any candles?"

"No, but there should be some in there," he replied, his voice already sounding muffled as his large bottom disappeared into the tunnel.

Tutting impatiently, Carmel waited a few minutes until the flickering glow of candlelight tinged the blackness with a golden glow. Getting on her hands and knees, she too began to crawl into the cave.

It was time for Thor to face his demons—and take his punishment.

"Ugh!"

Carmel grimaced as she stood up and took her first look around the ghastly, gloomy cavern. The air felt dank and putrid; and stank of human excrement and the sickly sweetness of rotting flesh. The atmosphere was filled with the stench of death; and the view was no less unpleasant.

"What are these?" Carmel enquired waving her sword at the bloodied and broken remains of three stone slabs.

"Um, that was Loki's bed," Thor replied with more than a hint of embarrassment.

"Hmmm," Carmel scowled. "And these?" she continued, waving the sword authoratively at smaller, shattered coils of twisted rock.

"Those were the enchanted bonds that held him captive," he replied balefully. Carmel was saving the worst for last.

"So if that was Loki's bed and he was tied up; then whose grave is this?" she yelled suddenly and angrily, banging her sword against a pile of rocks that had been heaped up over a shallow grave.

"I'd rather not say, my lady." Thor replied meekly, hanging his head. He felt so ashamed. *How could he have let it happen?* He would rather Carmel whip him now than admit the hideous truth.

"Well, you're going to have to tell me if you know what's good for you," Carmel fumed angrily.

What was her lover hiding?

What terrible evil had happened here?

"It's, it's—" he stuttered, beginning lamely. This was going to be painful; very, very painful. "It belongs to Loki's son. Odin made them fight, and Vardi killed Narvi. I begged my father not to, but in the end I couldn't stop him. I just stood by and let it happen. I'm so sorry; so very, very sorry."

To Thor's surprise, instead of hitting him, Carmel spun on her heel and hurried away down the tunnel. She didn't come back. After waiting a few minutes longer, he followed her outside. When he finally emerged from the tunnel, she was standing some distance away with her back toward him.

Her shoulders were heaving.

Drawing closer, he could tell that she was crying; sobbing actually. Deep, uncontrolled gulps of air followed by long, stifled bursts of weeping.

"Oh, my dearest darling, what have we done?" Sighing deeply, Thor took her in his arms and pulled her toward him. She turned and buried her face in his chest, hugging him close and holding him tightly.

When at last her grip lessened, Carmel looked up and forced a weak smile. "I'm so sorry, my dearest," she mumbled. "I've been such a thoughtless, mean, selfish bitch. Here, please, take this. I don't deserve to wear it anymore."

To Thor's amazement, she pulled him close once more and after caressing his face with her hand, she pressed his ring into his palm.

"Narvi's death must have hurt you so much," she continued tremulously. "What with Thrud being the same age. No wonder you've been feeling so guilty." Wiping her eyes, she kissed him tenderly on the lips.

"So, you're not going to flog me?" Thor enquired in bewilderment. He thought she would have been furious; not all tearful and loving.

"No, don't be so silly," Carmel sighed, squeezing him tightly. "Your guilt is more than enough punishment. How could Odin have done such a thing? He's the one at fault, not you. Why didn't you tell me he'd killed a child? He's such a monster; you should have known that I'd understand. I'm not an ogre, and I certainly wouldn't have blamed you—you silly man."

Thor laughed and hugged her tightly. Sometimes he underestimated the Valkyrie. Even with all eternity, he would never fathom her out. She was an angel and a devil all rolled into one; impossible to predict and harder still to resist. He felt like a child in her arms, helpless and hopeless; slave to her every need and whim. "I love you so much," he whispered without thinking.

Carmel giggled. "You realise that's the first time you've said that to me," she quipped, wiping away more tears.

"I know," Thor replied, as he helped her in this task. "But I'm sure it won't be the last." Laughing with relief, the two of them took stock of their situation.

Thor knew that Odin wouldn't have bothered to bury Narvi, so it must have been Loki and Sigyn who had done so after he'd been freed. How the bonds had been broken was a mystery at first, until an obvious solution slapped them hard across their faces.

It had to have been the earthquake.

This must have shattered Loki's bed, liberating him. Once freed, it would have been easy to dig their way out.

Surprisingly, both Thor and Carmel were relieved that Loki had survived. Thor's relief was founded on guilt, whereas Carmel's was fuelled by lust. Loki's drunken protestation of love in Aegir's palace still bothered her, rekindling a twisted desire. Secretly, she still yearned to have both her godly lovers; her silken stallion and her rampaging bull. Blushing at these sudden carnal cravings, Carmel shook her head as she tried to focus on what to do next.

Loki had escaped and could be anywhere. However, if they had to hazard a guess, it was most likely that he would have headed toward Jotunheim—the realm of his giant ancestors.

Mimir's prophesy had been correct. Loki had indeed survived Ragnarok.

Looking around them at the grey and overcast skies, Carmel and Thor decided that to return to the castle today wouldn't be sensible. It would soon be dusk, and what had been a difficult journey by day would be impossible by night. The lodge at Franang's falls was much closer, and they could find shelter there.

Climbing back into the chariot, it was another two hours before, in the final, fading gloom of dusk, the pair eventually arrived at the crofter's cottage. It was deserted but well endowed with a stack of tinder-dry logs.

Setting to work enthusiastically, it wasn't long before Thor had the doors and windows shuttered and a large fire crackling and hissing merrily in the middle of the room. Drawing up a chair and balancing a skillet of mead over the fire, Thor settled down with Carmel curled up upon his lap. Pouring two tankards of warm mead, they snuggled up tightly together, sipping lovingly at the deliciously warm, soothing liquid.

They were cosy, safe, and alone.

"You know," Thor began slowly. "I know you warriors all hate Odin now, but he really isn't so bad."

"How can you possibly say such a thing?" Carmel retorted, tapping his face playfully. "He abandoned us and left you here to die. I know he's your father, but come on; he really is a monster."

"No…not a monster," Thor mused thoughtfully, "more a perfectionist. All he's ever dreamed of and striven for is perfection. To know my father you need to understand him, to appreciate what makes him tick. He loved this realm, and he loved you, all of you. You were his chosen ones, the mightiest of the mighty; his beloved Valkyries. I know he was devastated when he found out that that lambda thingy was all wrong. He was furious; his hopes and dreams ruined by a single shake of the dice; a quirk of fate. He was devastated."

"Okay, my darling, daddy-defending hero," Carmel teased playfully. "So why did he abandon us? Why didn't he try to fix the problem?"

"He couldn't, not without Mimir. He was the brains of the outfit, the genius with all the answers and unfortunately, according to Odin, he'd been decapitated before they discovered the fatal flaw. If that terrible tragedy hadn't occurred, then we might all have been spared the horrors of Ragnarok."

"Then why didn't he take us with him?" Carmel continued provocatively. She wasn't going to let his father off the hook that easily.

"He had to draw the line somewhere. If he took the Valkyries as well as the gods, then why not take the Aesir and the Vanir, too? I'm sure this decision really hurt him. He really loved you. The Valkyries were part of his dream; his beautiful, powerful killing machines; warriors loyal to the last."

"Why thank you for your kind compliment, sir," Carmel jested, nibbling at an earlobe. The warmth and the mead were beginning to get to her. "But that still doesn't explain why he abandoned you and why he treated Loki so despicably? What he did was inhuman."

"I know, I know: but to be fair; both he and I had it coming," Thor retorted, chuckling as so many mischievous memories flooded into his mind. "I can tell you a good story sometime if you like."

Carmel nodded, although by now she was barely listening. Her mind had begun to drift as feelings began to stir.

"Anyway," he continued blithely. "We both angered him and now we've paid the price. Once you get on the wrong side of Odin, you can never get back into his good books. He bears grudges, bitter grudges; and he never forgives and he never forgets. He'll just keep on coming at you; again and again and again; wearing you down until you surrender. He won't give up until he's won, ever. That's why he's such a powerful god. Yggdrasill only knows what he'll do to Midgard. He'll conquer that world as easily as breaking wind."

Carmel stood up and repositioned herself on top of Thor; her legs now straddling his as they faced each other. Slowly, she began to grind her bottom firmly and rhythmically into his lap. "Are you done talking?" she enquired cheekily, caressing his face.

Thor nodded and closed his eyes, savouring the thought of where Carmel's body was tempting him.

"Ahhhhh, now doesn't that feel better," she cooed seductively, having reached inside his trousers to liberate his bulging manhood. This had been growing increasingly impatient under the sensuous thrusting of her hips.

Guiding him with her hands, she bore down hard upon his strength, letting it fill her as suddenly as it did completely. Carmel gasped and bit her lip. His abruptness thrilled her. Digging her nails deep into his flesh, she moaned appreciatively.

He felt so good, so huge, and so deep inside her.

Thor's hands now clenched at her bottom as his lips roamed tenderly over her breasts. Pinning him back into the chair, Carmel rode him hard. Here beneath her was her raging bull; and she ground her body powerfully against his, forcing his hips to rise and fall as hers did. Writhing faster, she begged him to take her; to consume her with the fury of his love. Climaxing together; they jerked long and hard as violent spasms rippled exquisitely through both their aching bodies. Carmel held on tight; digging her nails deeper and deeper as she exploded in a crescendo of elation.

Thor was hers to command, and she clasped him firmly between her legs. The god was her lover, her captive, and her slave; and his powerful strength lived only to satisfy her desires.

Moaning gratefully when she eventually collapsed into his embrace, Carmel prayed that this rapture would last forever.

46

The Lay of Harbard

"**S**o come on then, my mighty hero; tell me this great tale of yours."

Carmel knelt down beside Thor on an inviting pile of straw she had prepared for them. Tossing another log onto the roaring fire, Thor slipped his arm around her waist and pulled her close. Leaning over, she poured them both another flagon of warmed mead.

By now, the two of them were both pleasantly pickled; having enjoyed an excellent supper of barbequed goat—courtesy of one of Thor's long-suffering pets. The other animal, Tanngnost or Tanngrisni (Carmel couldn't remember which), was tethered in the corner of the room merrily munching a pile of hay.

Thor, being the hell-raising god he was, never liked to travel dry and, after making love, he had retrieved a large bodn of mead from his chariot, and they had proceeded to down pretty much its entire contents; hence their current state.

The warmth of the fire, the warmth of the mead, and the warmth of their entwined bodies had turned a cold, desolate evening into a magical one; a dream neither wanted to end.

Tired but happy, Thor settled back and, with Carmel wrapped snugly in his arms; he began to recount his tale.

The events of his story happened a long time ago, even before he was married to Sif. It was an era when, as a young and adventurous god, he liked to while away his time, hunting and fishing in the mighty forests of Jotunheim. He was fearless then as he was today;

but the follies of youth led him to take risks he wouldn't countenance nowadays.

It was a day in mid summer, and the sun was beating down fiercely upon his back when he reached a wide sound. Thor was tired and hungry, and after having had a successful day of hunting, he was carrying a large stag slung across his broad shoulders.

The place where he was standing was a treacherous strait; one laced with haphazard, oozing, mudflats threaded by steep-sided channels of water that ran fast and deep. Concealed beneath the water's calm and innocent face lay dangerous currents. These revealed their deadly intent as intermittent whirlpools and eddies that twisted and twirled enticingly as they drifted lazily past the banks of tufted reeds and tussock grass.

On a swelteringly hot day such as this, a dip in the calm and soothing waters would tempt the unwary—and terrify the wise.

The bank on which he was waiting was a well known crossing point; and a length of rope stretched across the sound to the other side. There; Thor could just make out the shape of a man standing in his boat. He believed the fellow to be Harbard, the ferryman.

For a fee, he would pull you safely across the dangerous waters.

It was too hot to work and too humid to walk; and Thor dreaded the prospect of spending three or four hours trudging around the sound to a shallow ford that lay several kilometres from where he was standing. He would pay the ferryman for his labours; and in a short while he would be on his way once more.

Thor hailed the man loudly; shielding his eyes from dazzling reflections of sunlight that burst in lithe ripples from the mirrored, watery expanse. The air was still and languid, with giant dragonflies darting impetuously as they scavenged for midges and other tasty titbits.

Settling down on the bank, he waited for Harbard to drag his boat across.

Now, unbeknown to Thor, Odin had seen his son returning from his travels and had decided to play a little trick on him. Bribing Harbard with gifts of gold and alcohol, he had taken his place for the afternoon. It was his father and not Harbard who was now lazily pulling the ferry through the water; and taking one hell of a time about it, too.

"Can't you pull a little harder, my good fellow?" Thor quipped impatiently when the ferry was about halfway across.

"Can't you stink a little less grossly, my irksome traveller?" came Odin's reply.

Thor was astonished. Quite clearly the ferryman hadn't noticed whom he was speaking to yet. He would almost certainly have shat his pants if he had known that the person he'd insulted was the mightiest god in Asgard.

"Do you not recognise me?" Thor bellowed as the ferry drew nearer. The sun was behind the vessel, so it was hard for him to make out the features of the man who had affronted him. It was impossible to tell that the ferryman was Odin in disguise.

"Yes, of course I know who you are," his father retorted crossly. "You're that impudent braggart, Thor; the cowardly son of our god of gods."

"What?" Thor shouted in amazement. He was on his feet now, and his face had turned puce. When the ferry arrived, he would beat its loudmouthed owner senseless—and then some.

"Look at you," sneered Odin, pausing in his journey such that the ferry came to rest a safe distance from the shore. "Strong as an ox yet with brains so feeble; it's no wonder your father despairs of you. You're such a mess; all bare-chested, unshaven and with shit on your breeches. I can see now why the other gods make merry at your expense. You're only fit to lay with serfs and thralls*."

"Hey, that isn't a very nice thing to say," Carmel interrupted as she gave Thor a big hug. His breeches were still disgusting, but it was pretty mean of his dad to be so offensive; he could have been way more tactful.

Thor nodded before placing a finger over her lips. "It gets worse, just wait and see," he whispered knowingly. "Anyway," he continued returning to his story, "I decided to bite my lip and hold my tongue. If I'd lost my temper, the ferryman would have turned tail and headed back."

"So what are you going to pay me for my services?" Odin had asked scornfully, taking up the rope's slack once more. "With dirt from your boots and rank sweat from your armpits, I shouldn't wonder; you penniless oaf. You beggars are all the same."

Seething with rage, Thor kicked a hailstorm of dirt and pebbles. These ripped the silken waters.

"Temper, temper!" goaded his father, laughing gleefully at his son's fruitless rage. He was safe on his boat, and he certainly wasn't going to risk coming any nearer.

"Look," Thor offered as he counted slowly to ten. "I can give you fresh salmon from my knapsack and a leg of venison from the stag that I've killed. That should be more than wages enough."

"We shall see," chuckled the god. "I doubt, however, you'll be able to open that knapsack of yours. You couldn't open Skrymir's, now could you?" he gloated.

"Who's Skrymir?" Carmel asked. The name rang a bell from other stories she had heard.

"He was an enchanted rock giant," Thor replied, hoping to jog her memory.

Carmel remained puzzled, but Thor decided to carry on with his story anyway.

"How dare you," he raged at the ferryman. "That knapsack was wired shut with an enchanted thread. No one could have opened it; not even Odin himself."

"I doubt that very much," his father sneered. "That's just an excuse. Go on, admit it; you're a weakling Thor; a dirty, cowardly, weakling. You couldn't even win that wager with the giants, the one where you failed to down a tiny horn of ale. Even the youths of Asgard could have done better."

Thor picked up a large clod of dirt and hurled it at the boat. The man dodged sideways as the sod whistled past his ear. "For your information," he fumed, "that horn was also enchanted. It was connected to the ocean, and I damn near drained it dry."

"Okay, well explain this," the fake ferryman jeered, continuing his torment. "How is it that the foster mother of the giant King beat you in a wrestling match, hey? If you're so big and mighty, how could you lose to such a weak and wizened old woman?"

"That's easy," Thor scoffed, amazed by the ferryman's ignorance. This contest was well known and widely respected. "Elli (that was the old woman's name) was enchanted, and she didn't beat me, she wrestled me down onto one knee, that's all. I would have beaten her if the giants hadn't stopped the fight."

"Rubbish!" his father snorted contemptuously.

"Rubbish! I'll give you rubbish, you miserable, old bastard. Do you know who Elli was or are you too stupid to remember the tales of your forefathers?" Thor bellowed angrily. He was tired of being trashed by this puny mortal. "Elli was old age in human form," he continued furiously. "I damn nearly defeated the mother of time herself! You really are an ignorant fool."

"Oh, yes, that reminds me," the ferryman yelled. "What about the cat you couldn't lift. You have to admit it; that was pretty pathetic, even for a wimp like you."

"You're making this up now, aren't you?" Carmel teased as she took another sip of mead. Running her hand lazily across Thor's chest, she absently twirled some of his hairs around her finger.

"Well, maybe a bit, here and there," he chuckled merrily. "But the story about the old woman and the cat are true. You have to remember, this was an age of enchantment. Gulveig and the other black witches still held sway, and their magic curses ruled the realm; torturing us all with evil spells and potions that nearly brought us gods to our knees."

"Okay, so what about this cat then; what was it?" Carmel enquired. She was getting tired now and the warmth of the fire and Thor's body was making her eyelids feel dreadfully heavy.

"The cat was the four pillars that support our world. I managed to raise one leg and trigger a massive earthquake."

"Oh, you fibber," Carmel giggled as she slapped him playfully. "Now I know you're making this up. So come on; let's get to the end of this porky pie so we can both get some sleep."

"All right, all right," Thor chortled, tickling her tummy and making her squeal. "That really did happen, but the details of the story aren't really important. It's the principle; that's what matters."

"Okay, so skip to the end already," Carmel sighed. "Did Odin own up to his disguise and ferry you across or did he make you walk all the way around?"

"Well, after trading a few more insults, he pulled himself back to the far bank and sat there laughing. The swine made me walk all right." Thor finished with a satisfied grin on his face.

"You're joking?"

"No, I'm not." He smirked, gleefully.

"Well that was a bit mean, especially as he's your dad and all. What a bastard," Carmel mused angrily.

"Exactly; and that's my point. We've never got on. Odin was jealous of my popularity and fearful of my strength. We're like chalk and cheese. My success threatened him; denting his pride. He has to be the best at everything, the greatest of all the gods. That's why he left me here to die. Sadly, no world could ever be big enough for the two of us." Thor paused; and then added, "I guess if the situation had been reversed, I would probably have done the same."

"No, you wouldn't," Carmel admonished him. "You may have a wicked temper, but you certainly wouldn't have done that. You're far too kind and gentle and loving and cuddly and..." her voice tailed off as she leaned forward and kissed him tenderly on the lips. As she did so, she felt him slip something onto her finger.

Looking down, she was wearing his ring once more. "No, Thor, you mustn't; I don't deserve it," she murmured apologetically as an image of Loki flashed briefly in her mind.

"Yes you do," he replied, placing a finger to her lips once more. "We're good for each other, you and I. You keep my temper in check while I keep your arrogance at bay." He slapped her bottom cheekily. "Besides," he whispered lovingly as he kissed her forehead. "I love you. You're my mighty queen, and I'm proud to stand by your side."

Carmel sat up slowly. She had had a worrying thought. "What about Sif and Thrud? I know you love me, but what about them; won't you miss them now that they're gone?"

"Of course I'll miss Thrud," Thor acknowledged solemnly. "But not my wife. We've grown apart over the years and have different interests and ambitions. Other than our daughter, we don't have anything left in common."

"All the same; don't you want them back, here, with you in Asgard?" Carmel asked thoughtfully.

"No, I'm glad they're gone," he muttered soberly. "If Asgard is truly doomed as Henry has said; then I'm glad they're safe in Midgard."

"Well, wouldn't you like to be with them, too; all safe and secure?"

"What's this, my talkative queen; twenty questions?" he teased, tickling her once more and play wrestling her into silence.

Giggling frantically, Carmel begged him to stop. She was too tired to retaliate. The good food, fine mead, and exquisite lovemaking had put her in the mood for sleep, not playfulness. Settling down once more, she decided to repeat her last question. Would he prefer to be in Midgard with Sif and Thrud?

"No," her lover replied emphatically. "Asgard is my home, and I will never leave it. If the realm is to perish, then I will die with it. A captain never deserts his ship; ever. Besides, where would I be without the woman I adore?"

"Thank you, my sweet," Carmel purred as she settled back contentedly into his arms.

The fire was beginning to fade; its embers spitting noisy clouds of sparks as one by one the smoldering, orange logs flickered before collapsing abruptly into a bed of glowing ashes. It had been a lovely evening and one they would remember for a long, long time.

"Don't worry about Asgard," Carmel whispered wearily, closing her eyes as she began to drift into sleep.

"We Valkyries, we'll save it—we always do."

*Author's notes: Thralls was a term the Norsemen used for their lowest cast of slaves. Intriguingly, Habard was one of many aliases Odin used as a disguise. I have also taken the liberty of fusing elements of another saga—Thor's journey to Utgard—into this tale.

47

Bad Pennies

"**H**ey Finch, how's it going?"

Woods knew that that was a stupid question even before he asked it. Squatting down beside the dishevelled, huddled figure in the corner of his harshly lit padded cell; Marcus looked a mess. His eyes were barely open, and several days of stubble pockmarked his face. Trussed up in a straitjacket, it seemed such a sad end for the New York detective.

Drugged, bound, and banged up in a loony bin.

If Woods had had a heart, he might have found Marcus's predicament upsetting. As it was; he just found it annoying. Of all the people in all the world; why, oh why, had his first assignment for the Dragza Corporation been to pick him up?

Marcus was his nemesis and, quite frankly, Woods was getting sick of him. He didn't exactly hate him, but Marcus was, well, like a bad penny—always there, lurking somewhere around the corner; just waiting to be picked up.

What the hell had he got that the Corporation wanted?

This question stumped Woods. Looking at the mess before him, he was inclined to turn around, walk away, and lock the heavy iron door behind him—permanently.

Who cared if the loser had shot Herr Flöda?

If picking him up and taking him back to Crescent Cay was all about punishment and retribution; Woods would be more than happy to administer that here—or better still at thirty thousand feet. A bullet in the back of Finch's head and a five-minute tumble into the Atlantic, mission accomplished. No loose ends and no comebacks. It would be easy.

Fuck! This was infuriating. Finch always stole his moment of glory. He had spent ten years culturing a relationship with the Contessa and then, one phone call, and she was all over the detective; inviting him to her island and parading him about like some strutting peacock on her arm.

The bastard.

And what about the Valkyries?

In the same ten years, he had only met one Valkyrie; and yet within the space of a couple of weeks, Finch had met two—and fucked one of them!

Where was the justice in that?

Now this; he damn nearly gets hacked to pieces by a speedboat, endures a spine-tingling injection of liquid shit to join the Club, and what does Finch get? Sprung from jail and escorted back to the Island in a private jet to be the Count's honoured guest.

Shit! Life really wasn't fair.

Getting up, Woods turned to the door and banged angrily on it with his fist. A few moments later, two burly FBI Agents—both loyal Dragza men—joined him in the room.

Their paperwork was in order, and permission had already been granted to transfer Finch into their custody. They were good to go. Indicating to his colleagues that he was ready, the two men tried to drag Marcus to his feet. He couldn't stand. Head flopping like a rag doll and with eyes rolled to the back of their sockets; Marcus was barely conscious.

It all seemed such a ludicrous waste of time.

Just what the hell did Finch have that was so fucking valuable anyway?

Without Odin's eye to guide it, the well in the Chamber of the Valkyries was playing up; or so it seemed to Kat.

Yes, the three of them had arrived safely in New York; but dressed like this? It was madness; there simply had to be a glitch in the system. They looked so out of place it was comical. If the aim of their plan was to meet up discretely with Marcus; then they couldn't have got off to a worse start. Dressed up as cheerleaders, with hair pulled tightly back into bunched plaits, ribbons, and glittering, golden pom-poms; it would be a miracle if their picture didn't make the front page of the *New York Times.*

What a choice in clothes.

Kat was livid, Jess was amused, and Hel, well; she was ecstatic. Jumping about like a lunatic, she simply refused to ditch her pom-poms. Dancing along the streets and saying "Hi" to as many people as she could; the former Queen of the Damned was in paradise. Midgard was beyond her wildest dreams, and she couldn't help but twirl and admire her reflection in each and every window they passed. A jour-ney to Marcus's flat that should have taken half an hour swiftly turned into a two-hour marathon.

Hel wanted to visit every shop and gave a continuous, running dia-logue of questions and comments on everything they saw or did. She was like a small child in a sweet shop; there were just so many candy jars to dip into that she didn't know where to begin.

After feeling initially annoyed and embarrassed, Kat gradually lightened up and began to see the funny side.

Hey! It was summertime and this was New York—so get real.

The streets were hot and heaving, and nobody gave a damn about Hel's curious antics. She could have pranced naked in the middle of the road, and no one would have batted an eyelid. The crowds around them were completely self-engrossed; sipping skinny lattes, texting, hailing cabs, or just rushing around from A to B. New York was a vibrant, living, happening city, and Hel was its newest, most exuber-ant arrival. Her enthusiasm was infectious, and the city embraced her with open arms.

Hel loved New York—and New York loved Hel.

Breaking their original agreement, both Jess and Kat relented and allowed Hel to buy one or two knick-knacks. "Souvenirs for Henry," she pleaded as she tried on T-shirts and kiss-me-quick hats that were so obviously meant for her.

Sensibly, the girls paid for these items with cash from their Val-kyrie purses; neither wanted to use their credit cards. It was a near certainty that Odin would have detected their arrival, and they didn't want to provide him with a paper trail. This would give him their exact location. Somehow, they hoped that, with Marcus's help and connections, they might just make it to Odin's Island undetected.

This was their objective.

To look for clues; anything that might help them understand what the heroes and gods were planning in Midgard.

Arriving at the entrance to Marcus's block of flats, a resident kindly let them in without having to buzz up to first. Jess wanted to surprise Marcus, so it was with mounting excitement that the three of them lined up outside his front door. He was going to be amazed to see her again; so young, so healthy, and so pretty. It was all so very different from their last, sorrowful parting.

What then had been a frail, greying, infirm Jess; was now replaced by the powerful and bubbly Valkyrie.

Marcus was going to be so pleased to see her, she hoped, keeping her fingers crossed tightly behind her back. He may not be a hero to save anymore; but the memories of their night together still lingered on; sending goose bumps shivering up and down her spine. She still loved him; and she hoped he would feel the same way, too.

KNOCK—KNOCK!

Jess had tapped cautiously; but the knock still caught Anna unaware. Motioning for Lia to stay seated, she got up and made her way over to the front door. Squinting through the peephole—she grimaced.

"Tusk, tusk," she tutted, undoing the chain before turning the lock. "That figures," she spat irritably as she pulled the door open.

The face through the peephole had been hideously distorted but still instantly recognisable. Anna hadn't needed Lia after all. Instead of searching for the Valkyries—they had come to her.

"I might have guessed you would turn up," she sneered dryly at Jess, trying to maintain her cool.

"Hi, Anna, is your husband home?" the warrior enquired with a broad and cheesy grin. Jess knew Anna hated the sight of her, but she held her hand out to shake Anna's all the same.

Anna didn't take it. "No, he isn't; but I guess that won't stop you from coming in, will it," she muttered crossly, standing aside to allow Jess past.

"Who's there?" Lia enquired, trotting eagerly into view.

"Oh, just some old friends," Anna retorted. "Meet Jess, she's a, she's a—" she faltered, "—she's a fucking Valkyrie," she blurted, venomously.

"Hi, I'm Kat. May I come in, too?" Kat asked politely, holding her hand out.

"And you are?" Anna enquired, as if she really needed to ask.

"Another fucking Valkyrie," Kat mocked sarcastically, before entering the flat.

Marcus's wife needed a lesson in manners.

"And I suppose you must be another fucking one as well?" Anna scoffed as she greeted Hel. The wretched cult was winding her up nicely; three for the price of one—how very thoughtful.

Hel didn't offer a handshake. Thrusting out an arm, she pushed Anna roughly backward; pinning her hard against the wall. Before the woman could blink, Hel's blade was at her throat.

She pressed deeply, drawing a bead of blood.

"Hi, I'm Hel, former Queen of the Damned," she growled. "And if I hear you utter another profanity I'll cut your tongue out and make you eat it." She pressed her face closer to Anna's. Smiling malevolently, Hel flashed her eyes a violent shade of red.

Anna blanched a deathly white before collapsing limply to the floor. She was out cold.

This shock had been too great.

When Anna eventually came round, she found herself lying on the floor with her head cradled in Jess's lap. Kat was holding her legs high in the air. She felt sick, she felt dizzy, and her heart was skipping beats.

"Who are you, and how did you do that thing with her eyes?" she asked weakly, looking up at Hel.

"Oh well, here we go again," Jess smiled taking control. She was getting a little bored of explaining about Valkyries. "We're undead warriors, and we need Marcus's help," she began with a sigh.

"I don't understand, what do you mean?" Anna enquired in a daze.

"Look." Jess replied, taking Anna's hand in hers and placing it on her chest. "No heartbeat."

Putting Anna's legs down, Kat knelt beside her and placed Anna's hand on her chest, too. "Ditto," she laughed.

Hel nodded that she was one, too. "I'm sorry about what happened back there," she added with a sheepish grin. "I just don't like swearing, that's all."

Anna tried to get up. Her head span sickeningly, so she lay back down again. Her body was still in a state of shock.

"Would anyone like a cup of tea?" Lia offered hopefully as she started toward the kitchen. She was intrigued by Anna's guests. She had heard stories about Valkyries from the Contessa and some of the hostesses with tattoos, but had never actually met one.

"When's Marcus coming home?" Jess asked sweetly as she eased Anna's head onto a couple of cushions.

"He isn't. He's in jail." Anna replied curtly.

"What? You mean he's at work, surely?" Kat suggested quizzically. Marcus was a detective, not a criminal.

"No, he's been locked up in prison. He shot someone, but I don't know why," Anna continued desolately. "And it gets worse. He went mad and has been transferred to a psychiatric unit. He was raving on about protecting his queen; or some such rubbish."

Hel pricked her ears up. "When was this?" she enquired eagerly.

"A couple of days ago, I think," Anna retorted a little unhelpfully.

The warriors looked at each other in amazement.

Ragnarok.

It couldn't be, surely?

"Did he have one of these?" Hel asked as she hitched her sleeve a little higher, exposing the tattoo at the top of her arm. It had faded badly since the battle, but it was still just about visible; the scar from Kat's knife carving an ugly gash that mutilated the flower's heart.

"If that's a tattoo of a poppy, then yes, yes he did."

"My queen!"

Lia, who had been eavesdropping on their conversation, suddenly dashed into the room and fell to her knees in front of Hel. Clasping Hel's hand in hers, she kissed it fervently. This must be the woman who the Contessa had served; the Black Valkyrie, the living, breathing Queen of the Angels.

"You see," Hel beamed ecstatically as she soaked up Lia's adulation. "I'm such a famous god!"

Anna stared at her in bewilderment. "Are you saying that you're the one responsible for the shooting?" she asked as anger replaced the confusion in her voice.

Hel blushed.

"No, well, not exactly. Frigg, I mean the Contessa, was in charge of day-to-day operations here, in Midgard. I didn't get involved in the details," she mumbled apologetically. "By the way, did Marcus actually kill him?" she added with an excited twinkle in her eyes.

"No." Anna replied grumpily. "But he'll still get life behind bars unless you can help me get him out of there."

"Hey, no problem," Hel replied flamboyantly before turning to the others for moral support. "That won't be a problem, will it?" she asked cautiously as she caught the expression in Kat's eyes.

Kat shrugged and pulled a face. "In for a penny, in for a pound; what do you reckon Jess?"

"Well, we've done it before, so I guess we can do it again; but it won't be easy, it never is." Jess thought for a moment. "Where did you say he was?"

"Some psychiatric hospital," Anna replied hopefully. "It's a secure unit not far from here. I have the details somewhere, but I haven't been allowed to visit him yet."

"Good," Jess concluded with a smile. "Hel; why don't you get your devoted servant up off her knees and let her carry on with making the tea? We probably won't have time to spring him today, but if we can bash our heads together, maybe we can come up with a plan for tomorrow."

Hel clapped her hands gleefully. "Does that mean we can stay the night?" she asked breathlessly.

"Yes, Hel, it does."

"Can we go out?" she gasped excitedly. "Oh, do say we can, please, please."

Jess inhaled slowly. This could be awkward. Hel definitely couldn't be trusted. She had been bad enough on the streets by day— so what in Midgard would she be like by night? "Depends on what you want to do?" she enquired tactfully.

"Oh, Kat, please, can we go and see Dolly Parton?"

"Um," Kat paused as she tried to stifle a smile. "We don't know where she lives, and it probably is too far away, anyway."

"Oh," Hel sulked momentarily before breaking into a smile once more. She had had another idea. "Well, what about Hollywood then? Surely we could go there and see Rhett?"

"Um," Kat paused once more and then giggled. "I think you'll find that Clark Gable is dead, and besides, Hollywood is also far too far away."

"Oh, rats!" Hel huffed dejectedly, plonking herself down into a chair. "I'm going to get so bored just sitting around here in this miserable flat."

Jess looked at Kat and shrugged. A happy Hel had to be better than a disgruntled one. There had to be a middle ground; something that would keep her amused but out of trouble.

"I know," Lia chimed in as she returned from the kitchen carrying a tray loaded with steaming mugs of tea. "Why don't we go clubbing together? You'll like that, your majesty, I promise."

"Brilliant!" Hel squealed, jumping up and down before hugging Kat excitedly. "That sounds fantastic. Will you come with us, too, Kat?" she pleaded, fluttering her eyes like a puppy dog. "Please, please—pretty please?"

Kat looked at Jess and Jess looked at Kat. Their expressions said it all. The thought was horrifying.

Quite possibly; this could be the worst night imaginable.

The ex-Queen of the Damned let loose on the streets of New York?

The mind just boggled.

48

Giants Waving Flowers

"**M**ight have guessed you'd turn up sooner or later," Ruby sneered as the man who had been crossing the Bifrost Bridge finally set foot on their side. "Shouldn't you be rotting somewhere in a nice, dank cave?"

Loki smiled as he twirled Odin's spear provocatively in his hands. "Lovely to see you too, my dearest Valkyries," he bowed, mockingly.

"Nice toy," Silk commented, stretching out a playful hand to snatch at Gungnir.

"Where'd you get it?"

"Sons have their uses," Loki joked, laughing as he plucked the item out of her reach. Relaxing a little, he decided to gloat over how Odin's spear happened to come into his hands.

Vardi had charged beside Fenrir and his pack during the battle of Ragnarok. Seeing Gungnir miss when Odin hurled the weapon, his son had seized the initiative. Realising its worth, he had snatched the spear from the battleground and raced away with it. This had been an unusually smart move; particularly as no one had noticed him leaving.

Travelling fast, he had retraced his steps to his father's tomb before nightfall. There, he had shaped shifted back into human form and used the spear's power to drive a tunnel through the rockfall. Once inside the cave, he had smashed his father's bonds and between them, they had buried his brother, Narvi.

"How's Sigyn?" Ruby asked mischievously after his wife. "Busy serving broiled leather boots for you and your starving companions?" She motioned toward his giant accomplices.

"That's rich, coming from you lot," he growled. "The Aesir will weep with hunger long before any giant farts from an empty belly."

"So where is she?" Silk repeated Ruby's question.

"Safe in Midgard with Vardi; Asgard is going to become an ugly place, now that there aren't any gods to defend it."

"It still has the Valkyries," Ruby hissed angrily. "We warriors are more than a match for you and your pathetic friends."

"Maybe," Loki chuckled arrogantly. "But with Odin and Thor both dead, you're not going to last long."

Ruby and Silk exchanged hurried glances. Loki was unaware that Thor still lived and their destinies had been rewritten.

Neither warrior chose to enlighten him.

"You'll find the realm has many enemies," Loki continued. "Giants, dwarves, dark elves, and witches; they all covet its riches, and I'm not just talking about its gold, diamonds, and trinkets. They desire the land, the hunting, the water, and the warmth. These are Asgard's priceless gems, and they're there for the taking. Come spring and the winter's thaw, you'll face a landslide of hate with wave after wave of invaders besieging your realm. Pretty soon you'll be begging me to conquer you rather than face enslavement by other, more repulsive masters. You'll weep with joy when eventually you hand back what was taken from me."

Pausing to gauge their reaction, it was Silk who broke the brief silence.

"So what exactly was it that was stolen?" she asked. "Perhaps we can come to an agreement; trade Gungnir for whatever it is that you've lost."

"PAH!" Loki exclaimed with an explosive guffaw. "Do you think I'm daft? Gungnir is mine now, so get used to it."

"Come Silk, I've heard enough from this braggart. Let's finish him." Ruby drew her sword, and Silk followed her lead. The drunken insults of Aegir's feasting hall had left deep scars, and their bloodlust yearned for satisfaction.

"Oh yeh, come on girls," Loki sneered, tapping Gungnir lightly on the ground. A ripple of thunder shook the frozen earth. "Do you really think you'll fare any better than the watchtower over there?"

The warriors paused and exchanged glances once more. It was Loki who had levelled the fortress, not the earthquake. This was a worrying turn of events, and they sheathed their weapons. Now was neither the time nor the place to take him down. Frigg and Thor needed to learn of this new and sinister development.

"A prudent decision, my fair ladies; and one your sisters would be wise to follow." Folding his arms defiantly across his chest, Loki stared scornfully at the Valkyries. For once, he had the upper hand.

Gungnir was power.

It was a weapon he could not only use to destroy Asgard but also to rule the giants. Suddenly, he was not only the most powerful god in the realm; he was, quite possibly, the only one, too.

"Here's my deal, and it's nonnegotiable," he commanded as the girls nodded for him to continue. His words should prove interesting.

"I'm going to leave now and return to my kinsmen in Jotunheim. If we are not provoked, I swear I will not step foot in Asgard until after the winter's melt."

"Sounds reasonable," Ruby interrupted. "What's the catch?"

"I'm so glad you asked," Loki chuckled cheerfully. He was just getting to the good bit. "As soon as the road to Utgard is passable, I will cross the high plateau and take my rightful place as the King of the giants. Then, with Hyrokkin by my side, we will return with a mighty host, and I can promise you; we won't be bringing flowers."

"And?" Silk urged him impatiently to continue. Spring couldn't come soon enough if it brought the promise of 'Ugs' for the slaughter.

"Then, my dearest Gunnr," he continued angrily. "I will seize Asgard and lay claim to my prize; the one that was stolen from me by that squat, ugly, two-faced, fat-arsed, shit of a god."

"You mean Thor?" Ruby added with a snigger; Loki's description was not only amusing but in some ways pretty accurate.

THUD!

Thumping Gungnir furiously on the ground, Loki made a violent 'zip it' gesture with his fingers. He was irritated; and demanded a much more respectful silence from these insolent girls.

"Of course I mean Thor, Prudr; who else would I be talking about?" He snarled angrily. "I want fair Carmel back. He stole her when she still belonged rightfully to me. Together, she and I can rule an empire that stretches from sea to sea. Asgard, Jotunheim, Muspellheim, and Nidavellir; all united under one, omnipotent ruler."

"Yeh, yeh, yeh. All hail the great Loki. Loki the magnificent, Loki the terrible," Silk mocked with a slow and sarcastic handclap. "Your delusions make me want to vomit."

"You may sneer now," Loki snorted arrogantly. "But come springtime, I swear you Valkyries will be begging to lick the filth from my boots."

"How dare you speak to us like that, you foul-mouthed cur," Ruby cursed. "Odin should have killed you instead of chaining you up."

"For your information," Loki retorted grimly. "Odin did kill me when he murdered my son and sealed me in that disgusting tomb. The Loki you once knew is long dead and gone. I go by another name now; one that will make the gods tremble in their graves," he threatened malevolently. "Go tell your friends and your sisters, all of them. Loki is dead, but his vengeance lives on. Death has a new name, and it is one you will come to fear and hate. It is a word that will redefine pain and suffering. You and the people of Asgard will cry rivers of tears, and your blood will pour in torrents from the wounds I inflict upon this, the most cursed of realms."

Loki paused before raising Gungnir triumphantly above his head.

"Be afraid; be very afraid as the mightiest of kings arises from Ragnarok," he roared.

"Here stands Utgard-Loki; the slayer of gods and the most ferocious destroyer Asgard has ever known."

49

Clubbin' Hel

*A*fter persuading Hel that she really didn't want to go out on the town dressed as a cheerleader; Jess and Kat rather wished they hadn't. A quick rummage through Anna's wardrobe confirmed what Hel had already suspected. There wasn't a single thing she wanted to wear.

Nothing was, well; quite 'slutty' enough, to give her the buzz she was craving.

There was only one thing to do.

With a shrug of tired resignation, Kat headed back out onto the streets with Hel and Lia to buy some clothes. Jess stayed behind, as she would do for the evening's entertainments. Somebody needed to keep an eye on Anna, and Jess decided it would be her. After what had happened with Marcus on that memorable dawn raid; Jess didn't want history repeating itself.

Anna might be on board; but she couldn't to be trusted.

Several hours and many hundreds of dollars later, Hel, Kat, and Lia returned from their expedition festooned with designer bags. Looking like a trio of exotic Christmas trees; each girl dripped with parcels promising an explosion of fairy tale costumes. Disappearing into Anna's bedroom, the three emerged triumphantly several hours later. Posing and pouting and prinking and preening; they looked fabulous.

The fires of Niflheim would be scorching the sidewalks tonight.

With surprisingly good taste, Hel had bought a simple, but impossibly short, black, leather minidress. It fit like a glove. With elegant stilettos, matching leather choker, hooped earrings, and hair piled high in a cascade of ringlets; she looked a million dollars.

Kat had decided to play safe; buying a chic, figure-hugging blue and white striped dress, which was both timelessly elegant and considerably less revealing. She left her hair down and wore a sparkling, diamond-encrusted pendant. This was a fake, but with the ornament nestling provocatively in her cleavage; the effect was sensational.

After initially being overawed by her queen, Lia quickly relaxed in her company. Hel was unlike anybody she had ever met before; and certainly the most fun. Egged on by her childlike enthusiasm, Lia had bought a denim miniskirt with a black, sleeveless crop top. She kept her hair pulled up tight in a ponytail, which complimented her face. Black leather boots and the same choker as Hel's completed her killer look.

Waving goodbye to a dubious Jess, the girls stepped out into the cauldron of a night on the town. Hailing a cab, Kat took them to a club that was both discrete and not overly popular. Hel's exuberance was at bursting point, and Kat needed to keep a tight eye on her.

Too big a crowd, and her excited friend might lose the plot.

Getting into the club for free, Hel begged Kat to let her buy the first round of drinks. Kat decided to accompany her to the bar, which proved to be fortuitous. After ordering a *Margarita* and two *Slow Comfortable Screws,* Hel dropped a clanger. In an exceedingly polite and accentless voice, she asked the barman for some coke. Fortunately, misunderstanding her request, he returned with a glass of the bubbling, sugary variety.

After dropping the drinks off at the table, Kat escorted Hel to the toilets for a chat. The club was beginning to fill, and Kat didn't want to risk any accidents. Locking a cubicle door behind her, it was time to read her sister the riot act.

"Hel, this isn't your harem back in Niflheim," she began authoritatively. "You can't go asking waiters for cocaine. It's illegal."

"I'm sorry; it was a slip of the tongue. It won't happen again."

"Thank you." Kat paused. It was difficult to get angry, because she could see that Hel was having a wonderful time; her eyes were twinkling like stars and her face was alight with a smile that stretched quite literally from ear to ear. She was ecstatic, and Kat didn't want to rain on her parade. Hel had never been to a night club before and quite probably would never do so again. However, the last thing any of them needed to do was to get arrested and spend the night in jail.

"Look, Hel, there are three simple rules to enjoying this evening," Kat volunteered, deliberately settling for a softly, softly approach so as not to upset her friend.

Hel nodded; she was listening.

"Rule one. No getting naked."

"What?" Hel looked up in astonished. "Have you seen some of the girls out there? They're practically naked and definitely wearing less clothes than I am."

"I know," Kat interrupted. "But if you start stripping off, you won't know where to stop, will you? So promise me, you won't take off any clothes."

Hel nodded reluctantly. This didn't seem fair.

"Rule two. No drugs, they're illegal, and we don't want to get busted."

"But!" Hel gaped in astonishment with her mouth open wide. Her look was that wonderfully, Hel-licious expression that Kat so adored. "I've seen loads of people taking them," she pleaded.

"I don't care," Kat scolded. "No drugs, okay? I don't want you high as well as drunk."

"Oh, so I'm allowed to drink; well, thank goodness for that small mercy," Hel huffed sarcastically. It really wasn't fair. *Why shouldn't she have the same fun as all the other people?* "What's the last rule then, Auntie Katkin?" she whined grumpily.

"No sex, please; especially not on the dance floor."

"Oh, come on, why not?" Hel was mystified by this rule.

"Because, because—" Kat decided to put this rule tastefully. "Because it might upset other people, and again; it's illegal in public."

"Oh, booooring," Hel moaned. "So what can I do? I can't smoke, I can't snort coke, and I can't even—"

"—You can dance Hel," Kat interrupted before she got to the sordid bits. "That's fun, really it is. Just copy what Lia does, she's an excellent dancer."

Hel pouted and scowled at the same time. It was looking like it was going to be a rubbish night, and she'd been so looking forward to it.

"Oh, do come on, Hel," Kat softened, giving her a sisterly cuddle. "We'll have some fun, I swear."

"Promise?" Hel asked with a tiniest flicker of a smile.

"I promise. So come on; why don't you buy me another *Slow Comfortable Screw* and see if you can get me legless."

After commenting words to the effect that she would much rather *have* a slow comfortable screw than drink one; the two returned to the dance floor.

Things were beginning to hot up.

With the bass pounding, the floor pulsating, and strobe lights flashing in all the colours of the rainbow; nudity, drugs, and sex were quickly forgotten as Hel plunged headlong into the spirit of the night. Joining Lia and Kat, she danced her heart out; gyrating wildly to song after song after song. Hour after hour they danced and drank, until Kat too became lost in the pleasures of the evening.

Relaxing more than she should, Kat didn't notice the danger lurking in the shadows until it was too late.

Pouncing with the audacity of a pack of wolves, a gaggle of 'Hooray Henry's' invaded the dance floor. Like bees drawn to a honey pot, they headed straight for the girls; thrusting their hips and baring their chests in a mating display that was as outrageous as it was cringe worthy.

Young, flash, and loaded with cash; the well heeled city types were out on a stag night; and the three women were just what they needed; the answer to all their prayers.

The boys could smell sex—and they were more than up for it.

Silver tongued and completely arseholed, Kat tolerated their drunken attentions for an hour or two. They were show-offs; harmless kids flush with their youthful success. Cocksure, the fresh-faced yuppies were obsessed with the power of their wallets and the labels on their fancy, designer shirts. It was fun to spectate, watching them strutting like peacocks as they plied the girls with a conveyor belt of expensive champagne.

Hel was in heaven; centre stage and loving every minute of their testosterone-fuelled attention. Grinding her hips against boy after boy, she wove an allure that drove the men wild. A torrid, naked orgy may have been out of the question, but dancing was legal; no matter how dirty it got.

She was sex on fire—and the boys drooled.

By 3.00 AM, Kat decided it was time to go.

Motioning to Lia and Hel, Kat shepherded them discretely in the direction of the toilets. They would leave by the back door without saying goodbye; which seemed a sensible precaution. Hel's dancing had inflamed some serious passions, and Kat didn't want to provoke any ugliness. By the time the lads had noticed they were gone, the girls would be safely in a cab and on their way home.

Unfortunately for Kat, Midgard men had smartened up considerably to feminine tactics.

"Hey, laydeeessss! Wheredya think urgoin?" one of them slurred as a gang of about ten of the drunken youths stumbled into the alleyway. The men were swaying horribly and unfortunately blocking the girls' way.

"Going home, as you should," Kat suggested hopefully. This was awkward. Perhaps they should have used the front entrance? They were hemmed in, and the alley was sheltered and hidden from the street.

"What about a goodnight kissshhh?" one of the men enquired.

"What about a goodnight shag?" another shouted less tastefully.

"Yeh, how about a good fucking, hey, sweet cheeks?" said the guy who was standing nearest to them. Staggering forward, he fumbled a grab, which was easy to avoid.

Standing her ground, Kat struck a pose. Attack was the best form of defence.

Hands on hips, she scowled angrily at the gang. "Come on boys, we've all had too much to drink. Why don't you clear a path and let us through? We don't want any trouble, do we?"

"Oh yesssh we do," came a catcall from the back of the pack.

"Get 'em lads, they owe us," came another, far more sinister, jeer. The gang looked nervy, but they began to creep closer.

Sensing trouble, Hel strutted forward to join Kat. Her eyes had widened and were beginning to spark. She smelt blood. "How many are there," she whispered excitedly in Kat's ear.

"About ten, but shush! We don't want a fight if we can help it."

"Fight, what fight?" The ringleader nearest to them had eavesdropped on their conversation. "Who said anything about fighting? We want to fuck, not fight; don't we lads, hey? We want a fucking, a damn good fucking," he hollered, exhorting the others.

"Then go home and have sex with your wives," Hel blurted sarcastically before turning to Kat. "Oh, come on, Kat, let's take them, it would be fun."

"You, bitches, take us?" the cocky guy had overheard Hel's suggestion and wasn't amused. "You're avin' a laugh," he continued, pulling a blade from his pocket and chuckling as he flicked it open. *Stupid bitches!*

Things were getting dangerous.

"You whores are all alike," he continued with a sneer. "A bunch of fucking prick teasers happy to drink our money before fucking off. We've given you a good time, now it's your turn to give us one, too."

Hel reached behind her back for her knife, but Kat put her hand on her arm and stopped her. "Look fellers, this is getting out of hand," she warned. "I really think you should go, now; before you get hurt. You don't know who you're dealing with, and you really don't want to know, either."

Kat took a pace forward as she finished speaking, and the guy with the knife backed away.

That was a good sign. Her speech had unnerved him—just a little.

"Hey Stu; are you really going let that piece of pussy speak to you like that? You fucking gutless motherfucker."

Another heckler from the back of the gang had just poured petrol on the situation. Two other lads drew their knives; alcohol, lust, and the power of steel in their hands buoying their confidence. They would fuck these bitches right there, right now.

Kat looked at Hel and shrugged. Trouble seemed inevitable, and her bloodlust was rising, too.

Hel's eyes flashed red as she grinned mischievously. "Hey sis, this is going to be fun," she chuckled, clenching her fists.

"Hel? Kat? What are you doing? You aren't seriously going to fight them, are you?" Lia gasped anxiously. "They're too many of them, you'll get us killed!"

Kat threw her head back and howled with laughter. A point not lost on the gang swaying drunkenly before them. "Lia, we eat wimps like these for breakfast," she chortled. "Get back and stay down. You're in for a treat." Turning to Hel, she nodded that she was ready.

It was time to get physical.

"No knives and no killing sis," she muttered before squaring off to stare 'Stu' down. "Hey you, shit-for-brains," she yelled mockingly. "Are you going to use that blade or am I going to have to come and spank you for it?"

Whooping with joy, Hel and Kat let out blood-curdling screams before smashing headlong into the stupefied gang.

It had been a while since they'd scrapped, and a good fight would make a perfect end to a Valkyrie evening.

50

Where Eagles Dare

Both Kat and Hel woke the following morning with sore heads and sore fists.

The two warriors had done their best, but the fight had been a disappointment from start to finish, and they felt sorry for Lia. They had let her down badly. Far from being a spectacular showcase, it had been a damp squib.

Nervous, drunk, and completely overawed; the boys had scattered before them like confetti. Pouncing like tigers, the Valkyries had torn into the men with overwhelming ferocity—which was probably a mistake; particularly as the girls had intended to enjoy the tussle.

The violence they had unleashed ruptured the boys' courage.

With teeth and blood spattering from the first to fall, the rest of the gang turned tail and fled. The warriors wanted to give chase; but high heels hampered their progress. With two men unconscious and two more writhing in agony; the fight was over almost before it had begun—which was a pity. Had the boys shown a little more spine, Kat and Hel might have given Lia a much more memorable display.

Not that Lia was complaining; far from it.

Open mouthed and with eyes popping out on stalks; Lia had watched incredulously. Such power and vengeance were beyond her imagination. She now wanted to become a Valkyrie more than anything; and she begged to follow her queen wherever that might lead. This show of unbridled adulation fortunately offset the warriors' disappointment.

Both Kat and Hel were warming to the girl.

"Good morning ladies," Jess beamed when the two Sangrids eventually emerged from their bedroom. "Breakfast?" she enquired in a voice that seemed way too cheerful for the state they were in. Hair tousled and last night's makeup still smeared across their faces, the pair looked a mess.

Slumping into the armchairs, they muttered a cursory "hello" to Anna. She was watching the news while slurping noisily at a coffee. This smelt delicious.

To their surprise, Lia was already up and seemed considerably less shattered than they were. She had already told Jess the story of their fight and was busy tidying the sitting room and opening the windows.

It was a glorious June morning, and the sun streamed in with a youthful vigor. Cars hooted, vendors hollered, and cabbies cursed as they battled to be heard above the hubbub of city noise. The sounds drifting up from the street more than rivalled the warmth of the sun's golden rays.

"Oh, could you please close the window, just a little?" Anna pleaded as she looked up from her coffee. "That racket is giving me a headache."

Lia turned and smiled. "In a minute, I'm just waiting for someone."

Anna furrowed her brow.

What was the girl on about?

Suddenly; and with a dramatic fluttering of wings; a large bird of prey alighted on the sill. It was the one they had seen the other evening. Folding his feathers, he hopped carefully into the room.

The bird was an eagle owl, but his appearance was too brief for Anna to take pleasure in his magnificent plumage. Within an instant the creature was gone; replaced by a burst of blinding light. From this emerged the figure of a man.

"That's not possible," Anna gasped, blanching once more. She must be going mad—and she looked like she was going to faint again.

Leaping to their feet, Kat and Hel took up defensive positions. Jess was quickly at their side. Not only was this possible, they knew the identity of the man who had emerged from the starburst.

"Hello, Vali." Jess grimaced as she clenched her fists. His presence was unwelcome and confirmed her worst fears. Odin had tracked them down.

"My ladies," Vali bowed low in a mock gesture of politeness. "What a lovely surprise to find you here."

"I wish we could say likewise," Kat replied as she crept menacingly forward.

"What do you want?" Hel growled aggressively, following her lead.

"Please, dear ladies," Vali began, backing away cautiously. "No violence. I mean you no harm. I've come with an invitation from Lord Odin."

"Oh yeh, so that cockroach really is alive," Hel spat disgustedly.

"Very much so, and he is delighted to learn of your excellent health," he continued, trying to retreat further but finding his path blocked. He was now standing with his back against the window. "Please, let's all be civilised, let's not behave like you did last night," he added with a wicked smirk.

Kat and Hel exchanged glances. "Did you see what happened?" Kat enquired inquisitively.

"Absolutely; and may I say what a shame those cowards didn't stand their ground. You must be awfully disappointed." He giggled nervously.

"Let's grab him and chuck him out." Jess suggested scornfully.

"Good idea; I've kicked his arse before." Kat pressed forward once more.

"Ladies, please; let's not jump to any hasty decisions. Besides, do you honestly think that I've come alone?" To his great relief, Vali heard a loud hammering at the door. Reinforcements had arrived in the nick of time.

"Don't answer it!" cried Hel, but her shout was too late. Lia had bounded across the room and undone the locks.

THUD!

With a sickening crash, the door flew open. Four uniformed men burst through with their rifles cocked and hunting for targets. Within moments, laser dots converged ominously on the girls' heads.

One false move—and the Valkyries were dead.

"Hey, Vali," Hel hissed as she raised her hands slowly in the air. "I won't forget this."

Vali didn't reply.

Motioning urgently to the men, one of them stepped forward and secured the warriors' hands behind their backs. Signalling when this was complete; Vali let out an audible sigh. He could relax at last.

"There we go," he smiled as he beckoned to the girls to sit down once more. "I knew we could all be friends. Now, if you'll just be patient; I have a quick phone call to make. By the way," he nodded to Lia. "Nice work."

Stepping into the kitchen, Vali closed the door behind him. His conversation was private.

"Traitor," Hel muttered as she caught Lia's eye.

"I'm sorry," Lia stuttered. "I didn't realise how nice you would be."

"Ah, well that's a comfort, you filthy, cheating snake," Kat added caustically.

"Look, don't blame me, I had to do it," Lia whimpered, lowering her voice. "All the other girls had been killed; I was the only one left. If I hadn't agreed, I would have been murdered."

"You'll soon wish you had been," Hel fumed. "How much are they paying you for this betrayal?"

"Immortality; that's my reward," Lia replied with a nervous grin. "I'm sorry, but you all have that gift, and I want it, too. You can't blame me for wanting to live forever."

"Are you telling us that these men are immortal?" It was Jess who had spoken, and her voice sounded perplexed.

"Yes," Lia replied not realising the bombshell she'd just landed. "They all bear the mark; the scar on their chests."

The girls looked at each other in amazement.

"Heroes!" They whispered hoarsely in unison.

"Oh, come on, Vili, surely you can play better than that?" Odin chuckled gleefully as he watched his brother scuttle off to recover the ping-pong ball.

"You're rubbish," sniggered Ve.

"Am not," Vili retorted as his head disappeared into a bush.

"Boys, you're both useless," Odin sighed putting his bat down. "I do hope my new toy is coming along better than this," he continued poignantly, mopping his brow.

It was hot, desperately hot; and although they had placed the table in the shade, it was now definitely time to take a break. They'd been playing for an hour, and the three of them were sweating hard.

"It's nearly finished," Ve volunteered as he stood up; the white ball glistening in his hand. "Well, almost."

"And it's better than the other one," Vili chipped in, eagerly.

"Brothers, I don't need it to be better. I just need it to work. Can you at least promise me that?" Odin asked anxiously. Time was of the essence.

"Of course, you can trust us." Ve answered with a confident smile. "We're always good at what we do."

Odin raised his eyebrows.

Hmmm—if only.

"By the way, what time are they arriving?" Vili asked in a voice tingling with excitement. "I can't wait to see them again."

"Soon, I should think." Odin smiled as he glanced at his watch. Vali had phoned mid morning with the news of his success. So allowing an hour or so to get to the airport; the jet should be touching down pretty much now.

To be truthful, he shared his brothers' excitement.

He had so many questions to ask his Valkyries and, of course, with Anna coming along too; he had an excellent bonus. She would make a wonderful insurance policy and ensure her husband's cooperation. That was why he had sent Vali to track her down. Marcus had arrived earlier in the day and was already recovering from his sedation. It would be interesting to see his reaction; being reunited with his wife—and his Valkyrie.

Vali had done well, and what a wonderfully, fortuitous surprise to have the warriors there in Anna's flat. Lia's telephoned tip-off had paid up handsomely—not that she would get the reward he'd promised her. *Immortality be damned!* He couldn't abide sneaks, even when they were working for him.

Relaxing into a recliner, Odin took a contented sip from a chilled orange juice.

Since his departure from Asgard, he had had a change of heart. Along with Gungnir, he now regretted his decision to leave his loyal Valkyries behind. That had been a stupid oversight and one that hung heavily on his mind. He missed them. It had been a mistake; and one he hoped he would soon be able to rectify.

He had a proposal to offer and was cautiously optimistic of its success.

Not that getting his warriors to forgive him would be easy, though. They were going to be sore, big time; and they would have many questions that he would have to answer with care. Too much information and the deal would be off—period. The girls were proud and noble, both qualities he adored; but if he pressed the wrong buttons, his Valkyries would become obstinate and obtuse. He had to make sure that they first understood and then sympathised with his side of the story.

As he mulled over what to say, one issue stuck out like a sore thumb.

How much did they know about Ragnarok?

If he told them the truth, they would be angry, very angry; and unlikely to agree to his offer. Unfortunately, with the two Sangrids present in the Valkyrie party, negotiations looked set to be tough.

Hel would definitely say "no" to any proposal he put on the table, and Kat was likely to follow suit. The two of them were close, too close; and that worried him. Kat was too easily led. Brynhildr, on the other hand, would be fine, she was malleable; but he knew that she would also side with Kat. Warriors and their former maids always did.

Kat therefore was the key to success.

Convince her to say "yes," and a bargain could be struck. If she voted against; then that would be a disaster. With time running out, his deal was going to be unique; a one-of-a-kind opportunity that they mustn't refuse.

The Valkyries had one chance to live.

That was his deal.

To say no would mean death—and dying in a far more horrific and ignominious way than any of them could imagine.

51
Ultimatum

"To my beloved Valkyries!"

Odin raised his glass and to a rousing chorus of "Hail Odin," most of the guests at the magnificent, marble, dining table drank a toast to his mighty warriors.

Kat, Jess, Hel, and Marcus remained silent—and they didn't raise their glasses.

In fairness, they couldn't.

Odin wasn't taking any chances. Although they were guests at his table; they remained bound with their hands tied securely behind their backs. Numerous armed heroes surrounded the area, and their weapons were prominently on display. He was delighted to see his Valkyries; but he wasn't stupid.

"So tell me, Sangrid, how did you stop the Guardians from destroying the realm?" Odin enquired as the guests sat down and began to tuck into their hors d'oeuvres.

Hel didn't reply.

"Okay," Odin decided to try a different tack. "Brynhildr, have you found Gungnir yet?"

Jess, too, remained silent.

Odin paused and studied the three girls carefully. He was being stonewalled.

"Ladies, please," he began plaintively. "It isn't going to be a very pleasant evening if you don't talk. Look, I'm sure you have many questions, as do I; so why don't we make a deal. A question for a question; how's that?"

Kat, Hel, and Jess exchanged looks. It seemed a reasonable solution; after all, that's what they were there for.

Answers.

"Why did you abandon us?" Jess blurted as Vali tried to feed her a spoonful of the starter. Vili and Ve were likewise engaged, gleefully taking it in turns to cram prawns into Kat's mouth. Sitting next to her and Lia on the far side of the table, the two were in paradise—a peculiar, blond-coloured, breast-ogling sort of paradise.

"I think abandon is such an ugly word," Odin mused slowly and deliberately after considering Jess's question. "Why don't we just say that I accidentally left you behind, sort of, shall we say—by mistake?"

"You filthy coward!" Hel cursed as she spat out the food that Thirle was feeding her. "You left us there to die; that was your plan. Everybody dies at Ragnarok, except the gods. They just used their grubby little rings and its goodbye to Asgard and hello paradise."

"Sangrid's right, Odin," Kat mumbled as she turned her head to avoid another spoonful from Ve. "Why weren't you honest with us? Why didn't you just explain the problem with lambda rather than shroud it in deceit?"

"Lambda; now there's an interesting word," Odin replied inquisitively. "So what do you know about its meaning?"

"Only that it's the Cosmological Constant, and you got it wrong. That the universe you and your crazy brothers created is collapsing and will end in a couple of billion years." Kat looked at Jess and Hel as she spoke. Maybe she shouldn't have said so much; but there was a key question that they still needed answering.

"Clever girl, Katarina; what a clever, little girl," he applauded. "Now did you figure that all out by yourself or did someone else give you a little bit of help?"

"Henry worked it out," Hel chimed in with a smirk. "He's a genius."

"He certainly is," Odin mused. He was one person he should never have allowed Frigg to get her evil hands on. "Did he say anything else about lambda?"

"Nothing, except that we must be missing something." Kat decided to strike to the heart of her question. "If the universe still has two billion years to run; why did you abandon it now, Odin? Why? Maybe we could have fixed the problem. After all; there's still plenty of time, surely?"

"Oh, Sangrid, how I wish there were, I truly do."

Odin waved his hand to Vili and beckoned him over. After whispering something in his ear, Vili clapped his hands excitedly and hurried away from the table. He was off on a mission, and while he was away; Odin decided to pose his first question.

"How did you stop the Guardians?"

This question had been bugging him since before their arrival. They were ghostly, unstoppable shadows; so how could they have failed?

Hel decided to answer this one.

"It was your dragons, you idiot," she retorted gleefully. "They were from a different universe, so the Guardians didn't affect them. I cut a deal with their leader—and they sent them packing. In the end, stopping the Guardians was a piece of cake."

"Bravo, bravo Sangrid," Odin commended her. "I hadn't thought of that. That really was a rather stupid mistake of mine, don't you think; so well done, you." Odin decided to be generous for a change. Perhaps stroking Hel's ego would make her soften.

"My lord, you still haven't answered our question yet," Jess interrupted politely. She couldn't help being courteous; the habit was just too ingrained. "Why did you abandon the realm you love and leave it to be devastated?"

Before Odin could answer, Vili returned to the table with the present he had hastily wrapped. He had done the job very badly, but it was just done well enough to hide whatever it was that was inside the box. After thanking his brother for his efforts, Odin passed the gift along the table to Kat.

"Here, this is a present for your friend Henry," he volunteered. "Let's see if he can work the problem out for himself." Odin paused and, as an afterthought, he took the plastic disk from his pocket and passed that along as well. "I'm spoiling you now. Here's another clue for your clever little whiz kid friend."

Kat studied the disk carefully. It was a beautiful green colour—but sadly didn't have any answers printed on it.

"I've decided not to respond to your question directly," Odin began cautiously, turning to Jess as he returned to her question once more. "But the answer can be deduced using the contents of that box. The reason why I left Asgard is also the reason why I have invited you to dine with me tonight. I want my Valkyries to come and join me here in Midgard; just you, my dearest Valkyries—no one else; that's the deal."

"Does that also include your very own, personal favourite warrior?" Hel quipped mischievously.

"If by that question you mean you, Sangrid; then my answer is still, with reluctance, yes. Oh, and you can bring that Henry chap along with you, too. His brains might come in handy."

"What about Frigg?" Kat asked pointedly.

"No way, my Lord, I forbid it!" Freyja spoke up for the first time, and she scowled angrily at the girls.

"You heard the boss," Odin chuckled as he raised his glass to his lover. "Oh, and one more thing; Freyja must be reinstated as your queen."

Kat, Jess, and Hel looked quizzically at each other. His offer was certainly tempting.

"What happens if we say no?" Jess asked; voicing their concerns.

"Then you will all die a horrible death." Odin replied grimly as he folded his arms across his chest. "Of that you can be assured. That is why I created the prophesies; a self-fulfilling lie that would lead to the end of Asgard in an epic and heroic battle. Believe me when I say this. Dying at Ragnarok would have been infinitely more honourable than the death that lies ahead if you reject my offer."

"So if we say yes, then the Valkyries will live; but everybody else still goes ahead and dies?" Kat felt angry and she wanted to clarify this point.

Odin nodded that this was so.

"I can't believe I'm hearing this," Kat exploded as she looked at him in amazement. "Do you have no shame? Do you expect us to flee like cowards and leave the Aesir to their doom? That isn't the Valkyrie way, you should know that by now. We won't run, and we definitely won't hide. There has to be a way to stop whatever disaster is going to happen; there must be."

"My dear Sangrid," Odin began apologetically. "Please believe me, if there was a way, then I would have found it and used it. Unfortunately, there just isn't, and time has sadly run out." Pointing to the disk, Odin hung his head mournfully.

A silence fell upon the diners as the gathering digested this sobering revelation—and their starters.

Asgard was doomed, and the key to the riddle lay hidden in the box.

Waiters came and removed their plates, and as wine glasses were refilled and the main course was served; a gentle ripple of conversation stirred amongst the guests.

Apart from Thirle, the girls knew everybody at the table.

Vili and Ve were sitting next to Kat and Lia; with Mimir propped up in a wheelchair at the end on their side. Hel had already greeted him with the quip "you've put on weight," and this had cause a weak smile to flicker briefly across his face. Mimir said little, but a brightness in his eyes hinted that reason might be returning to his addled brain.

Odin was seated at one end of the table, and Freyja was sat at the other. Thirle was sitting next to her, and he was on the opposite side of the table to Kat, Lia, Vili, and Ve. Hel, Vali, Jess, and Marcus were seated on the same side as Thirle. Both Anna and Woods were absent from the table; much to Woods chagrin. As he'd predicted; Marcus had stolen his limelight yet again, and he'd been relegated to the beach—albeit with the consolation of a beautiful hostess for the night.

It was about eight in the evening, and the patio was flooded in artificial light that cast eerie shadows amongst the palm trees. These swayed excitedly all around them. A freshening breeze had picked up before sunset, sending delicate wisps of grey cloud scurrying across the sky. The weather was on the change, and in a few weeks the hurricane season would be upon them.

"So how's Frigg?" Odin enquired jovially as he restarted his questions and tried to avoid a frosty glare Freyja had hurled in his direction.

"Oh, she's fine and sends her love," Hel replied sarcastically as she swallowed a spoonful of food. Nodding her head, she motioned for Thirle that she was ready for more.

She was hungry, and the lobster tasted delicious.

"Do you know what? I've got a little present for her, too." Odin offered, waving to a servant who hurried off in the direction of the mansion. "I'm sure she's going to appreciate it," he continued smugly.

"Is it her ring?" Kat asked scornfully. "Or are you too scared to return that?"

Odin chuckled as he waited patiently for his servant to return. His warriors were so spirited and feisty; he missed them so much. "Careful!" he yelled, standing up in alarm as the servant who was carrying the casket stumbled on the patio. Recovering his balance, the man placed it cautiously on the table.

"I'm sure you all recognise this box?" Odin enquired as the girls nodded that they did.

"Home sweet home," Hel muttered with a wicked grin, poking her tongue playfully in Mimir's direction.

"Well, tell my ex-wife that her ring is inside," Odin leered as his face dissolved into an expression of satisfied smugness. "Along with another dear, little keepsake."

The girls tried to press him for details, but he refused to let on. Like the present for Henry; the contents of the cask were a secret for now.

"How's Balder?" Hel asked, believing it was probably their turn for a question.

Odin and Freyja exchanged hurried glances, which instantly aroused her suspicions.

"He's all right, isn't he?" she continued with alarm.

"Yes, of course he's all right, he's just fine; absolutely," Odin replied much too hastily and in a voice that lacked conviction.

"He doesn't want to be here, does he?" Kat suggested shrewdly. Something wasn't right, she could sense it.

"Look," Freyja decided to join the conversation. "You've got Hod, isn't that enough? At least let Odin keep one of his sons."

"Maybe we could exchange them?" Hel suggested cheerily. She much preferred Balder to Kat's dolt of a lover.

"No, definitely not." Odin retorted, squashing that suggestion. "Hod chose to stay in Asgard, and he must live with his decision. Besides; he would never leave you, his darling Sangrid, now would he?"

Kat nodded her head slowly. Yet again, her relationship with Odin's son was dominating her life. *Make him hate you!* Frigg's words echoed briefly in her mind. *How, Frigg, how?* That was the conundrum she still couldn't resolve.

It should be easy being cruel to him—but it wasn't.

"So what do you want with Marcus?" Kat volunteered, trying to redirect the conversation as she forced her mind away from Hod.

"Hang on a minute," Odin laughed. "It must be my turn to ask a question. What happened to my spear?"

The girls looked at each other once more. This time, his question had the three of them stumped.

"We thought you took it with you," Jess suggested hopefully. "If you didn't, then I guess it's missing. Now that could be our little secret," she smirked, nodding in the direction of the presents on the table.

"That's a shame, but it doesn't really matter." Odin shrugged. "What was your question again, my dear Sangrid?" he enquired absently.

"What's Marcus doing here?" Jess repeated on Kat's behalf.

"Ahhh," Odin replied mysteriously as he sat back with a strange smile on his face. "You have Hel to thank for that."

"What?" Hel looked up in amazement. "I've got nothing to do with him, I swear."

"Maybe not directly," Odin continued. "But correct me if I'm wrong; isn't Marcus one of your Angels?" Motioning to a servant, he got the man to roll up Marcus's sleeve so that his poppy was visible. Like Hel's, it was fading, but still obviously present.

"I loved the stunt you pulled at Ragnarok with your Demon Angels," Odin congratulated her with a twinkle in his eye. "I want that power, and Marcus will help me get it."

"Why use him, what about Hel's other Angels?" Jess interrupted anxiously. She didn't like the sound of what Odin had in mind for her hero.

"Unfortunately, I can't use any of them," Odin replied with a sigh. "You see, I killed them all before I realised the poppies' true power. My ex-wife left such an excellent database on her computer. Only Marcus, being her latest recruit, was missing from that list. I guess that was another lucky escape for you," he suggested, motioning with his hand in his direction.

"What are you going to do to him? Don't you dare hurt him," Jess hissed protectively.

Marcus smiled weakly. He was still dazed, and his eyes were half open; but he could just about follow what was going on. It was good to hear Jess's voice and to see her so strong and so beautiful again. Their love still smouldered, and he could feel its warmth burning a hole in his heart.

"Of course I'm not going to hurt him, provided, of course, Sangrid cooperates," Odin began as he tried to reassure Jess. "I only need a sample of ink from the tattoo, and I'll have the formula for the poppy extract. Then, all I'll need is the spell of enchantment from Sangrid."

"Don't give it to him," Marcus mumbled. "I won't let you."

Hel giggled; the poor man could barely sit, let alone defend her from Odin. It was a mad gesture, but one that was really sweet and well intended, too. Jess's lover was a true hero, and she liked him already.

"I'll give you what you want," Hel began, looking Odin squarely in the eyes. "Provided you let Marcus and his wife go free and you tell us what you intend to do with its power."

Odin returned Hel's gaze. "My dear Sangrid, you are in no position to demand such terms, but I'm happy to give you my word; both Marcus and his wife can leave this island unharmed."

Odin paused for a moment, allowing Jess to begrudgingly nod her thanks. "As to why I want the power of your poppies," he continued. "I would have thought that was obvious. I want its control."

"I thought you already had control," Kat retorted, butting in. "What with our mead and whatever it is that you do to our heroes." She decided to dig for more answers and, to her astonishment, Odin provided a lengthy and revealing explanation.

Control, as he had stated, was the power he craved. Over the centuries, he had tried many methods to enslave his subjects. The Mead of Valhalla and the halos he used on the heroes were two such examples; but both had their limitations.

The Mead of Valhalla was hard to produce (though Odin wouldn't explain why), and worked better on women than men. It was potent in its effects, but it was also unpredictable and had the terrible, destructive cravings as a side effect. When it worked it worked well, fostering a slavish loyalty and devotion; but it was a crude and old fashioned instrument of power.

The haloes had been a necessary refinement and one he and his brothers were particularly proud of.

Odin could control large numbers through its tangled mesh of metallic nerves. It was also reliable and predictable. However, despite these advantages, it had some weaknesses. It worked better on men, and its level of control was limited. To change his commands needed complex reprogramming of each hero in turn.

Hel's transformation with the poppy extract had given Odin a glimpse of true omnipotence; the ultimate control that he craved.

Using its power, he could be inside each and every one of his heroes; controlling their moves—heartbeat by heartbeat. This prospect had him drooling, and with Hel now conveniently in his hands; the ultimate power of Niflheim was his for the taking.

Odin's reasons begged a question that Kat was quick to ask. "What do you need all this power for?"

"To control Midgard, of course," came a predictable reply. Odin smiled; he had anticipated that question. "There are far too many problems in this world; war, disease, pollution, and overcrowding to name but a few. There needs to be some changes, some reduction and redistribution. That's why I need control. I want to build a new paradise, a kingdom of true perfection that I can rule over forever."

Thirle nodded sagely as he raised his glass in salute. He was back in the guise of Herr Flöda and was more than grateful for that fact. Changed by the well, his true identity was once again mercifully hidden.

"I think you're missing an important consideration, you maggot." Hel interrupted, speaking up with her customary lack of respect for the god of gods. "You didn't create this world. How do you think its founders will react when they find you've stolen their realm? Do you reckon they'll be pleased?"

Odin chuckled slyly; Hel had a good point, and it was one he was eager to refute.

"The gods of Midgard don't care about this world," he retorted haughtily. "They abandoned the place long ago. Sure, they provided crowd pleasers like Krishna, Buddha, Jesus, and Mohammed; but these were just grandiose gestures; a placebo for the masses. If they had any serious intent, why haven't they intervened in all the floods, earthquakes, and the terrible wars?" Pausing, Odin gave his warriors time to digest this awkward question. "I'll tell you why they didn't," he continued. "They couldn't be bothered. They just left Midgard to fend for itself; naked and ripe for invasion. Short of dropping me an invitation or advertised the planet in a *situations vacant* column; they practically begged me to come and conquer it."

"So that's your plan?" Kat retorted venomously. "You're going to use your heroes in a battle to destroy Midgard, and when it's conquered, you and your foul cronies will reign supreme."

"Oh no, Kat, no, no, no! You've got me all wrong," Odin replied with a sneer. "Why should I waste my time fighting when the war is already won?"

This question caused a sudden, hushed silence that lasted until well after their main course had been cleared. It continued eerily as a selection of gorgeous desserts was placed enticingly on the table. Hel found these irresistible, and she announced to Thirle that she wanted to try them all—or die in the attempt. This made everybody laugh; which felt good while it lasted.

Returning to their interrupted conversation, it was Jess who took up his question.

"What do you mean that the war is already won?" she enquired quizzically.

"My dear Brynhildr," Odin began in a patronising tone. "I don't need to wage war, as my heroes already have control of the world's armies. I've been inserting them into positions of power for the last sixty years. Once one is established, others join him in their ranks. In this way, I have amassed senior officers in all the significant forces in the world. They'll never turn on me and will always do as I bid; my haloes ensure their cooperation."

"So why do you need yet more power and control?" Kat enquired thoughtfully. It sounded as though Midgard was a done deal, so she couldn't understand his need.

"Because it's there," Odin replied emphatically. "Why do people climb mountains or travel to the moon? It's because there are always other challenges, and believe me; there are so many, many worlds that I wish to conquer. Midgard will be my base, and with its people transformed into an army of perfect warriors, I'll be invincible. My dear Valkyries; you too can join me in this quest. You can share in the riches and glory of war."

"I don't think so," Jess shook her head defiantly as the others nodded their agreement. "We fight to protect innocents and for a cause that is just. I couldn't fight by your side merely to subjugate here or any other world, for that matter."

"Well, that's a shame," Odin retorted ruefully. "But I still beg you to consider my offer." Taking a mouthful of crème brûlée, he decided to give his warriors a little more time to consider his deal.

"What exactly did you mean by reduction and redistribution?" Kat enquired. She was returning to a phrase that Odin had suspiciously skimmed rather hurriedly over during his explanation. Somehow, she felt the words were important.

"Oh, nothing really; the world is a little overcrowded and would be so much better if there was a slightly smaller, healthier population. This is something Thirle has some expertise in," Odin nodded as he tried to dodge this awkward question.

"So how many people might you be reducing?" Kat continued, pressing him for an answer. She could tell he was being evasive by the tone of his voice.

"Oh, just a few, not too many, really," Odin lied as he refused to be drawn. It was time to change the subject. "Well, my dearest Valkyries," he began as he got up from his chair. "Now that we've all finished dessert; do I have an answer to my offer? Do we have a deal?"

The three warriors looked at each other.

"No!" Came a unanimous and unrehearsed reply. Chancing death was preferable to fighting for a god they couldn't trust and a cause they didn't believe in.

"Is that your final answer?" Odin asked reluctantly. He had hoped for better from them.

The girls shook their heads. There would be no going back.

"Oh dear, well, that really is most unfortunate," Odin sighed as he wiped his mouth with his napkin. Motioning with his arms, he gestured for his warriors to stand up. "Vili, Ve; would you be so kind as to escort these two with Lia to the well? I will follow with Sangrid once she has given me the details of her spell."

"May I please say goodbye to Marcus?" Jess pleaded, and Odin nodded that she could.

Leaning closer to her lover, her nose rubbed his somewhat awkwardly before their lips locked in a tender and passionate kiss. "I will come back for you, I promise," Jess whispered as they finished their embrace. With arms tied behind their backs, their farewell looked rather comical.

"Yeh, and I'll be back too," Hel retorted loudly, having overheard their conversation. "You can tell Balder that I'll be coming back to rescue him."

"Hmmm," Odin paused as he waved for a servant to bring him a can of air freshener. As soon as the man returned, he sprayed some of its contents under the girls' noses, just in case.

"What's that?" Kat enquired. She was mystified by his bizarre action, and she knew Odin well enough not to take anything for granted. He always had a reason, no matter how obscure.

"Let's just say that it's an insurance policy," Odin replied mysteriously. "In case you really do all return from the dead." Waving his arms in front of him, Odin shooed the girls towards the mansion and the lift that would take them deep beneath the heart of the Isle.

Here in its bowels lay his well; the twin of Mimir's.

"What's she doing here?" Kat enquired angrily when Odin and Hel eventually joined the small party underground. The focus of Kat's enquiry was Lia; who was beginning to wonder the same thing.

"She's going with you," Odin announced smugly as he pushed the girl toward her.

"Why?" Kat enquired gruffly. "She's done your bidding, and you promised her a reward. She may be a snake in the grass, but a deal's a deal; you know that."

"Then you honour it," Odin replied nonchalantly. "She used to serve Frigg and is a turncoat. I don't have any room for traitors in my army."

"She betrayed us, not you," Jess sneered as she tried to nudge the bewildered girl back toward Odin, his brothers, and their two heavily armed guards. Her arms were still bound, and they ached terribly.

"Well, if you don't want her, then she'll just have die," Odin retorted as he indicated to one of his men to draw a pistol from his belt.

"Wait!" Kat cried in alarm. "You can't just shoot her, that isn't fair. We'd take her back with us, but we can't; she isn't a hero."

"You know, Sangrid, you're right," Odin replied reflectively as he stepped forward and took a knife from his belt. Drawing it swiftly across her throat, Lia collapsed gurgling and dying to the floor. "Perhaps that will make your decision a little easier," he scoffed. "Now you can save her, if you want to."

"You bastard!" Kat yelled, straining at her bonds.

"Temper, temper," Odin jeered as he pushed Lia's twitching body to one side. Walking past her to the well, he crouched down beside it and began tinkering with its control panel. After a few minutes, he looked up.

There was a wicked grin on his face.

"Right, my dear Valkyries, it's time to say goodbye; but I will give you one last chance to reconsider my offer." He paused, eyeing each girl carefully.

"Get lost, you arrogant pig," Hel cursed, spitting crudely on the floor.

The others remained silent.

With a resigned shrug, Odin pressed a finger against the panel. An ominous, red light began to flash slowly, forming a thin, coloured ring that ran all the way around the well.

"What have you done?" Jess asked anxiously.

"I'm blowing the well," Odin replied matter of factly.

"What?" Kat exclaimed in astonishment.

"You heard what I said," Odin retorted emphatically. "I'm blowing the well. That should focus your minds."

Staring hard at the girls, Odin motioned to the guards to place their Valkyrie artefacts and his presents on the floor.

"You can live if you want," he offered. "There is still time for you to return to Asgard with my proposal and bring your sisters back to Midgard. If you don't, then the well will open fully and implode. This will send a shock wave back to Asgard, which will destroy everything in its universe." Pausing deliberately, Odin decided to reinforce his ultimate gamble with a stark and chilling warning.

"Either you return to Migard and live, or you stay in Asgard and die."

Turning to his brothers and the two guards, he indicated that it was time to go.

"How long have we got?" Hel shouted after them as the men began to leave the room.

Odin turned and smiled. "Oh, a few minutes or so," he replied cheerily, before closing the heavy door behind him with a loud and resounding, metallic clang.

His offer was one he knew his Valkyries couldn't refuse.

52

Poof!

"For goodness sake, do hurry up, Hel!"

"Shut up, Kat. Keep still; can't you see I'm trying?"

Standing back to back, the two warriors were wriggling up and down in a desperate attempt to cut their wrists free. Between them, they had managed to retrieve one of their Valkyrie knives from the floor, and Hel was now busy trying to saw through the nylon strap around Kat's wrists.

She was doing a good job, but there was so little time. The red light on the well was already flashing faster. Time was running out.

"Uh—there you go!" Hel cried when the strap finally gave way.

"Ouch!" Kat cried as the knife dug into her wrist. She was free at last. Licking the blood oozing from her cut, Kat quickly severed Hel and Jess's restraints.

"We must get back," Jess breathed anxiously in a state of panic.

"We could always stay here," Hel suggested, deciding to play devil's advocate.

"What? And let Asgard explode?" Kat looked incredulous.

"I'm only joking," Hel chuckled as she gathered up her things and helped Jess with the cask. "What are we going to do about her?" she enquired, pointing to Lia's body.

"We have to save her," Kat insisted resolutely, kneeling down beside the girl.

"Stop, please," Jess pleaded; Kat already had her knife in her hand. "She's not a hero; you don't know what you're doing."

"I can't leave her, and I won't leave her; she doesn't deserve to die."

"I know, Kat, but there are rules," Jess continued. "Important rules. Only villains and heroes."

"Whose rules, Jess?" Kat turned and stared hard at her friend. "They're Odin's, not ours. Look, she deserves a second chance, just like I did. Even if she isn't a hero, I can still make her a maid; my maid, can't I?"

Neither Jess nor Hel replied. Kat had a point. There was a desperate need for more warriors.

"You could be bringing her back to certain death," Hel cautioned ironically.

"As opposed to what? Leaving her here, dead already?" Kat sneered. "At least this way she'll get a chance." Kat's mind was made up. Taking the dagger in her hand, she plunged it deep into the girl's heart.

Wow!

The sensation was indescribable.

Kat had seen the flash of light before and been warned of the warmth in the blade; but not this. Not the extraordinary feelings she was experiencing now.

It was as though the handle had burst into life; she could feel it quivering; pulsating as the strength and passion of Lia's soul coursed through her arm. In that instant, Kat kissed Lia's soul and felt her living and breathing inside her body. They were one, complete and inseparable. The emotion was eternal and exhilarating; a bliss beyond bliss; a heaven on earth. Kat's life had changed irrevocably as rapture filled her heart.

With a flash of brilliant light, Lia's soul exploded from her knife and fled into the well.

Jess smiled warmly as Kat looked on in disbelief. She could welcome her now into the ultimate privilege of the sisterhood; the joy of life; both the taking and the giving; the ecstasy of rebirth.

"Congratulations, my darling Kat," Jess stroked her face and then hugged her tightly when she stood up. "You're a true Valkyrie now."

"Come on, you two," Hel muttered, forcing the girls to snap out of their embrace. "In case you haven't noticed, we have a well that's about to explode and a world that needs saving." She slapped Kat playfully on her bottom. "Playing mummy to your new maid will just have to wait."

Gathering up the gifts and their belongings; the girls joined hands as they clasped their coins.

In an instant, they too were gone.

"Where's Henry?" Kat yelled at the top of voice as she emerged breathlessly into the castle hall. Hel was close behind her, and she had already picked up a hammer. Holding it firmly, she began beating frantically at the gong. Jess too had sounded the alarm; blowing a horn as hard as she could.

The castle erupted into a state of panic.

"What's up?" Henry shouted nervously as he bounded down the stairs, two at a time.

"Hi, darling," Hel squeezed him tightly as he flew into her arms. "A spot of bother, I'm afraid." She cried, dragging him by the arm down the stairs and into the Chamber of the Valkyries.

"Get Frigg!" Kat yelled to the warriors who were dashing into the hall. "We need her—now!" Turning tail, she too disappeared down the stairs.

The situation was critical.

"What's this?" Henry enquired as he looked at the egg-shaped structure in the middle of the chamber. He'd seen the schematics, but had never seen the well up close and personal before.

"It's Mimir's well, darling," Hel purred calmly as though Asgard wasn't about to be blown apart. "This is the thing that flies us all over the place."

"And the flashing red light?" Henry had noticed that, too.

"That's the countdown to oblivion," Kat retorted bluntly as she grabbed his arm. "Odin's going to do exactly what we discussed; he's going to open the well in Midgard and let it implode, destroying everything here."

"Oh, is that all? We can easily stop that," Henry began pompously with an annoyingly confident smirk on his lips. "We open our well first, and the blast goes in the opposite direction."

"Henry!" Kat slapped him hard in disbelief. "Wake up! Have you thought about what you're saying? If we do that, we destroy Midgard, Earth—*our* Earth! All our old friends and families blown to smithereens; we can't do that, I won't allow it!"

"Shit! I'm so sorry," Henry blanched as he rubbed at his cheek. "I'd forgotten about that. Oh dear, well, let me see; how long have we got?"

"I don't know, a few minutes at the most, perhaps." Kat gasped in exasperation. "Just look at that flashing light, its blinking like crazy. When it stops, that's it. Poof—and we're all dead, just like you said. You've got to think of something, anything, and you've got to do that fast."

Henry crouched down by the control panel and buried his head in his hands. He wished he hadn't drunk so much ale and mead at the feast that evening. *Shit!* There was a solution, there had to be. Their dreams couldn't end like this.

"Think, brain, think," Henry thumped his fist angrily against the side of his head. "If Odin opens his well first—poof—we explode; and if we open our well first—poof—they explode. They're the only options; it's all black and white. Heads we lose, tails they lose. We're screwed Kat; we're really, really screwed."

Kat's eyes opened wide. Henry had missed something obvious.

"What if we open both wells together, at exactly the same time?"

Henry's jaw dropped. "Brilliant, you're a genius!" Leaping up, he squeezed her tightly, kissing her hard on the lips.

"Hey, steady on," Hel interrupted. "That's my boyfriend you're snogging."

"Sorry Hel," Kat muttered as she pushed Henry away. "He's just overexcited."

"There is, of course, just one teeny, tiny but extremely important detail missing in your idea," Henry frowned, recovering his composure. "The timing and opening must be identical. Both wells have to open at exactly the same time and to exactly the same degree. Can you give me these figures, Kat?"

"Um, er—no."

"Fuck!"

Henry cursed loudly as he slumped irritably back on the floor. It had been a good idea while it lasted. Now, they would definitely all die.

"No profanities, please, Henry; you know the rules," Frigg interrupted, entering the chamber with Ruby, Carmel, and Silk close behind. She waggled a finger angrily at him.

"I'm so sorry your majesty," Henry stood up hastily and bowed deeply. "It's just so frustrating. The well is about to explode, and we could save Asgard if only we had an exact timing."

"Timing for what?" their queen enquired as she crouched down beside the well, pressed her ring into a hidden recess, and then glided her fingers across the touch-sensitive, flickering control panel.

"Timing for when Odin opens the well in Midgard!" he yelled in horror. "We also need to know exactly how much it will open, and we don't have either measurement!"

"We don't need them," Frigg interjected calmly, standing up with a smile. "Come on; the emergency indicator is flashing and I really do think we should evacuate the chamber."

"Yes, but, but—" Henry stammered as she took his arm and began shepherding him away from the well. "We haven't sorted the well out yet. We'll all be killed."

"No, we won't, Henry; everything's under control, so stop worrying."

"What? How?"

"Shush, you silly boy," Frigg scolded teasingly. "I'll explain everything as soon as we're out of the room." Forcing Henry firmly through the doors, and after waiting for the warriors to leave the chamber, Frigg closed them shut behind her.

"I'm so sorry, your majesty, but I really don't understand why you're being so calm. We're all going to die," Henry blathered, panic-stricken as they arrived in the hall where the other warriors had congregated.

"When did you say Odin's well was about to explode?" Frigg enquired sweetly, ignoring Henry's angst as she looked toward Jess and Kat.

"Any time about now, your majesty," Jess replied with a nervous gulp.

"Then may I suggest we all cover our ears?"

53

Moonbow

"**O**uch!" Hel cried, pinching herself hard.

"Ouch!" Henry cried, as she slapped him hard as well; just to make sure.

"Hey, everybody, we're alive!" Hel exclaimed, stating what was blindingly obvious. "Henry's done it, he's saved Asgard!"

Blushing violently, her lover looked around him in amazement. He hadn't done anything. The castle had shaken, the ground had rumbled, and a dull, muffled explosion had emanated from the chamber below; but other than that, precious little had happened. By rights; they should all be dead—but they weren't.

It was a miracle.

Frigg walked over and gave him a warm hug.

"Your majesty, thank you," Henry began sheepishly as he shook his head. "You've saved Asgard, not I."

"Au contraire, my dearest Henry; I only did as I was told."

"I...I don't understand?" Henry mumbled in bewilderment as the warriors around them started to shout and cheer. Although most of them still weren't too sure as to what exactly had gone on, they were going to celebrate anyway. Something big had just happened—or hadn't happened—and the castle was still standing; which was good enough for the girls. Hooting with joy, the Valkyries formed a scrum around Henry as they celebrated the hero of the day.

"What happened?" Henry bleated, submerging beneath a welter of hugs and kisses.

"You wanted the wells synchronised, and that's what I did!" Frigg shouted before picking up Jess's horn and blowing a loud blast. Feeling sorry for Henry, she stepped forward and cleared a small area around the beleaguered boy.

"Look Henry," she began as she added her small kiss to the copious smudges of lipstick adorning his cheeks. "You may be the smartest kid on the block, but I've been well hopping since before your great, great ancestors were born. I may not know exactly why they work; but I certainly know how to operate them."

"What did you do?" Henry shouted as he struggled to be heard above the hubbub of excitement gathering pace around them. All the warriors who had been on missions had returned to the castle; and there was plenty of gossip for the girls to catch up on. Chattering noisily without actually listening, everybody was fighting to be heard.

"Let's go over there," Frigg yelled as she motioned to Henry to move to a slightly quieter spot. "I can't hear myself think."

"Please, you must tell me what you did," Henry asked once more.

"Well, I changed Mimir's well from 'master' to 'slave'; that's all. A simple change in its command function, and the well just mirrors what another connected well does; it was child's play, really. All the wells are the same; they have very simple controls. They were designed to be used by some fairly stupid gods," Frigg added poignantly, nodding in the direction of Thor. He was now joining in the celebrations.

"So what happened to all its energy?" Kat enquired as she wandered over. Arm in arm with Jess, they had caught the tail end of the conversation. Thinking back, she could vaguely remember Henry's explanation about universes being slices of bread, all stacked one on top of each other. If both wells had exploded inwards and met in the middle; where had the explosion actually gone?

Asgard had been saved, but had Midgard been saved, too?

Frigg shrugged and shook her head. "I don't know where all that energy stuff went, and to be honest, I don't really care. We're alive, and that's all that matters. Perhaps Henry here might be able to enlighten us?"

Henry nodded excitedly; he was smiling once more and beginning to look very excited. The magnitude of what they'd just done had just hit him. "Guess what Kat?" he gasped with obvious glee. "We've become gods! We've created another universe; how cool is that?"

"I don't understand," Kat replied, somewhat mystified. He was talking in riddles again.

"Look; do you remember those slices of bread we talked about?"

Kat nodded that she did.

"Well; if Asgard is one slice of bread and Midgard is a slice of bread next to it; then where they touch, a new slice of bread gets formed. The explosion occurred where they touched, and because the energy had no where to go, it created its own place; a new slice of bread. We've created a new universe; one complete with stars and planets and people and a history all of its own. Just think about it; we really are gods!"

"Henry, if I hear you say that word again I'll wallop you." Hel had wandered over, and she slapped his arm playfully. "You may be the hero of the hour, but there's only room for one god in our relationship, and you're looking at her."

After planting a big kiss on his lips, she turned to Kat. "Hey, Kat, haven't you forgotten something, don't you have an announcement to make?"

Kat paused.

"Sweet Odin!" she exclaimed loudly, before immediately regretting using the ex-god of gods' cursed name. "You're right; hey everybody, shush! Listen up; I have something important to say."

DONG!

Thor hit the gong with his hammer. The racket of all the warriors chattering at once was giving him a headache. "That's better," he bellowed as silence followed the reverberations of his blow. "I believe the lady Sangrid would like to tell you all something."

Kat stepped forward excitedly. "Not only has Asgard been saved, but we have a new maid!"

The hall erupted into chaos once more as Jess bustled Kat toward the door. "You must go and get her now, quickly; before she freezes to death."

Looking around her, Kat caught sight of Hod. "Hey, Hod! Can you come and help me please."

"Hi, Kat," Hod waved cheerily as he started to make his way across the hall. Ruby intercepted him, blocking his way aggressively with her body.

SLAP!

"Ouch!"

"Remember your manners, you ignorant oaf," she scolded. "She's my lady to you, and don't you ever forget it; you're her servant now, not her best friend, remember?" Ruby had struck him hard as a warning.

Kat winced. *The poor boy.*

Obviously, hatred toward the gods hadn't lessened while she was away.

"I'm sorry, my lady, please forgive me," Hod mumbled, blushing angrily as he bowed low to both Ruby and then Kat. He was seething and wanted to scream; but he didn't dare. The warriors were too strong; and both Frigg and Thor were preoccupied. For now, he must hold his tongue and be humble.

"Don't worry," Kat whispered excitedly to Hod when Ruby's back was turned. "Please, can you get some blankets and mead—lots of mead—and put as many logs on the fire as you can find? I've got a maid!" she squealed delightedly.

"Come on, Kat," Jess laughed, dragging her out through the door. "I'll make sure Hod sorts those things out. Just you go on and get her; go and get your new baby."

Jumping for joy, Kat charged across the courtyard and leapt onto Sleipnir. Horns were already blowing in the castle and the town below. Grabbing two cloaks from Jameela, Kat cantered through the gates before breaking into a gallop. Charging down the hill, she tore past the ruins of Gladsheim and over the river Iving.

Hurdling a small gate, she urged Sleipnir up a small rise. *Where was her new maid?*

Craning her neck forward, Kat soon spotted where she lay. A bright moonbow had alighted at the corner of the field beside a small copse. It was cold, bitterly cold; and a full moon was shining amidst a star studded sky. A carpet of snow glistened all around. Ploughing on swiftly through the snowdrifts, Kat leapt from Sleipnir's back the moment she arrived by Lia's side.

Naked, shivering, and alone; the girl lay slumped and half buried in the snow—unconscious and bleeding. She looked so young, so peaceful, and so delicate; an innocent child born into chaos; a world bristling with war and seething in hate.

What would she think when she finally awoke?

Kneeling in the freezing powdery carpet, Kat threw a warm cloak around Lia's body and cradled her head in her lap. Tearing the cork from her flask, she trickled sweet mead fearfully into the girl's lips. *Wake up.* She begged.

Spluttering and coughing, Lia choked—and then swallowed.

Crying for joy, Kat held her close and cuddled her hard. She hummed a soft lullaby, one of Jameela's, as she watched a ribbon of torches wind slowly up the hill toward them.

I have a maid!

Kat threw her head back and shouted with joy. Tears rolled down her cheeks as she fought back her emotions. The wheel had turned full circle.

Now Kat knew how Jess had felt when she'd held her in her arms.

The passion and excitement, the thrill and the fear, the pleasure and the pain; all thrown into one; this was the true heart of a Valkyrie—the love that poured between a warrior and her maid. Nothing else mattered; not Asgard, not Odin, nor the bitter winter's chill. This was it; the moment of bliss that made the horror of war so completely worthwhile.

She had never felt happier.

Barking orders anxiously when they arrived, Kat fretted and fussed as the stretcher bearers gently lifted Lia into their cradle. Clucking like some mother goose, she walked beside Lia; coaxing mead through her lips as she plumped pillows and rearranged the blankets.

By the time they reached the town, people had started to line the square.

In spite of the cold, the arrival of a new maid was always a thrilling occasion. Beaming with pride, Kat waved and nodded as she acknowledged their cheers. Urged on by her mother, a small girl stepped forward and placed a dried flower on Lia's chest. Kat thanked her warmly and kissed her forehead.

Bursting with joy, she wanted to scream out loud.

I have a maid! I have a maid! I have a maid!

"Are you all right, darling?" Hel enquired sleepily as she joined Henry in the now silent great hall.

It was long after midnight, and the dying embers of the fire flickered yellow and gold, glowing ever more dimly as they slowly crumbled into the ash. The hearth had grown cold, just like the winter around them. All the candles that had burned so brightly earlier in the evening had long since been extinguished. The joyous celebration following Lia's arrival had ended many hours ago, with the exhausted warriors now all tucked up safe and warm in their beds.

The castle was at peace as Asgard slumbered through the night.

Henry didn't reply to Hel's question—he couldn't. Standing by the window, he stared blankly at Odin's gift.

"Is something wrong?" Hel whispered as she wrapped her arms around him and pulled him tenderly close to her chest. His body felt cold; he must have been standing there motionless for hours.

Henry sighed as tears welled in his eyes. It just wasn't fair.

How could he tell her?

How could he break her heart?

His love had dreamt of this moment for so long and now, in the very moment of her triumph, her dream would be destroyed. It just wasn't fair for the woman he adored.

Alone in the moonlight, Henry stood by the window and wept.

"We're going to be all right, aren't we?" Hel cooed encouragingly, nibbling softly at one of his earlobes with her lips. She smelt so good, so fragrant, and so warm, with her lithe body pressed tightly next to his.

Putting the box down, Henry wriggled round, and after wrapping his arms around her waist, he kissed her lightly on the lips. "Mmmmm, I don't know," he lied, holding her close.

Absentmindedly, he toyed with Odin's disk in his hands

Kat had been wrong when she had held it in hers. The disk did have the answers printed upon it, and their message was loud and clear.

Now coloured blood red with a spattering of black; Asgard was dying—and Henry knew why.

54

Mark 2.0

"Do you think we should have given them more time?" Ve suggested hopefully.

"No, I don't think that would have made any difference, I'm afraid."

"Oh, that's a pity," murmured Vili.

Odin and his brothers had felt the implosion of the well from the safety of the poolside. A gentle, shaking tremor that had vibrated glasses and cutlery as it rippled away from the mansion. The size of the aftershock had been much smaller than Odin expected; but he still chose to wait for half an hour before venturing back down to the well.

Better to be safe than sorry.

Standing there now, the three of them gazed mournfully at its smoking carcase, watching as a plume of black smoke drifting lazily from the blackened hole at its apex. Soot and deep cracks poke marked the concrete walls of the small, whitewashed room in which it had stood.

The well was dead; gutted and shattered beyond all hope of repair. Its powerful core had collapsed in the instant of the explosion; crushing and folding space time into a new and unchartered existence. The well was dead, but its heart lived on; pulsating now to a different beat. Its awesome power being reborn into an unknown—and unknowing—cosmos.

"Do you think they survived?" Ve asked, breaking the depressing silence.

"They could have," Vili suggested, optimistically.

Odin turned and stared hard at his brothers. "I hope not," he sighed. "For their sakes, I really hope not. Instant death would be way preferable to the slow torment they will suffer if they have."

The three fell silent once more, drinking in the desolate vision before them. Lia's corpse lay on the cold, concrete floor surrounded by a pool of congealed blood. Her body was silent and still. Crouching down beside the girl, Odin examined her chest.

"I see they took her with them," he mused, nodding to his brothers.

"That's nice," Vili blurted, without really thinking.

"Not really," Odin replied. "Dying twice won't be very pleasant for the child." He stood up stiffly and stretched.

"They could still come, couldn't they?" Ve asked whimsically.

"Don't be so silly," Vili scoffed, slapping his brother on the back of his head. "Even if they have survived, they don't have a well. Mimir's was destroyed along with ours."

"Oh," Ve hung his head mournfully once more as the bitter truth finally sank in. No smiling Valkyries would be popping out from behind their charred well, and no cheering warriors would be waiting poolside when they returned to the surface.

The Valkyries had gone.

Odin's proud warrior elite was no more.

"Come on, boys," Odin sighed desolately as he wrapped his arms around his brothers. "They were too proud and too obstinate to accept my deal. In truth, I should have known that that would happen. They were Valkyries, my Valkyries; the very best of the best. Of course they'd choose to stay and die."

"You did offer them a good deal, didn't you, Odin?" Ve continued as the three of them left the room.

Odin closed the door behind them. "Yes, my dear brothers; it was a good deal, a very, very good deal, but some things just aren't meant to be."

With a chillingly loud 'clunk' that echoed emptily down the corridor; Odin turned the lock. The gateway to their past had been sealed.

Asgard was gone.

"Come on, how about you two trying to cheer me up then, hey?" Odin exclaimed cheerily but unconvincingly as he slapped both Vili and Ve heartily on their backs. "How's my new toy coming along?" It was going to be tough, but he was determined to put on a brave face and bounce back quickly from this bitter blow. The Valkyries were gone—and he'd just have to get used to that fact.

"Oh, absolutely fabulous," Ve retorted gleefully; beautiful, blond women being temporarily replaced by his other obsession in life: science. "Would you like to see it?" he continued excitedly. "You're going to be ever so impressed."

Grabbing Odin by the arm, the two brothers dragged him along the corridor to another steel-shuttered door; one that smelt of fresh paint. Fumbling with some keys, it was only at the third attempt that Vili finally managed to turn the lock.

"What do you think?" Ve enquired breathlessly after they had bundled Odin into the room. "Isn't it beautiful?"

Odin stood still; stroking his beard thoughtfully. Little by little, a smile began to form on his lips. Its steely grey colour was certainly most beautiful, and its shape was sleek and shiny and new. Oh yes; it really was beautiful and maybe, just this once, he would have to admit to being proud of his brilliant but bungling brothers.

"Does it work?" he asked distrustfully, narrowing his eyes as he stared suspiciously at the boys. It might look the biz, but that wasn't the point. It would have to work—and work damned hard as well.

"Yes, of course it does," Vili grinned as he bent down and ran his fingers over an invisible panel.

Shuddering and vibrating, Odin's new gadget flickered and hummed as it stuttered slowly into life. Grabbing hold of the surrounding metal columns, the three of them struggled momentarily as a shock wave of gravity tore at their bodies; inviting them to come and play inside its fearsome new heart.

"Wow!" Odin gasped as the object began to stabilise. "Have you made it more powerful?"

"Oh yes, ever so much," Ve replied with a cheeky grin. Their brother was going to be able to do so much more with his impressive new toy.

Mimir's well—mark two—was good to go.

55

Love Hurts

*I*t hadn't been a good night for Kat and, as dawn broke, she awoke feeling irritable and in a bit of a strop.

She had lain beside Lia, who was fractious; tossing and turning uncomfortably throughout the night. Waking hourly, her new maid had coughed and choked and vomited up blood as the deep gash in her neck continued to ooze. Half delirious, Lia had called out in terror as vivid nightmares stalked her dreams; chilling images of damnation swirling inside her mind like a tornado; gouging great holes in her soul.

Lia's torment had become Kat's agony as she kept a constant vigil. Feeding the girl sips of mead, she soothed her brow and held her close. The job of coaxing her maid back to life was both terrifying and filled with fear.

So many ifs, buts, and maybes.

Kat felt like a proud mother but one riddled with doubt; so to calm her nerves, she sought Jess's advice as the rest of the castle slumbered. Mercifully, her best friend made for a patient and reassuring soul mate. Everything Lia was experiencing was absolutely normal and, no; no she wasn't going to drown in the blood that was pooling inside her lungs.

Jess's support had been invaluable, unlike Hod's. He had been as useless as he was selfish. Snoring soundly at the foot of the bed, he had stirred only briefly and muttered when Kat had tried to arouse him. She had done this on more than one occasion but to no avail. He was asleep, and damned if he would be getting up.

Kat's new maid was her responsibility—not his.

Climbing grumpily out of bed, Kat strode around the bed to stand naked at its foot, gazing down at her friend. She prodded his body with a foot. He didn't stir.

Typical!

He was supposed to be her servant, not a houseguest. Things were definitely going to have to change. She had Lia to look after and worry about now, not him.

She had a maid!

That very thought made her want to jump for joy. Lia filled her heart with such desire that there simply wasn't any room left for Hod anymore.

For a moment, Kat became lost in her thoughts; tingling at the memories of the shocks and the surprises she'd had during her first few weeks in Asgard. There had been horrors and fears and moments of great pain; but it had also been a joyous resurrection and a journey she now desperately wanted for her maid. With Jess beside her to guide her through the complexities of motherhood, her life was complete. Until her hero needed saving, Kat's soul would be at peace. Lia felt like a daughter, and that thought alone brought endless waves of contentment.

Kat stared long and hard at Hod.

Was he her hero or destined to be the love of her life?

She didn't know, and she couldn't tell; their chequered past had been far too tortuous. Yes, she cared for him deeply, even loving him more than she should; but his fall from godly grace had been a long and dangerous fall; and one that now made him a liability. To stay with her in her new life would require big changes and sacrifices. He was supposed to be her servant, not that he'd noticed, and he would have to wise up. Their past was their past, and a new dawn beckoned.

Kat nudged him harder, but he still didn't budge. It was time to get nasty.

Looking around her, she spotted the chamber pot close to the bed. Grinning impishly, she lifted it up and gave it a gentle swirl.

Ohhh—it was so tempting!

Crouching down beside him, she tipped its contents slowly over his head.

"AAARGH! What was that?"

Coughing and spluttering loudly, Hod awoke with a start. Sitting up, he bumped his head against the pot. He rubbed his eyes, then focused them first on Kat's face—and then on the pot she was holding in her hands.

"Ugh! Oooh, how could you?"

He felt disgusted as the unpleasant reality behind his awakening slowly dawned—and dribbled—offensively down his face.

Kat must be cross, very cross.

Standing up once more, Kat forced him roughly back down on the bed with her foot. She wasn't going to mess around. This was it. It really was time for change. "Did you sleep well?" she enquired sarcastically.

Hod nodded as he muttered an obscenity under his breath. He was livid and desperately needed to get cleaned up.

"I'm so glad," Kat mocked, digging her foot aggressively into his chest. She wasn't going to let him up until she was ready. "It's time we came to an understanding, wouldn't you agree?"

Hod nodded once more. Kat's foot was pressing down hard, and the tone of her voice sounded both harsh and intimidating. Her eyes looked angry—and scary.

"Look Hod, our relationship has got to change."

"Why?"

"Because our lives have changed, that's why," she seethed. "I've got a new maid, and you're no longer a god. We both have new roles. I can't keep worrying about saving your arse and dodging your kisses any more. I still care for you, and you're still my friend; but Lia has to be my priority. If you want to stay, you're going to have to knuckle down, and you've got to be helpful. I can't carry you anymore." Kat stared hard at his face, watching him flinch at her words.

Hod gulped, nervously. "So, what exactly are you suggesting?"

"That you do as you should; that you serve and respect me as my servant. That way I can look after you and keep you out of harm."

"And if I say no?"

"Then you're on your own." Kat pressed down harder until the pressure of her foot made him yelp. "You're no longer a god, and your ring has no power. The well is destroyed, do you understand? It died when your father blew it up. The past is over, Hod, things have changed. The gods are gone and they're never coming back. Without my protection, you'd be killed within days. You know what my sisters are like; you're Odin's son, and they're thirsting for your blood."

"It's all your fault," Hod huffed defensively. "I would never have stayed if it wasn't for you."

"I beg your pardon?" Releasing the pressure from her foot, Kat gave him a small kick. "I never asked you to stay, and I never begged you to love me. You chose this life, and now you've got to deal with it; so don't you dare try to make me feel guilty. That just doesn't wash, okay?" Moving backward, Kat planted her hands firmly on her hips. "Do we have a deal?"

"Yes." Hod replied slowly after a lengthy pause.

"Yes, what?"

"Yes, my lady."

"That's better," Kat retorted haughtily as she stifled a giggle. It felt good to finally get some respect. "Now get cleaned up quickly and start being helpful, because that's what I need from you now." Walking over to the window, she parted the curtains just a little. "Oh, and there's one more thing," she added frostily.

"And what's that?" Hod muttered belligerently before thinking the better of it. "Begging your pardon; what's that—my lady?"

"Thank you," Kat smiled, acknowledging his hasty correction. "You must look after Lia and help her, too. You must show her the same respect as you show me, do you understand? I don't want you grumbling or deliberately upsetting her with your sulks and tricks. She's the most important person in my life right now, and that means she has to be the most important person in yours as well."

Hod nodded without replying. His head was hurting, and an icy chill rippled through his body. His hopes of winning Kat's love seemed to have vanished forever.

Lia had stolen his dream.

"Well come on, then; what are you waiting for," Kat scolded, indicating for him to get up off the floor. "Go and get me my cloak, stoke the fire, and then clean yourself up."

It was time to put Hod to work.

The mood of the warriors gathering in the hall should have been jubilant—but it wasn't. The atmosphere was tense and desperately edgy.

Rumours were circulating about dark news that was yet to come.

Henry had been seen consulted with Frigg earlier in the morning, and this meeting had been both solemn and lengthy. Locked in her room, they had spoken so secretly that even Hel didn't know what words had been said. When Frigg eventually emerged, her face was sallow and mired with grief.

Something bad was about to happen, the Valkyries could feel it in their bones.

Filing silently into the hall, the warriors stood nervously as they waited for their Queen. Every Valkyrie and maid had been invited— save for Lia and Hod. Ben and Elijah were there too, squeezing the hands of their partners discretely. Nobody felt comfortable and nobody spoke. The euphoria of the night before had disappeared like the sun.

Leaden clouds now filled the sky, and a bitter wind had blown down from the mountains of Jotunheim. Both were omens that suggested the meeting today was going to be tough.

Thor got the meeting started by recounting the events of his trip with Carmel. Ruby and Silk confirmed the fact that Loki was alive and shocked the gathering with their news that Gungnir was now in his hands. Not that this mattered. With Mimir's well destroyed, both Odin's spear and Thor's hammer were powerless.

Jess, Kat, and Hel quickly retold their tale of their journey to Midgard. The gods were there and, much to Silk's relief, they believed that Balder was being held against his will. The heroes were part of a master plan; one that would enslave and decimate the population of that world.

This was bad news, but not totally unexpected.

Everybody knew that their former lord was both a perfectionist and a dictator; democracy not being a word that had any place in his vocabulary. Unless something could be done, the former world of the Valkyries would perish under his rule.

Stepping forward, Ben and Jameela confirmed their former lord's hold over his heroes; the vial of silvery goop and the 'haloes' being the source of this control. These would have to be broken if Odin's power was to be curtailed.

"What about the Mead?" Jess enquired with good reason.

The Mead from Valhalla was the source of the Valkyries power. Now that the link to that realm had been broken, she was fearful for their suffering. The cravings she had once endured had gnawed at her soul, reducing her quickly to a quivering wreck. Without Mimir's well, there was no access to Valhalla, and without this, there could be no mead.

Thor glanced knowingly at Frigg before reassuring the warrior. "My dear Brynhildr, both Frigg and I can provide you with mead."

"How?" Silk enquired.

"We know the recipe," he continued with some embarrassment.

"May we ask what that is?" Ruby was intrigued. She'd been drinking it daily for nearly two hundred years. Perhaps now was the time for its secret to finally be revealed.

Coughing nervously, Thor tugged at his beard. He didn't want to give an answer, and he looked pleadingly to Frigg.

"My dear Valkyries," Frigg began with a sadness in her eyes. "Now is neither the time nor the place to go into such details. The mead will continue for as long as we live. Of course, without the well, there can be no apples and without these Thor, Hod, and I will all die."

"Aaah," Carmel stepped forward with her hands behind her back. Of all the people in the hall she was the most cheerful and had the best news. "While you were all running around last night in a panic, I used my head, not my heart." Carmel winked cheekily at Thor. "Just look what I got for you."

Grinning broadly, she pulled a basket laden with golden apples from behind her back. "And I've got another full basket upstairs," She added with a twinkle. "That should keep you going until we find our way out of this mess."

"Hmmm." Frigg hung her head. When she looked up, her eyes were even sadder than they had been before. This was the moment of truth. "My dearest Astrid, thank you so much for your kindness. Unfortunately, events may unfold that will make our apples as unnecessary as your mead. Henry, would you please kindly step forward and tell everybody what you told me this morning. Don't be afraid. You're only the messenger of bad news. Odin's curse is to blame, not you."

Shuffling forward awkwardly, Henry stood alone in the middle of the hall. Gone was the cocky swagger of the rogue who'd said "bollocks" to Thor just a few days before. Now he looked gaunt and strained; and his eyes were red and tear stained. In his hands, he held a box.

Bowing stiffly, he coughed nervously before clearing his throat. This was going to hurt. "I would like to start," he began cautiously.

"By thanking you all for making Hel and I so welcome in your home."

Henry paused to allow a ripple of approval and clapping to echo around the hall. It was a good beginning to his speech, although everyone knew that he was only trying to delay the bad news.

Once the murmurs of appreciation had died down, Henry opened the box and took Odin's plastic disk from it. "Catch," he cried as he tossed it to Kat. "What colour was this when Odin gave it to you?"

"It was green," Kat replied quizzically, staring hard at the object.

"And what colour is it now?" he enquired.

"It's dark red, obviously," she scoffed a little too hastily, "and now covered…with tiny black dots," she continued much more slowly and curiously as the other girls crowded around her. Henry paused again to allow them all to have a good look before he took Odin's other gift from the box.

"Some of you may recognise this device from Midgard. Kat, do you know what it is?"

Kat screwed her eyes up and shook her head. The object he was holding in his hands was bright yellow and about twice the size of a mobile phone. *Damn it!* It looked so familiar; she knew she would kick herself when she found out what it was.

"Anybody?" Henry continued; looking around him as the room remained silent.

"Okay, Kat," he continued, forgetting as he usually did to use her formal, Valkyrie name. "Would you kindly come over here and help me with a small demonstration, please."

Kat stepped forward and Henry switched the device on. It began to flash and make a loud clicking noise; one that sounded a bit like hailstones pattering against a window, but more metallic and sharply defined.

Slowly, Henry waved the device over Kat, then the floor, the walls, Thor, the table, and even a loaf of bread. Everywhere he waved the device; the flashing and clicking remained the same.

Growing impatient with this display, Silk decided to taunt him. "So come on then, brain box; we've all heard your noisy new toy, but what does it mean?"

Henry chuckled. Trust Silk to be bitchy to the end. She soooo didn't want to know the answer.

"That, my dear ladies," he began soberly. "Is the sound of death: our death; everybody's death to be precise. This toy, for your information, Silk, is a Geiger counter, and we are all highly radioactive.

That's why the disk has turned red and why Odin and the gods were so anxious to leave."

Henry paused and, after deciding to dramatise this point, he held the disk up high for all to see.

"When this turns black—we will all die."

56

Odin's Curse

A long and eerie silence followed Henry's shocking revelation. It was punctuated by the continuous clicking of the Geiger counter until Frigg prompted him to turn it off.

They had all heard enough of its deathly sound.

Too dazed to think properly, Kat followed Henry's explanation of their predicament in a bit of a blur; although a few key words stood out—most notably that they had days, rather than weeks, before they started to fall sick.

At first, the suddenness of this disaster struck Kat as quite odd. Lambda, the Cosmological Constant was wrong, and their universe was collapsing. However, this still had several billion years to run. How could Odin's blunder make everything radioactive and cause a much more sudden and disastrous ending?

This just didn't make any sense.

The reason, as Henry helpfully explained, was all to do with the lack of energy again.

Asgard's universe had started without enough energy and from too small a big bang. Because of this, it was destined to end much sooner than Midgard's. This was the problem with the Cosmological Constant and was the cause of its large negative number. So far, so good; this had already been explained and was logical and understandable. Unfortunately, however; the troubles with their universe didn't simply end there.

Because there was too little energy, the glue that held everything together was weak. Its stickiness had been failing for aeons, but the process was accelerating at an exponential rate. This had now become critical.

The process of failure was exactly the same as doubling a number.

Each time it doubled—two, four, eight, sixteen, thirty two, sixty four—the jumps between numbers became bigger. This was what was happening now. Matter was failing faster and faster and, just like some gargantuan runaway train; the process had accelerated until it was out of control and now moments from doom.

Matter was decomposing, dying by radioactive decay. Atom by atom, each molecule was disintegrating; falling apart at an ever quickening pace.

This was what the Geiger counter was measuring; clicks from atoms as they ruptured at the seams; each disintegrating in a flash of radioactive decay. The rate at which this was happening had reached melting point; hence the black spots on Odin's disk. So much radiation was being released by the dying atoms that the level had become lethal to life.

It was a depressing thought; and Henry couldn't offer the warriors any hope. Death from radiation sickness wasn't going to be a pleasant affair, although he did, however, have one small shred of comfort. The gods and warriors would live longer than the plants and the animals; the healing powers of the mead and apples giving them some protection.

The full horror of Odin's curse was hard to comprehend. It wasn't just life that was dying; it was everything—absolutely *everything*—was dying.

This reality was hard to understand.

The soil, the water, the air, the rocks, the sun, and their universe; whichever way you looked, all matter was falling apart. In a matter of months, the light would fail from their cosmos as everything dissolved; crumbling into a cold, dark, shapeless, primordial, nothingness. According to Henry, their universe would disintegrate into a 'quark-gluon' soup; although the name didn't sound terribly appetising.

Still, they didn't really need to fret over this, as none of them would be around to see it. All life—including the Valkyries—would have perished long before.

"Isn't there anything we can do to stop it?" Hel entreated her lover as she put her arm around his waist. She could see how distressed he was at telling them this news. "What about the cask Odin sent to you, Frigg? Was there anything inside that that might help?"

Frigg blanched nervously and then lifted her hand.

"It had my ring in it, though fat lot of good that will do us all now." Attempting a weak laugh, she waved her hand vainly over the gems to emphasis the point. "I guess these diamonds will turn into soup as well; won't they Henry?"

He nodded. He could understand their confusion. Everything seemed so normal, so solid, and so true. Radiation was something they couldn't touch, see, taste, smell or feel. Yet it was there; and it was so horrifically real. People and animals were going to start dying—and soon.

"Was there anything else in that cask?" Silk enquired wistfully. Had Odin offered them anything at all; a glimmer of salvation?

"Um," Frigg paused, as she took a deep breath in.

Odin's cask—that miserable skunk. How could he have done such an unspeakable horror?

"Yes, but I can't say what it is," she began apologetically. "It's too terrible and not relevant to what Henry has just said. What we need is more energy and lots of it; am I right?"

"Yes, your majesty," Henry replied dejectedly. "But that's not possible. A universe is a closed system, and the *First Law of Thermodynamics* applies. After the big bang, no more energy can be put in or taken out."

Henry hung his head as Kat's eyes burst into life. He'd done it again—the silly boy! Henry hadn't listened to what he'd been saying and had missed the blindingly obvious.

"Henry, you're such an arse!" she cried gleefully, dancing across the floor and taking his hands in hers. Holding them tightly, she skipped a little jig as she pranced excitedly around him.

They were saved—and he'd just given her the key.

"Sangrid, settle down, have you taken leave of your senses?" Thor bellowed irritably as he looked on in amazement. Grief affected people in different ways, and it looked as though the warrior had gone insane.

"No, absolutely not, my noble Thor," Kat chirped joyfully as she ran over and hugged him enthusiastically. "Henry, you twerp," she continued, turning to flash Henry a mischievous grin. "Our universe isn't a closed system, so we can get more energy in."

"Oh, Kat, don't be so silly," he retorted sharply. "I know what I'm saying, and you can't just go breaking physical laws because you want to. That's just not possible, so do calm down." It wasn't fair to offer her sisters false hope.

"Henry," she warned as she wagged her finger at him in delight. "You're so going to eat humble pie when I tell you what you've missed. You may have a brain as big as a planet, but when it comes to common sense, you're as daft as a brush."

Henry stared blankly at her. *What could he have missed?* Kat sounded so confident; he could already feel himself blushing.

"How did we get here, Henry?" she gloated. "Think about it, you klutz; how did all the Valkyries get here?"

Henry opened his mouth, but no words came out.

"Go on, Henry, admit it, Kat is a genius, Kat is a genius; go on say it, say it, say it!" she crowed elatedly.

Henry continued to stare as a faint croaking sound emanated from the back of his throat. "Oh, dear lord, I believe she's right, I believe Kat's got it." He, too, was now beginning to jump up and down with excitement. "Dear Kat, forgive me, you're so damn clever!" weeping, he hugged her tightly. "We all came here as waves of gravitons," he continued excitedly. "Gravity can pass from universe to universe, and with gravity comes energy. We can get energy in; listen everybody, we can get energy into Asgard!"

A ripple of cautious optimism quickly exploded into howls of jubilation. Warriors were hugging and kissing each other as though they had just returned from the dead. It was a wildly hysterical moment and one to be savoured.

Asgard could be saved—may Yggdrasill be praised.

Laughing and giggling, the triumphant celebrations could have carried on all day if it wasn't for one small, niggling voice that struggled to be heard.

"Ahem."

It was Elijah who brought their celebrations crashing to an end; starting with a tiny cough that everyone ignored.

"Ahem! Excuse me everybody," he coughed once more as he raised his voice just a little.

It was no use, but he had to be heard.

THUMP!

Borrowing Odin's hammer, Elijah brought it crashing down as hard as he could on the floor. The wooden beams shuddered and shook; and the excited hubbub quelled on the spot. He had their attention.

Rising slowly from where he'd been crouching, all eyes focused expectantly on him.

"I'm so sorry to have to ask you this, Henry," he began politely. "But how exactly are we going to get all these gravitons into our universe?"

"With the well, of course, how else?" Henry replied blithely.

"Can you repeat what you just said, please," he enquired once more. "Just to make absolutely sure I heard it right?"

"With the well, you dummy, with the…" Henry's voice trailed off.

"Hmmm—my point exactly," Elijah replied with a sigh.

The well had been destroyed.

Asgard remained doomed.

57

Memories

"**A**hhh, this is the life."

Marcus echoed Anna's feelings as he took a deep breath in, stretched, and then yawned loudly. It was another glorious day in paradise; although thick banks of cloud could now be seen skidding along the horizon from the shores of Crescent Cay. A couple more weeks, and the hurricane season would arrive. They had timed their holiday to perfection.

"Would you like another beer, darling?" Anna enquired enticingly as she got up from her recliner and picked up her empty glass. It was later afternoon, and the sun had thankfully passed its zenith.

It was still very hot—but not quite so unbearably so.

"Tom's having fun again, I see," she added, nodding in the direction of Agent Woods. He was splashing about in the pool with a beach ball and a couple of coquettish hostesses.

"He certainly does all right for himself," Marcus agreed, sighing as he reluctantly sat up to look around for the suntan lotion. His chest and cheeks were beginning to burn.

"How's your arm?" Anna enquired as she sat down beside him and twisted his torso so she could see the bandaging better. "Does it still hurt?"

"No, not much; it's almost better," he reassured. "We were lucky though, getting away with just this gouge and a concussion. It could have been so much worse, any deeper and it would have meant plastic surgery."

"Hmmm," Anna nodded thoughtfully. "I do hope they find the Count's wife. It would be so awful if she were dead. He's been so kind and so generous; it would be so terrible to find out that the woman had died in the accident."

"I know," Marcus shook his head. "Still, it was all her fault. She should never have taken that boat out in the state she was in; legless and as high as kite. Just think, it could have been us lying at the bottom of the ocean instead of her, she only has herself to blame if she's now feeding the fish."

"Oh, shush, darling; don't say such horrible things." Anna slapped his good arm playfully. "Don't speak so flippantly about the dead; it's unlucky."

Anna put down her glass and picked up the bottle of suntan lotion. Pouring a liberal portion into her hands, she began rubbing it into her arms and then finished the excess off on her husband's legs. Marcus was naughty about staying out too long in the sun, and his shoulders were already a delicate shade of lobster. In some ways, it was good that tomorrow would be the last day of their vacation.

Picking up her glass once more, Anna paused for a moment's contemplation. "Do you think you'll ever remember?"

"Remember what?"

"About the accident; what happened and all that stuff?"

"I don't know."

Marcus lay back and adjusted his cushion. He must have hit his head incredibly hard when the Contessa's boat collided with theirs. There were so many blanks, not only about the accident but what happened afterwards and—before. His memory now felt like a string vest: all riddled with holes. Vast chunks of his life lost in a vacuum of blackness.

It was like losing fingers or toes; he would never feel whole until they returned.

Clasping his hands together, Marcus shut his eyes tightly and tried to focus his mind. It was odd, he couldn't even remember what boat they had hired or why. He loved fishing, but Anna hated the sport.

What had they doing so far from their hotel—and the shore?

He guessed it was a lucky break that their vessel had been mowed down by a billionaire. They had really rather landed on their feet. The Count's gratitude for their cooperation, and their silence, had been this; an all expenses paid, access all areas, extension to their holiday for as long as they liked. They were living the lives of gods here on his fabulous island.

Wow! What a life—and it was going to get better. That had been one hell of a compensation cheque he had given them.

To be truthful, Marcus had felt almost guilty putting so much money into their account. The Count had been overwhelming enough with his generosity; and to think that his wife had probably died in the collision, too. His kindness beggared belief.

Still, as he had said; tabloid publicity about the Contessa's state of mind would most probably have cost him a hundred times more.

Marcus rolled over onto his stomach and turned his head to one side. His chest felt nice and toasty, and it was time for his back to get a roasting in the sun. This was his last chance to soak up these rays, more's the pity.

Turning his thoughts back to his missing memories, Marcus felt a terrible pain. The Count's doctor had warned him about this; trying to force his mind to remember could cause blinding headaches. He must try to relax and let things happen naturally. The memories could return in weeks, or months, or possibly years; who could tell? They might never return, but as Dr. Nyran had cheerily quipped; those that didn't probably weren't important anyway.

He was a nice man, the Count's doctor; an Indian gentleman who spoke immaculate English with a polished, upper crust accent. He was very good at his job, too; so thorough and so caring. One thing about the man, however, irked Marcus, and he found it intensely annoying. The doctor looked strangely familiar. They must have met in the past; an encounter now lost in one of his many memory voids.

Damn! It was so frustrating.

He wanted those memories back.

"Here you go darling," Anna smiled sweetly as returned with a beer.

Marcus rolled onto his side and pushed himself up. His head was hurting horribly, but he had to keep trying. Something was stirring in the darkness, something important was screaming to be heard.

"Oh, darling, you're not trying to remember again, are you?" Noting his angst, Anna placed a hand on his cheek and stroked it gently. She could read his face like an open book. "You know what Dr. Nyran said about doing that," she scolded. "You really mustn't; it just isn't worth the pain. We're lucky to be alive, thank God; just focus on that, please, my darling."

Marcus nodded as he took the bottle from her hand. "It's just important to me," he replied irritably. "There's something there, I can feel it; something important. There's someone missing, someone I really cared about." His eyes lit up. "Hey!" he exclaimed roguishly. "What if I had a secret love child or a mistress or something? Wouldn't that be weird?"

Anna chuckled loudly. "Oh, darling, you've got such a vivid imagination. Do you honestly think if you had such a skeleton in your closet I wouldn't have found it by now? Just stop being so daft and relax. Do as Dr. Nyran has told you. Let your memories come back naturally, and for goodness sake stop worrying."

"I know, I know; but it's so frustrating!" Marcus retorted tersely. "I know there's someone out there, someone important who I've forgotten. There was definitely a person, a woman who was special to me. She had a beautiful smile and gorgeous red hair. Damnation! If only I could remember her name, I'm sure the memory would come flooding back."

"I tell you what," Anna joked. "If there really was some floozy or mistress with red hair, then you'd best pray that you don't remember. You'll get such a beating if you do; you cheeky man." Anna slapped him playfully on the cheek before kissing him lovingly on the lips. Of course he didn't have a child, a mistress, or a lover. He should forget such silliness at once.

"Excuse me, Detective Finch."

A servant had crossed the patio and was now standing beside them. "Begging your pardon sir, but the Count was wondering if you might join him for a spot of table tennis?"

Marcus laughed as he looked across the pool. He felt sorry for the Count. His brothers were useless, and he got so frustrated when he played them.

"Go on, darling," Anna smiled. "At least you can give him a good game; he so enjoys it. But remember, don't you dare start winning, or he'll never let you go. He's so competitive."

Marcus stood up and stretched.

"Hey! Don't forget your beer," Anna laughed as she handed it to him. "Cheers, darling, have fun." Raising her glass, Anna clinked this against his bottle.

In the warm afternoon sun, a brilliant ray of sunshine lit up the marks on their wrists.

Two little tattooed 'v's stood out silent, bold, and proud.

Marcus and Anna were part of the club—and one halo was shining brightly.

58

Hail Midgard!

Sometimes, the path to salvation can be a strange one. The journey can start with blind faith, a freak quirk of fate, or just occasionally from the tiniest spark of inspiration.

In Asgard's case, redemption sprang from the third kind.

It was a curious case of nobody seeing the wood for the trees; and it took a whole week for the penny to finally drop.

When it did so, it came from a most unexpected source.

Carmel pulled back the curtains of Thor's room with a tired yawn. It was still too early in the morning; although from the brightness of the sky, she guessed it must be a little after nine. They had both slept well; overcome by the lethargy and tiredness that held so many of the warriors in its grip.

None of the Valkyries had yet suffered from sickness and diarrhoea; but most were experiencing tiredness and hair loss, which were also early signs of radiation sickness.

Unfortunately, the Aesir weren't faring so well. The old and the young had been particularly badly affected, with outbreaks of fatal 'stomach bugs' erupting in all corners of the realm.

Frigg had made the painful decision not to tell her subjects of their impending doom. Death would come soon enough without the need for the panic and fear that would stem from its anticipation. An epidemic of winter chills and bowel infections would soon claim all their lives, allowing them to die naturally and oblivious of Odin's curse.

Lia and Hod, too, had been spared the bad news.

Kat's maid had already cheated fate once; and it seemed a kindness not to burden her with the knowledge of a second impending doom. Indeed, this deliberate concealment had been a tonic for the warriors.

Lia was fitting in perfectly.

Oblivious of the horror ahead and brimming with enthusiasm and wonder for their realm, she was helping the Valkyries to forget their coming dances with death. It was a struggle staying cheery and talking optimistically to her about the future; but holding onto these emotions helped the girls stay sane and uplifted their hearts. The warriors would stay proud and brave to the last.

No one would yield to the despair of their doom.

"Oh dear," Carmel muttered with a melancholy sigh. "There goes another cart laden with death. It's such a shame; I think the victim must have been a small child. Look, I can see her mother there beside the body, grieving."

Thor murmured something from beneath the blankets, but Carmel didn't hear him. She was gazing absently out of the window—and into the blankness of space. She was lost in deep thought

Who would bury her and Thor? She wondered; *when it was their turn to die?*

Who would load the cart and carry them to Niflheim?

She could picture the two of them now; her body lying next to his; sliding over the waterfall on their long, long, voyage to oblivion.

It seemed such a pity.

All their dreams of a glorious afterlife shattered. With no Well and Skidbladnir to carry them to Valhalla, they too would suffer the ignominy of a pauper's burial; slipping over the waterfall's lip with the old and the young; the meek and the mild; the weak and the disabled; all tangled together as they tumbled to their doom.

It seemed such a miserable end for so mighty a god as Thor.

Fully loaded with mourners, the cart creaked and groaned as it clattered slowly across the cobblestones before leaving the courtyard. It would be a long and lonely journey to the Valley of Sighs.

Turning back toward the bed, a tiny spark flickered from somewhere deep inside Carmel's head. Glowing brightly, the ember exploded like a firecracker; flooding her senses with a radiance that made her swoon.

How could they have all been so blind?

"Oh sweet joy!" Carmel whooped wildly as she leapt upon Thor. "I have it, I have the answer. Asgard can be saved!" Without giving him a chance to reply, she pulled on a cloak and tore out of the room.

She just hoped Henry and Hel were up and ready to travel.

Carmel was in luck. Arriving in the feasting hall, she could see Henry busily helping himself to the last of his *Cocopops.* He stared mournfully at the box as he shook the last of his beloved cereal into the bowl.

Strutting coyly over toward him, Carmel squeezed past Hel and lifted his hands to place them around her waist. Pressing forward, she pulled his head toward her and kissed him deeply and open mouthed on the lips.

"What was that for?" Henry gulped breathlessly when her fiery embrace finally came to an end. His cheeks were glowing fiercely. Hel would be furious at such a wanton gesture.

"That, my dearest boy, is to spare you the trouble of thanking me," she squealed before turning to Hel and giving her an equally exquisite kiss. "I have it, the solution; the answer to our prayers. If a well can save Asgard, then a well you shall have."

"Oh, don't be so stupid," Henry replied with a tut of annoyance. For a brief moment, he'd thought she was being serious.

"I have found a well, and I can take you there now," Carmel teased as other girls at the tables began to sit up and take note.

She was being serious.

"Where do the dead go?" she asked cryptically.

"Depends," Henry mused as he put his bowl down on the table. "Heroes go to Valhalla, and everyone else goes to Niflheim; but you know that already."

"And how do they get there?" Carmel continued pointedly, poking him hard in the stomach. Any minute now, he should catch on...

"Everyone knows the answer to that," Hel interrupted with a sneer. "By using the wells, stupid." She was a feeling a little out of sorts this morning and had a worrying looseness to her bowels. *Perhaps she would be first Valkyrie to die?*

"And are the Aesir still taking their dead to the Valley of Sighs?" Carmel enquired mischievously.

"Yes...absolutely..." Henry replied slowly as he stopped fiddling with his spoon. "Oh my—Ouch!"

"Foxy!" Hel chastised, interrupting his expletive with a violent dig of a fork into his thigh.

"I'm so sorry darling," he gasped with excitement. "I wasn't really going to swear, but didn't you just hear what Carmel said? The Aesir are still taking their dead to Niflheim. Think about it. How can they do that if there isn't a well?"

Hel's jaw dropped open. "Sweet mother of Niflheim, there has to be another one!" Jumping up wildly, she grabbed hold of his hand. "Come on Foxy," she squealed. "We have to find Frigg. Asgard can be saved!"

Kat heard the commotion going on downstairs but decided not to join in. Stopping an excited maid who happened to be thundering past her room, she quizzed the girl until she'd discovered what it was about.

Frigg, Henry, Hel, and Carmel were off to the Valley of Sighs. Asgard could be saved—as if.

Kat decided to keep this 'wonderful news' from Lia, who was sitting peacefully on her bed. She didn't want to explain what was going on just in case it turned out to be another wild goose chase. Lia should be kept in the dark unless, of course, a miracle really did happen.

Then all Asgard would join in the jubilation.

Keeping her fingers crossed, Kat closed the door behind her.

"Are you all right?" Lia enquired innocently when Kat rejoined her on the bed.

Kat nodded as she sat down and offered a weak smile. She was feeling so desperately ill. Her head hurt, she felt as sick as a parrot, and clumps of hair were beginning to fall out. She was dying—and she knew it.

Without trying to be too obvious, she studied her maid intently.

Lia was such a beautiful girl; so strong, so feisty, and so proud. She was a thoroughbred Valkyrie through and through. Her recovery had been meteoric, and she was now bursting with new life and fresh energy. Mercifully, she was still unaffected by the radiation and hadn't as yet noticed Kat's deteriorating health. Her gleeful mood was infectious, and Kat thanked her daughter for that blessing. She would make a magnificent warrior one day—if only that day should ever come.

Kat cursed herself furiously. She must hold it together, for Lia's sake.

Before the interruption, the two of them had been locked in a conversation about Hod, of all things. He was currently out of the room; busily filling a basket of logs for the fire. With their deaths looming large and Odin to blame; anger toward him was steadily rising. It was now only safe for him to venture out of the room either with her or Lia; or when running the briefest of errands.

Wandering the castle on his own, he ran a gauntlet of hate.

Hod's situation was the source of some confusion for her maid, and this was what they'd been debating. Aware of his godly past, Lia had concerns about his position. Like a square peg in a round hole, he just didn't seem to fit into the accepted hierarchy of the castle's inhabitants; and this was making her feel uncomfortable.

Beneath the warriors, maids, and gods, the cooks and servants held the highest positions. Servants were almost always women, and they were well paid and well treated. Hod was supposed to be a servant, but he wasn't paid, and he most definitely wasn't a woman.

At the bottom of the social pecking order were the slaves and prisoners. Slaves were ex-men, unpaid eunuchs who were whipped and treated like dirt. In many ways, Hod's status was closest to these, but he hadn't been castrated; so he must be a servant—which he so obviously wasn't.

It was a wonderfully illogical, completely irrelevant conundrum that left the girl in a state of bewilderment. How could the former god understand his place when she didn't?

His role was ambiguous, so it was no wonder that he was giving such dreadful service. Far from being helpful and polite, he was constantly surly and resentful. In her confusion, Lia had coined a childish new word for his position.

Hod was a 'slavant'—which made Kat laugh.

Lia's concerns, however, were less amusing. She was struggling in the way that she treated him—just in case it upset Kat; and this was becoming a bit of a quandary for her.

Seeing the door open and Hod returning, Kat decided to put Lia out of her misery. She had had a solution to this dilemma for some days now; although she very much doubted Hod would appreciate it.

"Hey!" Kat cried as he staggered into the room, straining under the load he was carrying. "Would you like to serve a new mistress?"

Hod looked up enquiringly.

"Lia's going to be in charge of you from now on," she continued.

His face dropped.

"What?" Lia exclaimed with an excited gleam in her eyes. "Are you sure?" she breathed incredulously as she clutched Kat's hands in hers. She was delighted and clearly overwhelmed. She'd never had power over anybody, ever. It would be such a novelty and oh—what a delicious thrill.

"Absolutely," Kat replied emphatically. Her mind was made up. "You're going to be moving into your own chambers today, and Hod can help you settle in. You'll need some help, and you're used to having him around."

THUMP!

Hod threw a large log angrily into the hearth. A great cloud of ash billowed into the room, and a cluster of sparks landed on the carpet. These hissed noisily, forming a small scorch before he could stub them out. Hearing Kat's offer, he hadn't been impressed.

How dare she treat him like some hackneyed old slave?

"Is there a problem?" Kat enquired mischievously looking in his direction. The former god might not like it, but she felt sure Lia would make a good mistress. Firm, confident hands were just what he needed; and she might just get him to behave a little less oafishly. It would be like a breath of fresh air for all of them; and would definitely give her some breathing space. His constant presence in her room, and that of Lia's, was becoming claustrophobic. Besides, a hideous ugliness was looming large in her mind.

Death.

She was succumbing to Odin's curse, and she needed rest and lots of it. Kat didn't want her maid or her friend to witness her death throes when her demise eventually came. With their own ends being not too far behind hers, Kat didn't want to impose her suffering on their own. She was too proud for that humiliation.

Hod might grumble and complain about her decision, but that really was of little consequence. His servitude to Lia wouldn't last long.

They were both dead already.

"Oh, thank you, thank you so much," Lia exclaimed excitedly, embracing Kat with a lingering kiss on the cheek. "I won't let you down, I promise."

"I'm sure you won't, but he probably will," she scoffed.

Indicating for Hod to come over, Kat commanded him to kiss Lia's hand. Muttering grumpily under his breath, he did so as a thunderstorm was erupting across his face.

He was furious.

Ironically, and Kat chuckled as she watched him bend stiffly and give a cursory bow, Lia happened to be wearing Kat's first warrior tunic. Its fit was a little baggy for the slender girl, but she still looked magnificent as she accepted his kiss. In a moment of déjà vu; Kat remembered the halcyon days when Hod once pestered her in those clothes. With an unpleasant jolt, she realised those days were such a long time ago.

Maybe Lia would command his respect?

Now that would be a first. Watching her maid wrestle with the truculent god would have made for interesting viewing; but sadly, that was a journey that would never run its course.

Asgard lay dying, and time had run out.

"Come on," Lia commanded abruptly, snapping her fingers authoritatively at the former god. "Pick up your mattress and get to my room already. I want to see a nice, roaring fire with plenty of logs when I get there." She was starting as she intended to carry on.

Glancing in Kat's direction, Hod threw her a filthy look.

"Don't look at me," she giggled. "I'm not your mistress anymore." His face was a picture. "But I suggest you do as you're told, or you're going to make fair Lia angry; and then you'll really be for it."

Muttering curses under his breath, Hod stormed out of the room.

"Don't worry," Lia reassured as she stopped Kat from apologising for his behaviour. "I'm used to his surliness, and I'll train him good. I'll make you proud, just you wait and see." Strutting gleefully over to the door, Lia stopped to ask Kat one last question.

"How would you like me to treat him?" she enquired.

"To be honest, I don't really care," Kat retorted, sighing deeply. She felt so tired. Radiation sickness was grinding her down, sapping her will. "You decide what to do with him," she continued. "After all, he's your slavant now so you can do what you want."

"Oh goodie," Lia squealed as she danced away. Breaking in Hod was going to be fun.

Smiling weakly, Kat closed the door behind her and then shut her eyes. Thank Asgard Lia was so bubbly. Kindness or meanness; quite frankly, she couldn't give a damn.

In a matter of days, they would all be rotting corpses anyway.

"So can you explain to me again, please, Henry dearest; just how exactly do you intend to get this gravity stuff into our universe without blowing us all up?"

Frigg decided to repeat a question that he had already tried to answer, as they sped through the snow on the road to Niflheim. Hanging on for dear life, Henry tried to concentrate and put his plan in a way that she could understand.

This was important.

He was confident he could succeed, but he had to get her approval before she would allow him access to the well.

The four of them, Frigg, Henry, Hel, and Carmel, had set out from the castle immediately after breakfast. Riding Sleipnir and Gold Mane, Hel and Carmel had galloped on ahead; whooping loudly as they raced each other to the waterfall. Henry was travelling a little more sedately beside Frigg in Freyja's chariot. He wasn't too clever with horses, but the two powerful black panthers were making short work of the miles. Bouncing over iced ruts and skidding on frozen puddles of water, their progress was both swift and terrifying.

Breathing hard, and talking between anxious gasps; Henry tried to dumb down his plan for saving their universe.

The concept was quite simple if you could imagine each universe as a balloon and the well as a small doorway. Asgard's deflating universe lay on one side of the doorway, and a great big bunch of other balloon universes lay on the other.

Henry's plan was to open the doorway—the well—and suck little bits of energy out of lots of these balloon universes to reinflate their own. If he could do it, then it would be a neat trick; and one that shouldn't end in an implosion like the one that had destroyed Mimir's well.

That implosion had happened because they had opened the well widely with it focused on only one other universe—the one with Midgard in it. By plucking only one balloon universe from the bunch of balloons, this had easily passed through the door and collided with their own—creating the implosion.

To avoid a repeat of this disaster, Henry had decided to open the well up wide but with its graviton beam unfocused. This was the critical part of his plan. By sucking energy in from as many other balloon universes as possible, all the balloons would rush together toward their well—the doorway—and get jammed up against one another.

Crowded tightly in this way, Henry reasoned, no single balloon— or universe—would be able to pass through the doorway. None of the other universes would therefore collide with their own; and because there would be no collision—there would be no implosion.

This was his plan, and it was the only game in town. It was simple, ingenious, and made good sense. Suck little bits of energy from lots of universes all at the same time, and disaster couldn't strike.

It sounded easy-peasy, lemon-squeezy except for one tiny, weany, little snag. It had never, ever been done before.

Henry's plan was a desperate gamble for the ultimate prize.

Life.

It was going to be an all-or-nothing turn of the card, where the winner takes all—and the loser gets blown to pieces.

Luckily, as Frigg had so succinctly put it; they would never know if they failed. Death would be instantaneous as a new cosmos exploded into theirs. This was a sobering thought and one Henry reflected on with increasing discomfort as they drew nearer to their destination.

What if his guesswork was wrong?

Arriving at the rickety wooden gate, they found Hel and Carmel waiting impatiently to greet them. They were both smiling broadly and had excellent news. Corpses were raining down into Niflheim like it was going out of fashion. The wormhole was open, and because it was; there had to be another well somewhere close by.

Hel could go one better; although she had never seen the well, she knew exactly where it must be.

Spurring the panthers into a charge, Frigg cracked her whip, and they sped down the valley like two bolts of lightening. Henry practically fainted; he had never felt so scared. Rounding the final bend, Frigg pulled on the reins hard. Rearing violently; the mighty panthers roared angrily as they brought the speeding chariot shuddering to a halt. Panting hard, the two creatures growled menacingly at the wooden bridge before them. The stench of death troubled them, and they pawed nervously at the ground with their claws open wide.

Seeing her former Queen, Modgud dropped a gracious curtsey as Henry, Carmel, and Hel hurried across the bridge. Frigg couldn't accompany them, as she wasn't undead.

For her to cross over would result in instant death.

Disappearing behind a rock, Hel returned triumphantly with two thumbs stuck up high. They had struck gold. Exactly as she had suspected, the well lay at the back of the small cave where Garm had once lain.

Hel shed a quick tear. He had been one of her hounds who had died so courageously in the last battle of Ragnarok.

Wasting no time, Henry crouched down beside the well and carried out Frigg's instructions. Using her ring to gain control, Henry moved his fingers over the flickering panel in the way that she had described. This would turn the machine from 'slave' to 'master.' With a tiny shudder, the ground quaked, and a few loose boulders tumbled from the cliffs.

The well had stirred into life.

Henry gulped and looked nervously at Hel. This was it, do or die. He hesitated.

The responsibility was too great.

"Come on, Foxy," Hel encouraged as she crouched down beside him and cupped his face gently in her hands. "Don't be nervous, just do it."

"I...I...I can't," he stuttered anxiously. "What if I'm wrong?"

Giggling girlishly, she pressed her lips tightly against his, kissing him so passionately that his cheeks flared a brilliant shade of red. "Look," she reassured. "We're dead if you don't, and we're dead if you've got it wrong. Either way we lose; but we won't, I just know we won't. I trust you, and I know that you can save us."

"I love you, Hel."

"I love you too, Foxy-Loxy," Hel replied as she gave him a little tickle. Standing up, she let out a wild yell.

"All Hail Foxy! Saviour of Asgard!"

Shutting his eyes tightly, Henry completed the final sequence of movements with his fingers.

This was it; the moment of truth, the river card.

Opening the well wide, Henry felt its awesome power throb under his fingertips. "One thousand and one, one thousand and two, one thousand and three—" he counted slowly under his breath. When he reached one thousand and ten, he repeated the sequence with his fingers, closing the machine. Switching on the Geiger counter, this clattered noisily into life. Clicking away merrily, its sound hadn't altered one jot.

Nothing had happened; Asgard hadn't been saved.

Henry looked up at his lover, panic stricken.

"Don't worry, Foxy," she reassured with a pat. "Just do it again but give it a little longer. Hey! Look on the bright side; at least you didn't blow us all up."

Henry grinned at that thought. Hel was right. It probably would take longer than ten seconds to save the world.

Repeating the sequence with his fingers, Henry opened the well widely before retreating out of the cave. This time, he was going to let it stay open for a full ten minutes.

"How's it going?" Frigg mouthed from the far side of the river. Her voice couldn't be heard over the foaming tumult of the water.

Hel stuck one thumb up. Something was happening, although it wasn't terribly exciting. The ground wasn't exactly quaking with fear. Just like the deadly radiation, the waves of gravity coursing into their universe were invisible. Only time, and Odin's Geiger counter, would tell if they had been successful.

After ten minutes, Henry shut the well down and nervously flicked on the counter. It still clicked away gaily, but maybe it was his imagination: *was the clicking slightly less?*

Crossing all his fingers, Henry returned to the cave and fired up the well for a third time. This time he was going to leave it open for a full sixty minutes.

Pulling Hel close, he cuddled up snugly against her.

This was going to be the longest hour of his life.

Carmel was the one who made the joyous announcement. With a new well now working, she had been able to put on her cloak of swans' feathers and fly back to Asgard with the fabulous news.

Asgard was saved!

Arriving breathlessly, she whipped the castle into a frenzy of activity. Food had to be prepared, tables needed laying, and fireworks begged to be set up. The realm needed to celebrate like it had never celebrated before.

Asgard was saved!

She could hardly believe her own words.

Henry's final run with the well had been a success; with the clicks from the Geiger counter slowing dramatically to a much more sedentary pace. Henry hadn't left the well open, because that would have been unwise.

His idea had worked; but pumping energy into their universe would out of necessity be a long and laborious process. An hour a day for many, many years would gradually strengthen the glue that held its matter together. This process would ripple out from Asgard, spreading healing waves from star to star and from galaxy to galaxy. It would take eons to stabilise their entire universe; but they had two billion years in hand, so time really wasn't an issue. Eventually, many millions of years from now, the galaxies would slow down in their race to oblivion and, with a little bit of luck, they might even reverse direction and start sauntering leisurely apart.

That, in Henry's words, would be a joy to behold.

This distant prospect, however, lay far, far ahead. For now, all they could confidently say was that their sickness and tiredness would come to an end.

The Aesir could rejoice in a new lease of life.

Asgard had been saved—so proclaim the news loud and with cheer.

Frigg, Hel, and Henry arrived back at the castle many hours after dark. They were exhausted but bubbling over with joy. They had heard the horns blowing from a great distance away, and the many torches that had been lit had caused an eerie glow to the sky.

As their party came into view, Thor ordered a round of fireworks be set off. These whooshed as they sped into the air and exploded with the loudest of bangs. Small children cried in terror, and women wept tears of great joy. The Aesir weren't entirely sure quite what they were celebrating, but Thor's insistence that their sickness and dying were coming to an end, would do nicely for now.

Shouting with joy, the townsfolk threw dried flowers and tokens of appreciation as the weary procession rode up the hill before passing through the castle's gate.

It was going to be a wild and victorious night.

"Hail Foxy!" Hel cried triumphantly as the girls hoisted him aloft and carried Henry into the feasting hall on their shoulders. Screeching with laughter, they gave him eighteen bumps; tossing him high in the air as though he was as light as a feather.

Henry was the hero of the hour, the day, and the year. He could do no wrong, and his stunning success finally cemented Hel's acceptance as a Valkyrie. Even Silk, who still hated her, gave them both a warm hug. The gods were gone, Asgard had been saved, and the Valkyries were in charge.

Life was wonderful, and victory couldn't taste sweeter.

Banging Mjollnir down hard on the main table, Thor beckoned for everybody to calm down. Frigg had a short but important speech to make, and he wanted them all to listen.

"My dearest Valkyries," he began to a rapturous chorus of clapping, screaming, and foot stamping. He paused and waited impatiently for the warriors to calm down. At this rate, Frigg's speech would take five hours.

"Ladies, please, I beg of you," he bellowed irritably. "Give your noble queen silence for a few moments. Her words are important as will be your reply."

Calming slowly, the girls settled back into their seats. Their lives suddenly had a meaning and purpose once more; and it was hard to contain their exhilaration.

They now had a future; one that had seemed impossible only hours before.

"My dear sisters," Frigg began as she raised her hands high above her head. The jewelled ring portraying her godly status sparkled with a breathtaking beauty.

"Asgard has been saved, but our journey mustn't end here. There are many enemies who intend to wage war on our realm and will do so when winter wanes. Many challenges lie ahead. The watchtower needs rebuilding, as does Noatun on the shore. A new army must be trained and equipped, and our boundaries have yet to be secured. Asgard lies weak and defenceless, but just like the phoenix, the Valkyries will rise from its ashes stronger and prouder than before."

Frigg paused to allow a loud chorus of "Hail Frigg" to run its course. As the girls calmed again, she continued with her speech.

"Odin may be gone, but his evil ambitions remain. Even now, he is busy in Midgard; building a new empire, enslaving its peoples, and laying waste to their land. Without Mimir's well, the realm now lies hidden from view. However, this won't always be so. With a new well to guide us, we can seek out that world, and when we find it; we will bring justice for its people. Odin must pay for his crimes as surely as Midgard must be freed."

Frigg paused and gazed solemnly and proudly around the hall. The warriors were magnificent, and their power exalted her.

"Only we have the strength to do this, my dear sisters," she continued as passion blazed in her heart. "Only the Valkyries have the power to bring Odin to his knees. So I ask you now if you will join me in this our last and most glorious quest. Dearest sisters, I beseech you;

please be upstanding and raise your horns as I offer you this toast. All hail the liberation of Midgard!"

Rising as one, the Valkyries roared their agreement.

"HAIL VALOUR!"

"HAIL VICTORY!"

"HAIL MIDGARD!"

The battle was on.

TO BE CONTINUED...